COCKsure

K.I. LYNN
OLIVIA KELLEY

Cocksure
Copyright © K.I. Lynn & Olivia Kelley
ISBN: 978-1-948284-01-1

This book is a work of fiction. Names, characters, places, and incidents either are products of the author's imagination or are used fictitiously. Any resemblance to actual events or locales or persons, living or dead, is entirely coincidental.

This work is copyrighted. All rights are reserved. Apart from any use as permitted under the Copyright Act 1968, no part may be reproduced, copied, scanned, stored in a retrieval system, recorded or transmitted, in any form or by any means, without prior written permission of the author.

Cover image licensed by: David Wagner @ Wagner LA
Cover design by: Letitia Hasser at RBA Designs,
www.rbadesigns.com
Cover Model: Steven Brewis
Editors:
Ellie McLove
Marti Lynch
Formatting by: Elaine York at Allusion Graphics, LLC,
www.allusiongraphics.com

Publication Date: January 08, 2018
Genre: FICTION/Romance
Copyright © 2018
All rights reserved

COCK sure

cock·sure
ˌkäkˈSHo͝or/Submit
adjective

presumptuously or arrogantly confident.

Synonyms: arrogant, conceited, overweening, overconfident, cocky, proud, vain, self-important, egotistical, presumptuous; smug, patronizing, pompous; informal high and mighty, puffed up

"he won't be so cocksure when he gets in the ring with our boy"

Chapter One

Niko

THERE IS NOTHING LIKE a night out. A couple of drinks, some pretty girls, and a whole lot of fun for my dick.

Lick, suck, and fuck, then I'm out.

This chick walking toward me right now, though, yeah. Something is telling me to get up and go.

I don't, of course. As she steps closer, I realize she looks familiar but I can't place her face. Yet.

"Hey, Niko," the blonde says as she steps up beside where I'm sitting. I stare at her, trying to jog my memory. Nope. I know I've fucked her, but for the life of me, I can't remember her name.

There's an empty seat I grabbed for Cam, but he hasn't shown up yet. *Please don't sit down*, I keep repeating in my head. I know it's an immature thing to do, but I don't care lately. I think it's time for a new hangout because as much as I love the pub, this place is starting to make me feel claustrophobic.

"Heidi," she says after a minute of my blank expression. "My name is Heidi. Did you forget?"

"Sorry, doll face, it's been a long day," I say and hope she'll move on. I don't want to offend her, but I was clear and to the point before I went home with her.

COCK sure

Whenever that was.

"It's okay. I understand." And she fucking sits down in the empty seat next to me.

Fuck! Cam needs to hurry the hell up and get here.

"Can I buy you a drink, handsome?" she asks me.

The way she says it makes me want to roll my eyes. Her seductive voice is just grating on me. Maybe it worked last time I saw her, but it doesn't work now. I'm not in the mood for seconds.

"No thanks." I raise my full glass of ice-cold beer that I literally just got a second before she waltzed over here. "I'm good."

"That you are, handsome. I was thinking maybe you'd like to join me for something a little stronger than that draft beer, though," she says as she drags her finger with a very long, very sharp red nail down her neck to her full breasts.

Shit. I remember her now.

This is the chick that had my back, chest, and thighs lit up like a fucking Christmas tree with scratches from those claws of hers. Took me almost two weeks before they went away.

I shudder from the memories of that night. It was good and, at the time, I didn't give a shit that she used those claws more like a female version of Freddy Kruger, but no damn way was I going there again.

Even if I didn't have my one-night rule, there is no way I'm letting her cut me up like that again. Definitely not my kind of kink. That's some shit Cameron would be into, though. I almost snort out loud when I think of some of the sticky situations Cam has gotten himself into with women.

Speaking of the devil himself. "Finally," I say out loud as I see Cam make his way toward where I'm sitting at the bar.

The woman next to me seems oblivious to my mood. She continues to molest her own tits in front of me as well as about seven other men sitting around us watching, those red claws of her move back and forth across her chest. Cam steps up and waves the bartender down as he stands next to Heidi.

"Sorry, doll face, but as tempting as you may be, I was waiting for someone." I nod my head toward Cam, who of course smiles his pearly whites at her, not getting that I want her gone.

She looks behind her at Cam, and I watch as she looks him up and down before looking back to me with an evil grin that matches those red claws of hers.

"I'm always down for two hot-as-hell men at once. He's wearing a fireman's T-shirt. I'm going to take that as confirmation that he's also a fireman like you. Two hoses are always better than one. He can play too, handsome," she says, and I won't lie. The thought of a threesome sounds hot as hell right now, but there's that shudder again as memories from our one and only night together assault my brain. I look up at Cam, who's now looking at me with a brow quirked, his curiosity piqued.

I shake my head no as he grabs his club soda from the bartender, a smirk now crossing his face. Whatever, buddy. I'm saving your hose, and you don't even know it.

"Hillary," I say to the woman.

"Heidi, but honestly, you can call me whatever you want as long as I can get a repeat of what you gave me a few weeks ago."

Yeah, that's not going to happen.

"Listen, you seem like a nice girl, but as I told you a few weeks ago, that was a one-time deal. I don't do repeats. It's nothing personal."

"You did, but I didn't think you were serious. I mean, I'm not trying to marry you, if that's what you're thinking, but what's the harm in you, me, and your hot friend taking a ride back to my place? I promise it will be worth your while." She winks at me.

"I'm sure it would, but no thanks. Enjoy your evening, doll. If you'll excuse me, I've got some things to discuss with my buddy here," I say, and she looks between Cam and me.

Cam shrugs his shoulders as if to tell her he's on my side, even though I know he'd be down to leave with her if I gave him the word.

She chugs back her drink, grabs her purse before getting off the bar stool, and huffs out, "Your loss," before stomping away.

Cam sits in her vacated seat and doesn't say anything for a minute or two. I wait for it. He always has to throw his two cents in. Why should now be any different? I take a sip of my beer, and still he stays silent.

"What? Not going to bust my balls? That's unlike you. You sick or something?" I say to Cam who's now watching Heidi across the room chatting up some poor guy that has no idea what he's in for.

"I just don't get you sometimes, man," he finally says.

"Yes, you do. I've told you before. Why do you always act surprised when I run into someone I've fucked?"

"You don't just run into them, Niko. You run them off. I don't get you. If I had as much tail chasing me as you did, looking for seconds and thirds, I'd be set for life," he says.

I almost spit my beer out of my nose. "You *do* have that much tail chasing you, asshole. Hell, even more than I do, so stop trying to make yourself sound like St. Dick, and shut up," I say with a slight chuckle under my breath.

Cameron just shrugs in that annoying way that only Cam can do, and I shake my head at him. "It's not the same for me, though. I'm ADHD. I get bored easier than you do, but yet I'm the one that tries to stick around."

"Yeah, if you call a week or two sticking around, then you are the poster child for serious relationships."

"Fuck you, Niko. I'm just saying."

"You don't have to get it, man. It's just how it is," I say to him. "How I want it. I have rules. Rules that I live by. Rules that I fuck by. I'm not looking for something long term, I'm looking for the here and now." I know he's heard me say this before. "You have a bad habit, my friend, that more than once has come back to bite you in the ass."

"Yeah, yeah. You and your rules, Niko. You just wait. One of these days, you're going to have to break those fucking stupid rules you live by, and I can't wait to get a front row seat at the fall of the great Niko Callahan," he says to me, and we are right back to the bickering I'm used to with Cam.

"Not stupid rules. *You* could use some rules yourself, moron. Might have saved you years of the guys busting your balls had you followed one of my two most important rules."

"Yeah, which one is that?"

"*Never* bring them back to my place—the number one rule."

"That's not entirely ridiculous, but what if they don't have their own place? I mean, shit, it happens," he says.

I want to laugh at the seriousness of his tone. "Cam, stop fucking girls. What happened to that chick that still lived at home with her mother?"

"She was taking care of her mother! Her mom had some kind of illness and needed the extra help, dickhead."

"Yeah, see, that's another issue. Why do you know this information?"

"Because she told me. What's wrong with that?"

"What's wrong with it is that when you talk, lines get crossed. Feelings start. That's rule two. Only one night—they get needy. You don't seem to understand that shit and end up meeting the mom and having fucking breakfast and shit."

"What's wrong with breakfast? I get Mickey Mouse pancakes," he says in reply, and I do roll my eyes this time.

"Man, if I have to hear one more time about those damn Mickey Mouse pancakes . . . you dumbass."

"You know what?"

"Nope, but I'm sure you're going to tell me anyway."

"Maybe if someone made Niko some Mickey pancakes with butter and extra syrup, Niko wouldn't be such a pussy downer. There is nothing wrong with how I meet the ladies. You want to live by your stupid rules, be my guest, but I get sex and a home-cooked meal. Breakfast is the most important meal of the day. We learn that early in life, so fuck you very much. Plus, I get it all in a twenty-four-hour time span."

"Whatever works for you. I'll stick with my plan and my rules. They work for me."

Rules:

1. Never bring them back to my place.
2. Only one night.
3. Don't catch feelings.
4. See all rules above.

COCK sure

I have no desire to change my ways. Not because Cam said so. Not because some chick agreed and then wanted more. I'm not the bad guy here. I was straight up. I'm always straight up with them. I'm not changing my rules for anyone. No fucking way.

Chapter Two

Everly

"FLIGHT 2295 FOR ATLANTA is now boarding at gate B29." Every thirty seconds for the last hour, some airline employee's voice has boomed over the speakers, which are *everywhere*. It's the reason I'm on my second cup of coffee, and why I plan to have some alcohol as soon as I'm on the plane. Too damn early to deal with all of these people.

LAX is just as busy as always, and I'll be happy to go from thousands to a few hundred where I can plug in with a movie or music and forget them all. The week has been long, the last three even longer. Everything in my life is being flipped.

It may seem like running, going back to Boston and my family, but it's not. At least that's what I tell myself. I've been gone for seven years, thousands of miles from everything I'd ever known.

My phone buzzes on the table, and I glance down at it in reflex. His name is on the screen. I read the first few words of the text before I can stop myself. ***Evie, talk to me. I love*—** I look away, unable to read any more. There is way too much I've learned about the man, about what he's done behind my back, that I can say if that's his definition of love, then I want no part of it.

It'll be good to return to Boston. As much as I love California, I've missed my family and friends. I'll miss the weather and the friends I've made here over the years, but in the end, this is the right move for me.

No reminders of him, the comfort of home, and a chance to start over.

It'll be evening by the time I arrive and my brother, Cameron, is going to meet me for dinner. The sad part is that I don't really want to. Not today. The day is going to be long, the travel exhausting, and I'm just not in the mood to dive into my sudden change in location.

I pull up Facebook on my phone, an app I rarely use, and check in on him. There is a new picture of him at the top of his profile. It's one of those cliché testosterone gym shots showing off his muscles, which look huge but are necessary for his job.

What makes me catch my breath is the man standing next to him. It's been years since I've seen him in the flesh, but from the pictures my brother posts, his best friend just gets better looking with age.

Niko was my childhood crush, my first love, and every time I see him, that feeling starts to creep back in. I've never stopped thinking about him. The romantic teenager in me is all hearts and love, but the woman in me is trying hard not to lick the abs he's showing off or notice how that smirk has me squirming in my seat. His eyes are hypnotic, his demeanor cocky, and he's a man I've fantasized about more over the years than I care to admit.

I'm sure I'll see him at some point and he'll make me a complete and utter blabbering mess, just like he used to. The two of them are practically joined at the hip, so it's inevitable. I go to sign off when my messenger app shows I have a message. I look to see who it's from and, even though I'm exhausted, I can't keep the grin from taking over my face.

Alyson Payne: Why the hell are you on Facebook when you and your two Christmas hams for an ass are supposed to be on a plane right now heading closer to me and my chicken bone ass?

I laugh out loud and then cover my mouth in embarrassment when a snort escapes. I look around to see if anyone sitting around me in the airport is looking, but if they heard, they don't care or they're just used to hearing crazy people snort all alone while they sit and wait for their plane. I type back to my best friend, Alyson. She's one of the people I've missed most since deciding to stay in California after finishing college.

I've seen her over the years, but those times have been rare as she's been working two jobs since leaving school when her brother died suddenly. I've missed her something terrible and can't wait to be able to see her more often now that I'm moving home.

Everly Hayes: Are you trying to say that my ass looks like Christmas hams? I think I might just be insulted enough to stay in California now.

Alyson: NO! It's a compliment! Your ass has always been better than mine! Get it on the plane lady! I'll be forced to drive my shit box of a car from Massachusetts to California if you don't!

Everly: I thought you said your car was gone?

Alyson: Yeah, the one I had is gone. The one I have now is worse. Probably wouldn't make it past Rhode Island, but I'd try if it meant I was closer to you guys ;)

Everly: You guys?

Alyson: You and your pigs! Pay attention Ev!

Everly: Smh You do like one thousand squats a day and run a million miles a week. I'm sure your ass is far from that of a chicken Al *rolling my eyes at you*

Alyson: Whatever. Just make sure you roll them at me in person and get on that damn plane!

"Attention passengers on flight 1247 to Boston, we will begin boarding in five minutes."

And that's my cue.

Everly: Well, would you look at that . . .

Alyson: HELLO! I'm across the country and can't see what you're looking at. Now I'm rolling my eyes at YOU!

Everly: LOL They just called my flight. I'm about to get on the plane and leave this life behind me, I say to her, and for the first time since deciding to leave California and the life

I built here, it hits me. I'm leaving this place behind me and all the memories that stay with it.

Alyson: Don't think about it. I know you and I know you're sitting in that airport right now second guessing yourself, but this is the right choice! You made it. YOU decided. No one made this choice for you and it's what's right or you would never have gone to the extreme of selling your home, leaving your job and a place you've loved and called home for years. Leave that fucker there and don't look back!

Everly: I'm not second guessing my decision.

Alyson: We'll talk when you get here. Call me when you land no matter what time it is I want a call!

Everly: Okay.

Alyson: GET ON THE PLANE! Grabbing my screwdriver if you don't!

Everly: Screwdriver?

Alyson: LOL It's how I start my new car. Don't ask! LOVE YOU!! XX

Everly: Love you too! See you soon! XX

She starts her car with a screwdriver? I think and shake my head. I'm not in the right mindset to think about Aly and all that seems to have changed with her, but I make a mental note to ask her more when I get back to Boston.

I call the waiter over and pay my tab before picking up my bag and making a quick pit stop. Ten minutes later I'm settling into my seat in first class, ready for the near six-hour flight.

I down a glass of wine during the hour-long tarmac wait, which helps me to relax.

When the plane finally rockets down the runway, I picture Niko in my mind, hoping for good dreams as I feel the lack of sleep take hold. No amount of caffeine can keep me up after being awake for over twenty-four hours.

Chapter Three

Niko

WALKING INTO THE PUB in Newton is like stepping into one of my happy places. It's been our hangout for years, starting when we were in training, spending every night we could pounding down pints after a hard day. Years later, we've officially become regulars.

It's oddly the same after a decade. The dark woods, rich hops smell, and the dim mood lighting set up a level of comfort and sophistication. Their level of snotty didn't always like our brand of celebration, but the ladies liked our energy over their stuck-up dates.

As we sit at the bar, I notice they've updated the menus in the last few weeks. The items look the same, with a few new dishes. It's always been great, which is one reason why we come so often.

"Thanks for coming, man," Cameron says as he signals to Mike, the bartender. "Coke and a Sam Adams."

I turn and stare at him. "You said beer. Do you think I'm going to turn that down?"

He lets out a chuckle and shakes his head. "Nah, but it's different since I'm waiting for Ev."

It's been about ten years since I last saw Cam's little sister, Everly. The last time I saw her, she was a teenager and the definition of geek: glasses, braces, messy ponytail, and clothes that were unflattering to her flat body. She used to follow us around, as much as she was allowed to anyway. I always thought it was funny, but Cameron, not so much. Kind of hard to make it to first base with your kid sister in tow.

"Red Sox are playing tonight," I say as I look up at the screen. The game, the second one of the season, is just starting.

"Why do you think I suggested here?" Cam asks. "Besides, it looks like we'll be waiting awhile. Her plane's delayed."

"Doesn't surprise me from what I hear about that airport."

"It's unbelievable, especially with all the construction. Then again, what airport isn't a nightmare?"

I shrug. "You fly more than me." The last time I took a plane was to visit my mom's family in Greece when I was sixteen. "I can't believe your sister has been in California for so long."

"Good thing technology is on our side."

"Facetime?"

He nods. "I don't think I'd even know Everly anymore if it wasn't for that."

"You have stayed weirdly close," I note before taking a sip of my beer.

"She's the only sister I have. Plus, once I became an official adult, she wasn't that annoying."

I tilt my head back in laughter. "You mean once you were off to college and away from her."

Cam's brow scrunches before he rolls his eyes and lets out a sigh. "Yeah. That. But then I did want to, you know, have a friendship with her."

"Guess I never really realized how close you were since she's not around."

"Don't act like I never talk about her," Cam says.

"Not saying that, because you do. Just, it's not a relationship I can understand."

He nods. "Charlie is like a brother."

"Same last name, different situation," I say. It's been weeks since I even talked to my cousin. He got a girl about a year ago and disappeared, only to be seen at family functions or when he's not all curled around her.

"How about this; when Everly gets here, she can be your honorary little sister."

I purse my lips and take another sip of my beer. I'll look after Everly because she is Cam's sister and Everly means a lot to him, so I suppose that works. Besides, how much trouble can she be?

The familiar sounds of Twenty One Pilots "Heavydirtysoul" blares from Cam's phone sitting on the bar in front of him. "Hayes," he says into the receiver. A small nod, quick, "Okay," and then he's hanging up, hissing, "Shit."

By Cam's tone, I know what the call was.

"That was fast."

He throws back the rest of his Coke. "I was hoping if it did happen, it could at least wait until Everly arrived."

I shake my head. "Fire waits for no man."

Cam stands and pulls on his jacket. "Are you cool with waiting for her?"

I nod. "No problem."

Cam pulls out his keys and unclips a single key ring with two keys on it. He holds them out and drops them into my palm. "Do me a solid, okay?"

"What?"

"Don't try and pick up my sister."

I roll my eyes and let out a very unflattering snort. "Seriously, man? We're talking about your little sister."

"Seriously. Ev's not the same girl she used to be."

"Dude, I'm not that big of a manwhore."

I watch as Cam purses his lips. "Yeah, I don't believe that for a second."

"Well, I wouldn't call myself a manwhore exactly, but, come on, man, you know me better than that."

"I do. You forget I've been with you when you have met many of your 'dates.' Not only that, but if you're not a manwhore, then what does that make me?"

I laugh at his statement, taking a swig of my beer before raising it toward Cam in salute.

"Touché, brother, but you, my friend, have nothing to worry about here. You know that out of anyone, you can trust me, and we're talking about your little sister. I would never go there," I say and look him directly in the eyes so he knows I mean what I say.

Cam isn't just my best friend; he's like my brother, which I guess already makes Everly my little sister.

"Besides, I've got my eyes on a few exciting prospects for tonight," I say as I eye the redhead that's sitting across the bar from us. She's been eye fucking me since I walked through the door. I'm not usually into gingers, but she's got a rocking body that I bet won't quit.

Cam stares at me a moment, looks over at the redhead, and then throws some money down on the bar while shaking his head. He smiles at me before holding his fist out.

"I know I can trust you; I just needed to say it. She's my sister, and she's been away from home a long time. She's . . ." he trails off when he sees my smirk, and then he turns and starts to make his way out, throwing me a look that says, "Just stay out of trouble for one night while I'm gone, would ya." *Asshole.* "Later, Niko. I'll see you at the firehouse tomorrow."

I continue to peruse the evening's prospects, noting the lack of options. Then again, it's a Tuesday.

The redhead from across the bar is a bust seeing as I watch a male companion join her only minutes after Cam leaves. Can't trust some women. I shake off the thought and order some food and another beer.

A meal later, and the Red Sox are down by two runs. Two hours have passed, and still no sign of Everly. I text Cam to see if he's heard anything but get no response, which means they're out on a call.

I weigh my options, which are slim to none, the bar filled with regulars and game watchers.

It's after nine and it doesn't look like Cam's little sister is coming or that I'm going to take home some dessert, so I pull out my wallet to pay. With a nod to the bartender, I let him know I'm ready to cash out, and he holds up a finger. I guess I should tell Cam that his sister hasn't shown and that I'm heading home.

Just as I'm typing the message and hit send, the sexiest fucking woman I've ever laid eyes on takes the seat next to me.

Brunette waves frame her face, which is full of large hazel eyes and full pink lips. Tits that could fill my hands, slender waist flaring out to hips leading to long legs capped with four-inch heeled boots. Sun-kissed skin that I can't tell whether or not that is her natural skin tone, but she looks like she's spent some time on the beach. The thought of her in a string bikini floods my mind and has my cock instantly standing at attention.

There is no fucking way this girl is single; she's fucking gorgeous.

I turn and put my wallet back in my pocket, deciding then that I'm not ready to call it a night after all when the bartender decides to come and close me out. I wave him off, but the hot-as-fuck brunette next to me stops him before he walks away and orders a drink.

"Can I have something fruity?" she asks the bartender.

"Sex on the Beach or a daiquiri?" he asks her back.

"Sex on the Beach sounds good. Reminds me of the night I turned twenty-one," she says, and before I can stop myself, I let out a groan. Sure, it's one of those drinks most girls ordered back in the day, but the thought of sex and the beach coming from those lips of hers just did something to me.

I take a moment to compose myself and try not to make it evident that I'm staring, but I can't help it, and my eyes roam, looking her up and down. This woman has fucking legs for days.

Another vision of those legs wrapped around my shoulders hits me, and I almost groan out loud again. I'm tired tonight after working a double shift, but I want this girl. I know I can work this to my favor, that being she warms the other side of my bed in the morning.

She clears her throat, pulling me from my visual assault and one hell of a fantasy. Busted! Of course I'd get caught. She smirks at me, and I know she knows that I just adjusted myself under the bar. Smooth, Callahan, real smooth. Bikinis, sex on the beach. I'm fucking done.

"Um . . . Hi, how are you?" *Um hi, how are you? What the fuck am I, sixteen?* If Cam were here, I'd never hear the end of this.

"Fine. Surprised to see you alone."

Wait, what? Is she serious? Is she pulling my lines on me?

"Well . . . I'm not alone anymore, now, am I?" And he's back!

I don't know what happened to me for a few minutes, but the shock of her seems to have settled down.

"I guess. If you call me company," she says as she looks around the bar before her eyes land back on me and I watch her mouth turn up into a half smirk. Oh, this girl is good, but I know I'm better.

"I'd like to call you a lot more than some company." What I'd like to call her is mine, for the night anyway.

Fuck, is she hot. Actually, for her, I'd reconsider my one-night rule. This chick is so sexy that I can see myself letting her knock on my door twice. Hell, the thought of taking her back to my place alone is enormous. I honestly can't think of anything to say right now, and for me, that's rare. What she says next has me completely struck stupid.

"Going to scream my name?" Right then the bartender brings her drink over and she immediately takes a sip while watching me, and I swear I can see the fire in those gorgeous hazel eyes of hers. They almost look like liquid gold.

Oh yeah. Trouble. This woman is trouble with a capital T. I almost get lost in those eyes, but then I find myself before I have a chance to make more of an ass out of myself and blow this.

Did I just say blow? Shit, now that's a visual I'd love to see become a reality. If I don't stop all these fantasies going through my head right now, I'm going to embarrass myself like a teenager about to bone his first chick ever.

"Baby, you tell me your name, and I'll scream it all night and pray to it all day."

She stirs the drink sitting in front of her, and I see her suck her bottom lip into her teeth, and all I can think is how great those full lips would look wrapped around my cock.

I feel my phone vibrate in my pocket and decide it's the perfect time to adjust myself under the bar again while reaching for my phone. I don't care at this point if she sees what she's doing to me, but I'm not too keen on Cam's sister showing up while I'm sporting major wood. I pull my phone out and see the message from Cam in reply to my earlier one to him about his sister not being here yet.

Cam: Dude, just head home. I'll text Ev to meet me at the station.

I type out a quick reply letting him know I'm heading out and I'll see him tomorrow, then look up at the sexy-as-fuck chick next to me who is staring at me.

That's right, baby. I'm game if you are.

For a second there I'd say she is surprised or shocked, but there is no way she's not used to guys zoning in on her. Not looking like she does. She's more than my type. I usually go for straight tens, but she's surpassed my female rating by twice that.

It looks like my night just got interesting. I smile and then wait for her next move while contemplating my own.

Chapter Four

Everly

I STARE AT HIM, not blinking. Is he serious? He doesn't seem to recognize me. Hasn't Cameron shown him a picture in the last few years? Granted, I don't post photos on Facebook due to my career. It is strictly to connect with my family since I was living three thousand miles away.

I hold out my hand and let loose a lie. "Alyson," I say, giving him my best friend's name.

His lip twitches up into a smirk as he takes hold of my hand and pulls it close, pressing his lips against my skin. If I weren't so mesmerized by his actions and his beautiful eyes, the heat from his touch traveling up my arm would feel like an inferno.

Ten years have passed, and in less than ten minutes, he has me hooked all over again. The last time I saw him was right after his dad died. He was the same energetic, bright Niko, but his shadow was filled with sadness. I wanted to hug him then, to take away his pain, but I was just his best friend's little sister. Nothing more. Apparently not even worth remembering.

Then again, a lot has changed for me in that time. I finally grew out of my awkward phase and gained the curves my teen years denied me. A little help from Alyson, who I met my junior year of high school, and I learned how to tame and style my hair and how to use makeup. With all that, I finally had the confidence to wear clothes that accentuated my body.

I'm not the ugly little duckling I was when we were kids, following my brother around. No, now I'm the swan my brother seems to think he is forced to scare princes away from.

"Niko," he says and lets go of my hand, his lips drawn up in a smile.

Oh, I know.

He hasn't changed. Same vibrant, piercing grey eyes, dark hair, and smile that makes me go dumbstruck. There is energy moving between us, and after the last few weeks, I'm more than ready to run with it. He's looking at me like an animal looks at its prey, and I want to be that so very badly.

Physically, he's bigger. Broad shoulders, thick arms, and pecs for days. I couldn't see them, but I was confident he had perfect abs and a beautiful V showing the way to what I'd always fantasized to be another ideal part of his anatomy.

Overall, his presence is even more significant than when he was a teenager. Sitting here, looking at him now, I can imagine just how large other things have gotten since back then.

God, he's just what I need right now after all the Tate shit I've been dealing with.

An hour on the tarmac and six-hour flight followed by an hour of Boston traffic made me nearly two hours late to meet Cameron. It's been four months since I've seen my older brother, and I don't want to think about what Cameron would do if he found out that Niko was hitting on me. I look around the bar wondering where my big brother is and wonder just how long I can keep up this act of being Alyson before Cam returns and this blows up in my face.

"So, where is your friend?" There. The only way to know is to ask. He'll think I saw him with someone and was here already.

He looks puzzled for a minute, and I know he's apparently stumped. After all, I am two hours late. Cam could be anywhere now. My damn phone died, and I haven't had the chance to check my messages.

"I have many friends. You're going to have to be more specific, baby."

I look at him and raise my eyebrow. I can't forget all the stories I've heard about Niko. Of course, he'd have been sitting here with another woman.

"You mean the redhead? She wasn't one of my friends, but I'd like you to be," he says with the cockiest freaking smirk I've ever seen on a man. True, he has a right to be cocky. After all, he's gorgeous. The epitome of tall, dark, and handsome, but I'm not falling for his shit. Let's see how cocksure he is after I've gotten up enough guts to pull this off tonight.

"Umm, no, not the redhead, but now that you mention it, I'm surprised you're here talking to me. I'm quite the opposite of her." It's a challenge just to get a better gauge on what he's thinking.

"Not that there is much to compare where you're concerned, but let's just say I've got an eclectic taste."

"Let me guess; you're a 'variety is the spice of life' kind of guy." It comes out more like a statement rather than a question, and I realize I sound a little snippy. Before he can respond, I keep going and decide not to touch that right now and move on to the more important things. Like the whereabouts of my big brother. "Ah, anyway, I was talking about the guy that was sitting with you earlier. That friend."

He frowns a little, and then it's gone. Back is that cocky smile he had when he told me he'd scream my name if I gave it to him. Oh, my God, do I want to give it to him.

"Ah. You mean Cameron. He's gone. Work, actually. You weren't waiting for him to come back, were you, because I can assure you that out of the two of us, I'm much better company." He takes a swig of his beer while looking at me over the top of the bottle.

He thinks I came over here for Cam? That's just gross.

"No, not at all. I was just thinking that it might be rude if I asked his friend to take me home without letting him know that you were . . . safe." His eyes go wide for a second before he recovers.

"Unless he's used to that? You taking strangers home for sex. If that's the case, then my mistake."

He swallows hard and places the beer down. Pulls his wallet out of his pocket, throws some cash down on the bar, and gets up.

Too strong? Shit! I've been with Tate so long that I think I forgot how to flirt right. I feel stupid now and feel the need to grab my bag and get the hell out of here.

Tate. Why the hell would he come to mind now, when I have Niko Callahan in front of me? Niko, the guy I have crushed on since I was around eleven years old. Niko, who is now standing in front of me with his hand extended like he's waiting for me to, what?

Oh, that's right. I said I wanted him to take me home so we could have sex, and holy shit! He's waiting for me to get up. What am I doing?

"You want to finish your drink first, or are you ready to go have dessert? I've been craving something sweet all night." He raises one eyebrow, waiting to see if I'm serious.

A challenge? Oh, he's got the wrong one tonight. I'm not going to back down now. The part of me that has wanted Nikolas Callahan for so many years is patting me on the back right now screaming, "Hell, yeah! You are totally about to bone Niko-fucking-Callahan. Screw his brains out, girlfriend!"

Then there's the other part of me, the part that knows this is wrong. I know this is Niko. I've known him since I was a kid. Hell . . . he practically grew up in our house. Wrong because although he was around all the time, he hasn't seen me in the past ten years and has no idea that I'm Everly Hayes. Not Alyson, the name I gave him when I sat down.

I sit for a minute and think about what it would be like if he hadn't known my brother since we were all kids. What if I was just some girl he found attractive and decided he wanted to hit on, take home, and then maybe see again in the future? That's not the case, though, and there isn't anything I can do to change the fact that I know this man even if he doesn't recognize me. He never looked at me as more than Cameron's kid sister. He probably never will.

Can I do this? Can I be *that* girl? I'm so tired of being little Miss By-The-Book. Miss Follow-The-Rules. Can I put myself out there and be someone wild, careless? A girl that sees what she wants and takes it, and says screw the consequences?

I look at him, and it takes me all of one second to decide which side I'm going to listen to. I grab my Sex on the Beach for some liquid courage, chug it down very unladylike, and then grab my bag before standing up.

Sex it is. I can worry about the rest later. The chances of me running into Niko are rather low once Monday rolls around. I'll be too busy with my new job even to see my family, never mind Niko. This is my life. My rules. I want Niko, and I'm going to enjoy myself while forgetting everything from my past. Time to leave that Everly Hayes in the rearview mirror.

"How about both?" I say, placing my hand on his, a spark of static electricity as we touch and the drink I just downed making me feel bolder than I've ever been in my life. "Lead the way." I'm so proud of myself right now. I didn't even stutter when I said that, and I sounded one hundred percent confident when I'm about two hundred percent nervous.

He chuckles at my statement, but with a squeeze of my hand, I know he's not laughing at me.

"My bike is out back. Did you drive?"

"Umm, no, I took an Uber." Another lie. My rental is around the corner, but there is no way I'm going to give up the chance to rub up on Niko's ass on the back of his bike by driving the rental car.

"Good."

Before I think about what I'm doing, I push Niko against the brick wall on the side of the pub and kiss him. He seems caught off guard at first, but that only lasts about a minute before his tongue decides to join the party, and I'm lost. I'm kissing Niko fucking Callahan.

"A girl that knows and takes what she wants," he says in between breaths. "I like it." I may have started this kiss, but it only takes a minute for me to realize that it's Niko who's in control now. He's demanding, hot, and if he tried, I'd more than likely let him fuck me right here against the brick wall.

He pulls away from me, eyes alive and bright with pure fire. God. Those eyes! I could drown in the pools of Niko's grey eyes.

"We need to stop before I rip your pants down your legs and fuck you right here, and baby, the things I want to do to you, well, they need to be done behind closed doors."

He's breathing as heavy as I am, lips swollen from that fucking hot as hell kiss, and I just want to go before I chicken out.

"I can see your brain working there, beautiful. If you don't want this, now is the time to say so." He raises one eyebrow, waiting for my answer.

"I'm not backing out. I'm wondering why we're still here talking when we could be at your house doing all those things you claim you can do to me, but only behind closed doors." I give him back his smirk, and he laughs.

"Well, let's go, then. My bike is this way." He grabs my hand, and I feel it . . . the electricity I've only read about in romance books. The ones I usually roll my eyes at when reading while thinking, *bullshit!* Silly authors and their arm zings. Doesn't happen in real life, but fucking hell if that's not what I just felt. Niko must have felt it too because his steps slow for a second and he looks back at me with an odd expression on his beautiful face, those eyes glancing down at our joined hands, and for a second he looks like he wants to pull away.

Niko's bike is all black, pure muscle, and sexy as hell. A shiver runs through me, my heart pumping even harder as I watch him swing one of his long legs over the body.

"That was hot," I say while wondering if I'm drooling.

His lip pulls up as he reaches for my belt and hooks a finger in as he pulls me closer.

"Don't worry about your hair. I'm about to knot it with my fist anyway," he says as he slides his helmet over my head.

The fire inside me explodes, heating my skin as I stare at him.

"I could straddle you right here, on your bike."

His nostrils flare as a groan vibrates in his chest. "Get on."

Using his shoulders to steady myself, I climb on behind him and wrap my arms around his waist.

"Hold on," he says as he starts the engine.

The vibration makes me gasp, and I slide my hand down just past his belt to the bulge I've been eyeing almost since I sat down next to him.

"How about here?" I whisper into his ear.

He moves my hand back up to his belt. "Safety first," he says, and I can hear the strain in his voice before he turns the throttle and we speed off.

I let out a gasp, my arms tightening around him as we rocket down the road. It's exhilarating and scary, the breeze cool and biting.

The roads have cleared, and it only takes a few minutes before we're pulling up to a parking lot of a two-story building.

"What do you think?" he asks as he turns the engine off.

"I think you need to warm me up."

He runs his hands up my legs. "Baby, you're going to be burning up in a few seconds."

There's no pause of touching as we climb off his bike. He rips the helmet off before his hands are cupping my ass, pulling me off the ground and up to his lips. I thought I'd known a good kiss, but Niko puts his whole body into it.

More than sensual, it's heady, clouding every thought while driving up the need to have Niko closer.

"Fuck," he groans and sets me back down on my feet. "Walls. Need walls."

It's all he can manage to say. Reaching between us, I get my first good feel of him in my hand. It's covered, but I can barely get my hand around it and even through his jeans, the heat is scorching. He's cussing, hips rocking.

Niko definitely is not cocky for compensation's sake.

"You were pretty much carrying me."

"Had to, or I'd fuck you against the side of the building."

"I like seeing you undone," I say.

His fingers flex against me. "Baby, get your ass moving so you can come undone around my cock."

"Think you can get me off?" I ask.

"No, I don't think I can." His lip twitches up, his tongue peeking out to wet his lips. "I know I can, but can you keep up?"

"Only one way to find out." I pull away from him and jog up a few steps before turning back to his confused expression. The drink I had is giving me the courage to be someone else. "Are you coming, hunter?"

"Don't have to ask me twice."

His long legs have him on me in a few strides. Swept off my feet is taken in the literal sense, his arm wrapping around me as he practically drags me through the front door and up the stairs to his door. A shiver runs through me at the feel of his teeth scraping along my neck. It's so intense I don't even notice that we're inside his place until he pulls my purse from my arm and tosses it onto the counter.

I don't care about it or anything else. Not with the dark eyes devouring me or the body melting me. The way he grabs my ass, filling his hands, and practically kneads it before pulling me up like I weigh nothing until we are face to face. Instinctively, my legs wrap around his hips, and he begins walking us, his cock pressing against my clit with each step.

Fuck.

I fist his shirt while I fuck his mouth with my tongue because I know it's the last time I'll be in control for a little while.

"Too much," I murmur. "Not enough."

Niko chuckles but doesn't stop. I don't want this to end.

"Baby, there is no such thing as too much. I'm going to show you that and then some in about ten seconds."

I grip his arms, pulling him closer. My fingers dive into his hair. My whole body feels like it's been electrified, and I start to pull back. Niko isn't having it as the kiss turns brutal. "Where do you think you're going? We're just getting started."

His hands are turning impatient, no longer playful as he starts tugging at my shirt. I lift my arms as he pulls my shirt up and away, tossing it somewhere behind me. He stops for a moment, taking the sight of me in, and I see it. Pure fire in his eyes, desire taking over. The look excites and terrifies me at the same time, leaving me to wonder what I've gotten myself into.

"Fuck, you're beautiful."

I feel my face heat and dip my head down, but then before I can start to think about what I'm about to do with Niko, the boy I've secretly crushed on since I was just a girl, I turn myself off and become an alter ego. Someone that can do this and not give a damn about the aftereffects.

"No sweet nothings in my ear. That's not why I'm here. You're either going to fuck me or you're not. Your choice."

"Well, all right, then," he says with a chuckle.

I'm not laughing, though. I don't want to think about this for more than what it is right now. The crush I had as a child was just that—a childish crush. Right? But this, this is sex. Niko is no longer that teenage boy I followed around as a goofy, nerdy, and shy kid. He's all man, and I intend to live out any and every dirty fantasy I've ever had when Niko has come to mind.

I want this man to drag me to the floor and thrust into me until my screams are heard all over the city. I still can't believe I'm doing this. Too late to turn back, and I wouldn't anyway.

I want this. Need him now. Niko is exactly what I need right at this moment, and I'm not going to allow myself to go there. There is no way I'm stopping this now.

"Let me down," I say as I unhook my legs.

"Don't want to," he groans against my lips.

I reach between us and pull his belt through the buckle. "I can't suck your cock from up here."

His eyes widen, nostrils flare, and I can feel him twitch against my fingers. In two seconds, my feet are on the ground and he's furiously grasping at his belt. Cupping my face, he brings my lips to his while he finishes getting his pants open. He curses when he does and I look down, my eyes popping wide.

"Oh," I say and look back up at him.

That smirk draws up again, and I gather up my courage before dropping to my knees. It's been years since I had a first time with a man, and suddenly I'm very insecure about my abilities.

The cock in front of me is even bigger than I imagined. I can't help but stare, my mouth slack as I run my hand up and down the length. There aren't many I have to compare him with, but it really is just as perfect as the rest of him.

"If you keep staring at it like that, I'm just going to shove it down your throat."

My gaze flashes up to him and I lean forward, pressing the flat of my tongue against him before giving it a little flick at the end. A groan falls from his lips as his hand moves to rest on the back of my head.

"That is the best sight I've ever seen," he says as I wrap my lips around the head, and I look up at him.

My hands are wrapped around his shaft, pumping him as I work him into my mouth. Maybe one day I'll be able to take him all in, but today is only the top three or four inches. I stop myself from asking the cliché, "How is it going to fit?" I'm far from a virgin and I know it will fit, but only now that I have him in my hands do I realize how much bigger he is than other guys I've been with.

A shudder rolls through me with just the thought of how good he's going to feel inside me.

"I bet you do some damage with this beast," I say when I come up for a breath.

He's breathing hard as he looks down at me, his eyes dark, and his lips twitch up into that sexy smirk that makes me wonder if I've just issued a challenge. Crossing his arms over his torso, he grabs the hem of his shirt and pulls it up and over his head.

I lean forward and absentmindedly suck on him while I stare up at his chest. It's just as muscular as I imagined. He's gotten broader in the shoulders, large pecs, and solid abs. There's a firefighter's emblem tattoo on his shoulder, and I spot some Greek lettering on his ribs.

"My turn," he says. He grips my wrist and pulls, helping me up before once again picking me up. His lips are immediately back on mine, but this time he holds me close, letting me hang as he walks me to the bed.

The mattress presses against my legs before he leans over and drops me the last few inches.

"You get the jeans, I'll get your boots," he says as he unzips one boot. A swift tug, and then he drops it to the ground before moving to the other boot.

All the while I've barely gotten my jeans unbuttoned, enthralled by the way his muscles flex. Finally, my jeans are undone, and I push them past my hips and butt. He doesn't let me get much further and tugs on them, taking my socks with them. They join the floor with everything else, leaving me in just my thong and my bra.

Hungry eyes take me in before his body is covering mine, lips crashing into me. His mouth moves down my neck, igniting my skin. A light scrape of his teeth, the softness of his lips, and the flexing of his touch has me in overdrive.

Niko is touching me like he's trying to devour me.

Nikolas-fucking-Callahan.

My crappy day, crappy month . . . maybe it was all worth it to have this man. Even if it's just one night, I'm all he wants.

"Fuck, Alyson, I can't wait to taste you," he says, and it's the cold reminder that he isn't with me, with Everly.

I'm Alyson, if just for the night. It messes with my fantasy night, which never included another woman's name. I push it away, instead focusing on his hands and the way he practically rips my panties from me.

There's no pause, the quick breeze against my exposed pussy before his mouth is on me. My back arches, and I cry out as his tongue flicks against my clit.

"Fuck!"

My outburst only seems to incite him, and he delves in with fervor. Not just my clit, but *all* of my pussy. Niko has a *very* talented tongue.

His whole mouth, whole body . . . Jesus, I'm so screwed.

Almost instantly I lose track of time. It could be hours, days, or even just a few seconds, but time seems to have no meaning under his touch.

One of his hands slides up my back, but I'm too focused on what he's doing to my pussy to notice until suddenly my bra is loose. The back is undone with one flick of his wrist, and his hand slides around and under the fabric. His fingers dance across my skin, spreading the fire until he ghosts my nipple.

A quick strum of his finger and my whole body jumps, my nipple hardening and sending a zing straight to my clit.

"Shit!" I cry out as I recover from the surprise and pull my arms from the straps, leaving yet another piece of clothing on the floor.

The double sensation is so powerful, his mouth so sensually aggressive, that my hands shoot to his hair, fisting it. It's leverage to pull him in, to move him exactly where I need him. He knows the sign and dives deeper, groaning against my clit.

There. There.

"Yes, yes," I whisper over and over until it's just sound that crescendos into a scream as I come against his mouth.

It takes a few convulsive jerks before my fingers release him and I relax back down on the bed.

Fuck. I can't remember the last time I came that hard.

"Damn, that was sexy," Niko says, licking his lips.

I'm trying to breathe again, a complete mess on his bed. In my periphery, I can see him pushing his jeans down his legs before climbing back on the bed and over me. He kisses up my body, nipping and sucking my nipples as he crawls up.

"Perfect tits," he says with a groan.

Warmth taps near my clit and I reach between us to hold him, but as I grab onto him, I immediately notice it's not skin to skin. He really is good if I didn't even notice he put on a condom.

His eyes meet mine, and I guide him closer until he's sliding against the wet mess he created. He never looks away as he rocks his hips, then drifts down and pushes in.

My eyes widen, refusing to look away from him, but the feeling of him stretching me is pleasure overload. Lips parted, I struggle for air as every nerve ending erupts in a mini-explosion.

"So good," he says with a moan, his hips pulling back before pushing in again, working himself deeper.

It's an erotic gratification I've never experienced before. He flexes his hips and I feel it, pressed against the deepest part of me.

"Ready?"

I stare up at him. *Ready? For what?*

My question is answered when he rears back, then slams into me. The sound that comes from me is high pitched and unidentifiable. His dark eyes hypnotize me, his hands a distraction, as his cock ravages me.

I'm still sensitive from my orgasm, but it wouldn't matter. It only takes a few good, hard strokes of him inside me to ramp me up toward a second wave.

"Niko," I say in a breathless whisper.

His hips pick up speed, tearing apart any last thought from me.

Nothing but carnal pleasure as I come again, clamping down on him.

I'm cock drunk. Completely and totally consumed by Niko.

All sense of anything other than his cock is gone.

"Fuck, baby, that's it," he growls. His sounds increase, and then, he slams into me.

I can feel him twitching inside me, deep in a place I'm not sure any man has been before. He's breathing hard, hot against my skin before he pulls back, hand on his dick, probably taking the condom off, before he falls down onto the bed next to me.

"Wow," is all I can say. My body has no strength at the moment.

Fantasy? No, my fantasies were a bland comparison, but I have new fantasies with actual memories to accompany them.

He chuckles, and I turn into his side and his rapidly expanding chest.

"Definitely wow."

We're both silent for a minute as we come down from our high. Strength starts to return as air pumps in and out of my lungs at a slower pace.

"You're going to make sure I can't walk tomorrow, aren't you?"

He looks over at me and smiles. "Challenging me again?"

I giggle and draw my lower lip between my teeth. "Maybe."

His head falls back down to the bed. "Five minutes."

I scrunch my brow. "Five wha—" I cut myself short and glance down.

My mouth drops open as I stare down in amazement. He's still hard. Maybe not fully, but as I stare, it twitches. I look up to Niko who is smirking at me.

"See something you want, baby?"

I straddle his hips and lean over to his nightstand and the box of condoms. A smile fills my face as I look down at him and I hold one up. "I challenge you to a round two."

"Fine, but round three's challenge is mine."

"Think you can take me?"

He grins at me. "I already did."

Chapter Five

Everly

A JOLT WAKES ME, my eyes popping open in the dark. It's a small moment of confusion as I process the room and the weight of the arm draped around me. The bedside clock reads almost three a.m.; its red glow lights up the face of Niko as I glance behind me.

That's when I remember why we're both passed out. I can feel it in my abdomen, the memory of Niko inside me. The strength needed to pull myself from the warmth of his arms is intense, but I manage. I spot a phone charger in the glow and pray that it's a match for my iPhone.

Each movement when prying my body from his is calculated so that I don't wake him. I don't want him asking questions. I got what I wanted from him, and I plan to leave the way I've heard that he usually does.

He doesn't move, his breath even. Why does he have to look so good even asleep?

A question for another time.

The bed that once had a place on the left side of Niko's large room is now almost blocking his bedroom door. We just fucked so hard that we moved his bed across his bedroom.

Holy shit.

Niko wrecked me. There is no way that any man will come close to what we just did tonight. I'm not sure how I feel about that considering I don't plan on seeing him again after this. The thought makes me sad, but I'm too tired to dwell on the feelings.

My legs are weak, making my steps unsteady. There are clothes all over the floor around the bed, a few condom wrappers mixed in, and I pick up my clothes as I make my way through. I'm almost tempted to stay until morning and wake him up just to see what sex looks like with Niko Callahan in the light of day, but I can't risk that. I let out a small sigh and turn away from him.

As I slide between the thin gap between the bed and the wall on my way toward the door, I notice the massive blackness on his back and wish the light was better so I could see the tattoo. Then again, I didn't get a good look at any of the ink covering his skin. Preoccupied with other parts of his body and all.

Quietly, I move about his apartment in search of my bag.

There's a nightlight on in the kitchen, highlighting my purse along with another phone cord.

Perfect.

I pull my phone out of the outer pocket and plug it in. Hopefully, it will give me just enough charge to call for an Uber and see if Cam sent me anything.

I slip my thong on and look back into the bedroom—no change.

My phone has just enough juice to turn on, and I nearly jump out of my skin as the startup music begins to play. Phone clutched in my chest, I frantically try to cover the speaker while pressing the volume button down.

Another glance finds Niko has rolled onto his back, but he's still sleeping soundly. I blow out a breath, my frayed nerves calming as my heart slams in my chest. Another glance at his sleeping form and the sheet that barely covers the lower part of his body has slipped, showcasing the V that leads down his happy trail. I should say my happy path. The tent he's currently sporting under the sheet has my hands itching to touch him, and my mouth salivates.

Holy shit.

I remember the last few hours. How my tongue owned every part of Niko's body, and I'd love to do everything again. I'm getting lost in the memories, the feelings, and the desire to pull the sheet down and straddle him again.

I can't. I need to leave, I remind myself.

Dragging my eyes away from the sex god in front of me, I look down at my phone. There are half a dozen texts from Cam along with a few voicemails, but he's not the only one. Thoughts of Niko completely disappear as I read a few and then scold myself for even going there. Cam's text message is all I care about. Screw Tate and his weak excuses. I've ignored his text messages this long. I've no plans on changing that now.

The last message from my brother says to go to the station. It's well past midnight—will he still be there? I've no idea what time they work till at a fire station, but I guess I'll find out when I get there. I also notice the messages before that.

Cameron: I'm heading to work, but Niko is going to wait for you with the keys. Let me know when you land.

Then another.

Cameron: I just looked up your flight. Says your plane is delayed due to weather. I'm going to let Niko off the hook so he can go home. Just in case you don't see this and head to the pub, call me and let me know you're safe. If you can't get me, I'm probably out on the job. Have Niko call the station. He can reach me faster.

God, he's like a mother hen sometimes. There are about ten messages from Cam.

Cameron: Niko went home. God, I hope you turn your phone on soon. Call me as soon as you land! You know I'll be worried until you do.

The night probably would have turned out a lot differently had I seen all those messages before getting to the pub. I let out a breath. There's no use thinking about that now. It's too late anyway.

Time is moving fast, and I need to get out of here. The Uber app is on the first page, and I quickly pull it up and input the address back to the bar and my rental car.

Seven minutes to get dressed and get out.

I keep my boots off; the heels make too much noise. I should probably let Niko know I left. Or acknowledge that I enjoyed my time with him. Is that what usual one-night stands do?

No . . . that's stupid, Everly.

I have no clue if there is some one-night stand etiquette, seeing as this is my first one, but I feel weird leaving without letting Niko know that I enjoyed our time together. I don't want to seem rude. That thought almost makes me laugh.

Only I would think it was rude not to say thanks for fucking the shit out of me. A flash of yellow in my purse catches my eye, and I know there's a pen near it, giving me an idea. A small scribble and I leave it with Niko before carefully making my way out his door and down the stairs.

Thirty minutes later, I'm in my rental pulling up to the firehouse. The engine is in the garage, multiple men folding up hoses and putting equipment away. They must have returned recently from a call.

The slam of my car door draws attention from the open door, and the familiar silhouette of my big brother turns toward me. His blue eyes find me, his mouth slipping up into a smile as he drops whatever chore he is working on to jog over to me.

I'm barely in the door when his hands are under my arms, and he's lifting me into the air. "Everly! Jesus, kid, I was worried the fucking plane crashed or some shit!"

I squeeze him hard. I love my brother, and I've missed him and my family. Sure, I've seen them every few holidays, but it's never the same. A wave of peace and the thought that I've made the right choice by coming home overwhelms me, and I almost want to cry.

"Hey," Cam says, pulling back to search my face. "You okay? I knew you'd be fine. You know how I feel about airplanes."

"Yeah, I know. I'm just tired. It was a long flight. Nothing that a shower and a few hours of sleep won't cure."

"You sure? We haven't had a chance to talk about you coming home."

"Yes, I'm positive. I'm just happy to be home. You know?"

He eyes me for a second, searching my face for any sign that something more is wrong. Cam has always been able to read me. We were always close growing up. Even though he is five years older than me, we have a deep sibling connection. He just always knew when I needed him and was there to fix things and still tried to make things easier on me.

"Well, if you need to talk, you know I'm here to listen. You only have to say the word, Ev."

I smile because I do know this. "I know, and I love you for it." I pull him back in for a hug. "God, I've missed you, big brother."

"Missed you, too, kiddo. Let's go grab the keys so you can go get some sleep and then get yourself settled in, yeah?"

"Yeah. Sounds good to me." We start walking toward the garage door of the firehouse. A few of the guys are still putting some things away while double-checking their equipment. "Eyes to yourselves, fellas. My kid sister is totally off limits to you fuckers."

I shake my head and giggle at Cam's words. He's ridiculous. I'm not sixteen years old anymore, but he still seems to think that his friends can't check me out. It was like that when he was home from college on break. I wasn't interested in his friends back then.

Well, not all of them anyway. Just one, and I was always disappointed when Cam would come home for break alone. Niko usually stayed in the dorm during breaks. I'd heard Cam telling my parents once that after Niko's dad died and his mom moved back to Greece, coming home made him sad, so he chose to stay at school.

God. My brother will flip if he finds out what I did with Niko only a few hours ago.

"So what happened?" Cam says, breaking me from my thoughts of Niko.

I wave my hand in the air and shake my head, adding an exasperated sigh. "Plane delay and a bunch of other stuff. Ran into an old friend before my phone died. It's been one hell of a day."

An omission isn't lying, right?

"I bet. Is your friend cute? Unless it was that witch of a best friend Alyson you insist on keeping around. Then I don't want to know. And how did you know to come here?"

"No . . . not Aly, but not your type. I was able to charge my phone some when I got to the rental. Took a few minutes, but finally got just enough juice to get your messages." I didn't lie. Niko is probably not his type. I smile to myself, and Cam blows out a breath.

"Good thing I didn't have Niko wait."

"Oh yeah. Niko was waiting for me, right? He wasn't mad, was he? I would hate to have ruined his night," I say, knowing that his night was in no way ruined while waiting for me. He just doesn't know exactly who it was that made his night. Good thing I'll be too busy working crazy hours once the new job starts on Monday. My chances of running into Niko are slim, and even if I do eventually run into him, well . . . I'll worry about that part later.

"Earth to Everly," I hear Cam say, bringing me from my thoughts and deception.

"Sorry, I'm just tired. What did you say?"

"I don't think anything ever ruins Niko's nights."

I'm sure that's true, but if he finds out that his latest flavor was me, he'll likely be more than a little pissed off.

"When is your stuff getting here?"

I need to stop with the Niko thoughts. It's over. No use crying over spilled milk.

"The moving company is packing up my apartment and then will head out, so I need to find a place soon. My car should be here by the end of the week. The rest shortly after."

"Your car? Seriously, Ev?" Cam shakes his head. "You could've just bought a new, more practical one here."

"It's a BMW Z4 convertible. No way in hell I'm leaving my baby."

"A convertible won't do you much good here."

"It's a hard top."

"Whatever. Hard top won't help you once that snow hits us, little sister, and it's rear-wheel drive so you'll get stuck for sure." Cam shakes his head at me before digging into a bag he obviously brings with him to the firehouse during a shift. He rummages through it for a second and then pulls out his keys, twisting a set off. "Mom and Dad left two days ago and won't be back for a few weeks."

"So specific."

Cam shrugs. "You know how they get when they're in Martha's Vineyard."

Our parents are third-generation owners of a good-sized estate, a place we spent every summer at when we were younger. We never fit in very well, not acting like spoiled rich brats like all our neighbors. I mean, the Kennedys have a place there for crying out loud. Not to mention all the other wealthy families. Money pours in there during the warmer months.

"When do you start your new job?" Cam asks.

"Monday," I say as I slip the keys onto my key ring.

"I'm booked solid this week, but let's get dinner on Friday or Saturday, fill me in on everything."

I step forward and wrap my arms around his shoulders. "It's a date."

His arms tighten around me. "Missed you, kiddo."

"Missed you, too."

"All right, get to bed." He pats my shoulder, then pushes on my back.

I give him a wave goodbye and head back out to my car. The firehouse is only a few minutes away from my parents', especially at this hour with the lack of other vehicles on the road. The driveway is dark, but a sudden flash of light as I punch in the security code for the gate surprises me. The exterior is suddenly blinding, the motion detection lights activating all around the property.

As I drive up and park outside of the garage, I see a camera at one of the lights and wave, knowing my dad will see it. Maybe not now, but he'll get the alert on his phone and see it when he wakes.

After unpacking the car, I flip through the keys Cameron gave me. When I moved across the country, there was no reason for me to have a set, especially since I didn't make it home very often. Mom and Dad always flew out to visit me. In fact, I am sure the set Niko was supposed to give me was the set I used to carry.

The house is still, the flicker of light bringing life to a lifeless, dark room. I flip more switches, lighting the house up as memories come flooding in. It's my home, my one real home. I grew up here, and while some of the decors have updated, it still holds the warmth and familiarity that sends a wave of calm through me.

"I'm home," I call out into the quiet.

There's no response, and sadness washes over me. No Mom to pop out and welcome me, no pitter-patter of Bruno and Sasha's nails on the hardwoods as they bound over for a lick attack.

My suitcase is heavy as I lug it up the stairs, a point that is proven by the "Heavy" tag the airline attached. There's still another one, and I wonder if it's needed tonight or if I can get it in the morning, because my legs are still on the weak side due to the night's activities. The laptop bag is a must, but I'll get it when I grab a snack.

Entering my room is almost like opening the fourth dimension. It has the same warmth of familiarity and security of the rest of the house, but laced in my eighteen-year-old self's sense of style. Is geek chic a thing?

Bookshelves covered in books, some shelves two deep. My sleigh bed is encased in a pink floral comforter that I think has been there since I was eight. Pictures from high school are on my dresser, and, embarrassingly enough, Niko's senior photo taped to the mirror.

I just did a fuck and run on him.

Holy shit!

My mind reels with the reality of my actions, a smile curling up and practically breaking my face in two. I want to scream it from the rooftops, let everyone know that I, Everly Hayes, was fucked senseless by Niko Callahan.

My eyes widen.

Alyson.

The night's namesake needs to be informed. I run back downstairs and grab my laptop bag. The phone charger is buried, knotted in with the other cords. I pick out the tangled mess and run up for my purse.

I'm a mess with my purse in one hand and a tangle of cords in the other, all the while my stomach rumbles because I never did get to eat dinner. A groan slips out, and I run back down and into the kitchen.

My fingers work at the knots that somehow happened during the security inspection because I was very meticulous when I packed the bag yesterday morning. Once I fish the charger cord free, I plug it into the nearest outlet and immediately plug my phone in.

Next item to find is my Bluetooth, which has me rolling my eyes on where it ended up. After five minutes of searching, I see it in an interior pocket of my purse, which is just enough time for the phone to get enough of a start-up charge.

The whole process takes longer than I think it should, but finally, the phone is on and I'm pulling up Alyson's number. She's working at the bar tonight, so I know she's still awake.

Three rings and then a distorted, "Hello."

"Hi."

"Oh my God, Everly! Are you here?" Alyson asks.

My lips pull up into a smile. "Yes."

"Thank God! Okay, I'm coming this weekend, and we're going to drink wine and play catch-up."

"Not too much wine," I say as I open the fridge, it's shelves empty except for condiments and about a case of wine. Seriously? There is a wine cellar in the basement. Why is there so much in the fridge? "You know I try not to drink that much and usually only a glass or two with dinner." Or one or two fruity drinks when I want to have hot sex on a platter with one of the sexiest fish in the sea, but I'll save that little tidbit for a few more minutes.

I close the door and move to the walk-in pantry.

"Boo. That's so lame, Ev. So I'll bring dinner!"

I laugh at my best friend and give in. "Fine, but only because it's you, and there is a lot to catch up on. I'll probably need a few glasses of wine once I fill you in."

There is silence from Alyson a beat longer than I expect.

"What does that mean? Everly Hayes, you tell me what you did, and you tell me now."

I shake my head, my gaze scanning the shelves. There are some necessities, but nothing dinner worthy. "How do you always know when I've done something worth talking about?"

"First, you didn't call me when you got into your parents', which means you are just calling me now, and therefore, you just got to your parents'. You should have arrived like, six hours ago, so what have you been doing?"

I'm completely shocked, unable to respond.

"Or is the question who have you been doing?"

Jesus. She's a little mind reader.

"When did you become the psychic Miss Cleo?"

I begin rifling through drawers. There used to be a stack of takeout menus, a few open almost twenty-four hours, but the usual stash place is empty. Maybe my parents have finally embraced Siri.

"Oh my God! You did do someone! Tell me all about it. Was it some hottie sitting next to you on the plane? Did you join the mile-high club?"

"No. I was going to tell you this weekend, but . . . Do you remember me talking about Niko Callahan?"

If she were sitting in front of me, she'd be rolling her eyes.

"How could I forget? He was who you measured all guys by. If they didn't make you feel as much or more of the butterflies, you bounced. The almost-as-much was the only reason you stuck with Tate for two years."

I lean over the counter as I thumb through my GrubHub app, searching for anyone who delivers.

"Yeah, well, let's just say that my childish crush on the boy he was has nothing on what he looks like now as a grown man."

"So, he's hot?"

"Hot doesn't begin to explain how he looks now. He's something, though." She chuckles in my ear, but she has no idea that I'm not kidding. The Niko then has nothing on the Niko now. He's like something off one of those men's fitness magazines that you see on the store shelves. No way does that man has an ounce of fat on his body. I know I didn't feel any.

"Okay, back to that later. What about Niko?"

"Well, he was waiting for me when I arrived."

Chinese, burrito, or pizza seem to be my only late-night options.

"Are you telling me you finally tapped that?"

"Multiple times." I scan through the menus, letting my stomach dictate.

"Holy shit. Holy-motherfucking-shit!" Aly screams on the other end of the phone. "Oh, yes, we do have a lot to talk about! First, how was it?"

I let the phone drop back against the counter, my mind swirling with images of him over me, the feel of him inside me, the way our bodies moved together. The look in his eyes as he stared into mine, the way he made me come.

It was...

"Perfect."

"Seriously?" she asks, sounding in disbelief.

"Yes." Did she think he'd be one of those cocky assholes who couldn't live up to his ego? Probably. She has more experience in that department than I do.

"Are you going to see him again?"

"No."

"Wait, why not?"

I blow out a hard breath, the euphoria of the night darkened by one small fact. "He didn't know who I was, Aly." My fantasy never included him calling me by someone else's name.

"What do you mean?"

My sudden shift in mood answers my early morning dinner debate and I pick Chinese. A big bowl of noodles sounds perfect.

"We were talking, and I stared straight into his eyes, and there was not a single spark of recognition. Not even a nod of familiarity." There is a part of me that is disappointed that Niko didn't recognize who I was, but the other part of me knows that had he known who I was, last night probably wouldn't have happened. Who am I kidding? There is no perhaps about it. Niko would never have looked twice at me had he known that I was Everly Hayes, Cameron Hayes's younger sister.

"I don't even know what to say to that, babe. I want to say that it sucks, but I'm jumping up and down here for you because you finally did something that I would have encouraged you to do! I'm so proud of you, girlfriend!"

I smile at my best friend's words, and I can't help it. She's right. I stepped outside my norm and entirely channeled my inner Alyson.

"I'm glad you mentioned that. I have to tell you something." I start laughing and clear my throat before I expose my lie.

"Tell me what?"

"Well, I told you that he didn't know it was me, so I didn't tell him my name."

"Oh! You did like they do in those erotic romance books you read! One night. No names. No strings. No repeats," she says like that movie guy that tells you what's playing at the theatre and then starts cracking up. She sounds like a kid in a candy store.

I shake my head even though I know she can't see me through the phone. "Not exactly, although I wish I'd thought of that now that you say it. Sounds cooler."

"Huh? So who did he think you were if you didn't stay anonymous?"

"I told him my name was Alyson." I wait a minute and then look at my phone to see if we are still connected. Aly says nothing, and then I hear her sniffle.

"Aly? Are you crying?" What in the world just happened? "Al?"

"Yes. I'm here. Sorry," she says, and then I hear her moving stuff around and then she blows her nose in my ear. "You lied to someone? Everly freaking Hayes *lied?*" she says, and I smile into the phone.

"Umm, yes. If I told Niko I was you, then I'd say that was pretty much a lie."

"Oh my God! Everly! I'm so proud right now. Let me enjoy my moment. You've finally been initiated into the bad girls club. My girl is growing up." I chuckle and blow her a kiss through the phone. "I can't wait for you to graduate," she says, and I start laughing with her. I can't help it; she's contagious sometimes. "I think you should tell him who you are."

"Are you crazy?"

"Okay, well then at least hook up with him again."

"No. That's playing with fire. If Cam knew what happened, he'd blow his lid right off!"

"Are you serious? You're not a kid anymore, and Cam needs to mind his own damn business when it comes to you and your sex life. God, he's so fucking annoying."

Oh God. Here we go. Alyson and Cameron have the worst hate-hate relationship I've ever seen. I am not in the mindset to hear another long rant again on my brother's faults and all the ways she'd love to boil his balls.

"First, I'm not getting into your thoughts and feelings on my brother. I still have no idea why the two of you can't be civil," I say to her. "Second, this is Niko. You know how he is. How Cam has always been when it comes to his friends. So that's not going to fly."

"Ev, it's not like his best friend had sex with your mom! Come on!"

"Okay, that's just gross. Don't say Niko and sex with my mom to me ever again. Jesus."

"I'm just saying. There is nothing wrong with two adults that were obviously into each other bumping uglies. I mean, you're in your damn twenties, not a teen."

"Thanks, Mom. I wouldn't get too crazy over this, but I have to go. Shit . . . now I have the horrible thought of Niko and my mother! You suck." Aly laughs, and I want to find bleach for my brain. "I'll call you later. I need to unpack some things until I get situated, and hopefully, the things I sent from Tate's place will arrive soon. Otherwise, I'll have to buy a few new things for my new job."

"Speaking of crazy, have you heard from the pond scum?"

I knew she'd ask, but I wanted to forget about Tate a little while longer if I could.

"I haven't spoken to him, but he's been calling every day. More than once a day. Leaving voice messages or sending me text messages. Nothing new," I say nonchalantly and hope she leaves it alone, but I know she won't. She is Aly, after all, and she hated Tate from day one.

"You mean he's still trying to get you to move back there, with him?"

I've added a truckload of food to my cart while talking, somehow racking up more than fifty dollars in Chinese cuisine. The good news is my stomach won't be roaring at me in twenty to thirty minutes.

"You know that's never going to happen. It's over. I can deal with a lot of things, but cheating and lying are not on that list. Tate is my past. I just want to move on, start new, and forget I ever knew Tate Matthews."

"Which is exactly why you should tap Niko again. I think he might just be the best medicine for you right now. At least don't rule the idea out. Trust me. I always know what's right, and this sounds right."

"No comment, but we can talk about that again later. I need to run."

"Of course! Call you later. If you need me, you know where I am. I didn't like Tate, but I know that was hard for you, and I'm here if you need me no matter what."

"I know. And I will, but honestly, I'm good. Tate just isn't the same guy he was when we met."

"I'm not sure he ever was that guy you thought he was, babe, but I'm just glad he's gone, and that you're back. Even if he is the reason you've come home, I'm glad you're here. Call me later; I have to get back to work. My asshole boss is giving me the stink eye. Love you!" she says before we hang up.

"Love you, too!" God, I love Aly. I've missed her like crazy. I know I made the right choice coming back. Everything just feels right now that I'm home.

My Chinese arrives, and after gorging myself, I throw the leftovers in the fridge and crawl into bed. It's been a long day, but possibly the most memorable in my life. One I will remember forever.

Chapter Six

Niko

"SOMEONE BETTER BE DEAD or dying," I say out loud as I blindly reach for my cell phone that has now vibrated so many times it fell from my nightstand to the floor. My eyes are still closed, and I plan to keep them that way until my alarm goes off in . . . I pull one eye open as I try to glance at the clock on my dresser, but it's not there. Whatever . . .

I finally manage to pull it up by the cord and see not only who's calling, but that it's early. Really fucking early. I look at the name flashing on my cell and contemplate ignoring him, but I know he'll just keep calling until I pick up. I put my head back down on my pillow and close my eyes before answering.

"What is wrong with you? I have two hours left to sleep. Are you bleeding?" I ask, Cam, before I bury my head back into my pillow. I hear his insane laughter come through the line, and I'm tempted to press end, but like the good friend I am, I wait.

"Get up, sleeping beauty!" he says way too cheerfully for the hour. Fucking morning people. "I'm about to grab my gym bag and head out in ten. You said you'd hit the gym with me this morning before your shift. Get up, get your shit together, Callahan, and meet me downstairs in twenty."

"Shit!" I say and pull myself up into a sitting position on my bed.

"Yeah, shit is right. I knew you'd try and back out. Not happening, man. No pain, no gain."

I lean back against my headboard and rub the sleep from my eyes. "Listen, man, I'm not going to be able to meet you until after my shift."

"Why the fuck not?"

"If you'd shut up and let me wake up, then I could tell you that I'm not . . . what the fuck?"

I was about to tell Cam that I have company, but it's then I realize that I am, in fact, alone, and my bed is across my fucking room. Holy shit! Thoughts on everything that happened last night begin to flood my brain and my morning wood is double the wood from images of everything we did last night. Speaking of my cock, there is something stuck to it right below my abdomen. On my dick?

"What? What the fuck? Dude, are you talking in your sleep, man? Wake up, Niko! Get one of your nasty green veggie shakes and get ready."

"Cam, hold on a second." I hear him bitching through the phone, but I've stopped listening and pull the phone away from my ear.

I get up and flip the light on, and just for shits and giggles I double-check to make sure she's gone. Nope. There is no Alyson in my bed. The floor is littered with my clothes having landed wherever she threw them when she ripped them off. However, hers are gone.

I pull the sheets back, ready to find her, and that's when I see it. The thing that is sticking to me—not just sticking to me, but stuck to my dick—is a piece of paper. No, not just a piece of paper, one of those yellow fucking Post-it notes with the word "Thanks" written on it. And a goddamn smiley face?

"Are you fucking shitting me?" I say out loud. Cam is going to bitch my ass out in a minute, but I need a second to process. The fact that this girl, this sexy-as-fuck, rocked-my-whole-world-last-night woman left before I woke, stuck a fucking Post-it note on my cock to thank me for the best sex of my life, and bounced without a word.

Well, that's a fucking first.

"Hello! Earth to Niko, what the fuck, man. You're not what? Get your ass up and let's go," Cam says from the phone.

"Yeah, okay. All right, just let me grab a quick shower first." *And push my bed back against the wall*, I think, but keep that shit to myself. I'm not one of those guys that need to tell my boys all about my conquests. That's a dick move, and I try not to fuck and report if I can help it.

"Niko, it's the gym. Don't be a fucking girl and get all dolled up before we sweat our asses off. Shower after, you pussy!" Cam says and laughs at me through the phone.

"Shut up. I was going to tell you I couldn't go because I wasn't alone, but apparently, she dipped out on me sometime during the night and didn't let me know she was leaving. I need a shower, man, so give me a few minutes, or you can go work out alone."

"Whoa! Someone's cranky this morning. Is big Niko pissed that little Niko didn't get his morning nookie with his Wheaties?"

"First of all, there is no 'little' Niko, asshole, and there is nothing small about little Niko. Worry about little Cameron." Cam starts cackling again, and I'm ready to throw my cell across the room.

"You said there is nothing little about little Niko! Bro, you called your dick little Niko!"

"Shut up, Cam, you're giving me a fucking headache." I rub my temples to try and relieve the tension building in my head, between Cam and his ribbing me before the sun is even up and then a Post-it on my fucking cock thanking me for sex.

"Suck it up, buttercup! Welcome to the mortal world, Casanova. Sometimes you can't always get laid twice in twenty-four hours."

"Listen, I'm not letting you screw with me today, you ass. Let me wake up first," I say. Cam laughs and then just as fast as he began to, he stops and is eerily quiet.

"Hello?" I pull the phone away to see if we're still connected when I hear him on the line.

"Dude, you just said that she left in the middle of the night."

"Yeah, and?"

"And . . . She didn't wake you up? She didn't ask for a ride, nothing?"

"That's what I just said. What the fuck, are you a parrot now?"

"Did you check the rest of your apartment? What if she ripped you off or something? Did you check to make sure your wallet is not missing?"

"I didn't think of that, but I'm honestly not worried about that. She didn't seem like that type of girl—"

"What type of girl?" He cuts me off, and I'm seriously thinking about kicking his ass today. "The kind that goes home with a strange guy she just met in a bar, has sex with the guy, and then leaves in the middle of the night without a word?"

"No, dumbass, she left a note!"

"Ohhhhh! Well, that explains it! You're right! She doesn't seem like that type of girl at all if she left you a note!" he says with nothing but sarcasm, and I want to put my fist through the phone. I'm kicking his ass today. "What did it say?"

"It doesn't matter. Just shut up, would you? She didn't steal anything, and she's gone. Mind your own business." There is no way I'm telling him what the sticky fucking note said. I'll never hear the end of it, and he'll run his mouth to the rest of the guys at the firehouse.

"Open the door."

"What?"

"I'm at your door, Princess. Open the door, I'll make you a protein shake while you wash the smell of pussy off yourself, and then we can go hit the gym."

I don't bother with a reply, and I hang up on him, throw my boxer briefs on and head to my front door. Cameron is standing outside with hair wet from being freshly showered himself.

"So it's cool for you to shower before the gym, but if I do it, I'm a girl?" I smirk at him and turn to head to my bathroom. "Unless you got caught in the rain, I'd keep your bitch-ass mouth shut while I take my shower," I say, only to have Cam flip me the bird before throwing his bag on the floor and closing my front door behind him. "I'll be out in ten."

"Yeah, yeah. Just hurry up!"

I'm rinsing the soap from my hair when my bathroom door slams open, causing me to jump out of my skin. The shower curtain pulls back, and for a minute I contemplate screaming like the chick in that psycho movie, but my eyes now have soap in them, causing me to reach for the towel to my right to wipe my face.

"What the fuck, Cam? Get out!" I yell at him, but he doesn't budge. No, what little I can see of him with the shampoo and water dripping into my eyes isn't right.

Cam, who is now standing in front of me, is grinning ear to ear. When I clear my eyes of shampoo, I look down at his hand where, sure enough, he's holding the yellow Post-it note that Alyson left on my fucking dick this morning. Great. I try closing the shower curtain so that I can finish my shower, but Cameron isn't going to let this go. He pulls the shower curtain open again and with all his pearly whites showing, finishes my fucked-up morning off, Cam-style.

"Dude! Is this the note she left you this morning?" he asks with the Post-it stuck to his fingers. "Looks more like she was telling you that last night was barely passable if you ask me."

"I didn't ask you," I growl at him.

"I mean, this note she left doesn't even qualify as a note. It's one word and a smiley face, dude. I'd say it was rather insulting your dick skills," he says, and as usual, I want to hit him. Only Cam can pull shit like this. We've been going back and forth like this since we were teens. He probably won't stop, even when we are both old and fucking grey.

"Give that to me, asshole!" I reach for it, but he pulls his hand back and the Post-it is too far away for me to grab it without busting my ass in the shower.

"Bro, wait till I tell the guys. You are never living this one down. This," he says, waving the Post-it note back and forth in front of my face, "is total payback for all that ball busting you and Bishop did to me when that redhead I fucked left me cuffed to the back of Engine Two. You didn't have to tell them that shit! I'm still dealing with Bishop and Jenkins and the beginner's bondage set they keep leaving in my fucking locker once a week."

"You called me while I was upstairs playing cards with both of them, dumbass. I didn't know you were downstairs on your night off banging some chick that wanted to play spank-your-ass dominatrix on the truck."

"That's not what she was doing, fucker!" he yells, and I want to laugh all over again because he was the dumb fuck that brought her there on his night off knowing one or all of us could have walked in on him at any time. Did he think that we wouldn't notice him fucking some chick if we got called out on a job?

"Cameron . . ." I growl. "Cut the shit already. I'm not in the mood for your crap today. Just get out."

"So, what did you do, leave her hanging? Forget that you're supposed to let ladies go first? Come on, man. You can tell me," he says with that stupid smirk on his face. "Might as well fill me in now because if you don't, I'm just going to make shit up as I go. You know that I'm going to run my mouth regardless, so might as well get the story right about how you performed so badly that the chick you brought home ditched your ass in the middle of the night and left you a cheap-ass version of a Dear Niko letter."

"Sticking a Post-it on my cock doesn't qualify as a Dear Niko letter, you moron. If anything, it proves that the night went well for her because she thanked my cock and not me directly, you dumbass. I was sleeping. Maybe she couldn't wake me up. You think of that? Now get the hell out so I can finish my shower!"

"Wait, wait. What did you just say?"

"Cam. Get. Out!" He looks down at his hand, the one with the Post-it stuck to it, and starts waving it around trying to get the Post-it to unstick from his fingers. Finally, he takes his two fingers on the other hand and peels the sticky paper from his hand.

"That's not cool, man. That shit was on your cock, and you're just now telling me?" He gives me a disgusted look before saying, "That's just rude," and then walks over to my sink to wash his hands.

I let out a sigh and shake my head. "I'm rude? You do realize you just barged into my bathroom where I'm talking a damn shower, right, but I'm the one that's rude? Maybe next time you won't go looking into shit that's not your business." He stops and stares at me through the mirror, so I close the shower curtain. "Close the door on your way out." As soon as my head's under the spray of the water, the curtain is once again ripped open.

"What is your problem?" I yell at him. "This is beyond fucking weird, man. Even for you."

"She left you a note saying thanks? She stuck a fucking Post-it note on your dick, a thank you for fucking her?"

"Get out, Cameron. Get the fuck out!" I yell louder while I rub at my eyes. "Now, Cam, or you're on your own today!" He ignores me, and his annoying laugh just pisses me off more. I'm tempted to choke him with the shower curtain, or better yet beat him with the pole.

Why, God? What did I ever do to you? I think to myself as I listen to him cackle.

"This has got to go in the Guinness book! This right here is fan-fucking-tastic! I can't wait to let everyone know what happened to the great Niko Callahan last night!"

"That's it!" I lunge for him, trying to grab the damn sticky note, but he moves before I grab him and I end up slipping on the floor, shower curtain and all crashing around me. Cameron laughs so hard, he sits down and holds his stomach. Tears are starting to stream down his face. I get up and turn the water off, saying nothing else. Grabbing a towel, I wrap it around my hips and walk out, leaving Cam's laughing ass on my bathroom floor. "Fuck you, Cam." He lets out another belly laugh.

"Oh, come on! Don't be like that, Princess. I was just playing with ya!"

"It's like your religion or something."

"What is?" he asks.

"Instead of saying you're a practicing Catholic, you should tell them your religion is assholian. As long as I've known you, I should know better by now. You're an assholian prick."

"An assholian prick?" Cameron stands there for a second pretending to consider what I just said. "Where do you come up with these sayings?"

I'm already feeling frustrated as hell, and I got laid last night. "Same place you go to get your ass spanked, that's where."

"Oh, come on! It's funny shit, and you know it. Stop being a girl. It happens to the best of us, man."

"Shut up, Cameron!" I yell from my room while I get dressed. He's never going to stop. This day just gets shittier and shittier.

"Can you spot me?" Cam asks just as I'm getting off the treadmill. I'm not trying to get huge, but I stay toned, and I love getting my heart rate up with a good run. Usually, I head outdoors, but Cam has this thing where he doesn't like hitting the gym alone, so here I am.

"Yeah, I'll spot ya. Might be worth it. I might accidentally drop the bar on your neck. That way I can watch you struggle to wiggle out from under it in front of the chick over there." Cam's been watching this chick for the last thirty minutes. I saw him watching her in the mirror. Part of me was secretly hoping he'd drop a weight on his toe and embarrass himself in front of her, but with Cam's fucking luck, she'd be a nurse and kiss it fucking better. I smirk and shake my head at the thought.

"You wouldn't do that to me, now, would ya?" Cam says, and I give him a look that says otherwise. "Niko, you wound me, brother. Stop being a baby and let's get this done. Good thing today isn't leg day. I've got that training this week with the rookie, and I need to be able to walk."

"Better you than me." Cam snorts but ignores me for the most part, lying back on the weight bench while I grab the weights for him.

"So Ev was delayed last night. She stopped by the station late last and grabbed my keys to my parents' house. When she's ready to move her things, she'll need some help. I told her I'd grab a few of the guys from work. You on board to help?"

"Of course. As long as it's not a day I'm scheduled to work a double, I'm in."

"Thanks, man. I'll let you know when."

"Shit. I can't believe little Ev moved away to California and stayed away for eight years, bro. I don't know if I could be away from home that long."

"I know. Me either, to be honest. I might complain about the weather here, and the snow in the winter, but New England is my home. She loves it out there, though. She always said she wasn't leaving her paradise."

"So then why did she move back?"

"She got a new job. I guess they offered her more money and a better position at the company she works for or some shit like that. There's more, but we haven't had the chance to sit down and talk yet. I'm meeting her for dinner this weekend before she starts her job on Monday we both get too busy to see each other. If you're off one night this weekend, you should come. I'm sure she'd love to see you after all this time."

I laugh because I remember little Everly Hayes had a crush on me way back when. I thought it was cute, but Cam hated it. He always said it was because he didn't want her following us around, that it put the girls in our high school off him when Everly's little awkward self would bounce behind us. She was everything the word dork or nerd had after it in the dictionary.

"Yeah, maybe. It would be nice to see Everly again. See how much she's grown up and shit."

"Dude, you have no idea. I told you she's not the same girl you last saw."

"Still shy and awkward?" I ask, chuckling. I haven't thought much of Ev over the years.

"Not at all, man. Everly is very different from the little pain in the ass you remember."

"Nah, bro, she always bugged the shit out of you. She didn't bother me. I always wanted a younger sibling."

"She bugged me because I knew she had a crush on your fucked-up ass! Plus, she was always cockblocking my game with Cassidy Rollins." I laugh because Cam is dead serious.

"Cam, she was a baby if anything. She was never even close to being on my radar at her age. I never understood you back then."

"If it were your sister, you'd have understood. Speaking of fucked-up guys."

"Hey! I'm not fucked up, asshole. If I am, then like equals like, fucker."

Cam shrugs my comment off and continues his reps. "She's been with this guy, Tate, for a while. I can't stand the guy. I met him last Christmas when the folks and I went to see her for the holidays. He just rubbed me the wrong way."

"She's got a boyfriend, then?"

"See, that's the thing, I don't know. She didn't tell my mom anything, and she hasn't mentioned Tate coming here. I'm waiting for her to let one of us know. Mom didn't want to seem nosy, but fuck that. I'm going to ask her when we have dinner. I'm hoping she kicked his sorry ass to the curb."

"Well, for his sake, I hope she did too." I laugh at Cam's protective streak for his little sister. "Let me know what the deal is. If he's coming soon, maybe you and I can go invite him out for a beer. You know, be all manly and shit. Scare the fuck out of him." I smile wide because Cam is thinking about it. So much for being the big thirty. He still acts like he's twenty.

"Whatever, bro. I'm going to hold you to that. Ev will be pissed as hell, though. She'll probably cuss me out before she throws me out if I do something like that. She raked me over the coals when we spent Christmas with them last year."

"I can't see that. I still see Everly with braces on her teeth and those big-ass Coke-bottle glasses she wears."

"Wrong. I told you, Ev is different. No more Coke-bottle glasses. Plus she's got this friend of hers, Aly, that has rubbed off on her in not so good ways. Now that one is a piece of work."

"You're ridiculous, but you usually are, so whatever. I need to grab a shower before we head out. You about done here, or do you need me to stay and spot you so you don't break a nail?" I'm done talking about Cam's little sister. All I can think about is Alyson and everything that happened last night. I can't believe I didn't get her number. Not a last name, nothing.

"Screw you, asshole. You're the pretty boy, but no. I'm going to stay and work out a little longer. You go on ahead, and I'll catch up with you later," he says to me, but he's looking at the chick that was eyeing him earlier.

"All right, then. Later." No use in cockblocking my boy. After all, I got some last night. Maybe if he gets laid he'll leave me alone. I head toward the men's locker room so I can hit the shower before I head out, walking past the girl that has been watching Cam and me since we walked in on my way to the locker room. No way can she compete with the hot-as-hell woman that rocked my world last night, but she's cute. Cam will probably hook up with her a few times, and then the awkwardness will begin once he ends it. I shake my head at the thought. I don't usually do second dates with the women I fuck. Once is often enough, or I'll cause problems for myself. Happens every time I've allowed a woman to overstay her welcome. Feelings get involved, and not mine.

I don't like disappointing the women I'm with, and I sure as fuck never intentionally set out to hurt anyone. It's better for us both if it stays casual. Just hook up and be done. No strings. It sounds cold, but it's honest, and it works for me.

I've had more than a few that claim they'd like a more extended arrangement, but it's too risky. Time equals talking, and talking leads to getting to know more about the other, and knowing more leads to catching feelings. I just don't have the time for that right now. It's hard not to come off as a dick, but I'm up front, and I tell them from the jump that this is how it is.

The last thing I need is some bunny boiler showing up at the station. The guys wouldn't let me live that shit down, ever.

Now . . . Post-it note girl, on the other hand. Well, I'd let her stalk me anywhere she wanted. How the hell did I not hear her leave? I'm a light sleeper—I should have heard her. I rub my hand down my face in the shower, letting the water run down my body. I'm hard as a rock just thinking about her, and I don't like it.

I should just pull up one of the chick's numbers from last week, call one of them, and get Alyson out of my head, but that would break my rule. Not only that, but I don't want to. I want to know why she left without saying anything. I know she had a good time. Hell, I know she had a great damn time. There is no doubt in my mind about that. I made her come at least five times. There is no fucking way that was it.

Maybe Cam is right. Perhaps it's just because she left me before I got up and had the chance to let her down. I know I have an ego, but damn if I've ever had a woman bruise it before. It sucks. I'm sure there are women out there that don't find me to their liking, but I have yet to approach one where the attraction wasn't mutual. It just is what it is. So why the hell can't I get this chick out of my head? I let out a puff of air, shutting off the water. This is going to be a long-ass day.

Chapter Seven

Everly

I'M EXCITED TO HAVE dinner with Cameron. It's been so long since I've gotten to talk to him face to face, and there's a lot I need to catch him up about. Not that it's a conversation I want to have, but rather one I know is going to happen.

What I'm not looking forward to is Cam touting his greatness of prophecy, rubbing it in my face that he was right.

My baby arrived yesterday, and I am oh so happy to be rid of the rental. "Gold" by Kiiara pours through my speakers. The music calms me, and ever since I got back to Boston, I've felt the best I have in weeks.

Maybe it was the great night with Niko when I first arrived, perhaps it's the mini-vacation, or just being home, but I've been relaxed for days.

The music cuts out, the phone taking over the Bluetooth connection. Loud ringing and Tate's name covers the screen.

"Go away," I say as I press the button on the steering wheel to hang up. I blow out a breath, my good mood spoiled. "Asshole."

"Everly?"

I jump, my gaze flying to the display. "Shit." I hit the wrong button and answered the call.

"Evie, wait! Don't hang—"

I don't even let him finish, ending the call.

My eyes start to water and I shake my head, trying to get them to stop. Hearing him call me Evie in that desperate tone, begging, tears at me. There was a time just a few weeks ago that his voice calling me Evie was my favorite sound in the world. Now it's the most disgusting, and I hate that he ripped that from me.

"Fucker."

I push the feelings down, just as I have for weeks. I don't want to deal with them or even acknowledge their existence. There should be no sadness in me, and really, there isn't, but what is there is an injury I'm not sure will ever heal.

I loved him, and he broke the trust I had for him. Words can never scrub clean the memory of his betrayals.

Instead of thinking of Tate, I focus on the music and let it take me over, settling me by the time I pull into the restaurant parking lot. There's an empty spot next to Cam's huge pickup truck.

Walking in, I spot Cam chatting up the hostess, giving her his friendliest smile. I make a fist, letting my middle finger knuckle stand out and then pop him in the ribs.

"Motherfu—" He manages to cut himself off, grunting instead. I quirk a brow at him. "Damnit, Ev, that . . . shit." He glances back to the hostess and grins. "My little sister is such a prankster."

Prankster?

I lean forward, my hand up as I whisper, "Did he tell you about how he left some girl's house this morning?"

"Everly! Jesus!"

I smile up at him. "Still miss me?" I ask as the hostess directs us to our table.

"You're still a cockblocking little shit sometimes."

"Yeah, well, this is *my* night," I remind him. "No picking up chicks when I haven't seen you in four months."

As we take our seats, the hostess hands us our menus before informing us our server would be right over, no longer seeming interested in whatever charm Cam was giving off.

"I invited Niko to come, but he's working so looks like it's just you and me, kid," Cam says as he opens the menu.

I freeze at the mention of Niko's name in conjunction with our dinner. "That's too bad," I say, trying not to give myself away.

Cam laughs at my statement. "There was a time when my having Niko along would have been great news to you. My, have times changed."

"That they have. How's he doing these days anyway? He planning on settling down and adding any little Nikolas Callahans to the world yet?" I say, laughing off the statement when in reality the thought of Niko settling down makes me a little ill. A deep laugh from my brother pulls me from my unwanted thoughts.

"Niko? Settle down and have kids?" He snorts and pulls the menu up to his face. "You've been away awhile, kiddo, but let's be clear. Niko has not changed one damn bit since I was in high school." I tilt my head, interest piqued. "I take that back. He's changed a little. He now has rules that the asshole lives by."

"Rules?" I ask, confused.

"Yup. The dude has issues," he says nonchalantly and sips his drink.

"What kind of issues? He seemed pretty solid when we were kids to me." Cam looks at me over his menu, then quirks a brow at me in question. Shit! I don't want to sound too interested in his friend, but he's the one that mentioned issues. "Hey, you said it, I'm just curious now. Didn't think you'd be around someone with issues." I shrug to show him that I'm being more playful rather than genuinely interested in the daily life of Nikolas Callahan.

"Mmm hmm, not still crushing on my boy Niko, are you, Everly?"

"What? No! Of course not, you dummy. I was just a kid back then. What was I, twelve, thirteen? I think you forget that I'm no longer that nerdy little girl with a mouth full of metal and glasses and over the age of eighteen now. I've also been living on my own for quite some time, old man."

"Old man? That's harsh, Ev. Anyway, I haven't forgotten, kiddo. I guess I just like to pretend that you're still young. Makes me feel young too." He smiles at me, and I can't help but smile back.

"You're not *that* old. Thirty is like the new twenty. At least that's what I hear. What's that saying? You're now in your dirty thirties?"

Cam snorts at me and then gulps down some of his draft beer. "Pretty sure I've been in my *dirty* whatever stage for a long time," he says chuckling, "but yeah, thirty is cool. So far so good. Anyway, enough about my age. How're things at the parents' house?"

"It's funny. It's like I never left. I expected them to turn my room into something more for themselves, but nope. Everything is still the same right down to the pictures on my wall from high school. I can't believe how different Aly and I looked back then. Speaking of Aly, you'd better keep my *childhood* crush on Niko to yourself or I'll sic Aly on you."

Cam shudders at the mention of Alyson's name as I knew he would. The two of them are like fire and gasoline, and to this day I have no clue as to why they have such a strong dislike toward each other. The hate-hate relationship they've had over the years used to drive me crazy, but I got used to keeping them away from one another. It was just easier than listening to them volley insults back and forth.

"That's a low blow, little sister. I wouldn't wish *her* on my worst enemy, yet you would do that to your loving, most handsome, hot-as-fucking-hell brother? Dirty!" he says in mock upset.

"I knew you'd see things my way," I say and smile, showing all thirty-two of my pearly whites. Cameron laughs at me, and it's then that I realize just how much I've missed being with him.

"Speaking of best friends," Cam says, and I'm all ears until I realize he's not about to mention more of Niko.

"What about best friends?"

"You're glad I didn't bring Niko. Well, I'm happy as fuck you didn't bring that crazy chick."

I laugh at the face Cam makes as he talks about Alyson. "First, don't call her that."

"Hey, she makes sure I know she's crazy every time I see her, so you might want to mention that to her before you tell me not to call her something that she calls herself. Just saying," he says and shrugs.

"Oh, stop it. Alyson is a great person inside and out, and you know it. I've never understood what your feud is all about. You're too old to still be like that, Cam."

"I'm sure she's still the same on the inside as she is on the outside. Honestly, Ev, I don't understand why you chose her of all people to keep in touch with all these years."

"Because she's always been good to me. Just because you don't like her doesn't mean I shouldn't. Seriously, Cameron. I don't understand the two of you. It's childish after all these years. Don't you think it's time to grow up and see her as the adult woman she is and not the teenager you taunted when you were younger? She doesn't even mention you, yet you rag on her anytime I've mentioned her over the years."

"Yeah, right. Like she doesn't say the same about me when I'm mentioned?"

"She doesn't. She hasn't mentioned you in years," I lie to keep the peace. The two of them bickering would drive any sane person to drink. "I don't even think she remembers that I have a brother, to be honest," I say and Cameron smirks at me, obviously sure that I'm not being truthful with him regarding Alyson's feelings on my big brother.

"If you say so. I'll just take your word for it."

"Anyway, I'm glad it's just you and me tonight."

"Not that I'm complaining, but why?"

"Because I'm not going to get to see my big brother much after tonight, and I'm glad we have this alone time together. How many siblings do you know that say that and mean it?" I smile; it's true. Many of my friends in college always fought with their siblings, but Cam and I never did. Glad that never changed.

"Plus, it gives us more time to catch up," I say, hoping he'll think I'd only like to spend time with *him* going forward and he won't go inviting his best friend along again.

Thank *God* Niko didn't come. I know it's an eventuality that I'll see him at some point, but I'm not ready for it yet. Hopefully I won't see him again for a long, long time. For now, I'm just happy being with Cameron.

"I missed this," I say and mean it.

"What?" he asks.

"This. Us. We were always so close."

"Are you insinuating that we are no longer and that I've slacked in my nagging big brother ways, because if you are, we will have to rectify that ASAP. I can think of plenty of womanly things that need looking after at my place."

"You wish! That's why you need a wife."

"Whoa! Shhhh," he says and looks around the room, pretending he's worried someone might have heard my comment about a wife. I shake my head at him, and again that feeling of missing our easy back and forth hits me. "I may not have Niko issues, but I'm not looking to settle down anytime soon, kiddo. Take that shit back right now before I embarrass you in this restaurant full of nothing but fine people just trying to enjoy their dinner."

"There you go again with the issues. You and Niko have the same issues, I take it?"

"No. Niko has issues with women in general. He feels that it's a bad thing to know more than a woman's first name, which he forgets half the damn time anyway, where I don't mind getting to know a little bit about the women I, ah . . ." he hesitates, apparently searching for a word that won't make him look bad.

Too late, brother. I shake my head at his lack of response and finish for him.

"Date?"

"That's it! Yes. The women I date." He smiles, going back to the menu, changing the subject on me. "What do you want? I think the prime rib here is pretty good and they do baked potato on Thursday nights."

"Nice switch up, buddy. Lucky for you, I'd rather not hear about your *dating* life anyway. I think I'm going to go the seafood route, though. I've missed that the most since moving away from New England."

"I forgot you didn't get the good stuff in California. We'll have to hit a Chinese joint soon. I remember when I came to visit you. Chinese food there is just gross," he says, and I have to agree. I'm no big foodie, but I'm sure I'll need to overdo all the foods I've missed being away from all these years until it's out of my system.

One thing I've missed most about Massachusetts is the seafood, and also Chinese food. Nothing can ever compare. California had nothing like this, and that made me yearn to be home. Well, that and Dunkin' Donuts. A girl can only drink so much Starbucks before she starts looking like some addict. It's not a pretty sight. After my third cup, I begin to resemble something out of a horror movie.

Thinking of the food here brings my mind back to the old pictures of my friends and me during our senior year. They still sit on the wall above my vanity. It's so crazy to look at them now. How different I was back then. Junior year is when I met Alyson.

She convinced me to ditch our last two classes for the day so that we could go hit up this Chinese place, Tahiti, in Dedham. It took us about twenty minutes to get there, but it was always worth it. I drove by just the other day, surprised to see that they were still open after all these years. I'll have to hit that place soon and drag Aly with me. Those were good times back then. I don't know how I'd be, or what kind of woman I'd have become if I hadn't met Aly.

You could see the changes in me toward the end of that first year, right before we left for college. The early two years of high school sucked for me, but then Aly transferred in from another town, and we hit it off right away. She helped me in ways I didn't know I needed help. Aly brought me out of my shell. Once we hit California, well, things changed for me.

For one, I lost my glasses and got Lasik eye surgery. I finally cut my hair into a style rather than pull it back into a ponytail like I usually did, and my clothing style changed dramatically. Aly was a huge shopping addict who'd rubbed off on me over time. It was nice.

COCK *sure*

Alyson also started dragging me out with her every morning at five-thirty to jog. I have to admit that at first, I was winded and so out of shape that I didn't think I could ever keep up with her, but she'd slow down and drag me out every morning. I'm glad she did because the little extra weight I had on me practically melted away with all that running we did.

The only thing I didn't let her drag me into was her vegan lifestyle. I tried, but I just never could give up my bacon or red meat. To this day, Aly will turn her nose up at me as I stuff my face with bacon and eggs in the morning.

I'm looking forward to being close to her again. It was hard when she left school and moved home. Daily phone calls became weekly, and then once Aly started working nights, they became monthly due to her sleeping all day while I worked.

"Earth to Ev."

"I'm sorry, what?"

"Where did you just go?" Cam asks.

"Nowhere. Just trying to enjoy the food, and time with my big brother."

"Nothing wrong with that. So what's your time frame for finding a place?"

"I'm working with a realtor here who's set up some showings for me over the next few days."

"Marcy from next door?"

I nod and laugh. "Hopefully something comes of it and I can get myself settled ASAP."

"So, you're buying another house here? Not going to rent first?" Cam asks, pulling me from thoughts of Niko, *again*.

Pretty sure that's a bad sign on my part, one I need to fix, and soon. It's not healthy to keep thinking of that man. Jesus, it's like I'm thirteen again daydreaming about my wedding to Niko and telling my Dad that I'm going to marry him when I grow up. Yeah, not telling Cam that. He'd definitely not laugh as dad did back in those days.

"Yeah. No need to rent. I know I'll be here for the long haul. I don't plan on going back to California anytime soon."

"What about your house there? You own it, right?"

"It's under the care of a realtor and was put on the market last week. It's a seller's market there, and I think it will sell quickly."

"Yeah. Hopefully. It was a great house. Perfect spot. Too bad you didn't want to stay," he says, and I'm sure he's picking to see what information I will throw at him.

Part of me doesn't want to think about why I moved home, but it's kinda hard to forget when Tate won't just let go and move on while accepting that *he* screwed up. I can tolerate many things and expect that in any relationship that you have to make sacrifices, but cheating is not and *never* will be something I accept. There are no second chances on something like that, and I'm done with him.

The phone rings again, and I close my eyes and let out a steadying breath, my finger hitting the side button to silence the ringer. I can't even count anymore the number of times he's called every day since we broke up. I don't want to shut my phone off in case the realtor calls or someone I need to talk to does.

"So, the elephant . . . what's going on with Tate?" Cam asks.

"Nothing."

"I don't call that nothing, Ev."

"You were right," I say with a shake of my head.

Cam stares at me as he slumps back in his seat. I thought he'd be happy to be right, to gloat about being right, but his mouth is downturned, eyes sad. "What happened?"

I take a large gulp of my drink. "He broke my heart. I caught him screwing one of my coworkers."

"That's why you came home?"

I nod. "He was popping up at my office, my house. There were constant calls and text messages." My phone goes off, and once again, Tate's name pops up.

"He's still been calling and texting you?" Cam asks, and I nod again. "Why don't you block his number?"

"I did. He just got a new one, hoping I would answer. He must be using some app on his phone to call. Anyway, it was better for me if I just moved to an area with a different area code. No reason for him to call. He'll get the hint eventually."

"Instead, you're stuck with that jackass constantly calling and texting you? Change your number, then."

"I will. I just haven't gotten around to it. Besides, I shouldn't have to change my number. I still have friends in California that I'd like to stay in touch with. I'm not going to let him get to me."

"No, I get it, but this guy doesn't sound like he's taking the hint, Ev. When did this all go down? You haven't mentioned him once since you told us you were coming home."

"Three weeks ago."

"Three weeks?" His eyes go wide. "Wait, you fucking changed jobs and moved in three weeks? We all thought this was something you had in the works for a while but figured you didn't say anything in case you decided not to take the job here, but now you're saying that this all came about in a matter of three weeks?"

"Well, almost four now, but who's counting? Anyway, that's why I hired movers to deal with packing up my place, and then they'll send it here and hold it in storage until I'm ready to get it. I'll just need to hire someone to help me unload it."

"Don't worry about that. I can grab some of the guys from work to help move you when it's time."

I wave off his offer because guys from work mean the possibility of one of them being Niko. Not going to think about that right now. "Work has been trying to get me to move to the Boston branch for a year. The spot was still open, so I took it."

"Not that I'm not happy to have you home, but you don't think that it's a little extreme to just pack up and move across the country, take another job, and pretend that you and Tate never happened? Seems like you did just that— let him win. My guess is he's probably going to keep trying to apologize and hope he gets you back," Cameron says, and I know he's correct.

As for the other? No, I know I made the right choice moving home. As much as I loved California, I really was missing home. I just didn't realize it until this crap with Tate slapped me in my face. I wanted my family. I wanted my best friend and not just by phone. I wanted everything from before I left home back. That feeling of peace and love and belonging.

"Personally," Cam says, "I'm happier than a pig in shit that you've dumped his ass. He was never good enough for you, but maybe just take his call, let him get out whatever he has to say, and then be done with him."

The waiter appears and we both give our orders, waiting until he is gone before I speak again.

"Honestly, I don't want to listen to whatever bullshit that will come out of Tate's mouth because I'm already done with him. It's obvious I was a stupid, naive girl who believed his every word," I say. I can feel the anger filling my eyes in the form of tears. Anger at Tate and anger at myself for being fooled.

"What did he do?" Cam asks.

"He lied to me, cheated on me," I hiss through clenched teeth. "And then he expects me just to forgive him and come crawling back to him on my knees ready to suck his dick after God knows how many women he's been with? No thank you."

I stop for a moment and look around, realizing just how loud my voice had gotten. The whole situation works me up, and I hate feeling like this.

"There are no second chances after that. I hear what you're saying, Cam, I do, but I just can't waste any more time on that man. I want to look forward, not backward. He'll just have to deal with it on his own. I'm not helping him feel better about what he did by talking to him and listening to whatever crap he thinks I want to hear."

Cam sits there, shocked and blinking at me. I'm sure he's going to lecture me further, but I just can't deal with the subject of Tate for long. It gets me so angry when I think about how stupid I was when it came to him.

"Still, to uproot everything over a breakup?"

"Cam . . ." I say to him in warning. I know how my brother is and if I say the word, he'll be all over Tate, but I just want to deal with him on my own. I don't need my big brother to fight my battles. "I thought you hated him? Why push me to talk to him?"

"You know it will always be *you* I choose over anyone, and I *do* hate the fucker, but you left your paradise just to get away from a guy, Ev. You loved California, so I'm thinking there has to be more that you're not telling me."

"He turned my paradise into hell. I don't need him. I don't need *any* man that lies or cheats. You mentioned rules earlier? Well, that's one of mine. No cheaters. No second chances. Maybe you had the right idea all along, Cam. *Date* with no strings attached," I say, using air quotes on the word date, remembering my brother's comments a little while ago when talking about his and Niko's issues with women. "Maybe that's all I need. I'm still young, and Tate was really the first guy I was in what I thought was a true relationship. If I'm more like Aly, Niko, and you, and just play the field, so to speak, I'll learn more and then know better when the wrong guy comes along. I'll know to keep walking and not give him the time of day."

Cam shakes his head. "Everly," he growls at me. "That's not who you are as a person. And like Aly? Seriously, Ev? That chick has a new boyfriend like once a week, doesn't she? How is that a good thing?"

"You forgot about the part where I mentioned you and Niko too, brother," I say, not letting him off the hook. "And how would you know that Aly has a new boyfriend every week? It's not like you two run in the same circles."

"Doesn't matter, I just know. And men are different," he says, blowing off my question about how he knows more about my best friend than I do, apparently.

I mean, I know she's dated a lot, but I didn't think she dated as often as my brother just said. I don't want to bring too much attention to that right now, though. Not when he's being a sexist bigot with his one-sided remarks.

"Really? Women are different? How so?"

"They just are. Women can't just do that shit and not get looked at the same way as us men do."

I snort. He can't be serious right now. I don't get the chance to dig into my brother like I want because the waiter is back with our food. I'm sure he just heard the dumb shit that came from Cam's lips but he stays professional, keeping the smile on his face and I'm sure being that he's male, silently agreeing with his fellow male human.

Ugh. Men are so dumb.

"That is the most chauvinistic thing that I have ever heard come out of your mouth, Cameron Hayes."

"Other than having you come do my laundry and clean my house because you're a woman?" he says with all seriousness written on his face, and I roll my eyes at him.

"Yes, that too, but you don't honestly believe what you just said, do you?"

"Ev, this conversation, your whole attitude right now is showing me more than your mouth just spit at me. For one, you have such a jaded view of men, or of me as a man . . ." Cam sits staring for a moment. I can tell he's searching for something to say that will make me see something his way, but I'm past that right now. "You're wrong. That's not all I need. You're looking at my relationships with a warped view. And yes, to answer your question, I do believe what I just said because it's true. Don't get mad at me. It is what it is. I don't make the rules, but it's a fact of life. Women can't just sleep around and not get called out on their shit."

Is he kidding right now? He sounds just like a typical man at the moment. "Called out on her shit? You mean she gets called a slut or a whore, right?" Does he forget that I was around when he and Niko were sneaking girl after girl into our pool house? I know he's still doing the same thing. The only difference now is he doesn't have to hide from my parents seeing as he has his own place and is thirty. I love my brother, but he's another manwhore and way off base right now.

I drop my fork and grab my drink from the table. Where the hell is the waiter? I need something stronger right now if I'm going to deal with this. Women get called whores, but men can screw their brains out with nameless women and they get high-fived by their boys. Bullshit!

"Fine. I know what you're saying is true. I don't like that it's true, but I accept that it is," I say, and he starts to say something else so I cut him off. "But I'm the type of woman that doesn't really care anymore what others think. I'm also smart enough to be discreet. Unlike most men, I'm not looking to let everyone know how many notches I have on my bedpost, so chill out, big brother, and stop raining on my parade. Be my brother and not my father. I have one of those already." I cross my arms while looking him in the eye. "Speaking of the differences between men and women, what is it *you* want, Cameron?"

I know it's not him I'm mad at, but I can't help it right now. Tate is a sore subject that gets me going every time. Plus add in the fact that my brother just told me that I can't do what he does and sleep around if I chose to, pisses me off. I'm not about to screw fifty guys in a month or anything like that, but sheesh! Sexist much?

"Same as you. I want to find someone to love, but I'm not going to waste my time dating girls that I know aren't the one for me. I'm not going to settle. You're right, though; honesty is key."

"*Dating* girls? The *one* for you? I thought we already established that the word *dating* didn't really mean dating. That's bullshit."

"Fuck, Ev. This is not a conversation I thought I'd be having with my kid sister my first night out with her. Besides, you're way too young to be this cynical. That son of a bitch fucked with your head so bad that now you are going to what, be like your buddy Alyson and throw every guy you meet under the damn bus?"

"No, Cameron. He woke me up. And what does Aly have to do with any of this? Jesus, I'm not blind anymore. That should be a good thing."

"Maybe you're not blind, but you are wounded, and you're wearing dark sunglasses so I'd say it's not very good at all."

"Of course I am. He broke my trust, my faith in men." I can feel the tears filling my eyes. Tears I don't want as they leak the pain from my chest. "How do you know they aren't the one after spending one night with them?" I ask, coming back to his response. "I don't like feeling this way. After finding him with that woman, he made me realize that I need to stop being so trusting. Tate showed me that more and more men only think with their head that's below the belt. The only thing they care to know about a woman is how good they feel wrapped around their dicks."

"Now see, that's not entirely true, Ev. I spend more time with them than that."

"See! You even call them 'them'! They have names, Cam. Or do you not even bother to ask before you go sticking your dick in random women?"

"Dammit, you make me sound like I'm some asshole who just fucks and runs."

"Okay. Not you, then. You did admit that you did like to know who you were dating so I'll give you that, but you said Niko had rules. One of them was what? I think you said he doesn't even remember their names, right?"

"Look, Niko is no saint, but he's honest with any woman he meets. The guys you're talking about give others a bad rap. Tate gave other men a bad rap. I understand where you're coming from, and I know this is fresh and raw for you right now. Time is what you need. It's what heals all wounds and shit. All I'm saying is don't go making any decisions based on one stupid fuck's actions, okay? He didn't deserve you from day one. I knew that when I first met the asshole."

"Well, then why didn't you warn me?"

"Because you wouldn't have listened," he says. "You needed to make your own mistakes, and you needed to learn from that one. That's what life's all about. As much as I hate that you got hurt and that I could have kept that from happening to you, you needed to learn that life lesson so that you can go forward in life. The guy for you will deserve you now."

"What makes you say that?"

"Because after that shit with Tate, the poor fucker that finally gets you is gonna have to climb mountains and put you on a pedestal. I'm sure all that will be after you've put him through many hurdles, rightfully so," he says and smiles at me.

"One day, it could happen, but for now, I'm going to join the stress-relieving fun club."

Cam nods and shudders at my declaration. "Whatever you want. You just need some more time. Once the hurt wears off, you'll see that this happening wasn't such a bad thing if it got you to see that fucker for what he was. For now, though, just keep me up to date on him, okay?"

"Up to date?"

"I want to make sure the jackass fades away. If he doesn't, if he comes looking for you, I'll make sure he understands in a much clearer way. And if he decides to see you face to face, you let me know ASAP, okay? I'll send his ass packing back to the west coast."

I agree with a nod. "Okay, but I don't think it will come to that."

"Yeah, well, let's hope it doesn't, but do me another favor, okay?"

"Yeah, sure. What is it?"

"Never mention the word dick to me again. I know you're not ten anymore, but Jesus, that's not something I want to think about my sister being near. Not only that, you sound like Aly. Please don't take on her bad habits. I meant what I said. That girl is a thorn you need to rip away from."

I roll my eyes at his comment about my best friend, but I giggle at the absurdity of my brother's statement. I nod my head anyway to let him think he's gotten through to me, but it's useless. "Whatever makes you happy, brother of mine, but you do know that I've been having sex since college, right?"

"Everly, I just fucking told you that I don't want to hear that shit! It's the same as that time we walked in on the parents when we—"

"Shut up, Cameron! Okay. Okay! Just don't remind me about that, please."

"Back atcha."

I almost laugh at the expression Cam has on his face, as if he's just sucked on a lemon, but I hold it back. Sometimes it amazes me that he's older than me by only five years. There was a time that five years seemed like twenty. When did life get so complicated?

"So, neutral ground, did you get a promotion or anything?" Cam asks.

"Kind of. I went from Business Analyst to Senior Business Analyst," I tell him. It is a promotion in a way as I'll be in charge of more projects and people.

"That sounds like a promotion to me."

"A small step up, but it was mostly due to the office change."

He shakes his head. "I'm still amazed you're so high up after only a few years."

I shrug. "Your sis's got skills."

"Yeah, nerd skills."

I toss a crouton at him, which only makes him laugh. "Jerk."

The waiter comes to clear away our plates, and I'm glad the evening is over. I'm ready to head home, take a long relaxing bath to ease the tension that now invades my body, and get ready for my first official day in my new office tomorrow. No matter the strain I now feel after my heated conversation with my brother, I know I made the right choice coming back to Massachusetts. It's always going to be my home.

"You ready to head out?"

"Yup. Big day tomorrow."

"Hey?" Cam says, and I look up from searching through my bag for my keys. "We good?"

"Of course. All is good." I smile at him because it's true. It will take more than conversations about Tate to pull my brother and me apart.

It's then that I sober, Niko coming to mind. Tate wouldn't do it, but Nikolas sure would. Jesus. I'm going to have to keep my distance. There is no way I want to worry about that scenario anytime soon.

Out of sight, out of mind works for me.

Chapter Eight

Everly

"**WELL, THIS IS IT!** Your new home away from home," Shayne from Human Resources says as he shows me my new office. "I know it's not what you're used to, compared to what you had back in California, but we are working on getting you into one of the larger suites upstairs. Mr. Singleton put the request in a few weeks ago, but we had no idea you'd be joining us so soon, or we'd have put off the renovations until later."

"No, this is fine. No need to go out of your way. I don't mind this at all." I walk over to the large window behind what will be my new desk and take a deep breath I hadn't realized I needed. The view of the Charles River calms me, and looking down onto the street, seeing the hustle and bustle of people going on about their day gives me more peace.

"It's just that this position has been vacant for so long and we didn't expect you to say yes after Mr. Singleton informed us you'd turned it down last year, but now that you're here, we can accommodate you in any way you need."

"Thank you." I smile and mean it. "Everyone has been very welcoming to me. I appreciate it. I'd forgotten how great Massachusetts folks can be. It's a pleasant change from California living." Shayne laughs at my statement.

I'm sure he thinks I'm just saying whatever to make small talk, but I mean what I'm saying. California was fantastic and I loved it there, but it took me a while to get used to how some of the people there were. Not everyone was friendly and at times came off rude and indifferent.

"I don't think I've ever heard anyone say people from Massachusetts are great. I mean, I still have my old T-shirt from college that says 'I'm from Masshole' on the front of it. I'm from Ohio, but I went to Boston University. It was an interesting four years," he says, and I laugh with him this time.

"True, but have you ever been to Cali?" I ask.

"Can't say that I have."

"Well, when you have, you'll understand." I give him a friendly smile. A smile he returns, and I can see that my accepting the office that is smaller than I'm used to without any complaint has taken some of the anxiety from his face. I'm sure that he's used to dealing with the higher-ups in corporate who have very diva-like demands. That's never been how I've acted. I may have a fancy title after my name, but I chose to be friendly with the office staff as well as be more of a hands-on executive rather than become someone that workers in my office want to run and hide from.

"Okay, well, if you need anything else, let Lance know."

"Lance?"

"Your assistant. Don't call him a secretary. It starts more than you can imagine. Trust me. He should be here shortly. You arrived here sooner than I was made aware of, but I was able to pull him in for you. He's the best. He's only been with the company a few weeks, and he already knows everything. Whatever you need, he can get it for you."

"Sounds good. Thank you."

I've never had a male assistant before. I wonder if he's gay. Would probably be better if he was. I don't need the distraction if Aly ever comes to my office to have lunch. Who am I kidding? Not if, but when she comes. I almost want to laugh, but I realize Shayne is still here and I've just zoned out on him.

"No problem, Everly. This is your security card for downstairs. Make sure you have this at all times, and here is your office keys and your company cell phone. I've gone ahead and programmed all the important numbers and added them to your favorites. Again, anytime, just call. IT should be here in an hour or so to get you all logged into your desktop as well as bring you your company laptop. Any questions for me?"

"No. I think I'm good for now."

"Okay, well, then. I'll let you unpack your office and get settled in. I'll let Lance know you're here. Welcome to Boston!" he says in a mock tour guide type of voice.

"Actually, I was born and raised here. Newton, Massachusetts to be exact."

His eyes widen in surprise. "Ah. You've lost your Boston accent. I had no idea."

"I don't think I ever really had one. That's more North Shore. I grew up just outside of Boston, but we spent a lot of time on the South Shore. Cape Cod, Martha's Vineyard, and a little in Marshfield. I do drop the R when I say peppah, though." I laugh because I didn't lose it just now.

"Peppah. Watah. I've even started doing those too words myself. I've only lived here about two years and have yet to hit Cape Cod."

"Oh no. We just say The Cape here."

"I knew that!" He laughs at himself. "I didn't, but I've avoided going. I've heard the traffic is terrible, so I avoid it."

"It can be, yes, but I've heard you can take the ferry now, or train." I smile at him. It's nice talking about my home. I've missed Massachusetts so much, and I didn't even realize how much until I got home.

"I don't know. I'll have to look into that," he says with a slight shudder. "I've enough traffic in my life. I have to say, sitting on I-93 every day during rush hour isn't a selling point for my staying here permanently. We didn't have traffic like this in Ohio. Everything was pretty much thirty minutes to and from home. We also had lots of nothing, so that might have had a part in keeping traffic to a minimum." He smiles, and I laugh. He's sweet, but I'm ready to get settled.

"Well, I'll leave you to it, Everly. If you need anything, just call."

"Great. Thanks again, Shayne."

"My pleasure."

Once he's gone, I flop down into my new desk chair and blow away the lock of hair that's come loose. I quickly pulled my hair up this morning, not wanting to have to deal with blowing it out.

I have a few boxes that were sent over from my old office in California to unpack. That should help me kill some time before IT shows up. I'm about to start on the first box when a text message comes through from my personal cell phone. I pick my purse up and pull out it out, putting it on silent while I'm at work. I look and see that it was a text from Cameron.

Cameron: Have a great first day at your new job, kiddo! Lunch today?

I smile and type a reply.

Everly: I wish, but I've actually got a lot to do. Going to just have a quick sandwich at my desk. You know, first day and all :)

Cameron: Tomorrow then?

Everly: Cam . . .

Cameron: What? I just want to spend some more time with my kid sister. Stay caught up, ya know?

Yes, I do know. Cameron wants to continue to grill me more on why I'm here and why he and my parents only found out about my coming home a week before I got here. I sigh and try to think of what to tell him. I've told him pretty much everything he needs to know already, and honestly, I'm just ready to forget about all the reasons I'm home. What's the point of starting new if all I do is continue to be reminded of the things I want to leave in the past?

I can't say that to him now. It will only make him more concerned, and then he'll hover.

Everly: You are caught up. I promise, and sister. Not kid sister. :/ I'm far from a child Cameron. You are

COCK sure

the only one that can't seem to remember that . . . BTW, don't you have fires to put out?

Cameron: Yeah, okay. I'm going to hold you to that. KID. And yes, but I'm on nights this week.

I shake my head even though it's impossible for my brother to see my frustration and annoyance at his constant reminder that he still thinks of me as the little kid that always followed him and Niko around. I'll be one hundred years old before he figures out I'm not her anymore, but that's a battle for another day. For now, I'll ignore it.

Everly: I know. Talk soon! Maybe next week?
Cameron: Sounds like a plan. :D

Thinking of Cam and Niko back then brings thoughts of the Niko of the present. I'd love to say that the night I spent with Niko has put me off wanting him again, but I'd be lying. If anything, I've had to wrestle myself from jumping in my car and showing up at his place in hopes of round two, but I stop myself. I couldn't do that again, even if Aly has been harping on me to let loose and screw everything else. I need to keep myself busy. No more thoughts of Niko!

I go to place my cell back in my bag when it vibrates in my hand. Expecting more from my brother, I'm surprised when I see a text from Alyson.

Alyson: Drinks tonight! Let's celebrate your new job and your homecoming!

I shake my head before typing a reply.

Everly: It's Monday.

I reply. Aly, never slow on the draw, my phone vibrates seconds later.

Alyson: What's your point?
Everly: It's Monday! That's my point. Unlike you, I can't sleep all day.
Alyson: Hey! I work nights. Speaking of . . . I rarely take a night off, but I am for you. So . . . Let's celebrate my dearest friend in the whole world comin' home :D

I'm barely through reading her text when another one pops through.

Alyson: Say yes. You know you want to. ;) Do it! Say yes! *Giving you my puppy dog eyes here* Pleaseeeeeee

I can see her face now, and I want to laugh at her antics, but instead, I give in. As usual.

Everly: Okay. But I'm buying dinner first! No argument from you! Then we can celebrate with one glass of wine. I still have to be up early tomorrow.

Alyson: Fine on the dinner :/ but Yay!! Promise I'll be on my best behavior . . . and I'll make sure you are too! ;) BTW we are so working on getting you to that bad girls club graduation! Even if it's not tonight! :D

Yeah, I'm sure she's going to try. I'm so not fooled, but I'll go anyway because I've missed Aly just as much as everyone else here. I know Alyson has gone through something. She's more than likely still dealing with it. I can't pretend to relate, but I have a feeling it's more than she wants to share with me, and Aly has used our distance over the past few years to hide it.

We were only in our sophomore year of college when the call came. I still remember the night. It was a Tuesday, just before midnight. We were watching a movie after finishing our assignments that were due the next day, nearly nodding off due to an early morning class and being up so late before that, studying for finals.

She left the next day rather than taking finals. Aly left school to bury her brother, telling me she'd be back, but she never returned. Since then our friendship has survived three thousand miles apart and a lot of change.

I'd still do anything for her, but she never allows me to help, so I just do my part as a friend, and listen whenever she needs me. That's not often, though, because Aly is as stubborn and proud as they come. I blow out a breath and type a quick text off to her.

Everly: See you tonight. Xx

Now, let me see what I can do with my office. My home away from home. Because come tomorrow, I'm sure I'll have the hangover from hell once Miss Alyson Payne gets done with me and her way of celebrating.

Chapter Nine

Niko

"LET'S GO TO THE pub tonight," Cam says as he falls on the couch next to me.

I shake my head. "Nah, not tonight."

"Not tonight? Bro, you haven't been interested in doing shit lately. What's your deal? How can you not be interested in having a few drinks and maybe finding some hot chick to work out your frustrations on? Seriously, what the fuck crawled up your ass? You've been a pissy, mopey shit for a week."

"Just not in the mood."

"When was the last time you got laid? Don't tell me it was the chick with the Post-it note."

Fuck him.

"Damn," Cam says with a shake of his head. "She fucked you good, and more than just the way she rode your cock."

"Mind your business, Cameron."

"This is my business. You're bringing down everyone around you, man. If that shit is contagious, I don't want it. You need something to counteract it, and fast before someone else catches whatever you have too!"

"Dude, you don't understand."

"You're right about that shit. I don't understand. It's not the end of the fucking world, Niko. Shake that shit off and do it fast. The guys are starting to talk."

Yeah, only because he went and ran his mouth to them all like a gossiping old lady, but I keep that shit to myself. I'm not in the mood for Cameron and his crap right now. He's not wrong about one thing. This has gone on too long as it is, but hell if I can stop my thoughts of her from popping into my head.

"I can't stop thinking about her."

"Seriously? You?"

"What?"

"You're the cockiest motherfucker I know, and you're telling me some chick finally knocked you down?"

"Shut up," I grumble as I grind my teeth.

"The world is coming to an end." He opens his arms and turns to the rest of the room. "Hear me, brothers, the world is ending! The notorious half-breed Nikolas Callahan had his ego torn in half by a woman."

I turn and glare at him. "I cannot wait for the day when a woman knocks your high and mighty self on your ass."

"Never going to happen," he says with a smirk and a shake of his head. "I'm too smart for that shit, unlike you. Apparently, I've taught you nothing." He stares at me with one eyebrow cocked, daring me to say more. I know this is pointless now, so I give in. Mostly to shut him up, and the other side is hoping I can snap myself out of this funk Alyson left me in.

"Fine, asshole, I'll go."

"There ya go! You just need to get back on the horse, man. I think your problem is she left you and not the other way around. She became a challenge to you, and one that you can't do anything about because you have nothing on her. Shrug it off, Niko. You'll meet another hot chick, get her under you, and Miss Post-it note will be history."

"Yeah. You're right. I know you're right." I nod, hoping it's true.

"Damn straight I'm right! I've never steered you wrong, and as long as we've been friends, that's saying something. All will be back to normal, and you, my friend, will be back to your old self in no time."

"Yeah."

There's a bar not far from the firehouse that is always full of prime pickup opportunities. I smile down at the blonde sitting beside me, not feeling her. She's all right looking, I guess, but I love the way her eyes widen and her cheeks flush when I speak to her. The problem is, my dick just isn't interested. Try as I might to be my normal charismatic self, it's just not there. I'm forcing it.

Yeah, I want to get off, but I don't want her. The problem is, when I'm home all thoughts turn to Alyson. Those thoughts turn my dick hard as a rock, and the fucked-up part is we only had one night together.

It's so bad that I have to take more than one shower to relieve the ache in my balls or I'm afraid I won't be able to walk. More than once since I've had Alyson, I've beat my cock senseless in the shower with thoughts of her and that night. Sometimes more than once.

It's fucking pathetic.

I want her. Memories of that night flood my mind. Those lips. Those beautiful fucking red lips! Jesus, this chick has me twisted. I hate it, but if I get the chance to see her again, I'm taking her, and this time she won't know what hit her.

Two beers down and I need something stronger, ordering two shots of cognac. While I wait, I scroll through my phone list, desperate to stop thinking about her. Valarie is always down to play, and so is Chloe. I don't usually hook up more than once, but I know that both women are on board with straight friends with benefits. No attachments, just always down for a good time. The way I've lived my life before I met Alyson.

The chick next to me continues to chatter away about this and that, and I'm at the point where I'm being rude and completely zoning her out. I should feel bad, but I don't. Something has to give. I can't keep this up.

Usually, I'm not still here conversing with a woman this long that I plan on fucking. We both know what we want, get going, get off, and then we both go our separate ways once we're completely satisfied. End of story, but I'm just not feeling this.

I look over to where Cam was only twenty minutes ago, and the spot where he was sitting is now empty. Both he and the brunette he was talking to are nowhere in sight. Well, at least someone is getting lucky tonight. Me, on the other hand, I'm done. I take my wallet out and raise my hand to the bartender. She heads over to me, and I settle out my tab as well as the woman sitting next to me. It's the least I can do after wasting her time.

She starts to grab her handbag from the back of her seat when I stop her. "Are we going to your place or mine?" she asks, giving me what I'm sure she thinks is a sultry sex look, but now that I look at her, I realize she's got a face full of some filler. And those lips of hers look so overfilled that I'm sure they'd either pop once wrapped around my cock or float into the air, taking my dick with them like some balloon festival. Not happening.

"Sorry, doll face." That's exactly what she reminds me of now that I've paid attention to her. "But I'm riding solo tonight. I've got an early shift in the morning, and I'm tired. Maybe some other time, yeah?" I say it, but I don't mean that shit. She pouts or tries to sulk, but she just looks wrong doing it. Her lips look like they're over-stuffed Italian sausages, and not the hot kind. There is nothing spicy about this chick.

"Raincheck, then?"

"Yeah, sure. I'll see you around, ummm, Carla?" Fuck, I can't even remember her name. I'm such an asshole.

"Carrie," she says with a little annoyance, but not enough to let me see that she's still down if I change my mind. Well, at least it started with a C. That's something.

She grabs a pen and napkin from the bar and scribbles something down on it before tucking the folded napkin into my pants pocket. She lingers close to my cock, and for a minute I think I feel him stir to life, but no such luck. Her strained smile ruins it, and I'm ready to get the hell out of there. "Call me anytime tonight if you change your mind or can't sleep. I've got all kinds of sleeping aides that would help someone like you."

"Yeah, sure," I say, not meaning a word of it. "I'll let you know. Enjoy the rest of your night, Carla."

"It's Carrie!" she says to my back as I walk away.

I don't bother looking behind me, praying Cam took off so he doesn't witness my great escape from thunder lips. I just need to go home. Maybe go for a run to burn off some steam. Hit the shower and head to bed.

I'm almost out the door when I hear a familiar laugh. I stop where I am, and I take a look around, scanning the bar. Nothing. Just the girl I left a few minutes ago giving me the death stare. I ignore her and start looking toward the other side of the pub where folks sit away from the bar to eat.

It's then I see her. My Cinderella. Only she didn't leave a glass slipper behind. No, nothing as classy and traditional as a shoe. My girl got original and left a Post-it note on my dick. Speaking of my dick, the woman I wasted half my night with put my cock to sleep. All of a sudden, my boy is wide awake and instantly hard as I watch her laugh and smile with her friend.

I'm struck stupid, and I have no idea what to do. I know what I want to do, but I'm pretty sure that won't go over well with her. I look around, again searching for Cameron, but he's no longer inside. Good, because I don't feel like dealing with his shit when it comes to this chick. He'd more than likely embarrass the shit out of me and say something to her. I don't want that.

I walk over to the other side of the bar away from Alyson and her friend's view, but I make sure I can still see them. I wave the bartender over, and the attentive tip-seeking woman that she is comes right away with her pearly whites flashing me. Not tonight, sweetheart. I've got my eye on a much bigger prize.

COCK *sure*

"Change your mind?"

"Not exactly." I smile. "Can you send over two more of whatever the ladies at that table are having and put it on my card?"

She looks over at Alyson and her friend, smiles, and then takes my card. "Sure thing. Want me to let them know who sent them?"

I think about it for a second when I see, of all things, a pack of pink Post-it notes next to the register behind the bar. That's when the idea hits me. "Actually, can I borrow one of the sticky notes over there?" She looks behind her and then back at me, grabbing the pack and placing it in front of me. I smile at her and grab the pen she places next to them before heading off to make their drinks.

I quickly scribble my note, smiling wide, proud of myself for having such quick wit. I'm no longer that guy that's been like the walking dead. Time to flip the script on this girl. The waitress comes over and grabs the drinks from the bartender to bring over to her table. I reach out and stick the Post-it on one, igniting the look the waitress is giving me before she takes her tray and leaves. I want to stick around and see her reaction, but I decide to leave it in her hands. At this point, I'm just happy to be on even ground again. Alyson-one. Niko-one.

Tomorrow is another day. We had one night, that's all. That's what I've been telling myself, but now that I've seen her again, I know that's not all. Let's just hope that Cinderella is ready to play another round.

I take off out the side door, completely avoiding Alyson and her friend. I reach my bike out back, pull my helmet on, and then throw my leg over the seat.

I love to ride. It's the one thing other than running that helps me clear my head. I start her up and get the hell out of there, heading for my place. It only takes a few minutes to get home, and, after parking next to my Tahoe, I head toward my front door, keys out, ready to walk in when I feel my phone vibrate in my pocket. For a minute my heart starts to race with the thought of Alyson actually calling me once she read my note, but the feeling quickly goes away when I see who it is.

The screen is lit up with an incoming call from Cam. With a push of a button, I send it to voicemail and stick the key in my door, flicking on the light once I enter. I'm not even going to pretend that I'm not disappointed it wasn't her, but I am. Honestly, I don't expect to hear from her right away, but hey, a man can hope.

After kicking off my shoes, I head straight to the fridge for a beer. I fall onto my couch and take a long gulp while I think about how fucked up this situation is. I'm sitting around pining for a girl I fucked once, know nothing about, and who left a Post-it note, mainly thanking me for my services.

I feel used. But fuck if I don't want her to use me again. Like some kind of a gigolo except the only payment I get is mind-blowing sex. Probably the best sex I've had in my life, and that's saying something seeing as I'm no saint.

The beer isn't going to do it, so I grab a bottle of Courvoisier from the cabinet, pour two fingers, and down it in one gulp.

A minute later, and there is a ping from my cell indicating I've got a voicemail. That took a minute, so I know Cam left me something long-winded that I don't feel like hearing right now. Soon after, I hear a different ping telling me I have a text message. Curiosity gets the best of me and I get up to grab my cell, wishing I didn't once I read it.

Cameron: You left???

Then four more come in one right after the other, indicating he's frustrated with my lack of company this evening.

Cameron: Alone???
Cameron: What the fuck, man?
Cameron: Grow a pair and snap out of this shit!
Cameron: There is no such thing as pussy whipped after one fucking night!

I decided to try and save face by replying, hoping he'll lay off me with the BS, but no such luck.

Niko: How do you know I left alone?
Cameron: Because the chick you were with all night just left with someone that wasn't you, dickhead.

Niko: Dude, there was nothing there of interest for me.

That's a lie, but he doesn't need to know that.

His reply is immediate, and I wonder why he's able to text me if he left with the brunette I saw with him.

Cameron: That's bullshit, Niko! You had one primed and ready to drop to her knees in 2.3 seconds. You are so full of shit!

She was ready. There is no doubt in my mind that I could have gotten her to do pretty much whatever I wanted, but it wasn't her that I kept looking for while we were sitting in the pub. I'm still amazed at the fact that I saw Alyson there after having her on my mind all night. It's a sign I'm going to take. I *am* meant to fuck this woman again, and I plan to do just that.

Niko: Not full of shit. Her lips looked like over-cooked kielbasa. Sorry, but she looked like she would have strangled my dick. I left her behind in case you needed a blow-up doll. Stop fucking with me. I'm heading to bed.

I send the fist pump emoji to lighten the mood, and in return, I get the eye roll emoji back from Cam.

Cameron: Whatever. I'll talk to you tomorrow. Unlike you, I'm not pussy whipped. I whip the pussy! Enjoy your night beating your dick, dumb ass!

Niko: You need to stop watching those comedy specials. You're not funny.

I don't bother with any more than that, and Cam doesn't reply again. He's right. Disgusted with myself, I throw my phone back onto the table and head for the shower. A date with my hand is about all I'm getting tonight, but I'll be damned if I'm not going to have Alyson's face in my head the whole time I pump my fucking fist. Fucking Cam.

Chapter Ten

Everly

"SO... ANY NICE LOOKING guys at the new J.O.B?" Aly asks as she holds the tiny straw of her drink, then takes a sip.

I give her a shrug. "I wouldn't know. I wasn't paying attention."

"How can you not notice if a man in front of your face is hot or not?" She rolls her eyes and gives a huff. "Seriously, Ev?"

"It was my first day there, Aly. Besides, I'm not interested in any man right now, never mind any that work with me. That's like Corporate 101. No fraternizing, Aly. You should try it sometime," I say, knowing that Aly has been screwing one of her coworkers on and off for a few months.

She laughs and takes another sip of her drink. "Ouch! That was mean, lady. I forgive you, though. You can't be part of the club if you don't learn to live a little. Easy access, I say. You just have to make sure you tell them you don't do relationships up front, like me. You become what they call people on Tinder a 'serial dater.'" She puts her fingers up in air quotes, and I just roll my eyes.

"You need to stay off Tinder. Jesus Christ! You're going to end up on some missing poster or worse."

"Oh stop it, Mom. It's not as bad as you think. I've met some pretty normal guys on there, for your information. Like this guy,

Louis. He works for an airline. Travels all over the world. There is nothing like a well-traveled man. He's been places I'd love to go to."

"Yeah, like the STD clinic in each state and country where he has probably fucked like every woman he's met on that damn app. That is just gross, Aly. Stay off Tinder."

"I don't fuck them. I have gone out with a few. Some were normal. Some were married, looking to cheat on their wives."

My mouth pops open. "Oh my God! You didn't."

"Of course not!" She makes a gagging face. "They disgust me. I don't do married men. Gross, Ev. I have morals, you know."

"Well, I'm glad to hear you have some," I say with a giggle.

"Bitch."

I cock a brow at her. "Slut."

"Cow."

"Nun."

"Now you're just mean." She sits back and crosses her arms. "I'm not telling you anything else so that you can live vicariously through me anymore."

"Well, that is going to suck totally!" I say in mock sadness. "Whatever will I do if I don't get my daily dose of Alyson Payne's sexcapades update?"

She glares at me. "Okay, enough screwing around, Ev. What are we going to do with you and your issues?"

I look away and stir the drink in front of me. "I can't sleep with just any guy because I'm horny, Al. I need to have some feelings toward him; otherwise, I can't do it."

"I knew it!"

I jump when she yells. "What the hell? Knew what?"

"When you told me you'd slept with someone that wasn't the pond scum. You have feelings for what's his name."

"First of all, let's not talk about the pond scum," I say. "I'm trying to forget that I ever knew him, and other than him, I've only been with Niko." Her face lights up, and I shoot her down before she can pipe in. "Once! It was my first, and probably only, one-night stand. I just don't think that's something I can do again with some random stranger. That doesn't mean I have feelings for the guy. Jesus, Aly. You're the one that kept telling me that the only way to get over Tate was to get under someone else. Well, I took your advice. It wasn't the best idea I've had, but it's over now. End of story."

I shift under her gaze. There's something about it, like she can see through my bullshit and to the truth I might not want to see.

"Like I said . . . you have feelings for Niko."

I shake my head. "I'm not arguing about this. I thought we were celebrating my coming home?"

"And the new job, but that doesn't mean we can't discuss your sex life. This is not arguing." Alyson sits there, stirring her drink that's almost empty, and I wonder just how many of them she had before I got here.

"Fine," I grumble. "I'll talk about my sex life as long as we talk about yours. Deal?"

Aly starts squirming in her seat, and I know she's uncomfortable but too bad. It's only fair I know what's going on in her sex life if she's insisting on making me share mine.

"Trust me; you don't want me to tell you about mine."

"What do you mean? You're always telling me about yours."

"I keep it pretty tame for you. I mean, I will if you really want to, but you can't even deal with what you did with Niko, so I know my kink would scare you. I vote that we keep this PG-13 and concentrate on Everly."

"What are you hiding, Aly? And why have you been running through guys like it's the end of the world?"

"I *can* tell you whatever you want. I've nothing to hide," she says and shrugs her shoulder. "I like sex and you already know that I've been fucking someone from the bar. It's not like I've hidden that from you, but what I'm doing is different than what you did with Niko. I don't *care* about anyone that I've slept with." She lifts a brow at me, daring me to tell her that she's wrong. She's not, but I'm trying not to think about Niko. Not while I'm busy settling into my new job and trying to find a place to live.

"Fine. Let's just enjoy the rest of our night, drink, and deal with the other stuff later."

"Fine by me, babe. I'm going to grab us more liquor. You want the same?" She looks at my almost-empty glass and then up at me to see if I'm willing to have more alcohol tonight. I almost want to groan out loud. I'm going to need lots of water before we leave, and tomorrow, I'm sure I'm going to feel like death. I don't want to look like something from *The Walking Dead* tomorrow.

"Just water for me. I told you. The second day on the job tomorrow. I'm positive that hung over employee wasn't in my job description."

Aly shakes her head at me but decides to ignore me. This I'm sure of because just then our waitress arrives with a tray full of drinks. She places two freshly made fruity drinks in front of us, and I immediately know I'm not going home tonight without marring my address to our Uber driver.

"Compliments of the very fine gentleman at the bar," the waitress says, and she sticks a pink Post-it note down on the table. I instantly sit straight up and look over to the bar.

"Gentleman?"

"Yes. He's directly behind me, but closer to the bar near the exit. Black shirt, dark hair, eyes like liquid silver. Oh, and an ass that I'm positive you could bounce a quarter off of. See him?"

Alyson starts laughing at our waitress's description of our mysterious admirer, but now I'm curious so I look to the area she said, but I don't see anyone matching that description.

"I don't see him."

She turns and looks herself, but then turns back with a shrug. "Not sure where he went, but if a guy like that sent me a drink, I'd be all over that. I'm just saying." She laughs and walks away to deliver the rest of her drinks to her customers.

"Eh, you won't see me complaining about getting a free drink," Alyson says and lifts hers to her lips.

I look down at the Post-it and peel it off the table where she left it to read what it says.

You're very, very welcome. Let's do it again sometime. ;) 617-554-1214.

It takes a second to sink in, and then I understand why her description seemed so familiar. I freeze. *Niko.*

"Holy shit!"

"What?" Aly asks as I sit there looking around the room, going into major freak-out mode.

"Holy fucking shit!" I yell as I frantically look around.

"What!"

I point to her purse as I stand and pick up my own. "Grab your bag; we need to leave."

"What?" Her forehead is scrunched in confusion. "Why? What the fuck, Ev? You only just got here an hour ago."

"We just need to go, because if he's here then that means my brother isn't far behind, and I'm not ready to deal with all that right now," I hiss. Anxiety pumps through my body. This is not good. "Especially not when I've been drinking with you."

"Wait. Ev, who are you talking about?" She snatches the Post-it from my hand and reads it out loud. "You're very, very welcome? For what? Everly, what's going on?"

"Niko!" I whisper-yell at her, then point to the note. "That's from Niko. The drinks are from Niko, and if Niko is here, so is Cam!"

The mention of Cam's name has her face turning sour, but then she replaces it with a look of indifference while focusing back on the reason for my distress. "Where is he? I so need to see the famous Niko Callahan." She starts to stand up to look over our booth toward the bar, but I pull her down.

"He's not there. I looked already! Stop looking," I say, grabbing her hand to pull her back down. "I don't know where he went, but please, let's leave before Cam comes with him and ruins my entire night. Please, Aly?"

"Oh, fine! But only because I don't want to see your brother's ugly mug, or hear any of the ugly shit that comes out of his mouth."

"I'm not even going to bother scolding you about my brother. Let's just go. We can go somewhere else, or better yet, go to my house. Yes, my house is safe right now, so let's go." I ball the Post-it note up and toss it on the table, grab my bag, and start to follow Alyson out, only to bang into her back when she stops short. "Ummm, what are you doing? Go!"

"I am. Just give me a second. I forgot something." She walks around me and then back to our table and grabs the crumpled Post-it I left with Niko's note on it.

"What are you doing?"

Alyson gives me her "I'm up to no good" smile and walks past me, grabbing my hand and pulling me along with her to the exit. "Helping you graduate, Everly. Mama wants to make sure you walk tall and proud across that bad girl's stage."

The Uber we called after our close encounter at the Newton pub earlier pulls in front of my parents' house, and I drag myself from the car. We didn't end up at my house after we left like I'd hoped. Another pub not far from where we were and way too many drinks I did not plan on having are not sitting well with me. The world is spinning, and I'm pretty sure that I won't end the night without throwing up. God, tomorrow is going to suck when it's time to get up for work. "Thanks, Ronnie!"

"It's Roland, Ev."

"What's rolling?" I slur at Aly. I only had three Sex on the Beach drinks, but I'm a lightweight when it comes to drinking. I always seem to let Aly talk me into more which is why I'm a little more than tipsy right now, but not exactly drunk to the point that I can't see straight.

"His name, Ev." She starts giggling. "You said Ronnie, but his name is Roland."

"Well that's a—" I stop trying to think of a nice way to say it's a strange first name, but Aly says thank you, closes the door to the car, and starts pulling me toward the front door of my parents' house.

"Hey! I wanted to tell him that it's okay if he had the last name for a first name!"

"Yup! He knows. Now let's get you inside. You've got work in the morning, and I've got to get some sleep if I want to get up with you at the ass crack of dawn and drive my happy-ass home to get a few extra hours in before my shift tomorrow night."

"Oh! That's right. You're staying over! It will be like when we were kids again. Sleepover!"

Aly laughs at me again, pushing the key into the door. "Yup. Like old times. Let's go, drunk lady."

"I'm so not drunk, drunk. I'm just tipsy drunk."

"Mmm hmm. Same thing. You're going to hate me tomorrow when your head is breaking in half. I'll grab you some Advil and water. Can you manage the stairs?"

"Pffffff I'm fine! I totally couldn't hate you! You're my best friend! You know that, right, Al?"

"And you're mine, but you are going to be Everly Hayes mad at me tomorrow, so do me a favor and head upstairs, get your jammies on, and I'll go get you something to help you in the AM."

"Okay," I say and drop my purse and phone on the stairs.

Heading up to my childhood bedroom, I turn and see Aly walk toward the kitchen. Once I get to my room, I face-plant on my bed. Screw the sleepwear. I can't move. The last thought I have before I pass out is of Niko. Maybe Aly is right. I think I still have feelings for Niko, although I'm positive they have gone from childhood crush to major adult lusting. We've only had one night together. One wild, crazy, hot-as-hell night full of sex. Yeah, not seeing that night as something I can forget anytime soon. Maybe not ever.

I'm so screwed.

Chapter Eleven

Everly

"WAKE UP, SLEEPING BEAUTY! Time to play grown-up by getting ready for work." Sunlight blasts through the room, and I pull my pillow over my head and groan.

"Close the curtains! Ow!" My goddamn head feels like someone is stabbing me with a pitchfork right now, and I want to cry.

"Advil and water are right next to you. Let's go! The second day on the job, can't have my girl late to work. Besides, I want to beat some of the traffic and head out. I can't do that if I think you're going to go back to sleep and miss your whole day. Wouldn't look good for the new boss. So come on, get up. Get up. Get up!"

"I hate you, Alyson Payne."

She sighs at my use of her full name. "I know, but you love me too, so let's go. I'll make you some greasy bacon and toast real quick and tell you why you'll love me even more when I tell you what I did for you." That gets my attention off my hung over state.

"What do you mean, what you did for me?"

She bites her lip and looks like she just ate a bird. "What did you do, Aly?"

"Okay, so maybe you won't love me more right away, but I'm such a firm believer in our best-friend status that I know you won't hate me forever."

"Alyson!" I yell and instantly grab my head. Fuck! "Just spill it! What did you do? It's not going to get me fired on my second day, is it?"

"No . . . nothing like that, silly girl, but hopefully it will get you laid again, and soon if I worded it right."

"Wait. What? Worded what right? Alyson, speak English. It's too damn early for me to speak, Aly, and I'm hung over thanks to you. Just spill it."

"Okay, okay," she says, but she's more hesitant this time. Aly is the type to tell you like it is. No sugar coating things, but she's not her usual, which makes my stomach drop. I know this is not going to be good. "So I might have sent a text off to Niko last night before I went to bed."

"You did what?" I grab my head in both hands. Oh, my head! Shit. Damn liquor is not my friend right now, and neither is Alyson, it seems.

"Calm down. Take your Advil and meet me downstairs. You'll feel better once you've eaten something. Oh, and take your Advil!" she yells as she runs out of my room to make me breakfast.

I grab the water and pills, down them, and then get up to search for my phone. Downstairs. I left it downstairs. What the hell did she do? I make my way to the main floor and find my purse. I pull my cell from it and open my text messages.

Nothing. Fucking bitch!

I toss it back down and head for the kitchen and the smell of bacon cooking. My stomach recoils, but she's right. The best thing for this hangover is to eat.

"Good job, Aly. That got me up. Now feed me so I can get in the shower and hopefully feel halfway normal by the time I get to work." I sit at my parents' breakfast bar and freeze when I see what Aly has in her hands.

"You didn't . . ."

"I did, and before you spaz out on me, just hear me out, okay?"

"Alyson! That's my company phone. What did you send to him?"

"Well, I know you said it was just a one-night stand, and given your whole bullshit relationship with Tate, I just think you need a little nudge in the Niko department. You've been pining for this guy since you were a kid, Ev, and you've finally gone after something that you wanted. Don't throw it away now that you've had the prize. Explore it. Enjoy it. Have some more."

"I don't want more. I just wanted something at that time, and Niko was in the right place at the right time. If it weren't him that night, it would have been someone else. It was just how I was feeling at that moment. I don't want a repeat," I say through gritted teeth. I love Aly, I do, but she's crossing the line on this one.

"I call bullshit, Everly Hayes. I've seen how animated you've gotten when telling me stories about things Niko did when you were a kid. Hell, you were giddy when you told me you'd slept with him recently."

"Whatever. Just give me the phone so I can see what type of shit you've gotten me into now." I'm mad and she knows it, so she hands the phone to me and I immediately pull up the text.

Alyson/Everly: Thanks for the drinks. Did you disappear?

Niko: Wow! I didn't think you'd use my number.

Alyson/Everly: Then why did you leave it if you didn't think I'd use it?

Niko: A man can hope. ;)

Alyson/Everly: Why did you disappear?

Niko: You were with your friend. Didn't want to intrude. Besides, I wasn't sure if you'd be receptive after the way you dipped out on me the last time I saw you. :/

Niko: Why did YOU disappear?

"Alyson!" I can't believe she sent him a text.

And she said it was me.

Oh my God!

"Stop freaking out."

"Don't do that. Why did you text him? I can't keep talking to him, or see him again for that matter. He's Cameron's best friend!"

"What's your point? You're an adult. Who you choose to screw shouldn't have anything to do with your moron of a brother."

"Regardless of your feelings toward my brother, for whatever stupid reason that you hate him, I care about him. He would freak out over this, and you know it. I don't want to cause any tension between him and Niko and believe me; this would do it. On top of that, I lied! I lied when I slept with Niko by not telling him who I was and by telling him that I was you, or did you forget that little part of the story?"

"I didn't forget."

"So then what? What the fuck am I supposed to do now? And you sent it from my new company cell phone! What if they monitor the calls? Or the text messages? Jesus, Aly!"

"You're making this more than it needs to be. Just relax. It's not a big deal. Here. Eat your breakfast before it gets cold." She places two plates down on the counter, but I can't eat now.

My stomach is in knots, and it has nothing to do with being hung over or being hungry. I don't know what it is, but I don't want to examine it at the moment. No. Right now I'm mad. Not mad. Pissed off.

"When are you going to get that everything doesn't just revolve around what Alyson wants, and stop being so fucking selfish with the things you do? What you choose to fuck up in your own life is one thing, but to start screwing with mine? Not okay!"

"Wow!" A look of hurt crosses her face. "I guess you're very mad at me if you're swearing, calling me selfish, and telling me what a fuck-up I am."

"Alyson, I didn't mean—"

"No. It's fine. I get it, okay? I just want you to come out of that shell and live a little, you know? You're my friend, and I hated hearing how you were becoming less and less of yourself while you were with that asshole, Tate. I know I wasn't there, but when we did talk, you never sounded happy with him. Now he's gone, and I have you back and home. I want you to be happy, and when you told me about Niko, well, you were you again. I can't explain it, but you were just different. That's all I want."

"Aly—" She won't let me finish, and I know what I said hurt her feelings. Shit!

"I need to head out. Traffic sucks this time of morning and I want to get a few hours before my shift tonight. Call you later, okay?"

I don't get a chance to say anything more because she's gone. Great! Now I feel bad. My phone vibrates in my hand, and I all but forgot that Aly was texting with Niko when I came in, pretending to be me. Shit!

Niko: Still there?

What do I do? I can't answer him. I should just ignore him. He'll go away, and all will be right again. I put my phone on the counter and get up to grab some of the bacon Aly left for me. I take a bite, and the flavor of it bursts in my mouth. God, I could eat this stuff every day! My phone buzzes again, reminding me that I have an unread text message, and I'm so damn tempted.

Fuck it.

I grab my phone, stuff another piece of bacon into my mouth and read.

Niko: Hello?

What did he say? I scroll back and see his message about the Post-it. It can't hurt to reply just once, right? I mean . . . that's rude.

Everly: Yeah, sorry about that, but I left you a note. Didn't want to wake you.

I also didn't want to be tempted by your glorious cock again, which would have more than likely had me at his house for the entire next day, but he doesn't need to know all that.

Niko: Yeah. I got your note. Did you really thank my cock or was that a mistake?

I laugh out loud. I can't help it. I didn't exactly mean to tag his cock, but it landed there, and I wasn't about to pull it off and the chance waking him when I was trying to sneak out and do my walk of shame alone. I'm sure that ego of his didn't like that very much. Maybe I need to remind him that it was me who decided to go home with him and not the other way around.

Everly: Why wouldn't I have thanked him? He's the one that actually did all the work. :D

Niko: LOL. Funny girl.

Everly: I try.

Niko: So, when can I see you again?

Everly: That's not a good idea.

Niko: Why not? I think it's a great idea actually, and so does my cock. ;)

Everly: Your one-eyed snake is going to get you in trouble one day, but not with me. I know this will sound ridiculous because we met at a pub and I went home with you, but I have never had a one-night stand. It was my first, and last. I've decided that it's not for me, but thank you. I had a rough few weeks, and meeting you that night helped take my mind off things that I'd been trying to forget.

Niko: One-eyed snake??? LMAO! I have NEVER had anyone call my dick a one-eyed snake. I like it.

Everly: I'm rolling my eyes right now.

Niko: You see, if you go out with me, it won't be a one night-stand at all. Come on! Your one-night stand record will stay clean. ;) We can have dinner first. I know this great place down by the wharf in Boston that makes the best-stuffed lobster. Do you like seafood?

Oh boy. I love seafood, but there is no way I'm going to eat some with him.

Everly: I'm sorry. I can't. I just started a new position with my job, and it's going to keep me busy for a while. Thanks anyway.

Niko: You have to be free at some point. Let me know when you are and I'll see what I can do on my end to make it work.

Everly: I'm sorry.

Niko: Think about it.

I start typing no again and get ready to hit reply, but I don't send it. Instead, I hit the backspace button and type out another, only to backspace that one as well. God, I want to, but I just can't make this any worse than it already is.

Niko: I know you're thinking about it. I can see that you're typing because the three dots keep popping up on my iPhone showing when you type. Just think about it . . .

Shit! I forgot about that. Most of my friends have Android phones except for Aly. I'm trying not to overthink it, but the truth is, I want to say yes. I'm not going to say yes, but I'm not telling him no. Not right now anyway.

Everly: We'll see.

Niko: Okay :D

Everly: I've got to run. Late night last night, and I need to get ready for work. Nice talking to you.

Niko: Did you think about it yet?

I bust out laughing at his persistence. I'm so tempted, but I can't do it.

"Everly, What the hell are you doing?" I say out loud. I look at the clock on the stove and jump up. "Shit! I'm going to be late!" I'll think about Niko later. No time for him now. My head still hurts, and I still need to figure out how to fix things with Aly. How did my life get so complicated so fast?

I hear the text message alert go off again on my cell and I can't help it, so I look.

Niko: Yes? No? One word answer. Not hard words.

Everly: No

Niko: No, to going out with me again, or no you didn't think about it yet?

Everly: That is more than one word answers.

Niko: True. So . . . which is it?

Everly: I don't know.

Niko: Now?

Everly: LOL No

Niko: OKAY ;)

Niko: I'll work on you later! We got a call. Keep thinking about it though ;)

I don't reply anymore. I'm sure he won't see it until later anyway if he's at work. Doubtful they bring their cell phones with them when fighting fires. I need to block his number and stop all temptation from my view.

I should, but I don't. What could it hurt at this point? I've already slept with him. Can't hurt to simply text with him, right? I shove my work phone in my briefcase and get ready for my second day at my new office.

This should be interesting.

"Good morning, Miss Hayes," my new assistant, Lance, says in greeting as I walk into my office.

I wince a little, still fighting the slight headache I have from last night's drinks.

"Good morning, Lance. Please, call me Everly. Miss Hayes makes me feel older than I am." I smile, and he knocks me over with his perfect white teeth.

Whoa. If he's not gay, I can guarantee he's broken some hearts during his life. Lance looks to be in his late twenties, early thirties if that. He's handsome at around six foot two I'd guess. Lean, but very toned body. Dark hair and eyes that only a bad boy would have.

Alyson is going to want to screw my assistant.

I sigh and walk into my office, Lance following behind.

"A Mr. Sinclair from MIT called. Said something about possibly having an intern here for the summer. Was wondering if you'd be interested in hosting and apologizes for it being on short notice. Word travels fast around here when someone new steps in, so I'm not surprised they are trying to secure a spot for one of their students."

"It's fine. We all had to start small and learn before we can move up. Give me his number. I'll call him later and get more information from him."

"Oh, I can do that for you, Miss Hayes."

I look at him as a reminder that he can call me Everly. He smiles again, showing me a dimple this time. Good Lord, he's pretty.

"Sorry. Everly. I can do that for you. Besides, you have your first monthly meeting in an hour. Thought you'd like to get your things together first? I wasn't sure what you do for coffee, but I can grab you whatever you like while you look over the files I've compiled for you, at least bring you up to speed on the minutes from last month."

"Thank you, Lance. I appreciate it. I'd love some coffee actually, but I can get that if you point me in the right direction. That and maybe somewhere I can grab some aspirin?"

"You want to get your coffee?" He looks puzzled. His blazing smile is gone, replaced now with a look I'm not sure I can understand.

"I'm sorry. I've got this friend, and well, we haven't seen each other in a while so I had a few drinks last night and I'm afraid I'm suffering a little this morning because of it."

He smiles again, and I can see the lights are back on in his eyes. "No worries. I know how those things go. That's why I'm here. I'll grab the coffee and some Advil. You just relax, take a look at my notes, and I'll be right back. Cream and sugar or black?"

"Extra cream and sugar, please, and thank you, Lance." He smiles and then he's off to get my coffee. This will take some getting used to. I've had assistants before, but never a man.

I grab my bag and place it in my desk drawer, but snag my phone first. I pull up Alyson's number and hit send.

It rings once, then goes straight to voicemail.

I know she's awake. I dial again, and she sends me to voicemail again.

Okay. She's going to make me grovel. Fine.

I hit redial again and again until she finally picks up.

"Aly?"

"That's who you called, isn't it?"

I sigh. She's still hurt. "I'm sorry. I didn't mean what I said. I didn't mean to hurt your feelings, and I take it back. Okay?" I sit there for a minute and then look at my phone to see if she's still there. She is. "Aly?"

"Yeah. Okay."

"So am I forgiven?" I ask.

"Nothing to forgive. All is good."

"Thank God! I don't like when you're mad at me."

"All is good . . . as long as you tell me that you continued my conversation with Niko."

"Always a catch with you, lady." I laugh, but I'm honestly really happy that we are talking again. "I did, actually." Aly screams in my ear, and I pull it quickly away to save myself from going deaf. "Jesus! Still hung over here and you're yelling in my ear."

"Oh, sorry. And I'm sorry that I made you drink on a Monday."

"You didn't put a gun to my head. I'm a big girl. I didn't say no."

"That's because peer pressure is a bitch," she says, giggling in my ear. "So what happened?"

"With what?"

"Oh, don't start playing dumb now, you bitch! You just admitted that you continued the conversation, so what happened?"

What happened is she has opened up a can of worms that I'm not sure I can close. It could get ugly, and part of me doesn't care. The other part wants to slap me and say, "What the hell, Ev! He's your brother's best friend. Oh, and you're a liar to boot!"

"He tried to convince me to see him again."

"And you said yes."

"I said maybe."

"Maybe is not yes, Everly."

"Maybe is maybe, but probably not."

She huffs on the other end. "Oh, come on! I lined it all up for you to get some more bow-chicka-wow-wow."

"You are so immature, Alyson."

"And you are so uptight, Everly. Take the stick out of your ass and fuck a little, would you."

"So crass."

There's a knock on my door.

"Just a minute!" I call out. "Adulting calls," I say to Aly.

"All right, go do that work thing. I'm gonna do the sleep thing."

"Call you later."

I hang up the phone just as Lance opens the door. "Coffee and aspirin. Is there anything else I can get you?"

I toss the pills back, swallowing them down with the glass of water Lance brought with him in addition to my steaming hot cup of liquid gold. I could get used to this.

"Thank you."

"How about you work on that coffee, and I'll come get you for the meeting?" he asks.

"Perfect."

He heads out while I take a long drink of my coffee and look down at the file. Maybe I should have taken an actual vacation before starting.

Chapter Twelve

Everly

OVER THREE WEEKS HAVE passed since I moved back to Massachusetts, to my hometown of Newton and changed positions at work. Not much in my job is different, just the location and clients. There are more responsibilities, and I do have more people under me, but it feels about the same. My office is a little bit smaller but has a pretty good view of the Charles River, so nothing to complain about. I'm just over the border in our Cambridge office, and other than the traffic, I love it. The problem is my lack of social life. Maybe I need to get myself back out there. Force Niko Callahan from my mind.

Easier said than done, especially with the way our conversations have turned as of late. Why did I let Alyson's texting him, behind my back, escalate to more than that one day? All it's doing is screwing everything up and making me lie to him more. When he finds out what a horrible person I am, and the biggest liar . . . I can't keep this up.

After that first day when Aly sent him those few text messages on my behalf, Niko has sent me a text daily. Multiple times a day.

First, it was just, **good morning beautiful.** Then, **good night beautiful.** Then he'd start with . . . **Can't stop thinking**

about you. Eventually, we'd started to get dirty, and as much as I wanted to be offended, I found his dirty texting kind of a turn-on. Like the one, he sent a little while ago.

Niko: You. My one-eyed snake. This weekend. We can do dinner beforehand. ;D

I can't help but smile at his persistence. A few times I've almost given in, but stopped myself. Eventually, things took a turn, and not in a bad way. At least I didn't think so at the time. I had my first sexting experience with him, which escalated quickly to phone sex with the man.

No. Not just any man. Nikolas Callahan and I had sex via text. Niko made me come over the phone the day before, his voice dark and delicious as he told me what to do. I pull out my phone and read the text messages I have yet to erase. While I'm reading them, a new message pops up from Niko.

Niko: What are you wearing right now?
Everly: What?
Niko: You read that right. What are you wearing right now? ;)
Everly: Why do you want to know what I'm wearing? What are you wearing?
Niko: I just got home from work. Took a shower and right now I'm completely naked stroking my cock with thoughts of every fucking delicious thing that we did the last time I saw you. You won't let me see you again and I'm hurtin' over here, so the least you can do, baby, is humor me by telling me what you are wearing right now.

"Oh my God!" I say in a whisper. I'm in my office alone, but Lance, my assistant, could walk in at any time. The thought of Niko mastrubating is so fucking hot that I can feel the wetness between my legs.

Niko: Do you like thinking about me touching myself?

My face turns bright red as I read Niko's next text. Just thinking about him wearing jeans and a T-shirt is enough to set me on fire. Naked Niko? That is like adding gas to the fire. Naked Niko stroking his cock, is a guaranteed explosion!

It's easy to forget everything when you're texting with someone you're not supposed to be talking to, but I put all thoughts of Cameron out of my mind when I talk to Niko. He's growing on me, and he makes me laugh with some of the outrageous things he says. Sure, he's arrogant, cocky, and sometimes a little more full of himself than I'd like, but he's also sweet and funny. I keep telling him that I can't get away, and for the most part, he's understanding. Until recently, that is.

Niko: Still with me, baby?

I know I should not even consider this while I'm at work, but I get up and walk over to my office door and open it to see if Lance is at his desk. He's not, thank God. I close the door and lock it before walking back to my desk and sitting down before replying to Niko.

Everly: I'm here. I had to lock my office door.

Niko: Fuck yeah! Now tell me what you're wearing?

Everly: I'm wearing my work attire. Nothing sexy about that.

Niko: You have no idea how sexy clothing can be so tell me what you have on . . .

Everly: Black pencil skirt, white blouse. Nothing sexy, trust me.

Niko: Fuck. I bet you look hot as fuck in your tight skirt. You wearing high heels?

Everly: Yes. Black ones.

Niko: You have no idea the dirty things I want to do to you. I'm stroking my cock while thinking about your long legs wrapped around my waist while I watch my cock going in and out of that hot, wet, beautiful pussy you have.

"Oh God," I say as my hand travels to the top of my blouse and rests there. I'm not sure if I can keep saying no much longer. The truth is, I don't want to say no, but I just can't see how this can keep going the way it's been. I read the last text Niko sent and reply with my response, smiling while I do so.

Everly: *I'm picturing you in my head right now.*

Niko: *Remember how it felt when I was inside of you? How your pussy would squeeze my cock every time I'd thrust back into you. I know I remember. I haven't stopped thinking about it since that night.*

Niko: *I wanted you again when I woke up, but you were gone. I wanted to hear you scream my name as I emptied myself in you. Don't you want that again?*

I don't answer him because the truth is, I do want that again. I want that and more, but it can never happen. I close the door on that thought and concentrate on the now with Niko.

Everly: *I'm so wet right now that I'm going to have to take my panties off because they're drenched. This is so unfair. I'm at work and you're at home with no chance of anyone walking in on you.*

Niko: *Did you forget that you locked the door? I want you to pull your skirt up to your hips, slide those wet panties off and pretend that your fingers are my lips and tongue caressing, kissing and sucking on your pretty pink pussy.*

Jesus! I'm not usually into dirty talk, but reading the words Niko just sent to me has me feeling as if I'm on fire.

Niko: *Did you do what I asked?*

Everly: *You're so bossy . . . Yes. Happy now?*

Niko: *Not yet, but this will do. For now . . .*

Niko: *Can you feel me, baby? Feel the way my tongue slides between your folds? Fuck . . . Your taste is so damn addicting. I could eat you for days and never tire of the taste of you.*

I was playing along at first, but there is no way I can't actually touch myself, and do what he asked. I look at the door and listen for a second before pulling my skirt up and removing my panties. Of course mastrubating isn't new to me, but I usually use my vibrator at home and usually late at night, not while I'm at work locked away in my new office.

Niko: I'd suck your clit into my mouth and at the same time I'd put a finger into your wet pussy then add another so that I could finger fuck you while licking and sucking your clit. Do you remember when I did that? How good it felt and how your hips rocked up and down faster and faster as I got you there? How fucking good that felt when I ate you like a starving man without food or water for weeks? Because I fucking do. It's all I think about lately.

Everly: Yes.

Niko: Fuck... I'm so fucking close at just the thought of you. You make me feel like a teenager all over again.

Niko: I'm calling you. I need to hear your voice, hear you come.

I don't get the chance to reply before my cell phone is ringing. I hit the green answer button and hold the phone to my ear.

"You there, baby?" Niko says into the phone. He sounds like he's breathing heavy, and I know that this wasn't just dirty text messages. He really is mastrubating.

"I'm here," I tell him and put my hand and fingers back between my legs.

"You still touching your pussy, baby?" he asks, strain obvious in his voice.

"Yes," I say in a whisper so that Lance or anyone outside my office won't hear.

"Tell me, just how wet are you?"

My fingers slide easily across my opening and I gasp. "I'm really wet."

"Fuck!" he hisses. "I want my mouth on you so fucking bad right now that it hurts whenever I think about it. Do you know how painful that is, baby? What you do to me?"

"I do now," I say and smile at the thought of Niko walking around with sporadic hard-ons. I almost giggle into the phone, but when I hear his breathing intensify, all thought of laughter leaves my brain.

COCK *sure*

"Next time I see you, and there *will* be a next time, I'm going to fuck that beautiful mouth of yours. The memory of your full, luscious lips, wrapped around my cock while I pull out and then slide back into your mouth is seared into my brain forever." I can hear his hand moving up and down on his dick, the lubricated sounds as he strokes and says the words. The struggle of his labored breath is accentuated in each word he speaks. "I want that again. I want to feel that warm mouth around my cock while you suck me fucking dry. Just like you did the first time. Do you remember that, baby? How I tasted on your tongue as I held your head and thrust in and out of your mouth?"

He's struggling to talk, but it's not stopping him and I'm so damn turned on that I think I might just come from hearing him get himself off on the phone. My fingers are rolling over my clit, making tiny circles as I imagine it's Niko's mouth there instead of my own fingers.

"Put your finger in your pussy. I want you to finger yourself like I would. Remember what it felt like when I fucked you with my hand. Hurry, baby. I need you there with me and I'm so fucking close right now."

Right then I hear voices coming from outside of my office, but I don't stop. I couldn't if I wanted to. The door is locked, so they'll just have to wait if they decide to knock. My fingers travel from my clit down lower to my entrance. I put one, then two fingers inside of myself and pump them in and out, just like I remember Niko doing to me the night we were together. My breathing quickens, and I can feel myself reaching the edge of a cliff I'm more than ready to fall off.

"That's it. In and out. I want you to bring all those delicious juices back up to your clit and circle her. You ready, because I'm fucking dying over here, baby. I've got pre-cum coming from the slit of my cock and he's ready to blow. I want you to come with me," he says, and I can hear him struggling to hold back and wait for me. "Tell me what's going on, baby. I need you to tell me."

"I'm so wet, Niko. I think even more than I was the night we were together. I'm remembering about how you felt. How your fingers and mouth attacked my pussy. Every time you pumped them in and out of me. How I screamed when you bit my clit and then sucked it into your warm mouth. I loved it all. Every. Fucking. Thing. You. Did. I've used my vibrator so many times since you fucked me that I've gone through four sets of batteries," I say, and my fingers continue to slide in and out, up and down, over and over again. My hips are rocking even though there are people standing right outside my office door. I'm about to come and it's killing me not to scream out loud and give myself away to everyone in my office.

"Fuck! I can't wait, baby. Fuck! Fuck! Come with me," he says, and I hear his hand strokes going faster and faster as he moans into the phone.

"Niko! Oh my God, Niko, it feels so good. So damn good."

"That's it. Faster. Rub your clit faster, baby. It's my tongue. I'm sucking your swollen clit into my mouth and my fingers are pumping that pussy so hard right now just waiting to replace them with my cock. Give it to me, baby. Let me hear you scream!" he says, and that's it.

I scream out as I push myself over the edge while listening to Niko fall over his own ledge. My body shakes as I continue to rub circles on my clit until it's too much for me, and I move back down my entrance, pumping my fingers inside myself and feeling the walls of my pussy pulsate around them. I continue to do this until I hear Niko's moan and his hand strokes start to slow down, and I know he's just exploded. As soon as I pull my hand away and sit in my office chair, boneless, there is a knock at my door.

"Fuck, baby. That was—"

"Oh shit! I have to go, Niko. I'll call you later," I hang up before waiting for him to say anything. As I stand up, I pull my skirt back down and try to rub any wrinkles that it might have. "Just a second," I yell to whoever is on the other side of my door. I round my desk and walk to the door, unlocking it before pulling it open. My assistant, Lance, is standing there with another guy that I don't know.

"Sorry to bother you, Everly," Lance says cautiously before looking behind me into my office. "We heard a scream?" It comes out as more of a question. I don't know if it shows, but I'm mortified that I allowed myself to do what I just did with Niko in my office. "Everything okay?"

"Umm, yeah. I just saw a really big spider. Dropped right down on my desk and scared the shit out of me," I say to Lance and watch as he quirks an eyebrow at my using the word "Shit." I'm always professional with everyone here, and swearing isn't something I do when I'm at work.

"Okay, then. I just wanted to make sure. Is it too hot in here? I can turn down the thermostat if you need me to?" he asks, and I'm confused by his question.

"No, it's fine. It's comfortable in here, but if you're hot, feel free to lower it."

"No, I'm good. I just thought maybe you were hot. You look flushed, so I just assumed your office was too warm."

"No, thank you for asking, though. I'm just going to make a few phone calls, so if that's all?"

"Of course. I'll be at my desk. Let me know if you need anything," he says and walks away with the man he was obviously talking to during my phone sex call with Niko. I close the door to my office and walk back to my desk and sit, blowing out a breath as I do. I hear my phone vibrate on my desk, and I reach for it.

Niko: Everything okay?

Everly: Yes. No. Someone knocked at my door.

Niko: I thought it was something like that. You good?

Everly: Yes, but I don't think we should do that anymore while I'm at work LOL

Niko: Well, at least you are saying there will be a next time. ;) Now if you'll just agree to let me see you in person, we'll be great. What do you say?

Everly: No.

Niko: Baby, I know you want to see me again, stop trying to deny it. What could one date hurt?

God, he's so cocky. One of these days someone needs to pop that bubble he calls a head. I laugh to myself, thinking of the night I went home with Niko and left him before he woke with nothing but a note saying "thanks!" At least I popped it once. I'm sure of it. Didn't stop the cocksure bastard from re-inflating that ego of his and I just helped that along by fucking him via text message and phone sex. Good job, Everly. Might have to do something about that soon, but first, I need to look at what could be my future home. The faster I get out of my parents' house, the better. I can deal with Niko and his dirty mouth later.

Everly: Love how you assume a date is the issue.

Niko: Considering how you were talking to me a few minutes ago, panting and screaming as you came, just from the things my voice told you to do, over the phone at that. I figured sex is a given. :D

Everly: I can't this weekend.

Niko: You said that last weekend :/

Everly: Because it was true.

Niko: I'll break you down soon, babe. You can't keep resisting me forever.

I've got my lip trapped between my teeth as I smile down at my phone. It's so incredibly hard to turn him down.

Everly: I bet that's something new to you, huh?

Niko: It is, actually.

Everly: Maybe it's a sign that you should give up?

Niko: Give up? I'm not a quitter.

Everly: No, but you seem to be a glutton for punishment. :)

Niko: I think I have to agree with you there. Considering the fact that I'm having a relationship via text and phone, I'd say you are right about that... This is crazy. Just let me see you. I can come to you if you can't get away.

Everly: This isn't a relationship, Niko.

He doesn't reply to my last text. I don't know what he's thinking, but it's not. It was only supposed to be one night. One extraordinary night to cleanse myself of every dirty little fantasy I've ever had about him, along with the new ones that popped up the second I saw him again. That was the plan once I made it, and then to move the hell on. The problem is that I can't stop thinking about him.

Every dirty little thing he did to me and every last inch of his delicious body that I touched with my tongue. It haunts me. I can still taste him after weeks, and it's driving me crazy.

He's in every dream, every fantasy. My battery-operated friends only seem to sour the memory, a poor substitute for the flesh. And he's funny. I find myself looking forward to our text messages and occasional phone calls. He sends most at night while he's at work and things are slow. I can see how dangerous Niko is, and why he's known as a ladies man. I'd fall every time if I were them. Hell, I was and am them. I'm addicted after just one night.

"Earth to Everly . . . Alyson Payne to Everly Hayes, come in, Everly." Aly's voice breaks through my Niko-induced trance.

It's been two hours and I'm still completely lost in Niko land.

"Sorry, what was that?"

"I asked if you liked your housewarming present, and I want the details on what's happening with Niko."

"I can't get into that right now. I have a meeting in a little bit, but I promise I'll fill you in."

"You'd better! What about the gift I sent you?"

I glance over at my stacks of rainbow-colored Post-it notes and smile. "I *love* it!"

"I knew you would, weirdo."

"Hey! I take offense to that."

"Ha! Says the girl obsessed with Post-it notes. You've got a sickness."

"Right back at ya, Miss Obsessed-With-Buying-Scratch-Tickets."

"Hey! You can't win if you don't play. I could win big. You can't win shit with Post-its. Sorry, sweetie." She giggles in my ear as we go back and forth with our usual teasing.

"No, but I like organization and my Post-its help with that. They keep me on track. Don't you say anything about my quirks or I'll start bringing up all of your weird idiosyncrasies. Not just your scratch ticket obsession."

"Well, tell me this, then. You zoned out because you were thinking about all the naughty-girl sex you had, aren't you?"

"I'm not going to confirm or deny it. Let's just say that I need to find a different guy to fuck that will help me get over him. That is one peen I'm not sure I'll ever forget."

The door to my office swings open and in walks Cam, his eyes wide.

"Whoa! Covering my ears. I do not want to hear about my little sister boning some guy! And peen? Seriously, Ev? If you call it peen, I can see how you'd never forget it. Hell, I'm scared, and I have no idea what the fuck a peen is. Sounds like some deformed dick that I certainly don't want to hear about."

I shake my head. "Aly, I'll call you back. Cam just walked into my office, and I think he needs a reminder that not only am I not a child anymore but that I'm also not the Virgin Mary."

"Love you, girl." She pauses, and I think she's hung up, but there's no click. "Grow a brain, moron."

Cam's expression drops. "Fuck off, Aly."

And there's the click.

"I told you she hasn't changed. Doesn't mention me, my fucking ass! I don't understand why you're still friends with her."

I stare at Cam, giving him my best disapproving look. "I really can't tell if you two are messing with each other or just hate each other's guts for some unknown reason."

"She's a crazy witch, and I'm not afraid to tell her. Someone needs to put her in her place, knock her off her high horse for once. I don't mind doing it."

"What's up?" I change the subject. I can't listen to the same thing I've heard from him forever. It bothers me that my best friend and my brother hate each other, and for the life of me, I have no idea why.

"Wanted to see if you were free for dinner," he says while looking around my new office.

"You couldn't use the phone for that?"

He shrugs. "I was in the area. Plus I wanted to see my sis's swanky office. Gotta say it's a bit smaller than I was envisioning."

"But I have a window."

"That you do. And you get to see the dirty watah that is known here in these parts as the Charles River. Or maybe being in California all this time has you forgetting about all the joys of living in Boston. Either way, go you, sis! This office is prime."

I laugh and shake my head at him and then I pull up my calendar as it's the only way I stay sane, and glance down. "I'm going to go see two places after work, but if you don't mind dinner at about seven, I'm good."

"Sounds perfect." Cam props his foot up on the edge of my desk, and I eye the boots he's wearing.

"Awesome. Can we go to Legal's?" I could go for some lobster.

"You haven't had your seafood fix yet?" Cam asks, surprised.

"Never. I've missed the food here. I want to inhale it all, and get your feet off my desk."

Cam laughs and shakes his head, dropping his big feet to the floor. "I thought we could do Bisuteki."

"Japanese steakhouse?"

"Yeah. We can hit the one over here on Memorial Drive. Save ourselves from traffic."

I nod in agreement. "Sounds good. I haven't been there in years, and I used to love their sushi."

"Great. I'll call ahead, so we get a table." He places his hands on the armrests and pushes out of the chair. "Good luck with the house hunting today. Hopefully one will work out."

"God, I hope so. I want my things. Living out of suitcases sucks."

"I bet. It will work out. One thing at a time, Ev. See you at dinner." He gives me a wave as he heads out the door.

Hopefully when I see him next, I'll have good news on the house front. I hope so, as the search has been killer. I thought

California real estate was crazy, but it was nothing compared to my current search.

The novelty of staying with my parents has worn off, and I'm ready to be on my own again.

"This is a three bedroom, three-and-a-half bath, just over nineteen hundred square feet semi-attached home that just went on the market today," Marcy, my realtor and my parents' neighbor, says as we stand in front of the third house of the evening. It's the twenty-fifth home she's taken me to in recent weeks. The problem isn't me picking one; it's the market. Taking a night to decide has cost me three different houses already. Things are flying off the market so fast I've upped my budget in hopes of snatching one.

"I love the front," I say as we head up the paved walkway. It's a freshly painted blue-gray with white trim. "The bay window is beautiful."

"It was just renovated, so everything is brand new down to the pipes and electrical, so nothing to worry about there." Marcy turns the handle and opens the door.

My mouth goes slack as we walk in. Light hardwoods run through the open floor plan, marble tiles wrap the fireplace, and in the back, there is what looks like a gorgeous kitchen. There's even a back porch leading to a private backyard.

I could get a dog.

I try not to show my excitement or how much this place feels like home. From the architectural details to the gorgeous finishes, there is still a warmth that calls to me. I let Marcy continue to show me around. The master bedroom is on the second floor with a huge bathroom and custom walk-in closet. Up there is a second bedroom and bath, then the third floor, which was once an attic space, has been finished out with another bedroom and bath.

When we return to the main floor, Marcy turns to me. "You've been quiet."

I nod. "Offer ten grand above list price, closing in a week."

Marcy's mouth drops open. "Really?" She blows out a breath. "Way to almost send me into a panic, Everly. I thought you hated it!"

A laugh springs out. "I thought jumping up and down screaming 'This is the one' might have been a bit childish."

"Childish, maybe, but I wouldn't tell." She winks at me.

I look around and heave a sigh, a smile on my lips. "You think they'd let me stay the night?"

Marcy chuckles and shakes her head. "Maybe in a week." She turns off all the lights, and we head out. "I'll submit the offer as soon as I get back to the office, so maybe half an hour, but I'll call the realtor on the way."

"Excellent. I'll be happy not to be living out of suitcases."

"I'm sure," Marcy says as she steps forward and wraps her arms around me. "Have a good dinner with Cameron, and I'll call you the second I have any news."

"Thanks, Marcy."

"Dammit, Jojo, calm down!" a deep male voice says, causing us to turn.

Coming onto the front porch from the other door of the large duplex is a tall man with a wiggly butt pit bull who is wrapping him up with a leash as she circles around him in excitement. The dog sees us and heads over, tightening the knot she's caused.

"Hi, baby," I say with a smile as I bend over to pet the taupe coat of the grinning canine.

"Oh! I'm so sorry," the deep, sexy voice of her owner says.

I look up, Jojo's tongue bathing my hand while she continues to wiggle. "It's okay . . ." I trail off, words leaving me as I stare into a set of beautiful green eyes on chiseled features.

Hot damn. His voice matches his face and body. I wouldn't say he's hotter than Niko, but he's close. Oh boy, is he close.

"Jojo!" He pulls on the leash, and she bounds over. "So sorry, I didn't see you. I'm Grant, and this hyper girl is Jojo."

He holds out a hand, and I slip mine in. "Everly."

Strong, firm handshake. I like that. Grant is confident, and it's showing. I'm sure he's broken a heart or ten in his lifetime.

His smile is brilliant, matched only by Jojo, who is tugging on his arm while she sniffs the grass.

"Are you here to look at the house?" he asks.

I nod. "Yes. I'm putting in an offer."

"Excellent. Well, I just moved in a few weeks ago. I love it here. I'm pretty sure I'll love it even more as the month goes on." He smiles at me, and I'm not sure if he's hitting on me or not. I've never been good at being able to tell when a guy is flirting or just being friendly.

Another tug on his arm, and he looks over to the dog before locking eyes with mine. "I better get going before she rips my arm off. Good luck—I hope you get it. I think it would be great to have you as my new neighbor."

I smile as I watch him as he heads down the steps, Jojo pulling him along. "Nice meeting you, Jojo!" I yell, and Grant turns to look back. A smile is stretching from ear to ear.

Damn. I'm sure he's got a lot of women falling at his feet. I would probably be one of them if I hadn't been ruined by Niko Callahan already, and as much as I'd like to date other people, right now I can't. I also can't date Niko, no matter how hard he tries to get me to give in. We started out with a lie, and that lie is still a big red flag when it comes to him and me. I need to move on.

"Do you think he even saw me standing next to you?" Marcy asks with a chuckle.

"Great neighborhood," I say with a wink. "I'm sure he was just being friendly."

"With the way he was looking at you? That was flirting," Marcie says with a chuckle.

Unfortunately for me, I can't seem to stop thinking about the flirting that another man does with me. Niko is the only man that I'm interested in flirting with at the moment, and that's bad. I might just have to force myself to look into other options. Force being the key word. God, I am so screwed.

Chapter Thirteen

Niko

"**W**HERE'S EVERLY?" I ASK, sitting down at the table next to Cameron. It's been two weeks since his little sister moved back. While I'd much rather be seeing Alyson, it'll be good to see Everly again after nearly a decade away.

"She was looking at some houses. Just texted me she's on her way."

"Did she finally find the one?"

He shrugs. "Who knows? Every time she submits an offer, it's already pending. Apparently, you no longer have the luxury of sleeping on it."

"This market is brutal. I'm glad I got in when I did."

I glance down at my phone. Alyson and I have been going back and forth all day, but she stopped replying a few hours ago after I sent my last. I'd be lying if I said that I don't look forward to her text messages. They're usually flirty and fun, like the one she just sent, but I did send her a picture of my cock, so I'd expect nothing less than the reply that comes through while I sit with Cam.

Alyson/Everly: I think you might be a bad boy. ;) Tempting me with such a beast. Keep it up, buddy and I might have to call animal control on you. :D

My lip twitches up. Finally, Alyson responds. I've always thought dick pics were stupid, but I'm at the point of desperation to see her again, so in the middle of jerking off, I texted her a pic.

That was two hours ago. I'm not above guilting her to help put me out of my misery after every conversation or text with her. I'm usually ruined for the rest of the day after our chats.

Niko: Animal Control, eh? Maybe I just need YOU to come control my animal . . . Dinner before dessert? You come work your magic on my one-eyed snake, and I'll eat you for dessert. Sounds good to me.

Alyson/Everly: Smh You and your dessert. LOL, Sorry, but I've got dinner plans. Text you later?

What the fuck? She can't see me, but she can have dinner out with someone else? I'm pissed the fuck off. I know I have no right, but this woman is killing me here. Is it another guy? I have this feeling of jealousy hitting me, and I hate this shit. I don't get fucking jealous, but apparently, someone forgot to tell the rest of me this shit. I try not to ask, but I have to know. I've been asking her to meet me every time we talk or text, and she's always got a reason to say no. She's saying yes to someone, though, and that just pisses me off. Fuck it! I'm asking.

Niko: With who?

Alyson/Everly: Niko . . .

Niko: You do realize that you seem to have time to go to dinner with everyone, but me. I'm starting to think that there is something wrong with me.

Alyson/Everly: Niko . . .

Niko: Alyson . . .

Alyson/Everly: I have to go. TTYL

As always, the brush off. I'm to the point I don't get this chick. She's interested, very interested based on our conversations, but unavailable. I'm beginning to wonder if she's married. I don't do married women. Then again, I don't think she'd be texting me back if that were the case.

"As a friendly reminder, don't hit on my sister," Cam says.

I put my phone back down on the table, and I roll my eyes. "How many times are you going to have to tell me?"

"Until it's through that thick Greek/Irish skull of yours."

I can't stop the roll of my eyes. How much could she have changed for him to be so damn adamant about me behaving? He acts like I fuck anything with a pussy.

"She's not my type, Cam."

Cam purses his lips. "Maybe she wasn't when she was fifteen, but now, yeah. Just behave."

I scrunch my brow and let out a chuckle. "What, are you saying that she . . ." I trail off, my gaze locked on a familiar figure walking through the door. My jaw drops as I stare at the woman I haven't been able to stop thinking about for weeks. The one I was just texting with. What are the odds? "Holy fuck."

Is it possible that she's gotten even more gorgeous in the weeks since I last saw her?

Cam slams his elbow into my ribs, pulling my attention from my Post-it note girl and to the pain in my side.

"What the hell, man?"

"Keep your fucking dick in your pants, and close your fucking mouth."

"How . . ." I trail off in confusion to look back toward Alyson who is headed straight for me, but the confident look from that night we met is gone, replaced by a wary, apprehensive one. Something feels off, and I have a bad feeling all of a sudden.

She looks to Cam and walks straight up to him, wrapping her arms around him, her lips against his cheek.

What the fuck?

"You're late," Cam says.

I'm dumbstruck staring at her trying to compute what the fuck is going on, though I think I know. And God do I hope it's not true.

"Sorry, traffic was bad," she says as she sits down, "and there was an accident on I-95 south. I had to get off and make my way through the back roads. I haven't lived here for so long that I got a little lost."

"No worries. I was just giving you a hard time. We haven't been waiting long, have we, Niko? You remember Niko, right, Ev?"

She nods and gives me a small smile like we haven't seen each other in years.

"How could I forget? How are you, Nikolas? You look the same as you did the last time I saw you," she says with that smile still plastered on her face.

Is she serious right now? The last time she saw me was a few weeks ago! I fucking talked to her on the phone yesterday. Shit, she sent me a text less than five minutes ago.

I look over at Cam and then back to her, and her face loses that pretty smile of hers. Yeah . . . she's worried now that I'm about to let Cam in on her inside joke. It wasn't funny, and I'm pissed.

Fuck. Me.

She already did that, though. More than once that night, in my mind every night since, and over the phone sitting in front of me.

She knew it was me. This fucking girl played me. No, not a girl. She's no longer a girl. Everly-fucking-Hayes is a full-grown woman and a liar. One that I have fucked without knowing that she was Cameron's fucking sister.

I can see it in her eyes. She knew who I was. From the moment she sat next to me, she knew, and I was fucking clueless.

She lied to me, fed me a line, and I didn't even notice. Even now I can't reconcile the memory of teenage Everly to the woman in front of me. Talk about ugly duckling syndrome. She passed average swan and went straight to a queen of the swans. There is nothing that reminds me of her when she was a kid. No, that's not true. Her eyes. Her eyes are the same hazel color that has always been unique to her, but I still had no damn idea it was her.

"It's that Greek and Irish DNA in his blood. Pure luck on his part. He might look like he hasn't aged, but trust me, he still can't hang with me at the gym." They both laugh. Everly's laughter is a lot lighter than her brother's, though.

"Oh, I'm betting he can keep up with you, big brother. You're all about bragging. You forget that I know how you are. I bet I can guarantee that Niko here doesn't brag at all, do you, Niko?" She stares at me. No. She's daring me.

This fucking chick!

Cameron is going to kill me. Rip out my intestines with his bare hand while he pummels my face with the other fist and stomps my nuts kind of torture death.

And I'm going to kill her.

I would never have fucked her had I known it was her. Fuck!

Cam kicks me under the table when I sit there staring at his sister, drawing my attention to him. I look at him, fuming until I see his face. I can't stay here with them. I need to get up and away from this whole fucked up situation, but I can't. Cam will have questions, and right now I'm not prepared to answer them. He gives me a look to remind me that this is his sister, and I know what he's thinking. I look away, not saying anything because I don't know if I can lie to Cam. He doesn't know that his warnings have all come too late.

Maybe he should have fucking warned his little sister not to fuck his friends instead of worrying about me. That might have been helpful. He said she changed, but I didn't expect sweet, shy, needy little Everly Hayes to have changed into a two-faced liar.

This is so messed up.

I shake my head and pick up the menu to pretend like I'm interested in eating. I'm not. I've lost any damn appetite the moment Alyson . . . No, not Alyson—*Everly*—walked through the door only to reveal herself as someone I had no business ever touching. And Jesus Christ, the ways I touched her. Shit! Cameron is going to flip his fucking shit. The things we did. My left leg starts to bounce, and I don't hear the waiter when he comes to take our drink order.

"Niko?" Cam calls.

"I'm sorry, what?" I ask.

"You want another beer or are you good?"

"Actually, I'll take one of those and a cognac. Thanks," I say, and Cam eyes me suspiciously. I've got nothing for him right now. Nothing I know he'd want to hear.

"You good, man?" he asks, and I still can't look him in the eye.

"Yeah, just hungry. You know what you're getting?"

"Nah, I need another minute. We can grab an appetizer if you want, while we wait?"

"Yeah, sure. Whatever you want is good."

Cam tells the waiter to bring us some Chinese wings and a California roll, then turns to Everly to see if she wants to add anything. She's also looking down at her menu, avoiding eye contact with me. Good. I hope her ass is just as uncomfortable as I am right now because this situation is pretty fucked up.

"Ev? Sushi?"

"Yeah, that works. I'll have the Arizona Maki, and can I have a glass of water?" she asks, finally looking up at the waiter. He nods and then is off to put in our order. I should just leave. Tell Cam I got a call or something. I'm not sure how long I can sit in front of her and her brother and not ask her what the fuck.

"How were the houses you looked at?" Cam asks Everly, pulling me out of my thoughts of strangling his sister.

"Great. I submitted an offer. It's vacant. Recently renovated, so hoping to close in a week."

"A week? That's fast. No issue with financing?"

"Diving," she says, which confuses me until Cam responds.

"Seriously?" Cam asks, his forehead scrunched up. "Your trust fund?"

"Cam, I love Mom and Dad, but they've been home for four days and are already driving me insane."

"Over six thousand square feet and you can't get away from them?" Cam asks with a laugh.

"You forget I haven't lived with them for eight years. Plus, I've already got it set up to repay it once my house in California sells. Besides, no judging from you. I know you took money from yours to buy your place."

I scrunch my brow. It's not new information about Everly having a trust fund because Cam has one, too. What surprises me, but shouldn't, is that she's going to repay it.

Cameron is one of the most level-headed trust fund babies I've ever met. Apparently, so is his sister. They make small talk while we wait for the food, and I'm counting down the minutes to when I can get the fuck out of here or get Everly alone.

Thank fuck Cam heads to the bathroom, because I can't take this shit anymore. I wait a minute until I know Cam is out of earshot, noticing all the fidgeting Everly is doing across the table from me. She's looking everywhere but at me. Good. She should be uncomfortable. I'm pissed!

"What the fuck, *Alyson*?" I ask with a sneer.

Her eyes widen at me before she looks around the room. "Keep your voice down," she finally says.

"Seriously? I think I've kept my voice pretty damn quiet for the past forty-five minutes," I say to her, and she just sits there like a deer stuck in headlights. "Well?" I press her, waiting for something.

"What do you want me to say?" she replies, her voice low.

Oh, no, woman. I need more than that shit.

"I want you to tell me why you didn't tell me who you were? Why did you lie to me and tell me that your fucking name was Alyson?" I ask. My blood is fucking boiling.

"At first, I thought you knew it was me. You were flirting, and even though I was surprised by your coming onto me, I liked it."

"So you decided to lie to me?"

"You wouldn't have gone home with me if you'd known that I was Everly Hayes."

"You're damn right I wouldn't have!" I yell at her, causing the table next to us to stare and then whisper. Fuck! I need to pull it together before they throw us out and I'm explaining why to Cam. I shake my head in disbelief at the whole damn situation and just how fucked up it is. "Cameron is my best friend. You knew that. You knew that when you decided to lie to me that night. Do you understand the fucked-up position that you've put me in here, Everly? How fucked up this is?"

"I do, and I'm sorry. That night, I was in a bad place," she says, and as I start to tell her off, she holds her hand up to let me know she's not finished. "I had a lot of shit going on in my life recently. I know that this is no excuse for lying to you, but it's what was going on in my head at the time, and I just want to explain. I didn't plan to lie to you, it just happened, and once I did, well, I couldn't take it back. Even now, as mad as you are at me, I wouldn't change it. I know that sounds selfish or stupid. Maybe even both, but being with you that night was what I needed."

I sit there with my mouth open. I'm completely dumbfounded at her response, and I honestly don't even know how to respond to her right now.

"That doesn't even make any goddamn sense!" I say to her, and it doesn't.

"I know, but it's all I have. You were there. Maybe if it were someone else instead of you, I might have gone home with them, but it was you. I know you would never have talked to me that way or brought me back to your place—"

"To fuck you? Because that's what I did, Everly. We fucked like rabbits and then you up and left in the middle of the night! You have been talking to me by phone and text messages ever since. Didn't you think that maybe you should clue me in on your lie then? Did you think that I would never find out that I fucked my best friend's little sister? What the fuck?" I drop my head into my hands and let out a long breath.

"Look, we had one night of great sex. I'm sorry that I lied to you. Truly I am."

"Seriously?"

"Yes, seriously. Why are you acting as if you've never had a one-night stand before, Nikolas," she says it like she knows all my dirtiest secrets, which I'm sure she knows some. Fucking Cam and his big mouth. "Look, I get it. You don't like it when someone takes advantage of you. I did that, and I was wrong. This situation is one hundred percent on me, and I own that. I can also empathize with you, but it's too late to take it back now, and honestly, I wouldn't if I could. I had fun."

"Yeah? Well, at least you had fun. That's the number one thing here, isn't it, Everly?" I say, drawing out her name in the most sarcastic tone that I can. "Tell me, though, what was your plan?"

"Plan? I'm not sure what you mean, I had no plan."

"Sure you did. What did you think would happen after we fucked the shit out of each other and you decided to string me along, pretending to be someone else? Your fucking plan!" I yell again, but I don't care. She looks toward the restrooms where Cam went and then lets out a breath before speaking.

"Honestly, I left your place with the intention of never seeing or talking to you again. I figured I'd avoid you by not being around my brother when I thought you might be with him. I don't know. I didn't think about after, but I do know that when I left with you that night, it was only for that night, Niko."

"That's fucking bullshit. If that were true, the last two weeks wouldn't have happened. You took my number. You reached out to me. Stop this shit. Fuck! The lies alone. Why didn't you tell me?"

She shrugs. "I didn't reach out to you."

Okay, now I'm about to lose my shit here. Cam is going to come out to me flipping out on his kid sister, and I don't give a flying fuck right now because what the fuck is wrong with her?

"You just said that with a straight fucking face. I'm concerned now because I don't think that Cam is aware of your mental health status. You do remember that I was there for all of this, right? I mean, you are lying to my face right now, knowing that I know the damn truth, yet you keep lying."

"There is nothing wrong with my mental health, Niko. I'm not lying. I didn't reach out to you. Well, not at first anyway. Aly did."

I look around at the people sitting at the tables surrounding us, enjoying their dinner as they make small talk and wonder where the cameras are. Cam hasn't come back yet, and I'm praying that this is a fucking joke.

"I'm being punked, right? Am I being punked?" I ask her, praying that this is another one of Cameron's lame attempts at being funny. I look back at her and look for a crack in her armor. She gives nothing away, though, and my leg again starts to bounce under the table.

"Niko?"

"This is a joke, right? Cam is hiding in the back right now with the guys laughing his ass off, and they've just been waiting for me to crack before they come out with a camera so they can play this shit on a loop at the station, right?"

"No. Cameron is not in on this. He knows nothing, and I'd like to keep it that way. Look, I said I was sorry. I didn't string you along. Maybe it seemed that way, but honestly, I just enjoyed our conversations, and I couldn't ignore your text messages when they came in." I sit there realizing that she's serious and that this is not a joke. "I wouldn't have used your number. I left it balled up on the table in the pub the night you sent the drinks."

"Do you have split personalities or something? I'm sure Cam would have mentioned something as serious as that, but maybe he was embarrassed."

"Well, kind of, she's just a real person."

"You are not making any damn sense. Jesus, right now I can see the resemblance between you and Cameron, and it has nothing to do with your looks. Speak English!"

"Alyson is my one of my closest friends. She was the girl you saw me with that night at the pub."

"Okayyyy. Other than the fact that you stole her name, what does she have to do with this?" I ask, wondering where she was going with this. She's confusing the fuck out of me.

"Well, I wasn't lying when I said that I didn't plan to see or talk to you again, however, you sending over your number with the drinks, well, Aly decided to give me a push," she says, and it's starting to make sense now. Well, just the texting and phone part. That doesn't negate the fact that she lied about who she was and that we've fucked.

"She's who I've been texting and talking with on the phone all this time?" I ask for clarification.

"Not the entire time, no. Just the first few the morning after you sent the drinks."

"This shit is making my fucking head hurt. You could have just told me."

"Truth destroys fantasy. I saw an opportunity, and I took it."

"What?" I can't believe this. Is this the same woman I've been talking to? "You knew who I was before you sat down next to me, didn't you?"

She nods. "I did. Like I said before, I thought you knew who I was. And that maybe you decided to treat me differently now that I was no longer that thirteen-year-old ugly duckling that used to follow you and Cam around, crushing on you like a lovesick puppy. Seeing you again, after so many years and as an adult man? Well, once I realized that wasn't the case, I knew that you wouldn't have given me the time of day if you'd known that I was Cameron Hayes's little sister. I decided to take a chance."

"Yeah, how'd that work out for you, Everly?"

"What do you want me to say, Niko? I've apologized. I'm only trying to explain."

"I think you've said enough, to be honest. You're right about one thing, though—I would never have taken you home if you'd told me who you were. I would never have done that to Cam. He's like my brother. You know this, and that is what I don't understand about this whole thing. You'd risk fucking with your brother like this, forcing me into a corner to either lie to him or tell him the truth and hope that he doesn't say fuck our friendship and believes me over his sister," I say, and she has the nerve to look contrite.

"I thought you knew who I was—" she says softly, but I'm done.

"I didn't," I say between clenched teeth. At this point, she's just saying the same shit over again, and she doesn't make any sense to me. Doesn't matter anymore. I just need to end this shit and get out of here. "Was it worth it, Everly?" I ask, throwing the contents of my drink back.

"What, using you for sex?" she asks, and I choke on my drink before spiraling into a coughing fit. She jumps up to do what, I don't know, but I don't give her the chance to touch me and wave her off. "I didn't mean I used you for sex! I don't know why I even said that. Forget I said that."

I watch as she turns a few shades of pink.

"Don't start lying again now. You meant what you just said, so own that shit! You did use me for sex. Pretty sure that was already established the night I took you home and we fucked."

Jesus, I was fucking used. What's worse is that I don't like how it feels. I'm stunned, in complete shock that the woman in front of me is the same girl that used to follow Cam and me around when she was a kid. A nerdy, but very sweet kid. She just stares at me, completely mute.

"Two weeks of text messages. Phone calls . . . Fucking hell, I was just texting you before you walked in here." I turn away from her, my jaw clenching. "I don't understand this. Did I do something to you that I don't remember doing, hurt your feelings when you were a kid or something? I'm seriously at a fucking loss here, Alyson. Oh . . . Not Alyson. Everly."

"Let's just forget that it happened," she says. "We keep what happened between us to ourselves. No harm, no foul."

"No harm, no foul?" I say incredulously. "Man, he said you'd changed, but I didn't realize you'd changed into a selfish bitch. Who are you?" I ask, and she doesn't respond to me at all. Just keeps looking at the food in front of her, picking at it.

"If that's what you want to think of me, fine, I'll accept that, but please, don't tell Cam. I'm not trying to come between the two of you. I didn't think about that when I decided to sleep with you. You didn't know it was me, I get that, but you could get to know me now, as a friend?"

I chose to ignore the last thing she says, focusing instead on the one thing I don't do with women. "No, I didn't know who you were, but you knew you were lying to me. That's all I need to fucking know about you. That you're a fucking liar. Maybe Cam needs to know that his sweet little sister isn't so sweet after all, eh?"

She flinches. Finally, a fucking reaction that makes fucking sense.

Cam walks back to the table just as I stand up and grab my jacket from the chair.

"Where are you going?"

"I got a call and need to take off, but you two stay. Enjoy the rest of your food. I hear the dessert here is fantastic. I'm sure anything is better than what we order at the pub," I say, referring to the fact that I called her my dessert when we were leaving the pub the night I took her lying ass home with me. "Take advantage while you're here." I grab my wallet to throw Cam some cash for my barely eaten dinner, but he waves me off.

"It's cool, man. I've got you. You sure you don't want to stay?"

"Nah, I'm positive. Apparently, I need to start watching what I eat. Seems to come back later to bite you in the ass when you cheat by having dessert." I can feel her eyes on me as I pull my coat on, and I know it's not lost on her what I'm referencing. It's been a running gag, but there's nothing fun or sexy about it right now. Whatever. I just need to get out of here.

"I'll talk to you later, Cam." I turn and look at Everly, my eyes I'm sure are blazing right now with the fury I'm holding in toward her. "It was fantastic to see you again, Everly. You've grown up into quite the lady. No. Lady is too much. Quite the woman." Cam is watching, confused by my statement. I've hardly said two words to her since she arrived other than when Cam left the table, but he doesn't need to know about that.

"You sure you're good?"

"Yeah. Enjoy your time with your sister. I know how much you've missed having her around the last few years. I'll leave you to it."

And with that, I'm fucking out. The faster I get away from her, the better it will be for Cam, because I don't think I could bite my tongue much longer.

There are two very dangerous parts of my job—going into a burning building, and venting. I'm on the roof, prepping to vent the two-story building that's home to four families. Every move is calculated. The section I'm on is slightly sloped, but takes a dive a few feet behind me. There are guys on the ground helping those who are in the building, and guys blasting water through a now broken window.

I'm trying to help those who are inside. Right now visibility is almost nothing; the smoke is black and thick. It and the gases cloud everything.

The smoke needs out.

"Get back!" Cam yells, the loud roar of the chainsaw engine drowning out everything else.

The chainsaw cuts through the layers of shingles, plywood, and rafters with variable ease. He steps back after the crude cut, and I swing the pike pole forward, grabbing onto the roofing and pulling until the hole is exposed.

Flames erupt from the new hole, oxygen feeding the fire. It's so hot I can feel it through my gear. Cam tugs on me, pulling me back to the ladder. The roof gives a little with each step, causing me to move faster as the thick, black smoke surrounds me.

Once on, we book it down the shallow angle, which still takes time with all the gear, ready to move on to the next task. A loud crash causes me to look up, and I watch as the roof collapses.

"Shit, that was close," Cam says when we get to the top of the truck. We look back and watch the flames shoot twenty or thirty feet up in the air, smoke billowing all around.

I nod, trying to catch my breath. "It went faster than I thought."

"Anyone still inside?" Cam asks Jenkins, who is putting a blanket around a shocked and crying woman once we reach the ground.

"Peterson was the last one, and all occupants are accounted for."

"Pets?"

"Jake's giving oxygen to a dog, and there was a cat who ran off."

It's always a good day when there are no casualties. There are some smoke inhalation and mild injuries, but that's common. Any serious injuries were avoided, which indicates that there were probably good alarms installed, considering the sun isn't even up yet.

"Good job, you two," the chief says as he takes the chainsaw from Cam. "There's another ladder coming, so get ready to help with the hose."

We nod and turn back to the house. Even thirty feet away I can feel the warmth against my face. One hose isn't enough to combat the plume of flames devouring the structure.

The truck arrives a few minutes later and we run around, helping to set up the hose segments and attach it to a fire hydrant, which is two blocks away. We've already tapped into the one closest to the house.

Eventually the fire goes out, white smoke is still escaping. The structure is a complete loss at this point. I won't be surprised if more of the interior collapses while we're here. The good thing is that it didn't spread. We were able to keep it contained and away from the houses that seem only a few feet away.

"That was best case scenario right there," Cam says as we watch the last resident head off. I nod in agreement.

Some occupants were sent to the hospital, and others were guided to emergency housing. They've lost everything they own, but they're alive. It'll be hard, but we've got a great team of support to help them rebuild.

"Fuck, I'm beat," I say, noticing how the sky is beginning to lighten. It's been a long day, and I'm ready for sleep.

Cam nods. "Chief is with the investigation team."

I work on intricately folding up one of the hoses. "Deliberate."

"Why do you say that?"

After every fire we speculate, using out years of experience, and wait to see if it lines up with the investigator's report.

I cock my head back to the building. It's evident at the front door, the door nobody could get through. "Alligator charring." I say. While it's no longer considered an indicator of an accelerant, there are other factors that coincide. The shiny alligator blisters on the door, and the fact that the fire moved quickly through the stairwell and into the apartments, meant that the fire burned faster than normal.

"Fuck," he hisses. "I hadn't taken a good look yet. Probably gasoline starter."

"Probably." It's the easiest to get hold of. "Real lucky everyone got out." With the way it spread, we had to pull everyone out through the windows.

"Now to find the bastard."

"I hope they do. The last thing we need is a pyro junkie."

We continue in silence, picking up the gear, getting the truck back in order, until everybody is ready to head back.

"I can't wait to crash, but after I shower," I say. The adrenaline has worn off, and I'm dead tired.

"Power nap," Cam says.

"What?"

"Dude, it's officially Saturday."

"And?"

"You're helping move Everly into her new place."

I let out a groan. "Fuck."

By the time I get home, it'll be almost seven, giving me two or three hours max. Maybe I'll shower and crash at the station and go from there. But I won't be the only one as Bishop and Jenkins also agreed to help. The rest of the guys had the night off.

Everly hasn't called or texted, and I sure as shit haven't reached out to her. My luck to finally meet someone, pursue her, and it blows up spectacularly in my face.

What I'm not looking forward to is seeing her. Not after her lies. I'm still pissed about that fucked-up dinner two weeks ago.

The only thing that hasn't changed is that she's still the chick I jack off to daily. Today is going to be interesting.

Chapter Fourteen

Niko

SIX HOURS LATER, I'M carrying a box labeled "Kitchen" into Everly's house and set it down on the counter. She found a nice place, and I can only guess how much it cost. Probably double my place, and worth every penny from what I've seen.

Due to the fire, and half the day's volunteers taking the call, we started with the unloading a few hours later than scheduled.

"Want a beer?" Cam asks as he heads toward the fridge.

"Nah, man, I'm still beat from last night. I don't need anything to relax me, or I'm gonna fall asleep on the floor."

"A Coke, then. I think I saw some earlier."

"Nah. Just water for me."

"You still on that bullshit about Coke taking inches off your dick?"

I look at Cam and smirk. I don't think it does, but I like screwing with him so I keep it up. "It's true. Keep drinking that crap, and you'll see when your dick starts shrinking."

"Where the fuck did you hear that stupid shit. I drink Coke all the time."

"Exactly! And you've probably got a small dick. Now we know why you can't keep up with the ladies."

"Fuck you, Niko! My dick is just fine, and I keep up with the ladies without any problem at all." Cam swings the fridge open and pulls out water for me. I watch him grab a Coke, but he looks down at his pants then grabs water for himself, bypassing the Coke he wanted to drink.

I turn my head trying not to laugh when he comes back and puts the water in front of me.

"Speaking of the ladies . . . I'm not the one who's on a pussy strike. After one chick decided to give you a taste of your own medicine, you've decided the world is ending."

Jake walks in right as Cam is running his mouth. I see the laugh he's trying to hold in, but he doesn't say anything. Whatever.

Yeah. Everly gave me a little more than my own medicine. Cameron's devil sibling did something I'd never do to anyone, and it stings. Especially with her nonchalance over the whole thing.

"Yeah, whatever. I'm not on strike. I've just been busy and distracted. I've got things on my mind." Distracted and pissed is more like it, but he doesn't need to know that.

"Busy and distracted with what? Jacking off to the memory of the girl that fucked your head up?"

"No. Just stuff. My stuff has nothing to do with her or any woman, so just mind your own business." I wish he'd shut up about this. The last thing I need is for his sister to overhear this shit and pump her head up with things. "God, you're an asshole. Just get moving so we can get this done today, would ya?" I don't think I can handle Cam's typical ball-busting today. Not while we are in his sister's new house and she's in the next room.

"Yeah, sure. You've been distracted by one chick. Stop denying it. You're pussy whipped. One night, and this chick has your head all over the place. Stop fixating on her, man. You were probably one of many. Just get over it and let's get you back to being Niko again. You're boring as shit lately."

If he only knew what he was talking about right now. I know he'd eat his damn words if he knew the woman he's referring to is his sister.

I've stayed away from any invites Cam has tossed out at me to have dinner with him and Everly since finding out she and Alyson were one in the same. Not only did she lie about who she was, but she apparently doesn't see much of a problem with what she did. At least that's how I see it.

The night I finally found out while at dinner with Cam was enough interaction for me for a lifetime. I tried hard to pick up one of the guys' shifts at the firehouse to get out of being here today. I'd promised to help move all Everly's stuff from storage to her new house, but no one wanted to switch shifts with the late notice, so here I am, stuck in front of a few of my friends from work as well as Cam and his sister that I banged without knowing who she was.

As mad as I am, seeing her this morning and having her act as if nothing ever happened between us both calmed and enraged me. I finally just gave up and decided to let the rage go, leave my friendship in the green zone and forget it ever happened. Everly has been different today than she was when we all had dinner.

She even thanked me for coming out to help on my day off, and it was sincere. Of course, she thanked the other guys too, but she didn't single them each out to do it as she did me. Being this close to her is screwing with my head again, and I don't want that. She walks in and out of the room that Cam, the guys, and I are in taking a break, and I can't help but watch her, the way her hips sway in the yoga pants she's currently wearing. I try and look away before she notices, but she's caught me twice now, and I've gotten nothing. No smirk, no smile, no blush, nothing. It's like she knows she's fucking with me.

Bitch.

"Hey, Niko! Like my shirt?" the rookie of our crew, but still one of my brothers from the firehouse, Jake Bishop, says while placing one of Everly's boxes down on the kitchen counter. I barely glance at him until he walks backward to give me a more unobstructed view of the shirt he's wearing.

"What the fuck?" I look over at him, and my fucking eyes feel like they've just popped out of my head. Printed on the plain white T is a photo of the note. *Everly's* Post-it note.

"Cam gave it to me this morning. Said to make sure I wore it for you today," he says while failing to suppress a laugh.

Fucking Cameron.

"Did he, now?" I push my chair back and stand up with the intentions of finding my best fucking friend when he walks into the kitchen with his fucking sister. His sister that fucked me ten ways to Sunday, and left a Post-it on my fucking cock before leaving without a word. Without telling me who she was. Great. Just add to my humiliation some more. This has got to be payback for something I did in my life.

Then it dawns on me that this could work in my favor even if it's making me feel like an asshole at the same time, but screw it. She's the one who lied. The one that didn't tell me who she was. I would never have crossed that line and risked my friendship with Cam. Now the can has been opened, and turnabout is fair fucking play!

"Hey, Cameron. Jake here was just showing me the T-shirt you gave him. Got one for me too?"

Both Cam and Ev stop talking and look over at Jake's T-shirt. I watch Everly's smile drop, and the color slowly fades from her face before she swings her gaze to me. Fuck her. I didn't do this, but let's see what she's going to do now. I raise my brow at her. Waiting for her next move. Daring her to ask or acknowledge that she's the person who wrote the Post-it note that her brother obviously saw at my apartment, took a snapshot of and somehow turned the goddamn thing into the T-shirt that not only Jake is wearing, but the rest of the guys are too.

Cameron starts cracking up, holding his T-shirt up to reveal his homemade Post-it shirt underneath, then falls over clutching his stomach and falling into fits of laughter while reaching for the chair I just pushed away from the table. Asshole.

"Look familiar, Niko?" Cam says when he catches his breath, a shit-eating grin that I want to punch right now spreading across his face.

"You went out and paid money to have shirts made with a note left for me by a girl I fucked?" He's taking this a little too far.

He says nothing, just wears that stupid smirky smile on his face. "Who the fuck does that?" I say, completely dumbfounded at the lengths my so-called friend would take to bust my balls.

"Cam would," Jake responded, "Pretty sure he's trying to deflect so that whoever keeps leaving the dominatrix shit in his locker will start fucking with you instead." This causes the rest of them to crack up.

"Fuck off! All of you can kiss my ass!" Cam replies, his laughter fading, sounding like a petulant child with a dirty mouth. It doesn't matter what he does; they are never letting him live that shit down.

"What's the story behind this, or do I want to know?" Everly asks. Her color still hasn't returned, but she's playing it off, not a single hitch in her voice.

Jake shrugs. "Apparently some chick left Callahan in the dust, from what I heard."

"I didn't finish telling you where she left it though, Bishop," Cam says through tears as his laughter picks up again. Jake looks amused, but curious now. This is bullshit. I will never hear the end of this shit.

"Where did she leave it?" Bishop asks, but it's not Cam that answers.

I'm so going to junk punch the fucker.

"Right on Callahan Jr.," Jenkins pops in.

"Thanks a lot, asshole," I say to Cam. "Did you have to tell everyone?"

Cam's almost rolling on the floor. "Priceless. Fucking priceless! She fucked you and thanked your cock."

Everyone's attention is on Cam, giving me a quick second to shoot her a glare. It was all her fault in the first place. If she'd just told me who she was, but fuck, I would have missed out on the best night I've ever had. I'm still pissed at her, but as mad as I am, I want her just as much. There seems to be a small bit of remorse as she looks back at me.

"Bro, you got cocktagged," Jenkins says with a smirk.

I shake my head and pinch the bridge of my nose. "Cocktagged is when someone tags your shit on Facebook, and it wasn't fucking posted on Facebook." Fucking Cameron!

"No, brother, this chick real life cocktagged you! Like . . . is it real, or is it Memorex?" They all start laughing, and all I can do is glare at her.

Motherfucker.

"So, what's up for later tonight, Hayes?" Jenkins asks, and I'm happy for the change of subject. "Club? Pub? I'm off for the next two days, and I have nothing to do. Damn sure don't want to sit around watching reruns of *Orange is the New Black* on Netflix. You game?"

"Nah, I'm working actually. Grabbed an extra shift down on D-Street," Cam says, and I ignore the talk of work and clubbing.

I see Everly from the corner of my eye, and I try to keep looking busy so that she doesn't notice that I'm watching her every fucking move. Fuck, this woman has me all kinds of fucked up.

"The only person that's in need of a club night is our boy Niko here. The boy is pussy whipped," Cam says, breaking me from my Everly-induced haze.

"Far from whipped, but whatever, Cam. I've snapped out of it. Matter of fact, I might have a date tonight, so let's get this fucking show on the road so I can go home and crash," I lie, but he doesn't need to know that. I notice Everly had stopped unpacking the box she was working on when she heard me mention that I had a date. Could she be bothered? I fucking hope so. Would serve her right after all this shit.

"You still have a ton of books," I say as I lug the tenth box into her living room. It's a good thing she chose a place with built-in bookcases.

She shrugs. "I like to read; is that a problem?"

"Nope. Just an observation. Just wondered if any of the old Everly still existed," I say, staring right at her.

"Ha! This isn't shit. You should see her shelves at my parents'," Cam says, oblivious to the meaning behind my statement to his sister.

"Cameron!"

"What?" he asks, halfway opening one of the boxes.

"Stop," Everly says, her eyes wide.

"Stop what?" he asks. He's been helping her to unpack a lot of the boxes as we bring them in.

"Just . . . leave that box, I'll get it."

Cameron's lip twitches up into a smirk, his eyes moving to slits, drawing me closer. I'm his best friend; I know he's about to let something slip.

"What is it, sis? Don't want anyone seeing your collection of bodice rippers? Or have you upgraded to some Fifty Shades of kinky shit?"

Everly's face lights up, a shade of pink that piques my body's interest. Fucking cock likes the embarrassed demeanor flooding her. It's different from the woman I spent the night with and more like the Everly I remember from my teenage years. She's flustered, pushing Cam over in an attempt to get the box away from him, but she's physically no match for him.

This small interaction brings back memories, makes me see her as still the shy, nerdy girl and not the cold woman who duped me. Those hazel eyes glance at me, making my dick fucking twitch. It's an innocent look, wide eyes and lips parted, which only confuses me more. Her fucking Jekyll and Hyde personality gives me whiplash. Which one is the real Everly? Because right now all I can think of is the innocent version on her knees in front of me, biting her lip as she works my dick.

"Callahan!" Jake calls, breaking me away from my fantasy.

I lock eyes with Everly, whose gaze flashes down to my crotch, before turning to where my name was called.

"Yo!" I turn to find Jake and Jenkins struggling to get a dresser through the front door and run to help them.

Grabbing onto one end, I lift while Jake moves back to Jenkins to help lift. The dresser is solid wood and weighs a ton, making me wonder if the drawers are even empty.

"Where do you want this, Everly?" I ask, drawing her attention.

Her eyes lock on me, mouth open to respond, but nothing comes out. "T-that goes upstairs, in the spare bedroom."

It doesn't go unnoticed how she's staring at my body, the way my muscles are flexed. At least to me. I don't think anybody else is paying attention.

It seems she's not as immune as she thinks.

Chapter Fifteen

Everly

"THERE ARE ONLY FOUR or five more boxes, and the label on this one is impossible to read. Do you know where you want it?" my brother asks from the doorway of my new place. Cam and his friends spent a few hours helping move me in. Most of them left a few minutes ago once the beer and pizza were gone. Now only a few remain, including Cam and Niko.

Jake and Niko walk in behind Cam, both carefully placing my flat screen TV down. I turn the box in Cam's arms and stare at the squiggly line. The movers packed up a lot of my stuff, and by the handwriting, this is one of them.

"I think it says office," I tell Cam and turn away so I don't stare at the bulge of Niko's arms as he and Jake make room for my television. I hear Cam walk down the hall and try to focus on anything but the man in front of me.

"Hey, sunshine, you want me to set this up for you while we're here? I've got my tools in my truck. I'm not working tonight. I'm pretty sure Niko and Cam are both scheduled to work tonight, but I'd be more than happy to stick around to give you a hand with all this," Jake asks me, and before I can say anything, Niko replies to Jake.

"Actually, Jake, I'm not working tonight, but it's nice of you to keep tabs on my schedule."

I look over to where Niko just spoke, Jake standing next to him. Although Niko has his back to me, I can see that his body appears rigid, like he's tense and ready to blow up. I don't know what he thinks, but what happened between us was indeed a one-time thing. I also get the feeling that Niko and Jake don't care for one another. Interesting. Niko or no Niko, if I choose to get to know Jake, or any other man for that matter, it's my right. I'm single.

After what I've dealt with in the past few months, I deserve to put myself out there. Play the field, so to speak. If Aly were here, she'd be pushing me to step out of my comfort zone. I know Jake is waiting for a reply, and when I look up at him, he winks at me.

"Um, sure. That would be great. Usually Cam does all that for me, but I'm sure he'd be happy to be let off the hook." I smile at him, and Jake smiles back.

"We could grab dinner too. That way I can set up your surround sound. You know, take my time. Make sure I do it right and all that."

Of course, Niko chooses that comment to turn around and glare at Jake, but I don't care. He needs to mind his own business.

Jake is outright flirting with me now, and I'm honestly not feeling it, but I refuse to back down or let Niko know that I'm not interested in other men, especially while he's standing here listening. I know I shouldn't, but I want to push this. I want to see his reactions. See what Niko thinks.

"Sounds like a plan. Do you like Thai food?" I ask, grabbing my cell from the table.

"I love Thai. Whatever you get works for me. I'm not a picky man."

I smile and then press the home button on my iPhone. "Hey Siri, find me a number for Thai food that delivers near me."

"Why are you looking for Thai? We just had like twenty pizzas, Ev," Cam says as he walks back into the room. Niko crosses his arms and smiles over at me before opening his big mouth, and I want to throw something at his smug face.

"Well, Sunshine here is planning on eating dinner with good old Bishop tonight while he helps her set up her surround sound and flat screen. Weren't you doing that for her, Cam? That's dirty of you to pass the job off on poor Jake here."

"Sunshine? Who the hell is Sunshine?" Cam looks over at Jake and then to Niko, confusion written all over his face. Niko, the asshole that he is, moves his head toward me. Cam's eyes light up as he swings his head toward Jake. I watch as his eyes narrow once it clicks for him. "Like hell he is! That's my sister. My little sister." He drags the word little out like we are all in special ed or something.

Really? And of course, Niko turns his head away, but not before I catch his smirk. Real mature, Nikolas.

"Well, your little sister isn't so little, Hayes, or have you not noticed that we're all here today helping her move into her own place?" Jake fires back, and I know this isn't going to be good. My brother has always been protective of me, but he's even worse now that he knows what's going on with my ex. As much as I'd like to stick it to Niko right now, this isn't a battle I want my brother to have with one of his firehouse buddies.

"It's fine. It wasn't like a date or anything, Cam. Calm down. I just figured I'd save you the time. I know you're working tonight. It can wait if it's that big a deal. No reason for you two to go all crazy over nothing," I say, trying to diffuse the tension that Niko caused for nothing other than the fact that he's a jerk. "He was only offering to help."

"I bet he was," my brother says to me, but he's still giving poor Jake the famous Hayes stare down.

"Everyone is calm, Everly. No worries," Niko says with his hands up as if he were surrendering.

Yeah, right.

Cam grabs the box from where he dropped it a few minutes ago and stands to eye Niko and Jake. Finally, he lets it go, bringing another box to me and placing in on the table.

"This one has no label. What do you want me to do with it?" Happy to change the subject, I grab the box cutter and walk over to Cam and the box. I ignore the testosterone levels in the room and try to forget that Niko is not even ten feet from me. I swear I can smell him from here, and it makes me remember things I shouldn't.

I pull the box open and realize it's some office items I packed last minute. I must have used this as my miscellaneous box when I got tired of packing.

"It's just odds and ends. Mostly office things. This can stay here on the table until I get my desk and everything in my office set up." Cam pulls the flap open after I just closed it and started pulling a few things out.

"Everly Hayes! Do you collect every colored Post-it known to mankind? What is your deal with them?" He's sarcastic, but I don't care. I don't judge him for being the most unorganized slob ever known to mankind.

"They keep me organized. Just put them back, okay?" I pull the brand new rainbow-colored package of Post-it notes from my brother's hands. He's always teased me about it since I started doing it in junior high school.

"I don't understand you. We live in a time where we use Siri to set reminders for us on our cell phones, but yet, you have a paper calendar and Post-it notes all over the place to remind you to take a piss at certain hours of the day. I told Mom and Dad they should have had you evaluated. It's just not normal."

"Bite me, Cameron. You're not normal. You'd forget your name if someone wasn't constantly saying it to remind you of who you are, so shut it and put my stickies down. I don't need to ask Siri everything all the time. Sometimes you need an old-fashioned reminder rather than to rely on some computer or electronic device. You should try it sometime. Maybe then you'd remember more than your birthday!"

Hands up, he steps back, laughing at my outbursts. "Touchy, touchy, little sister. I'm just saying. You need to step into the now and leave 2005 behind you. Times have changed, and I have to say for the better. And I already said I was sorry about missing your birthday. I was on call that day, and it slipped my mind. I did call you, though."

I roll my eyes and stuff the pads back in the box. "Whatever, Cameron. You called me at one in the morning the next day. You know what? Niko was right—you are an ass." The mention of Niko causes Cam to laugh harder, and I want to punch him in his neck. Niko, who is helping Jake with some of the bigger stuff, seems to be ignoring us, but I know he's listening. You can just tell.

"Speaking of Niko." Cam says and claps his hands together. "Where do you get your supply of Post-it notes, Ev? Niko here had his bone broken by some hooker at the pub not too long ago. She left him high and dry after a wild, rock 'em sock 'em night of dirty sex and had the nerve to leave him with nothing but a Post-it note thanking his junk for his services."

My eyes grow wide, and I look over to Niko who stiffens and then tells Jake he needs a break. They put the treadmill down where they're standing, and Niko turns to glare at my brother while Jake smiles, trying to hold in a laugh I'm sure.

"Maybe Ev can give you her supplier, and you can track down the chick that wrecked you for all womankind. You can track her down as they do on that damn CSI show you watch, bone her again, and get that shit out of your system so we can all get back to normal, eh?"

"Fuck off, Cam. Cut the shit already, would you? This is getting old." Niko storms off and heads outside.

I don't blame him. My brother is being a total dick, and I'm basically to blame for it. I hit my brother on the back of his head for being rude.

"Ouch! What was that for, dammit!" he says, rubbing the spot I just smacked.

"For being rude. Niko is here on his day off, helping me, your sister, move into a new place. He doesn't have to be here, and you've been giving him a hard time all day. Cut it out before he leaves, and then you'll be stuck here helping all alone." A throat clears behind us, and I turn to see Jake sitting on one of the breakfast stools.

"I just want to state for the record that all is normal on my end," Jake says with a mischievous grin.

"Shut up, rookie. Don't get Niko fired up again. I'll have to hold him back from kicking your ass when we all leave. Trust me, he's a dirty fighter."

"Seriously, Cameron? You're telling other people not to antagonize Niko, but you haven't stopped since you guys got here. What is wrong with you guys?" I don't understand men sometimes. It's like having third graders in front of me all day and having to play referee or they'll kill each other. This is why I'm never having kids. I'd be too afraid of having a child that would turn out like my brother.

"I've got no plans tonight, so I can stay and help with whatever you need. I'm just letting you know. All's good here." Jake says as he smiles at me.

"Yeah? Well, you don't have to go home, but you can't stay here. So whatever thoughts you had about Thai tonight for dinner with Sunshine here, you can go get it on your own, because my sister is off limits, Bishop."

"I was just offering to help, Hayes. I figured if you and Niko are working tonight, I'd be a gentleman and stay. I was only being helpful."

"I'm sure you were, but actually, Niko's not working tonight. I am, and Niko already offered to stay and help my sister with the rest, and setting up, so you can get gone anytime you'd like. She's all set."

I glance over to the door where Niko is coming in with another box and raise my eyebrow. Niko looks like this is brand-new news to him, but he doesn't say anything to correct Cam. Good Lord. What am I missing?

I look back toward Cam and Jake, only now the two of them seem to be having some standoff in my new living room, and I'm not sure what to do. Niko notices the tension in the room. He looks at Cameron, then Jake, and then over to me. I shrug, and he narrows his eyes at me. I don't think he likes when I do that, but whatever.

"All good in here?" he says and looks at Cam.

Cam pulls his eyes from Jake and nods his head. "Yeah. Everything's good. We about done out there?"

"Yeah. Just two more boxes and then she's golden."

He looks around at the mess of boxes piled everywhere. "Well . . . all the lifting is done anyway."

Chapter Sixteen

Niko

CAM BREAKS DOWN THE box he just emptied and sets the utility knife down on the counter. "All right, man. I'm about to head out. I want to shower and grab a nap before I head to the station. You have anything important to do tonight?"

"Nothing that can't wait. Why?" I look at Cam and wonder what he's up to. I overheard some of the spat between him and Bishop, but I have a feeling it has to do with Bishop staying around.

"Do me a solid?"

"What's up?"

"Hang around awhile. Make sure all the guys leave before you do."

"What's a while?"

"As long as the rookie is here, I want you to stick around." I follow Cam's gaze to Jake and watch as Everly laughs at something he just said to her. I won't lie, I want to punch the fucker's smile right off his face. Even after Cam told him to back off, the asshole is disregarding everything he said and openly flirting with his sister.

I don't blame Cam for being worried. If Cam and I have a reputation with the ladies, it's nothing compared to Jake Bishop. The ladies flock to him like starved birds in the Boston Common.

As long as he gets them into bed, he doesn't seem to care. The dude is full of that pretty-boy charm, and he uses that shit to his advantage. At least that's how it appears to us when we watch him in action.

"Yeah. I'll stick around. No worries, brother." Cam claps me on the back and then heads to the door.

"I'll see you sometime tomorrow, Ev," he says with a wave.

"You're leaving?" Ev asks, her gaze flickering to me.

What, is she scared to be alone with me?

"Yeah, in a second, but Niko had a change of plans, so he's going to stick around and help you get the big things set up," Cam says, and I want to laugh as I watch the look on her face and her eyes grow wide.

"Oh, he doesn't have to do that! I'm sure he's got other things he can do on his night off."

With that reaction, I'm staying until she forces me out the damn door.

"Actually, I'm good. Nothing planned until much later, so I'm all yours." I smile my famous megawatt smile that is sure to render little Miss Everly Hayes speechless. It never fails. She doesn't say anything at first, falling into the typical Niko zone that I knew she would, but shakes it off faster than I expect. Whatever. She doesn't need to know that my plans for later are made up.

"Okay, then. I guess I could use the extra help." She does that goddamn shrug that I can't stand, but I'm starting to get the feeling that it's all bullshit. I'm just not sure yet.

A few minutes later the boys start to move out, Cam hugging Ev goodbye as he goes, but a few linger. I see the way Jake keeps glancing over at Everly the second Cameron is out the door. The way he moves closer and closer to her. The fucking way she smiles at him every time she catches him looking at her.

She's fucking smiling at him, while I get jack shit. I'm the one that's pissed off. I'm the one she should be smiling at, thanking me for the best night of her fucking life, but no. She bats her eyelashes at him, the same way she batted them at me while she screamed and begged for more. Why the fuck am I thinking about that night?

Shit.

I crane my neck and let out a deep breath; my eyes close as I try and calm myself and my dick down.

Yeah, my pride is wounded, and I want to fucking pound her with my cock out of fucking anger. Why the fuck did she have to be Cam's sister? I've promised him, but her lie voided that. Would another night make the situation worse? She's not telling him, and I'm sure as hell not going to tell him what happened. It's already being kept from Cam, so what harm could come from me pursuing her one more time? Would it stop me from thinking about her non-fucking-stop?

She's exactly what I want right now. A challenge. Her whole attitude has me on my toes ready to pounce, but can I chase her and keep my friendship with Cam intact? I mean, technically we've already been together, and that wasn't my fault. I would never have taken Everly home had I known who she was. However, now that I have, what's stopping me from pursuing her again?

I just need to get her out of my system once and for all. Turn the tables, so to speak. There is no way she can resist if I give her a repeat of what we had that night. It was in no way fucking forgettable, and I know, regardless of her aloofness toward me and our situation, I know for sure that she was right there with me. I have the texts to prove it.

She can try and deny it all she wants, but I'd know she was lying. Time to even the playing field and get back in the game.

Everly Hayes, one.

Nikolas Callahan, zero, but not for long. I'm about to score . . . once I get rid of Jake's lady-killing ass.

"I thought you had a date," Everly says from somewhere behind me.

Jake just left, so I'm sticking around to make sure he stays gone. It'll also give me some time to talk freely.

"Actually, something came up last minute. I'll just be meeting my date a little later than planned. It was planned last minute, so don't worry your pretty little head about me. Everything's good." I give her my teeth and blind her with my pearly whites. It's one of those smiles that I've used to render women speechless. Everly is no different than they are when it comes to it. I'm not surprised to see that she's essentially zoned out on me while staring.

"Earth to Everly." I snap my fingers, causing her to blink a few times. Yeah . . . she's not as immune as she tries to act. She turns away from me and starts pulling the top off another box, trying to play off her reaction to me. Good. I'm already starting to feel better. This is precisely what I needed. I've been so busy being obsessed with the fact that she left me without a word after one of the best nights of my life, then pissed at her when I found out that she lied to me about who she was.

It's time to turn the tables on this shit. Get back to being me and not this fucked-up version she left me with. She wants to act like she was just looking for a hookup? Well, I'll give her what she wants, but this time I'm going to put her on her ass. After all, this isn't my first rodeo, and it won't be my fucking last. Let's see how she likes it.

"So, something else came up, and just like that you're free for the evening, huh?"

"Well, not the entire evening, but yup. Just like that."

"Right . . . So my brother didn't happen to talk you into babysitting by sticking around, maybe make sure Jake was on his best behavior?" she asks, her brow quirked up. She knows, but I don't think her brother knows who he needs to watch out for.

"Maybe it's *you* that he wants to ensure is behaving. I'm starting to wonder now if maybe Cam should have warned me about just how much his little sister's changed over the years," I say and pull the leveler from the tool bag on the floor.

"Don't you think it's *you* that my brother should be worried about and not just Jake?" She stresses the word 'you' like I'm some villain in this situation. I want to snort at her, but I don't. I can be just as cool as she can. However, that won't get me what I want right now, so I answer her honestly.

"Maybe, but then again, Cam and I have been friends a long time. He knows that I'd never intentionally hit on or hook up with his kid sister." I look directly in her beautiful hazel eyes, eyes that a man could drown in, but then I snap myself from the thought and make sure she knows what I'm saying. "The key word there, sweetheart, is intentional."

"Look, I know that night we all had dinner was all kinds of crazy."

I stop what I'm doing and shake my head at her words. "Not crazy, Everly. Fucked up is what it was."

She waves her hand in the air toward me and then goes right back to unpacking her books. "Okay, fucked up. I apologized. I know I was wrong. I've been in a bad place lately, and I meant what I said. You were in the right place at the right time. I don't want you to take it personally. I mean . . . if it were someone else that I'd gone home with, I'd have left the same way. It wasn't you it was *all me* so don't be too hard on yourself or let the guys get to you."

My jaw ticks. "It wasn't just the night you *used* me for sex. You led me on for weeks. You flirted. You didn't just flirt; we had phone sex. We talked, and not once did you think it was a good idea to tell me who you were?"

"No, because that's all it was," she says, and I want to strangle her. I know what the fuck it was.

"It wasn't *just* sex and you fucking know it," I say, cutting her off, but she ignores me.

"I should have told you who I was." I glare at her for a second, and she ignores me. "But I didn't, and we can't change what happened now. Can we just start over and move on from here? I get it. Cameron would be pissed if he found out about what happened between us, and even though I'm obviously a grown woman and can sleep with whoever I want, I don't want to cause problems with the two of you."

"Everly, I think you are missing some major points here."

"Look, you told me to own my shit, and I am. I used you for sex, and it was wrong. I lied, and that was wrong. I'm sorry. The last thing on my list of crimes is my brother. Other than thinking of my brother's feelings on my hooking up with his friend, I don't see what other major points matter now," she says, and I'm shocked into silence.

Well, it's about damn time she said that shit on her own.

"I knew he wouldn't be happy with the fact that I'd slept with his friend. I just didn't realize how much of a problem it would be until now. After today, seeing how he's acting with just the thought of Jake hitting on me, I know he'd be upset. I honestly wasn't thinking about Cameron at all when I decided to go home with you."

"You should have. Cam should have been the first person you thought of when you decided to lie to me. And Cam wouldn't *just* be upset; he'd be *pissed*! Do you know how many times he had warned me off of you before you even arrived?"

"I know," she says softly, and it brings my attitude down a little bit.

"No, Ev, but you're going to know once he finds out. As for those being the last things on your list of crimes, well, you're wrong about that. What you did, the night in the pub, that was wrong, but after?"

"After?"

"Yes, after. The texting. Getting to know me more. Letting me get to know you, and not telling me. It shouldn't have happened."

"I agree. We can't change it now. What good would come out of telling my brother? We can still start over, Niko. Water under the bridge and all that. You've known me since I was a kid. We can be friends. What do you say?" she says, and again she's throwing water on my fire, but only a little bit.

Eyes on the prize, Callahan. I already know I can't do the damn friends thing with her. Not after our night together, and not after all the time we've already spent on each other these past few weeks. No, friends with Everly Hayes is *not* going to happen. I'm not sure what my plan is, but seeing her fucking flirting with Jake is first on my list. I'll figure the rest out as I go.

"Well . . . for starters, you need to stop your flirting with Bishop. Cam is going to end up breaking his neck, and you're going to stomp all over poor Jake's heart. So cut the shit and be an adult. Whatever bad time you've gone through that had you hunting me down like prey only to use me and then ditch, get over it."

"I just apologized, and that is what you come back at me with?"

"I'm just saying, Everly. You're playing games, and you said it yourself, you're a grown woman now, so why the childish game playing?"

She doesn't answer my question, but she's staring at me, making me think she's got an answer but just doesn't know how to word it. Finally, she lets out a sigh and walks into the kitchen. I'm starting to think that my not talking to her after her big reveal that night at dinner with Cam might have bothered her more than I thought. When I got here today, she was cool but polite. Like she was okay with the fact that our little chat sessions had ended. I think that little Miss Indifferent isn't exactly who she's pretending to be. She's nowhere near the Everly I knew years ago, but she's in there somewhere. I see her every so often when I'm watching her. She lets her guard down for a few minutes at a time, but that's it. I just have to catch her at the right time, and then I can spin this in my favor.

Challenge accepted.

I slide up behind her, my hands on her hips, loving the way she freezes under my touch. That buzz I felt the first night is still there, and it sets my veins on fire. I swear she's in my damn blood after only one night.

"Ya know," I whisper into her ear, sliding my hands around her waist, pulling her closer. "If you need help christening this place, I volunteer my cock, since you had so much fun last time."

She draws in a sharp breath as I rock my hips into her. I've been half hard all day and now with her so close, in my arms, I'm fighting with myself to not just take her right now. There's no resistance, her body pliable in my hands.

Her hands clench on the counter, back arching. Fucking erotic, and I'm a second from pulling down those ass-hugging yoga pants and giving her what I know we both want.

"Damn," I hiss, forcing my body from hers.

When she turns, her look of indifference is gone—her cheeks are bright red, pupils blown, lips parted.

Yeah, baby, there you are.

I smirk at her, and she blinks, schooling herself. She clears her throat and looks away.

"I'm good."

I nod. "Yes, you are."

It's not the fuck I want, but at least I'm finally on the scoreboard. The problem is, I'm now stuck with a raging hard-on, and I'm not sure I can stop myself.

I want her. More than I should. More than I can stand.

How the fuck am I supposed to survive Everly Hayes with my friendship with Cam intact?

The Red Sox are up by two as I sit at the pub waiting for Cam. It's been a week since we moved Everly, and things have shifted again. I'm still mad at her for lying, but I can't stop myself from texting her. Not since her response when we were alone. By the time I left, we were both so turned on I had to pull myself away from her. One kiss of those fucking lips, and all promises would have gone out the window.

Not that I'm keeping to them anyway. A fact that tears me up, but I'm fucking addicted to her.

Niko: What are you doing?

I only lasted a day before I began texting her. She said she wanted to be friends, to start over. Well, here I am, starting over.

Everly: Work.
Niko: What are you wearing?
Everly: Pervert.

Niko: Pervert? I didn't realize that was an article of clothing.
Everly: You=Pervert
Niko: *shrug* Maybe.
Everly: Definitely.
Niko: Why do you say that? And can I get more than a one word answer.
Everly: Shouldn't you be putting out fires or saving a cat from a tree.

I fucking love it when she's feisty.

Niko: Nah, I'd rather set a certain pussy on fire. You don't happen to have a kitty that needs saving do you? ;)
Everly: . . . . . .
Niko: That all you got? I'll take a cleavage shot if you've got no comeback.

The problem is with the "friends" aspect of her proposal. In less than twenty-four hours after she finally responded, things turned back to the way they were before I found out who she was. In a way, having her still in my phone as Alyson makes the whole thing not seem as trust breaking as it is.

When a picture pops up, I let out a groan, my dick waking up. It's from above, obvious she just pulled her shirt back and snapped the pic, but it's almost the same view I have standing behind her, looking over her shoulder. Her perfect, suckable tits are tan mounds against the white lace of her bra.

Niko: That bra is a little virgin white for you.
Everly: Vixen red would show through my light grey blouse.
Niko: Please tell me you have said vixen red.
Everly: I have every color of the rainbow ;)

Fuck. Me. Seriously, I need her to come and take care of the hard dick I've got now.

Niko: I really think we need to schedule a fashion show. That way you can model them for me and I can let you know which ones to keep.

Everly: What will I do with the others?

Fantasies of fisting them in my hand, shredding them before spreading her legs wide, fill my brain. I need to taste her again just to end this sickness. This need for her.

But I'm beginning to understand the truth—there will never be enough of her. Never enough to quench this deep thirst that I have for her. One that goes against my core values of friendship and loyalty.

I'm a desert without her, dry and wasted. She is the rain. The only thing that brings life to my world.

Niko: Oh, don't worry about those. They'll be trash once I rip them off you.

Everly: Then what will you do when I'm all naked down there?

Niko: Down there??? Fuck, your innocent act . . .You've got me all hard in a public place.

Everly: There is always a dark corner.

Niko: But you're not here to help me find it.

Everly: Guess you're on your own.

Niko: Tease.

I'm five seconds from getting up and going to the bathroom to call her and take care of my cock problem. A few words from her and some quick strokes, and I'll be coming all over the tile walls.

Before I can push back from the bar, Cam walks up and pulls a chair next to me, his face scrunched in the most pissed off expression I've ever seen. I toss all ideas of getting my rocks off out the window and resign myself to blue balls. As I drop my phone down on the bar, he calls the bartender over, and I work on calming down my dick that desperately needs some attention.

"What's wrong?" I ask. It's not often I see him like this, so something's not right.

He huffs and narrows his eyes at me. "What's wrong with you?"

I shift in my chair as I take a sip of my coffee. "Nothing." I knew the question was coming at some point.

"Nothing? Man, you've been off for over a month. No girls, not going out . . ."

I run my hands over my face. "I can't stop thinking about this chick."

Cam's eyes shoot open in surprise. "Who?"

"I'm not going to tell you if you plan on being a dick about it."

"Fine, I'll be serious. Spill."

"Post-it note."

"Oh, fuck. Still?" He stares at me before tilting his head back in laughter. "The great half-breed finally got served his karma for all the chicks he has walked out on."

"You're a fucking asshole. Forget I said anything."

"Shit, man, I needed the laugh."

"Yeah, whatever. You going to shut your yap and tell me what crawled up your ass?"

His laughter dies down—and a sneer crosses his face before straightening. "I'm worried about Everly."

I scrunch my brow, my fucking heart jumping in my chest at the mention of her name. "Why?"

"Remember me telling you about her boyfriend, Tate?" I nod my head, letting him know that I remember the conversation we had. "The reason she moved here so abruptly is that he cheated on her. And he's not taking the hint."

Wait, what? Does Tate think they're still together? Did Ev not break it off? Neither Cam nor Everly ever mentioned her still being with this guy, and I'm going to hope that it was over before we got together, but I just need confirmation right now. It sounds like this moron that cheated on her had it coming, but I don't do cheaters, even if she would have been justified. End things, don't go out and revenge fuck only to go back to the same shit later.

"I thought you said she came here to get away from him. Is she still with him after he cheated on her?" And why the hell would someone cheat on her?

He shakes his head. "They broke up before she moved here. Thank God. From what I knew of him, and the one time we met him, I couldn't stand the guy. He was never good enough for my sister. Had she lived closer, I'd have hunted him down and kicked his ass."

I'm positive he would have, and a little surprised he still hasn't set off on a trip to do it now.

"Okay, but he's not taking the hint now, how?"

"Calling her, texting her. He's blowing her phone up multiple times a day. When she's at work, home, and whenever. She's not reading or listening to them, but he's not letting up. I listened to the voicemails . . . I'm worried he's going to come out here and try something."

"Try something? What the fuck does that mean?"

He shakes his head. "Some of the messages are bullshit, like begging for forgiveness, shit like that, but then there were others . . . The tone sent a shiver down my spine. Something is just off with this guy. I don't want him anywhere near her."

Cam's description lights up my protective side, and not just because she's his sister. "What is she saying?"

"She's blowing it off. Says he'll stop eventually, but asked me to leave it alone. I can't do that. It's a feeling, man. He's a manipulator, and I just don't want him near her again."

"Then we make sure he doesn't get close."

Cam nods as he takes a swig of his beer.

"I'll tell you this, though. This asshole has fucked up things for the next guy who comes into her life. I didn't want this for her."

"You think?" Well, shit, that's not a good sign for me.

He nods. "I just want her to be happy even though she's old enough to handle her life on her own. I still feel the need to protect her. She's still my kid sister, and I don't like seeing her get hurt. After talking to her about some of what this guy did, she's guarded now."

"Guarded how?" I ask.

"She's always been a little naive when it comes to boys, and now as an adult, men. It's one of the main reasons I didn't want my friends checking her out." I freeze at his words. This would be the perfect time to mention something, but I can't find the words. "Whatever guy she meets in the future is going to have to climb a fucking mountain for her to let him in and trust him."

Fuck.

I want to be that guy. It seems I'm going to have to invest in some good hiking boots.

"Just for the hell of it, what is the issue of your friends checking your sister out? I mean, I get what you're saying, but I'm wondering if I should feel insulted, man." I laugh it off so that it sounds more like I'm busting his balls, but I want to know why he feels like he does. Why Everly is off limits, exactly. Maybe it will help me decide what to do with this situation I've found myself in with his sister.

"You're kidding, right? My friends are pretty much your friends, bro. Would you want them dating your family, or a sister if you had one?"

"I guess not, but if she's not a kid anymore, what choice do you have?" I ask.

"I know that, but take Jake, for example. He was hitting on my sister when we moved her into her new place. She had no clue that he was hitting on her."

"I know that. I told you what was going down, remember? And I think you're wrong about her not knowing. I'm pretty sure she was on the same page. Either way, you know I'd never knowingly do that shit to you, and never in your face like that," I say, and I mean it. He doesn't catch the key word I used there, and I'm not going to stress it any more than I already have. I just hope that if Cam ever finds out what happened between his sister and me that he'll get over it.

He nods. "I know, and I'm glad you did. I knew that out of anyone, I could trust you. Jake is new to us. He's the rookie, but he's been around long enough now to know better. I didn't like that shit, and I already chewed his ass about it."

Oh shit. This is news to me.

"When did this happen, and why am I just hearing about this now?"

He narrows his eyes at me. "Because, you've been acting like you have a mangina instead of a dick, and haven't been paying attention to anyone or anything except your fucking phone and your right hand, asshole."

"What the fuck are you talking about?"

"Niko. We've all noticed. You come to work, but you spend more time looking at your fucking cell phone, texting. If you're not texting, you're over in some corner, talking low and laughing like some teenage boy who's about to score with the head cheerleader for the first time in his life."

Jesus. How did I not notice my behavior? Am I that consumed by her?

"I don't do that. What the fuck, man. I come to work, and my attention is on work. Always." Everly and I have only begun talking again on text.

"I know that. I know you have my back when we get a call. That's not what I'm saying, though."

I'm seriously clueless now, and I'm afraid to say much because I'm not sure where he's going with this. I honestly didn't think he noticed the back and forth I had going on with Everly all this time. I need to be more careful around Cam. He's obviously paying more attention to the things going on around him than I thought.

"Look, man. I know I've been screwing with you a lot when it comes to this chick you've been all fucked in the head over, but I'm just me." He gives me his half smirk, and I just shake my head at him. Yeah, he's him all right. "But seriously, bro, all jokes aside, I have never seen you act this way about a chick. Like ever. If she has you this consumed with her, then go and get her. If it's going to improve your moods and shit, then I'm all for my boy catching himself a permanent fish. Just keep that hook and line over there because I'm not ready to be caught." We both crack up at his statement, but I sober once I get to the root of the problem in my case.

"It's not that simple, Cam."

"Why isn't it? You got her number, right? I mean, I see you on your phone and shit." He gestures toward my phone which lights up with a new message from "Alyson." "There is no way you're talking to someone else."

"No, it's her, but it's just more complicated than that. We have obstacles in our way that kind of makes going forward impossible."

Like you.

Shit, this is bad, because I really can't stop thinking about her.

"Then remove the obstacles. I can't see anything in the way that would stop you of all people from getting something that he wants. Make it happen, man. Trust me. You'll be happier if you do."

God, do I wish it was that simple. Other than her big lie, there is also one huge obstacle that is preventing me from getting what I want, and it's standing right in front of me, telling me to take what I want. Pretty sure he wouldn't feel that way if he really knew.

"Anyway, let me know when you plan to bring her around so I can meet the woman that has brought my friend, Nikolas Callahan, to his knees. I want to let her know that she has officially fucked up my rotation by pulling you out of the game."

Yeah. Like that will ever happen.

Chapter Seventeen

Everly

LEFTOVERS USUALLY AREN'T BAD, but for some reason, I can taste what the reheating has done. Rubbery chicken is not good. Maybe it's a texture thing.

Sitting at my kitchen island eating my unappealing leftovers, I also notice just how quiet it is. There are cars passing by, but besides the tick of the clock on the wall behind me, there is nothing but silence. Suddenly, I feel . . . lonely.

Cam is meeting me at The Sinclair at eight, and he's bringing Niko. I'm tempted to start in on the drinking some liquid courage based on that fact alone, but I need to get out of my house, and if I dive in now, I won't make it out.

I need this night. I've spent all week working followed by every spare minute devoted to unpacking boxes and locating everything. Box after box, and still there are more boxes, but I'll worry about them this weekend. For now, I need a drink and a few hours to let loose. Besides, I'm the one that said we should start over. Be friends and forget things happened. Easier said than done, but I'm going to try my hardest to stick to it. Niko is always on my mind, but thoughts of him are always being interrupted by the nagging from my cheating ex.

It's been just over two months since I walked in on Tate fucking Shannon, and I've been going full speed ahead ever since, barely stopping to take a breather. Every moment has been filled with packing, unpacking, work, setting up my office, and getting used to the time zone difference. Even when I was at my parents' when they weren't, I was always busy with something.

For two years, Tate was my world, and it's just now hitting me hard that I'm single again. Not that it's a bad thing that he's history, but I miss sharing my time with someone.

Aly is about an hour away, but she works two jobs, so getting together with her is more difficult. I'm happy that at least the calling between us has gotten easier. I have no other friends here. High school was filled with a lot of self-centered assholes who I don't care about reconnecting with, and any adult friends I have are back in California.

What needs to happen tonight is a good time, and hopefully, an added good time. I told Cam I wanted to join the fun club, but even after over a month, the only sex I've had was with Niko that first night I got here.

Even if I can't admit it to myself, the truth is Niko never left my mind. I can't get over that night.

It shouldn't be surprising. Because he's Niko. Man of my dreams who showed me why after so many years that he will always be that. They are altered, dirtier than ever before, and make my previous view a sugar-coated candy crush in comparison.

I do worry, though, about tonight. He's almost gotten me to cave in the last few weeks, and a little alcohol could have me giving in to him. Then again, Cam will be there, and they will be in full pick-up mode.

Fears that I'll have to watch Niko in action, in his prime, picking up another woman, makes my stomach turn.

Maybe that drink isn't such a bad idea.

At just after seven-thirty, I'm in a dress I forgot I owned until I found it while unpacking, and some strappy heels. Pretty basic

COCK *sure*

wear, but perfect for the night's objective. The dress, however, has nowhere to put anything, making me find a clutch in the closet. At least my new closet is huge, unlike the one I had in California. All my clothes, shoes, and purses are perfectly organized, the only section in my home to be fully unpacked.

I step outside and turn to lock the door. Right as I get the key turned, I feel something nudge me and a cry of surprise leaves me.

"Oh! Jojo!" I lean down to pet the taupe head while I look around for Grant. Instead of a tall man, I'm met with a girl who can't be more than six or seven with curly, light brown hair and large green eyes. Where did she come from?

"Well, hi, what's your name?" I say to her.

"Ella Prince." Her voice is light and sweet.

"Ella!" Grant pops out from his door, his eyes wide and frantic. He zooms in on the little girl and runs forward, scooping her up in his arms. "Baby, you can't go out the door like that. You scared Daddy."

Daddy?

It hits me then—Grant Prince.

He lets out a hard sigh and blinks as he looks at me. "Everly . . . I'm so sorry. I turned my back for five seconds and she was gone. It took me another minute to realize Jojo was gone, too."

"So . . . you have a daughter?" I ask, still surprised by the revelation. From the moment I saw him, there was never any indication.

He nods and turns her in his arms. "Ella, this is our neighbor Everly. Can you say hi?"

She waves at me, her green eyes a perfect match of her father's. "Hello."

"Why don't you go inside and wash your hands? We're going to Grandma's for dinner."

She pads off, and Grant turns to me, a sheepish grin. "She's six. I have family that helps me out a lot so I can get some work done."

"She's yours, full-time? What about her mom?"

I watch as something flashes across his eyes, his lips forming a thin line. "It's just Ella and me."

Such an open sentence that doesn't answer much. By his reaction, I decide it's best not to pry.

"Are you headed out?" he asks as he looks me over.

I nod. "Going out with my brother."

"He's the firefighter, right?"

I nod. "How did you know?"

"I'm not stalking you or anything; I just saw them when they were helping you move in."

"Yeah, the T-shirts with the firefighter logo on them were hard to miss. A couple of the guys were on backup."

"Yeah, that kind of gave them away. Either that or they all give a lot of money to the fireman's association." He smiles, and I have to admit, he's charming. Too bad.

"Well, I should get going. It was nice meeting you, Ella Prince," I say and smile down at the cute six-year-old who is back and standing next to her dad.

"Enjoy your night, Everly," Grant says and ushers his daughter back inside.

"You too." I walk down the front stairs to the Uber that just arrived, and I can't imagine being a single mom. I can't imagine that being a single dad to a six-year-old girl is easy. Then again, I can't imagine much of any childcare. I don't ever think that is something I want in my future. I'm sure he must find it difficult to date with having his daughter full-time.

I don't know why I'm thinking these things. He's my neighbor. It's not my business. Time to meet my brother and Niko. Get my head back in the game, so to speak.

Less than ten minutes later Emily, the night's Uber driver, drops me off outside our meeting point. The Sinclair is packed, but thankfully Cam already has a table. Too bad Niko is sitting next to him. I want a relaxing night, but I'll have to make the best of the situation.

"Excellent table," I say as I climb onto one of the stools and cross my legs.

Cam's eyes go wide, and he nearly spits out the brown beer he was drinking. A Guinness, I'm assuming, and gross. I don't know how anyone can drink that stuff. "What the fuck are you wearing?" my big brother asks, and I want to laugh.

I glance down. "A dress?"

"You call that a fucking dress?"

I look down, then back up. "Yes."

Cam rolls his eyes and shakes his head. "Fucking California. That shit isn't Boston wear." he says, and I glance around at the other woman in here who are dressed similar to me or worse. He's so full of shit.

"Is it warm out?" I ask him sarcastically.

"Yeah."

"Then it's fine."

I glance over to Niko who is staring at me. "What?"

He looks to Cam and shrugs. "You got your bat bag from the baseball game today in your truck?"

Cam nods. "Good call. Gives us something to beat them back with."

It's my turn to roll my eyes. "Oh, please. Enough of the protective theatrics. I already told you, Cam. I'm ready to play, and I plan to learn from the best."

"It's a little different from the male side of things. And for fuck's sake, I don't want to fucking witness someone hauling my little sis off to a dark corner to do shit she shouldn't be doing."

"Shouldn't be doing?" I ask.

"Yes, you're too young."

I roll my eyes. "What age is appropriate, then?"

"Thirty. Maybe forty."

I lean forward, narrowing my eyes at him. "And how old was the last girl you went home with?"

His lips form a thin line. "Irrelevant."

"How so?"

"She's not my sister," he says and shrugs his shoulder.

"Um, ew," I say, my face scrunching up. "That's gross, but you know, she was probably somebody's sister."

"Nope. Not going to change my view."

"What about when you have a daughter of your own someday—then what, brother?"

"Won't happen."

"Why the hell would you say that—you not planning on having kids?"

"Sure, but I won't have any girls. God is going to bless me with my own football and baseball team. He would never leave me responsible for a daughter. He knows I'd fuck that job up, so I'm good when it comes time to procreate," he says, and my mouth drops open as I process his statement. "Besides, I don't plan on kids for a very long time, so for now, I'll just practice the act of creating my very own sports team," he says with a huge smile and then takes a swig from his bottle. I look over to Niko to see if he's thinking the same thing that I am right now, and that is that my brother is a moron.

"Don't look at me, Ev. I agree with him. Men like us shouldn't have daughters. What do we know about raising girls?" Niko says to me, and then he and Cam clink their bottles together in agreement.

"Amen, brother," Cam says to Niko, and I want to smack them both in the back of the head right now.

"That is the dumbest shit I think I have ever heard come out of your mouth, Cameron Hayes. Am I ever going to get it through your thick, warped mind that I'm not a child anymore?"

"Probably not. Last time I was around you for any measure of time you were a teenager, and that is how I will always remember you. Tonight, you're following us around just like you always used to do. The only difference is you're not crushing on Niko."

My eyes go wide. "Cam!"

"What? Everybody knew."

I look to Niko. "Did you know?" I ask, curious about his response. Did he know?

"Yes."

Heat floods my cheeks. "Well, that's embarrassing."

"You were a pre-teen, Ev," Cam argues.

"And that makes what difference?"

"Just like your awkward phase, you grew out of it."

Oh, if my brother knew just how wrong he was. In fact, my crush is on fire and looking at me like he wants to rip my dress off.

He's covered it well, but I see the innuendo, hear it in his words, the pause as he speaks. As Cam looks around for his target for the night, I lock eyes with Niko. The corner of his mouth slowly slides up, and I shift in my seat.

I clear my throat and look down at the drink menu.

"What do you drink to let loose?" I ask, looking between Cam and Niko. They glance at each other and in unison, hold up their beers. I narrow my eyes at them. "Really? You're no fun."

"And you've been hanging with fucking Alyson too much," Cam says, and I ignore his jab at Aly.

"We've learned how to pace ourselves," Niko says. "We're older and wiser now. Besides, too much of the sauce and you can't get it up as well. Don't like to leave them with a lackluster performance."

I roll my eyes. "Unbelievable."

"What are you getting? Sex on the Beach?"

Cam starts laughing while I glare at Niko. "Dude, nobody drinks those. Such a fucking cheesy name."

I purse my lips and glare at my brother. Not the best name, but it's a good drink. Probably the only real drink I will order with alcohol in it other than my glass of wine here and there.

The waitress pops up beside me and looks around, her gaze lingering on Niko and Cam. It's hard not to roll my eyes.

"Hi, I'm Lindsay," she says once she makes her way back to me. "I see they already have drinks. Is there anything I can get you from the bar?"

"Yes." I stare directly at Cam. "I'll have a Sex on the Beach."

Cam lets out a chuckle and shakes his head. "What did you learn in California?"

I glance over to Niko. "That sex on the beach is the best." There, buddy. Take that.

Niko's tongue slips out to wet his lips. It's slow, seductive, and I can't keep my eyes off the way his teeth scrape across his bottom lip.

"Maybe you should try something different, then. Like a *Screaming Orgasm*. I hear those are good."

Fuck. He did not just say that in front of my brother. I shift in my seat, suddenly wishing I'd worn at least a thong.

Another point for Niko.

He makes me want to pull out my phone and text him, but that would be too obvious with Cam so close. Plus, my reduced purse for the night does not have room for two phones, meaning my work phone is at home.

"What are you going to have with your frou-frou drink?" Niko asks, teasing me to cover up.

"I had some leftovers at home. I didn't realize we were getting food so I might get an appetizer, especially if I plan to drink more."

"Burger for me," he says.

"So, when do you two work next?"

"I'm free until tomorrow night," Niko says, his tone still flirtatious.

Can he be any more obvious? I glance at Cam who doesn't even seem to notice as his phone goes off.

"Shit," he says with a huff as he looks down at the screen before answering it. "Hayes . . . mmm hmm . . . be there in ten."

Niko glances at his watch, then to Cam. "Really? Your on-call shift ends in less than two hours."

Cam stands up and grabs his wallet, pulling out a few bills. "That's how it rolls. You're up on Sunday."

"Yeah, yeah."

"How can you go when you've been drinking?" I ask.

He holds the bottle up. "I'm not, Ev, this Root Beer is non-alcoholic. I'm more than good," he says and smiles at me. I glance over and notice that his glass of water is empty as is the brown bottle he just held up that I assumed was a Guinness beer.

"Oh, I didn't realize. I thought you'd be drinking with us tonight."

"If it got to ten o'clock and no call came in, I would have, but the call came in. Sorry, baby sis, but work calls. Have fun with Niko. I'll apologize for him ahead of time, though. He may ignore you for the night's pick," Cam says and slings his arm around Niko's shoulders.

"Make me sound like an ass." Niko shakes his head and tips back his beer.

"What? It's true."

"Yeah."

Cam leans down and whispers something into Niko's ear. I can't hear it, but when Niko looks my way, I know it's about me.

"Everly," Cam says as he leans in for a hug. "Have fun, but not too much, okay? Be a good girl."

I shake my head. "I'm going to be a very *bad* girl tonight."

Cam rolls his eyes. "Just don't tell me anything that happens."

"Deal. Stay safe." I wave goodbye as he steps away, then turn to Niko as soon as he's gone. "What did he say?"

"He said to keep an eye on you."

I scrunch my brow. "And you agreed."

He nods and takes another sip of his beer. "I'll keep both eyes on you. Such a beautiful sight, why would I look elsewhere?"

"Ooh, bringing out the smooth talker now that the brother is gone."

"Been forced to keep comments to myself. Something that is hard when you're teasing me with sex on the fucking beach."

"It really is the best." I give him a wink and love the way his eyes darken.

"Ev, there are beaches in Massachusetts. Don't make me take you to one right now to try it out."

I'm tempted to do just that, but then Cam comes to mind. If we continue down this path . . .

"What about your friendship?"

His eyes narrow on me. "Yeah, well, you're the fucking iceberg in that situation."

"The iceberg? Does that make you the Titanic?"

His lips twitch up into a smirk. "I do like to go down."

I squirm again in my seat, remembering how good he was at just that. "How many beers have you had?"

"Three."

"Seems I need to catch up."

Over an hour, three more beers for Niko and two Sex on the Beach drinks for me, we pop off the dance floor and back to the table for some water.

The songs playing have been upbeat and fun, but the lights dim even more as the DJ begins to pump out more sexual songs. Bodies come together, and I look to Niko. Going out there would be dangerous for us, but I want to.

I want his arms around me, his hands all over my body.

I notice Niko looking around; a pretty blonde a few tables away is making bedroom eyes at him.

"She's pretty," I say.

Niko turns back to me. "Yes, she is."

"Do you want to fuck her?" There's more venom and hurt in my tone than I mean, and I blame it on the booze.

He scrunches his brow as he stares at me. "What if I do?"

"Do whatever you want, I'm going to go dance." I grab the new drink the waitress sets down in front of me and stand, my legs pushing the stool back.

I quickly down the rest of my drink, and I'm gone. I don't look at him, not even a glance back as I make my way into the sea of gyrating bodies.

Let her have him, so maybe I can move on.

The music is loud, hypnotic. The lights flash to the beat, displaying an array of colors out into the crowd. I don't even know the song, but my body knows the beat, swaying and moving. I'm just like everyone else, caught up in the current, the booze releasing the stress of everything.

I feel the spark before his hands slip around my hips, his powerful muscles drawing me back against his chest. There's no need to look back. I know the body holding me close, moving in time with my own. The cock that's pressing into me.

Fuck!

The bastard is going to tear me down. Especially when his warm breath is against my neck, sliding up to my ear.

I want it. Want him.

"Those fuckers are looking at you, Everly," he hisses.

My lips pull up, and I turn my face closer to his. "Good."

"But none of them are me," he says. It's a statement. He's not fishing, backward asking me if he's above them because he knows. God, he knows what he does to me, what he's doing to me.

"No, they're not you," I whisper, my head falling back against his shoulder.

"I don't like it."

There's no stopping the need now. Arms around me, lips grazing my neck, and his body grinding against mine in time with the beat are all overwhelming feelings colliding, stealing all thoughts from my mind.

"You were looking at other women," I remind him.

"I only want to touch you."

I've fought it ever since he touched me on the day he helped me move. The need for him. Feigning annoyance to cover fear and desire.

"I'm going to take you home," he says, "and remind you who I am."

"I know who you are."

"I don't think so, baby, but you will."

Oh Jesus! The promise in those words sends a shiver down my spine. Home? That's too far. I need him now. "We could just find a dark corner."

"No, Everly, I don't want a quickie. I need an all-nighter."

"Yesss," I hiss. "I can totally do an all-nighter."

I'm too attached to Niko's mouth to understand how we made it up the stairs to his place, let alone *to* his place, but as soon as we're through the door, he grabs my ass and picks me up. I love how he can do that so effortlessly. My legs wrap around him, pulling him closer as he slams my back against the wall. There's fire from his hands on my legs as they make trails under the hem of my dress.

"Fuck," he hisses as his hips rock into me, fingers digging into my ass. "Are you fucking bare?"

I groan and rotate my hips against him. "Can't wear panties with this dress."

He crashes his lips to mine, and I can feel his hand between us. I'm wet, ready, and desperate for him to fill me. A month's worth of teasing texts has us both so worked up.

"I need inside you, Everly."

Fuck, the way he says my name.

No pause, clothes still on, he presses his lips to mine as he pushes inside me. Stretching, full and deep, and exactly what I need.

Every nerve ending lights off, sending a spiral of what feels like an electrical charge racing through my body. It feels so good. Too good.

I whimper when he pulls out only to thrust forward, smashing me into the wall, igniting me all over again. My head falls back, and I close my eyes, listening to the erotic groans leaving Niko with each thrust that slams into me harder and deeper.

Everything is Niko. All I feel, hear, and smell is him. My fuzzy mind can only comprehend the pleasure, his cock rocketing me toward a mind-blowing orgasm.

Nothing but carnal bliss as he pounds into me. My whole body tightens, and I scream out. Fire rips through me, whiting everything out as my muscles snap, releasing all the tension in my body.

"Fuck," he curses as his hips crash into me, his back arches, muscles jumping.

I can feel his cock twitching inside me, coming. Filling me.

His head falls against mine, our breaths harsh. This is what I so desperately needed. Release.

After a moment of rest, Niko pulls back, his hands still holding me up as he steps away from the wall.

"Wha . . ." I trail off, wondering where he's taking me. His cock twitches inside me again, and I realize he is still hard.

"All-nighter. I'm going to make you come until you pass out," he says as he lays me back on the bed.

He strips off his shirt, giving me a full view of his chiseled physique. One that I love to rake my eyes over.

"Keep looking at me like that, and I'll never let you leave," he growls, making me shiver and clench around him. His head falls back, and a groan vibrates in his chest. "Fuck, baby."

The fire is back in his eyes, consuming me.

Never leave.
Never, ever leave again.

The need to pee wakes me, and I try to roll out of bed, but a weight around my body stops me from moving. I pick up the arm and turn as I sit up, my head spinning from the movement. I blink, the action taking longer than usual.

The neon light from the bedside clock hurts my eyes, but I'm able to make out that it's just after four in the morning. Looking over, I have a sense of déjà vu. Niko is asleep next to me, naked as the day he was born. So am I.

"Shit," I hiss.

Standing up is a challenge, and I'm still too drunk to walk straight. Not being able to walk in a straight line seems to help avoid some of our clothes on the floor, but not all. A pair of jeans almost sends me falling on top of Niko, a guaranteed way to wake him, but I manage to steady myself on his dresser.

Thankfully there is a nightlight on in the bathroom. My mind is hazy, memories of the last few hours nothing but a blur, but I know as soon as I'm done, I have to get out of here.

The déjà vu of the situation doesn't go unnoticed, even in my current state.

I locate my dress and heels on the floor and pick them up before walking out into the living room.

Somewhere I vaguely remember dropping my clutch. The problem is where. Luckily, I spot it right away, the silver sparkling against his navy blue couch.

My phone still has half of its battery power, and I immediately pull up the Uber app. There's someone ten minutes away, which is just enough time for me to get my clothes on and get out.

I want to leave him a note, but without my purse, I'm low on options. Carefully and quietly I pull open drawers until I find a thin stack of Post-it notes that can't contain more than two or three pieces. Niko probably doesn't even know they are there, buried at the bottom of a drawer.

I'm tempted to put the Post-it on him again, but instead, I choose someplace a little more conspicuous. All I need is a repeat of last time.

Dress on, heels in hand, hair an absolute mess, and with my clutch in hand, I walk out once again on Niko.

Chapter Eighteen

Niko

I STARE AT MY fridge, at the stupid yellow Post-it note. It reads, "Thanks again." I'm beginning to hate her notes. At least this time she didn't leave it next to my dick, but this shit is seriously fucked up. Where is she getting all the Post-its? I don't even think I have any.

It's then I remember her conversation with Cam when we moved Everly into her place. She is still a bit weird if she's carrying them around with her, but I have to admit, I like it. Some of the old quirky Everly is still there.

After filling a glass with some water, I quickly down it and refill it before walking back to my bed. The chime of my phone goes off, but it's not on my nightstand. I dig around on the floor for my jeans, tossing clothes everywhere until I find it.

A missed call from Cam by the time I've got it in my hand. It's then I notice something is off.

My dick shows and feels signs of usage, but what I'm not seeing is any condoms. No wrappers and no used rubbers anywhere. I've never fucked anyone without one. I've never even had the urge to fuck a woman without protecting myself. Even with protection, I get tested once a year when I go in for a physical just for peace of mind. The thought of Everly and me, together, with no barrier between us has my dick twitching. I am suddenly pissed I don't remember fucking her bare. The thought of being able to claim her, mark her in such a way, has me feeling like a fucking caveman. I keep trying to remember.

The memories are there. I remember us coming home, stripping her, and fucking her over and over, but it's clouded by an alcohol-induced haze.

One thing is for sure—round two didn't dispel my want for her. It feels like she's in my blood now, a vital part of my being. Round two secured her spot as more than a good time and worth the risk to my friendship.

I'm not letting her note stop this thing between us.

After slipping back into bed, I pull up my contacts list. I haven't changed the name yet, so "Alyson" still shows up. I contemplate whether to text or call, and finally hit the call button.

"Mm, hello?" she answers after the third ring, her voice groggy.

"How was the walk of shame this morning?" I ask.

"Not bad," she says before a screeching yawn comes across. "It was long before the sun was up. The Uber driver was a little creepy with the way he looked at me."

"Pretty sure you had just fucked-hair. You shouldn't have left like that, Everly. That time of night, it's not always safe, and you were alone."

"Mm hm. What do you want, Niko?"

"Seriously? That's how you're going to act?" I'm getting tired of her aloofness toward me and our situation. It still doesn't stop me from going after her. Somehow I know if I can just break past her walls, her mood will improve. Problem is, it's hard on a guy's ego when the chick just up and leaves every single time and acts like you're the shit on the bottom of her shoe.

At least in bed, she's honest. The taste of her lips, the feel of her in my arms, and the look in her eyes when she comes all tell me she hasn't stopped lying. Only it's not to me; it's to herself.

"I'm looking for fun, just like you. Nothing more."

I clench my jaw and close my eyes. She's not in front of me, letting me read her reactions. Then again, that hasn't helped me in the past. She's very good at pushing me away.

"I'm not looking for fun, Everly, I'm looking for more than a quick fuck and a sticky note."

"W-what?" she asks with a stutter. A fucking stutter. There's Everly.

"You heard me. You. Me. Dinner. Or lunch, I'm not picky."

"Niko, not to stroke your already humongous ego, but you are fantastic in bed. We had fun. The end."

"Not the end. I want more," I say. "More sex, more you. And to find out which of your fucking personalities is the real Everly."

"Why?"

"Because I liked Alyson, and I have a feeling you were true to me then, even if your name wasn't."

She's silent for longer than I expect. "I don't know."

"You don't know that you have feelings for me?"

"Why would you think that I have feelings for you?"

"Because if you didn't, you wouldn't have kept up the lie. You wouldn't have kept contacting me." She says nothing, so I take that as confirmation. "Soon, Everly. This isn't over. It's just starting."

"Niko, this can't happen."

"It already has. Stop fighting it, and just let the cards fall where they do. I'll see you tonight." And with that, I hang up. Let her crazy little mind marinate on that for a bit. I'm starting to see that when it comes to Everly, I have to take the choice away from her or she will keep trying to push me away. Not going to fucking happen. New point for me.

The second night with Everly did nothing but fuck me up even worse. Weeks have passed, and every text I send goes unanswered. The last fucking thing I want to do is come across as some needy wimp, but this woman has me so twisted. My whole body aches just to touch her again, and it has never done that before.

Emotions I don't understand, feelings I've never had, and they're all because of her.

I need another drink. Something to dull this hum running through me.

As I pull up to our usual haunt, I spot a very familiar car in the parking lot. There aren't a lot of BMW convertibles out here, especially not with that sexy black and red interior.

After parking in the open space next to her, I pull off my helmet and toss it onto her passenger side seat. That way, no matter how it goes in there, she won't be rid of me when she walks out the door.

I'm prepared for hostile, for her walls. She's a pro at trying to push me away, but I'm not going to be pushed back anymore. Doesn't mean I won't play the game with her. I love it when she's feisty, and it makes the chase that much more infuriating and the reward sweeter.

She's sitting at the bar, her back to me, when I walk in. The seat to her left is empty, and I walk right up and slide in. The movement catches her eye, and her head reflexively turns toward me.

I don't register. It was just a quick glance, but then comes the double take.

"Fuck," she hisses under her breath and turns back to the drink in front of her.

"Another Sex on the Beach?" I ask, just to tweak her.

She adjusts her position so that she can look at me a little easier. "Raspberry tea, if you must know. How did you even know I was here?"

I raise my eyebrow at her but don't answer her question. "You're at a bar, drinking tea?"

"I don't have to explain."

"No, you don't."

"Besides, it's a pub and grill. Do you have to sit next to me?"

Fuck. She makes me want to lean forward and take her lips just to shut her bitch up. Horny Everly is so much easier to deal with.

I lean in closer, loving the way she tenses. "Do I make you nervous?"

"No." There's a force behind her words, but pink spreads across her cheeks, giving her away.

I place my hand just above her knee, making her jump. "Do I turn you on?" I ask, having more fun than I should be.

Her eyes are slits, but she doesn't faze me. The deepening pink in her cheeks tells me I'm right.

"Go away," she hisses as she swats at my hand.

"No."

"Leave me alone!"

I stare at her. "I don't think you really want that."

"Hey! The lady said to leave her alone," a guy at the other end of the bar yells out.

I like that he's looking out for a lady, but he's barking up the wrong tree. "Hey, man, this is between her and me."

The guy stands, the bar stool screeching against the tile floor. "Yeah? Well, now it's gonna be between you and me."

Everly holds out her hand for him to stop. "Thanks, but I can handle him. I don't need your help."

The guy rolls his eyes and turns his attention back to the beer in front of him.

I quirk a brow at her. "What are you doing here anyway?"

"Seriously? The Red Sox are playing. I need food. Am I not allowed here?"

"Of course you're allowed here. You should have called me. I would've joined you."

"Yeah, right. That sounds a little too much like a date, and I'm looking for dessert."

My jaw ticks. She thinks she's got the upper hand here, but I'll show her. I lean forward, getting in close to her. So close I can feel her body heat, and I know by her sharp intake of breath she feels mine.

"There's no dessert here better than me, baby." I slide my hand up her leg, to the interior of her thigh, and press the seam of her jeans up against her clit for a few quick pulses before pulling away.

It's not something I would ever do normally, but she's driving me insane. "But you already know that, don't you, Everly?"

Her lips are parted, and her breath has sped up. "Niko, whatever it is that you think is going on here, it isn't."

My eyes drop to her full mouth. I almost groan out loud at the memories of that sexy as hell mouth of hers, and all that it did to me, especially the way it stretched around my dick.

"Yes, it is."

"It's not, and the sooner you realize it, the better off we will be." She rifles through her purse and throws a couple of twenties down.

I tilt my head, watching her. I hear what she's saying, but her body language is screaming that she's lying. She fidgets in one spot before squaring her shoulders.

"Enjoy the rest of your night, Nikolas." And with that, Everly hops off the stool and walks away, cool and calm, as if the idea of us being an us isn't on her radar.

I don't bother protesting her exit. She's back to feigning disinterest in me for more than just sex, like she was that first night that I found out who she was, but I know better now. She can't hide her body's response to mine when we are together. I'll let her run, for now. I know that there is more between us than she wants to admit, but I'm a patient man, and I'm willing to bide my time until I can make her see it too.

It doesn't take long before I find I've broken her to some degree. An hour later a picture comes through my phone. Everly's jeans are gone, her legs spread, a hand covering her mound.

Everly: *You fucking suck.*

I smile down at the message, then set my phone back down on the bar. Let's see how she likes it when I don't respond.

Chapter Nineteen

Everly

NIKO: WHY IS IT that even while watching an entire structure burn to the ground this afternoon, all I could think of were your eyes.

I stare down at my phone and the random text from Niko. It isn't the first text I've gotten from him this week, but it is the hardest to understand and I have no idea how to take it. A compliment?

Everly: Ummm I'm not sure where to start with that.

I text back.

Niko: It's true

Everly: I believe you, but you thought of me while watching a fire?

Niko: No.

I blow out a breath and roll my eyes. Is he drunk again?

Everly: No? That's what you just said.

Niko: What I said was, while watching an entire structure burn to the ground this afternoon, all I could think of were your eyes.

My chest tightens as I read and reread his words. It's not like I can let on how affect me, though.

Everly: *Rolling my eyes here* You might be crazy.
Niko: Crazy for you.
I laugh out loud at his text. Oh, he's breaking me down again. Damn him and his charm.
Everly: LOL Cheesy. Is that all you've got?
Niko: Not even close, baby. I've got so much more for you. ;)
Niko: I'm off in a few hours. What are you doing tonight?
You, is what I want to respond, but that is *not* a good idea. He is way too addictive for his own good.
Everly: Actually, I have plans.
Niko: With who?
Everly: Another man, but I'm sure you don't know him. He's bald and a little older than I usually go for.
Niko: Your dad?
I roll my eyes as my fingers fly across the glass.
Everly: My dad? My dad isn't bald. lol I might have to tell him you said that.
Niko: Okay, WTF Everly?
Oops, he may be mad I played with him.
Everly: I have plans with Mr. Clean! I did a little painting last night. I have more to do, but after that, Mr. Clean and I will be getting very close.
Niko: I don't think you're funny, little girl. And why are you painting? You can hire someone to do that.
Everly: Because I like to personalize my own space. That's why . . . and little girl??? Not you too.
I'm getting tired of Cameron calling me that and the last thing I need is Niko jumping on that stupid name as well.
Niko: Yup. Me too. Think you might need to be punished for teasing me. Now that you bring it up, I can think of all kinds of dirty things I'd like to do to punish you.
The way my body heats up reading his words is almost too much to handle. I can't go down the dirty rabbit hole right now, but I can't help goading him for more.

Everly: Punished?
Niko: Babe.
Everly: Babe? That's it? You're not going to explain?
Well, he's no fun tonight.

Niko: See you after I get off work. I'll show you how I clean up things that are dirty.

I slap my hand against the wall to hold me up. Just the bait makes me remember all the very dirty things we've done together. The promise of how dirty they could be tonight turns me into a mess. Damn him.

Everly: Who is the tease now?

A few hours later, and I'm covered in paint. I'm wearing what I call farmer pants. Overalls, but that's what I think they should be called. I've finished two rooms all on my own, but the ceilings need to be done in both rooms. For some reason, whoever rehabbed this place painted them off-white versus bright white.

Maybe I should have hired someone, but I wanted to do it myself. I always feel like a place feels more like home when you have a hand in the decorating, right down to cleaning and painting. Since this place was done when I moved in, I found some colors I liked to warm it up a little more.

I walk over to where I left my cell and picked it up to check the time. Shit! It's already close to seven o'clock. Maybe Niko was just screwing with me and isn't going to show up after all. Either way, I should just finish up what's left and call it a night. I haven't eaten, and I need to wash the paint out of my hair.

I put my phone back on its dock and then smile as I remember our earlier text messages to each other. Things are better between us now that Niko knows the truth of who I am. We've broken the just-friends rule, but I can't seem to care about that right now. I'm done feeling guilty about it and worrying that Cam will find out. There is no reason Niko and I can't be friends.

Friends with benefits works too.

I know Niko isn't the type to look for more, regardless of what he's been saying. Plus, I'm still in my "be like the big boys and play the field" phase. Although I haven't dated anyone or slept with anyone else outside of Niko, I've decided that's okay, though. If Aly asks, I'll just let her know that I'm a work in progress. Baby steps and all that.

I pick up the rolling paintbrush and start to screw it onto the broom handle so that I can attempt to reach higher on the wall that I'm finishing up when my doorbell rings. Instantly my heartbeat starts to pound in my chest, knowing that it has to be Niko. I'm a mess, but the truth is, I shouldn't care if we are just staying friends. At least I should act like I don't care. Nothing I can do about it now anyway, and hell, that's on him if he thinks I'm not up to his normal standards. I told him I was painting and then cleaning.

The bell rings again, and I walk a little faster to the door. "I'm coming! Hold your firehouse, buddy. My house isn't burning down." Okay, that was corny, but I don't care. I pull the door open, flashing all of my teeth in a big smile, but it drops just as fast. I'm completely surprised by the fact that it's not Niko, but Jake at my door.

"I was in the neighborhood, and thought I'd see if you were in the mood for that Thai food we were going to get before your brother decided you were grounded for being an adult." He smiles, but it's quickly replaced with a smirk at the mention of my brother.

"Ah, hi, Jake. Grounded, huh?"

He laughs. "Yeah, sounded like the best analogy to me. It summed up how your brother was acting the day we moved you in."

He's not wrong about that, but I grew up with him, so I already knew Cam didn't like his friends snooping around me.

He holds up the bags in his hand, and I won't lie, I pretty much drool at the smell of the delicious food coming through my front door.

"If you've got basil fried rice in there and steamed dumplings, you can come in." I raise a brow, waiting for the magic words that will gain him entry to my home. He opens one of the bags, sniffing the air before pulling up a container so that I can see.

"Would you look at that. Those both just happen to be two of my favorite Thai menu picks. I knew we'd have something in common, Sunshine."

I laugh at his nickname for me, and then step back, allowing him to come in. He walks past, and I grab the container he still has in his hands, causing him to laugh at me.

"What's so funny?" I ask, and he just shakes his head at me, smiling, a dimple I hadn't noticed before popping out on his cheek. He really is cute, but he's not making my heart race. Maybe if I'd met him before I'd slept with Niko. I think about that for a moment, but decide that no, not even then. Oh well. "You have no idea how happy I am that someone showed up with food! I haven't eaten anything since early this morning."

"Always happy to feed a starving damsel, but it's almost seven thirty. Why haven't you eaten all day?"

I spin around in place and hold my hands out, gesturing to the mess I've made. Old sheets all over the floor, tape on the woodwork, and paint cans at my feet. "I've been busy painting. I guess I forgot until about ten minutes before you rang my bell. I was just about to find a menu soon, but I wanted to get the ceilings done first. I was just getting ready to start them when you got here," I say and walk toward my kitchen. "Want something to drink? It's the least I can offer you, seeing as how you've brought food."

"Sure. Whatever you've got is good."

I grab two plates and a couple of waters before heading out into the living room again. When I get there, Jake has laid out all the food on one of my covered tables, but he's no longer in the room.

"Jake?"

"In here," I hear him call out. That's weird. I walk into the den, or family room, as some people call it, and Jake has his sleeves rolled up and is holding the paint roller I was putting together right before he got her.

"What are you doing?" I ask.

"I figured since I'm here, I'd help out while you get something into your stomach."

I shake my head. "You don't have to do that. You brought me food. I don't expect you to work."

"I don't mind, honestly. Go ahead. Get something to eat. I'll finish this up for you, and then I'll join you."

"Are you sure?"

"Yup."

"Okay, then. I'll be right back. Would you prefer a beer over the water?"

"Both would be great." He smiles, and I can't help it. I smile back. Maybe this isn't a bad idea. I mean, I said I wanted to play the field, and if Aly were here, she'd tell me to make more friends. I grab two of the beers Cam left here from the fridge and head back toward the food.

I don't usually drink anything but wine or the occasional fruity cocktail, but I feel like I should have a beer and kind of let Jake know that I just see him as one of the guys. I don't know what he's thinking by showing up here like his, but I like Jake. I just don't think I like him in the same way I would someone I'd want to sleep with. Aly would be rolling her eyes at me right now, but I told her that I couldn't just decide to sleep with anyone. I need an attraction. I need pull.

Jake is attractive, but he's not pulling me. Besides, I don't think he's here with the intention of he and I being just friends. Cam would be pissed. I can only keep one of his friends a secret right now, and even that is stupid on my part. Right as I head back toward the den to give Jake his beer and plate, my doorbell rings again.

Now what? I walk back to the door only to freeze when I see the silhouette of the man on the other side. I'd know that shape anywhere. Jake managed to distract me with food, and with the time ticking, I honestly didn't think Niko was going to show. This probably is going to look bad, but is that a bad thing?

I need Niko to know that what happened between us is sex. Just sex. Him seeing another guy here will only solidify that, right?

Guess we shall see. I pull the door open, and as it usually does, my heart beats harder, and I feel butterflies in my stomach. God, he's so damn pretty to look at.

"Hey. I didn't think you were actually coming by."

"I told you I would. I wanted to get a shower first." He looks me over from my feet all the way up, and I see it. That fire in his eyes whenever we're in the same room together. You can feel it. The air becomes heavy, almost as if we've sucked all the air out of the room and replaced it with combustible energy just waiting to ignite.

"You look sexy as fuck in the overalls, Ev."

"I'm covered in paint, and the overalls are two sizes too big. You hit your head today fighting fires, Niko?"

"Nope. I just know what's underneath those big clothes and all that paint." He's still staring at me when Jake yells out from the other room.

"You didn't order pizza too, did you?" He laughs, and I turn toward Jake's voice but turn back when I hear Niko growl.

"Who the fuck is that?"

Oh, shit. Maybe him seeing Jake isn't such a good idea.

"Jake came over and is helping me."

"Jake? Seriously, Ev?"

"I didn't invite him, Niko, but he's not unwelcome. He's a friend."

"I can see that," he says as he looks at the two beers I've been holding in my hands. "Did I interrupt something, because if I did, I'm not fucking leaving."

"Well, well. Look who's here. You are definitely not the pizza guy. Can't say that I'm surprised," Jake says as he enters the room Niko and I are in.

"What the fuck does that mean, Jake?" Jake laughs. Is he serious right now? Niko looks like he's ready to pummel Jake, and he's standing in my front hallway, paint-spattered on his shirt, but looking as cool as an ice cube. Maybe Jake's not playing with a full deck. That couldn't be possible, though, because Cam would never have brought him into my home if he had issues. Either way, he's either very stupid, or he's positive that he can take Niko in a fight because that is where this seems to be headed. I'm starting to think he's not that smart.

"It means, I had a feeling you'd be heading here," Jake replies to Niko.

"Wait, what? How did you know Niko would be heading here?" I ask, and both men ignore me. I'm about to stomp my foot like the child my brother keeps believing me to be when Niko throws ice water on my internal tantrum.

"Does Cam know you're here?" he asks Jake, and the hostile vibes pour off both men in waves.

"Does he know you're here?" Jake replies sarcastically.

Niko takes a few steps forward, but I step in front of him. "Stop! This is my house. I'm not sure what's going on here, but I don't have one of those things swinging between my legs like the two of you do to measure against yours, so stop."

"It's called a cock, Ev, not a thing that swings between your legs," Niko says in a menacing tone. "And he's not getting his anywhere near you. Cam might not be here right now, but I'm the next best thing to her brother, and I have no problem playing his part while kicking your ass, Bishop."

"That's rather incestuous, isn't it, Callahan?" Jake says with a small smirk on his lips. "Oh, and watch your mouth, Niko. There is still a lady present, or didn't your mother teach you any manners?"

Niko steps aggressively toward Jake, but I grab his arm, stopping him. Jake's hands go up in surrender, but I'm pretty sure he's goading Niko. The question is, why?

"You better watch yours, rookie. I don't know what your game is here, but trust me, you don't want to open door number two. Cam warned you once already. He finds out you're sniffing around his sister after he told you to fuck off, and things are going to get real ugly, trust me."

"My apologies if I offend you, Everly. That's not my intention, but would you mind if I spoke to Callahan here for a minute alone?" Jake asks, but it's Niko who answers.

COCK sure

"I don't need to speak to you alone. Whatever you need to say, just say it." Jake stares Niko down for a full minute before he swings his gaze to me. What in the hell is going on?

"Okay, then. Your brother finds out that the two of you are screwing around, and all hell is going to break loose. You know that, right?"

"What the fuck are you talking about, Bishop?"

"I saw you two at O'Malley's pub."

I can feel the blood fall from my face.

"I didn't know who she was at the time so I didn't think anything of it, but the day we moved her in, I knew she looked familiar, then I saw you two together, and it clicked. From your reaction that day we got her all set up, I knew I was right."

Niko doesn't say anything. He looks at Jake and then to me. "So what? What is this all about then if you're not trying to get in her pants, Bishop?"

"I wanted to be sure, man. I know I'm the newest one in our crew, but you guys are still my brothers. All of you. Cam finds out about you and his sister, and shit's going to get worse. It's going to cause a lot of shit that the guys and I feel would put us in the middle of the two of you. We don't want that. I don't know what the status is between the two of you right now, but the fact that you're here tells me enough. I know for a fact that Hayes doesn't know that you're here. Whatever this is or isn't, you need to figure it out, fast, and then either tell Cam or end this now."

"I don't need you telling me what I need to do, Bishop," Niko growls at Jake.

"Hey, man. I'm just passing your own advice back to you that you started to give me no more than ten minutes ago. Shit's going to get ugly. Trust me," Jake says, and Niko's nose flares. Time to wrap this night up before these two go any further.

"Look, Jake, I appreciate the advice, dinner, and for helping me paint, but I think we should probably call it a night."

"Of course. I don't want to wear out my welcome. Maybe we can do something another night?" He smiles, but it's directed at Niko. Jesus, this guy is something else.

"Un-fucking-likely," Niko growls at Jake.

"Yeah. That's what I figured." Jake grabs his keys from the table and heads toward the door. "See ya around, Everly." He closes the door behind him, and I walk to it, locking it.

"What the fuck just happened?" I ask as I turn to Niko.

"We were just officially told that everyone except your brother knows that we've been fucking around. That's what just happened."

My eyes go wide. "Everyone?"

"That's what he said. This is not good, Everly. Not at all."

"Now what?" I ask, but I'm not exactly sure what I'm asking. Do we keep going, or stop this once and for all?

"I don't know." He steps closer, his hand reaching up to cup my face. "But I don't think I can stop."

His hand is warm against my skin, comfort seeping in as I lean into it. The warmth is potent, causing me to step forward in search of more.

I shouldn't want this, but, brother forgive me, I do.

Chapter Twenty

Everly

A GROAN CRAWLS UP my throat as I wipe my mouth on the back of my hand. I barely made it to the kitchen sink in time. A few seconds later, and there would be a mess all over my floor.

If I hadn't been feeling bad the last few days, as well as feeling off the last few weeks, I would blame my stomach issues on the seafood I had at lunch. After washing my hands and rinsing my mouth, I pull down a glass and fill it with water, an itch scratching at my mind.

Halfway through a large gulp flushing the taste away, the scratch breaks through as a chilling idea sets in.

It's late July, and the last time I can remember having my period was in May when I moved in. Two weeks later Niko and I . . .

The glass slips from my fingers and crashes to the ground, shattering.

I draw in a stunted breath, my hands shaking as I instinctively grab for my phone, the glass forgotten. My fingers are clumsy and fumble the phone as I attempt to unlock it.

Three rings, and Aly's cheerful voice comes over the line.

"Hey, doll," Aly says. "How are you?"

"Hi, Aly. Are you busy, or um, what are you doing right now?"

"I just got home, actually. I have a shift at the bar tonight. Why? What's going on, Ev? You sound funny."

"I need you. Can you come over?"

There is a pause; then she's back. "Yeah. I'll call out and then be there in an hour."

Every part of me is shaking. What am I going to do if it's true?

"Can you pick up a pregnancy test on your way?"

"Shit, Ev," she hisses. "I hope you've got some wine because I'm going to need it for this story."

"I don't feel so good, Al."

"Go relax. I'll be there as soon as I can."

I can't believe I didn't notice, didn't remember, but as I think back, unlike the first night, there were no condom wrappers sprinkled in with our clothes. How could I be so reckless and stupid? We. How could we be so stupid? What am I going to do if I'm pregnant?

An hour and five minutes later, Aly and I stare at three pregnancy tests, all with the same response—positive. Three different brands. Positive, two pink lines, and a plus sign. No way they're all wrong.

I'm pregnant.

Fuck.

What the hell am I going to do?

"How did this happen?" Aly asks. I quirk a brow at her, and she rolls her eyes in response. "I know how it happens, but how did it happen to you? Oh my God! Please tell me there is no chance it's Tate's?" Her face pales, and I understand her concern, but I know it's not Tate's.

I shake my head. No, there's only one man responsible.

"Niko. There's only been Niko. Tate and I haven't been together like that in months, and I've had my period twice since he and I broke up. There's no way it could be his." I shudder a little, thinking to myself that would be the only plus to this right now. That it wouldn't be Tate's baby.

Oh my God! A baby. The words are wrong and confusing, and I'm at a cross between crying and throwing up . . . again.

"That night we went dancing I was so in the moment and more than a little tipsy . . . You know I don't usually drink much. I don't think we even thought about a condom."

"What about birth control?"

I shake my head. "My prescription ran out, and I just haven't had time to find a new doctor here. I'm not dating anyone, so it wasn't even a concern."

"Not dating anyone, but you've been with Niko, Ev. Obviously more than once."

I give her my *no shit* look, and she just shakes her head. I'm acutely aware that this is a huge screw-up on my part. Shit. "Sex does not equal dating or any type of relationship."

"Who said relationship?"

I let out a sigh before I answer her. "He did, but I'm not going there."

"Everly! You didn't tell me that!"

"I know, but you've been working nonstop. It wasn't a big deal. I told him that I'm not looking for more than sex."

"I'd say it is a big deal, and that you got way more than sex, Ev." She holds up all three pregnancy tests, showing me the results.

"You do know that I pissed on those, right?" She drops them, and I start laughing even though there is nothing funny about this.

"What are you going to do?"

I shake my head. "I have no idea."

"Have you seen him since then?"

I let out a loud sigh. It's been almost two months, and after Jake was over, I've avoided him at every opportunity, but he is seriously wearing me down. "He called and asked me on a date the day after."

"And you turned him down? Why?"

"Because it's Niko Callahan! He's a manwhore, and I'm not ignorant to that or to the fact that he is too good looking. I'd be stupid to think that he never has women throwing themselves at him on a regular basis. I just don't know if I could ever trust him, not after everything with Tate."

"That asshole," she says in regards to the mention of Tate's name before taking a sip of her wine, and sighs. "Has he tried to reach out to you since?"

"He's called a couple of times, and texts every few days. I've even blown my brother off, afraid that Niko would tag along just to get in front of me. I ran into him once, and he came over after an afternoon of flirting that was diverted by another of the guys from the firehouse."

"Do you text back?" Aly asks, skipping over all the other information I just unloaded.

"Sometimes." Well, more than sometimes. In the beginning, no. Lately, yes. So that all evens out to sometimes, right?

She holds her hand out for my cell. "Let me see."

I hand my phone over and watch as she reads, the ever-changing expressions on her face entertaining.

"Um, Ev, girl . . . you need to give this man a chance."

"Why? To prove myself, right?"

"Because, and I quote, 'Stop ignoring me. I want you, and I know you want me. Or are you afraid I'll make you weak again?' Weak, again? I can only imagine what that means. Chick, he isn't walking away. You seem to be the one trying to run, and he is still chasing. You have to put that fucking asshole Tate out of your mind and stop thinking that every guy in the world is going to do to you what he did. It's just not how all guys are."

"Maybe."

"No, babe. Not maybe. You have a kid coming now. You owe it to yourself and this kid to give its father the benefit of the doubt. Stop being so guarded and let some of those walls down. If he fucks up, then I'll kick his ass and your brother's. No worries. I'll even take care of both bodies for you."

"Hey! How did Cam end up dead and buried in this scenario?"

"Because he's fucking Cameron, that's why. I'd bury him just for PC."

"PC?"

"Political correctness, Ev. Pay attention." She shakes her head at me, and I'm speechless at the way she manages to throw my brother under the bus at every turn. For a moment I forget about the fact that I'm pregnant, but it doesn't last long.

"Time to figure out what I'm going to do with the rest of my life."

"Yeah. It's going to be okay, Ev. I have a good feeling about this. I'm never wrong. Ya know?"

I snort, and we both start laughing.

Aly is the rock I so desperately need right now.

A week later, I've avoided the reality inside me and the bottle of wine I desperately want to drown in, though I did order some baby books that are still in their Amazon box sitting by the front door. It's as if I open them, I'll have to accept their meaning.

What to Expect When You're Expecting—the pregnant woman's bible, along with a few others. I have no idea what I'm doing, and I need all the help I can get.

Nothing in my fridge looks appetizing. Then again, my stomach has been revolting at an increasing rate with each passing day.

I thought it was morning sickness, but apparently, it's an all-day event, and sometimes night.

After closing the fridge, I move to the pantry and the package of saltines I've almost gone through. Just as I'm about to slip a cracker in my mouth, the doorbell goes off, startling me. I try and think if I'm expecting anyone when the ring happens again, then again.

My lips curl up into a smile as I hear the familiar SOS code starting to be played out over my doorbell. I walk to the door and fling it open to find Cameron with his finger still pressing the button.

"Hi."

"I feel like you've been avoiding me, little sis," Cam says from the other side of the door, wasting no time getting to the reason he is here.

I blink at him. "Avoiding you?" I shake my head, trying to throw him off on just how right he is as I step aside to let him in. "It's just been busy at work. I have this intern I've been helping."

"But you have time for the royal Payne."

I roll my eyes. "She's my best friend."

"I see where my importance with you lies."

I shake my head. "Drama queen."

"Hey, that's drama king. I want to bang a queen, not be one."

I begin to laugh, but it quickly changes. A wave of nausea rolls through me, and I blow out a breath and close my eyes, hoping it will pass. My mouth begins to water, and I'm a second from tossing whatever may be left in my stomach, which could just be acid at this point.

"Ev?" Cam asks.

I hold my hand up, then shake my head before turning and running into the powder room. Another close call and my stomach heaves, but all that lands in the toilet is some bile. I can't seem to keep much down, so I've got nothing in my stomach to expel. After a few heaves, my stomach settles down, and I sit back against the cool tile wall and draw my legs up.

"Are you okay?" Cam asks from the door to the bathroom. "If you're contagious, I love you, but I'm out." He holds his hands up as he backs away.

I start to laugh, but it quickly morphs into sobs, tears streaming down my face. I'm exhausted, scared, hungry, and out of my depth.

"Ev?" He steps forward and squats in front of me, his hands running up and down my arms. "What's wrong?"

"I'm sorry," I say as I try to pull myself together. I don't know if it's a combination of hormones and knowing my brother is going to kill Niko, or the all-out scared-to-death feeling of what is growing inside me.

A baby was not in my five-year plan.

Seeing Cam only intensifies my guilt for what I know is a coming storm.

If I tell Niko.

It was my fault, after all. My responsibility. I seduced him that first time and gave us both a taste of something that couldn't be satisfied in one night.

"Do you need to go to the hospital?"

"Because I'm crying? Jesus, Cameron!"

I shake my head, my lips forming a thin line. Cameron's blue eyes are scrunched in concern, sending another knife into my heart.

"You should go. You don't look so good, Ev. It's more than the tears. You're white as a sheet."

"There's not much they can do for morning sickness," I say in an unsteady voice.

His expression falls from concern to shock, and he pulls back. "Morning sickness?" He blinks a few times, and I wait for what I said to set in. He stays quiet, and I know I'm just going to have to say the words for him.

I swipe the hair from my face and purse my lips together as I nod. "I'm pregnant."

"Jesus."

"Not quite. My name is not even close to Mary, and in my case, there was sex involved." He ignores my attempt at a lame joke, instead of asking me the question I've been dreading since I found out.

"Who is the father?" Cam asks, his words calculated.

I stare at him, unable to tell him what I did with Niko. For him to know about my lie. That I'm the author of the infamous Post-it note.

"Does it matter?" I say almost in reflex. I'm too freaked out to come up with some other response.

"It fucking matters, Ev! It's Tate, right?"

I don't deny it, but I don't exactly say it is Tate's either. I'm not ready to deal with Cameron knowing about Niko and me hooking up.

"It's been months, Everly."

"I'm going to hell," I say out loud.

"I'm pretty sure we're past the days where people expect you to be married before getting knocked up, Ev, but I'll agree with you on that where Tate is concerned. Fuck!"

Cam grinds his teeth and looks away. "Are you going to tell him?"

"I don't know." With lots of burning hell flames that will roast me for all eternity.

He blows out a breath; his jaw jutted forward. "This is such a fucking shit storm! How could you let this happen?"

"Don't yell at me! It's not like I wanted this to happen! I didn't plan for this. I didn't even think this was a possibility in my future. I don't even think I want kids! I'm not ready to be a mother."

"Ev . . ."

"I'm scared, Cam, and I don't know what to do. I can't tell Mom and Dad yet, but I needed to tell someone other than Aly, and you're yelling at me!"

His brow furrows, and his eyes soften. He moves to lean against the wall and slides down next to me. "We'll figure it out, don't worry." He throws his arms around my shoulders and pulls me in. "You've got me and Mom and Dad. We're here for you. Anything you need, okay?"

I lean further into his shoulder and nod. "Don't say anything to them yet, okay? I'm just not ready."

"Okay, but soon, Ev. They'll support whatever you decide. You know they love you."

"Yeah, but I'm not ready to see the disappointment in their eyes when they find out their daughter got herself knocked up and is currently single." Cam doesn't say anything, and I know he knows what I said is true. I'll deal with them later. For now, I've got bigger fish to fry, and that's figuring out how to tell the baby's father. The real one.

Chapter Twenty-One

Niko

"**E**VERLY IS PREGNANT," CAM says, and I know that I must be hearing shit. "She says it's her asshole ex, but I don't believe her."

The iced coffee I just grabbed from Dunkin' Donuts slips from my grip and drops to the ground. I hear the cup hit the concrete floor and watch as some of it splatters up and onto Cam's shirt. Not a single muscle twitches to try and stop it from happening. I just stand there, shocked and a little dazed by what I just heard.

I stare at him, his words filling my head. Those words, "Everly is pregnant," and the knowledge that the last time we had sex, we didn't use any condoms.

Holy shit. She's pregnant.

For over a month I've been trying to get her to talk to me, to go out with me, but she keeps refusing. Is this why? She's pregnant and doesn't know or maybe want to tell me?

"Dude! What the fuck? This is a clean shirt," Cam says, pissed off as he swipes at the spots that I'm sure will stain his perfectly ironed shirt. I don't fucking care right now. He's ridiculous for ironing a fucking T-shirt anyway.

"She's pregnant?" Maybe I imagined him saying it.

He grabs a towel from the chair and walks over to the station's kitchen sink to wet it.

"Apparently. She just told me today." He's wiping the little spots of coffee from his shirt, his strokes on the stains angrier than anything. Nope. Not my imagination.

"Okay, so you say you don't think it's her ex's baby. Why don't you believe it's his kid?" I ask while throwing paper towels on the liquid mess on the floor.

He stops suddenly, throwing the towel back on the chair, and stalks toward the window to stare. The rest of the guys are outside sitting on chairs while enjoying the early evening weather.

"Hell, I don't fucking know! I guess I just don't want it to fucking be his. It would mean she'd have to deal with that fucking asshole for the rest of her and this kid's lives. I don't want him anywhere near her, and if it were his, you bet your ass he would try to manipulate her into taking his lying, cheating ass back. I also keep thinking that she wouldn't keep it if it were his."

My eyes grow wide at his last statement, and I can feel my heartbeat just a little bit faster. Surely she wouldn't consider terminating, but what do I really know about adult Everly Hayes? Honestly, I know next to nothing about Ev. She's so far from the little kid she was when she followed Cam and me around, back in the days when she wore those thick-as-hell glasses and had two braids on her head. Not the one who walks into a pub and goes home with her brother's friend for a night of mind-blowing, unforgettable sex.

"What did she say when she told you? I mean, Cam, she's not a baby anymore. You know that, right?"

"Of course I know that! And she may not be a baby to you, knowing how you treat fucking women and seeing how you can't keep your fucking dick in your pants long enough to care about anyone for more than a night, but she's my baby sister. This fuck doesn't deserve to have his DNA sharing hers!"

"Whoa! Back up, Cameron! I was just trying to say that it's not like she's sixteen and can't handle having a child of her own. Everly is smart. She'll make the right choice."

"Fuck! Niko. Look, I'm sorry, man. I didn't mean that. I shouldn't have said that. I know that's not the case. I'm just frustrated at the thought of her going through this with him or if she decides, alone. She hasn't even told my parents yet. Just me. I'm worried about her. I know you don't understand because you didn't grow up with siblings, never mind a younger sister, but I'm always going to worry about her, and I want to protect her from assholes like this fucking guy, Tate."

"No, I get it, man. It's fine. We're good." Cam shakes his head, and I decide to keep him talking. It's not like I brought it up, and to be honest, now I'm itching to get the fuck out of here and speak to Everly myself. I have to know. I need to see her eyes when she answers me. I want to call her right now and ask her if it's true—is she carrying Tate's baby, or is the baby mine?

God, this is some Maury Povich type shit, but I know already. I don't need Maury for this. We didn't use any fucking condoms the last time. Deep down I know this is my kid. The question is, why hasn't she told me, and why is she telling Cam it's her fucking ex's baby?

I'm calm as I park my bike in front of her house. Her car is here, so I know she's home. I slide my leg over my bike, standing face forward toward her house. Pulling my helmet off, I hold it and walk toward the front door. I notice the curtain in her front window move, and I know she's aware that I'm here. I get to the door and don't bother knocking. I wait for a beat, then two before hearing the lock on the door click before she opens it.

"Niko," she says, her voice giving a small shake. She knows why I'm standing at her door, especially when I glance down to her abdomen and I have my answer.

"It's mine." I lock eyes with her as I walk in. "It's my baby, right?"

She blinks and nods, locking the door behind us. "Yes," she whispers, passing by me.

"Were you going to tell me?" I ask as soon as we enter her kitchen.

"Of course. I just needed to figure it all out first."

"How long was that going to take?" I ask. Anger is boiling up inside me. Why didn't she call me?

"Jesus Christ, Niko. I just found out a week ago."

"You could have called me, we could have talked about it, and I would have been with you."

"It's still settling in. I've been trying to figure out what to do."

"Figure what out? What is there to figure out, Everly?"

She lets out a sigh. "It's not the best timing or the best situation. I honestly didn't plan on having kids. Not anytime soon, anyway," she says this all in one sentence, almost like she's trying to breathe on cue. "Don't worry, I'll take care of everything. You don't have to be involved."

My stomach drops, and a wave of nausea rolls over me. She wouldn't get an abortion, would she? Cam said that he didn't think she'd keep it if the baby were her ex-boyfriend's, but what about mine?

"What does that even mean, Everly?"

"That I don't need you. I am financially capable of taking care of a child, so you don't have to be involved."

"What the fuck, Ev? You're going to keep me from my kid?"

She shakes her head. "That's not what I'm saying. What I'm saying is this was a fluke. I'm letting you know I wasn't trying to trap you or bind you to me. You're free to keep fucking around and doing whatever else you do. You won't be burdened by a baby."

"Fucking around? Seriously, Everly? That's all you've got? The only fucking I've been doing is with you!" I can't believe her. There is no way I'm letting her push me out of this situation. It's my kid. "So I'm supposed to take this as a fucking favor? To be able to live the single life without being 'burdened' with a kid? Or is it I'm an unfit parent in your perfect eyes. That I don't make enough money."

"Stop twisting my words, Niko! That's not it. I'm telling you I don't hold you responsible."

"That's my child, my family, and I'm just as fucking responsible as you are. I will be in his or her life no matter what, and I will fucking fight you for that," I growl through clenched teeth. My muscles are tight, ready to claw tooth and nail to be in my kid's life. I'm not ever going to walk out on a child of mine. Ever! She needs to fucking get that through her thick, stubborn head right now.

She blinks at me, clearly stunned. "I thought you'd be happy," she says in barely more than a whisper.

"Why the fuck would I be happy about not being in my child's life?"

Her eyes narrow on me. "You think my brother didn't tell me about all your escapades together? All the girls you went home with, together or alone, and the girls chasing you. You've been spreading yourself around since you were a teen, Niko. The only thing that's changed is your age and the fact that the ones that chase you now are women. You're just a manwhore, always have been, always will be."

"Wow! Just wow, Everly. You don't know anything about me. Which was fucking obvious when you left a Post-it note with the word 'Thanks' to my dick. Who does that?"

"He did show me a good time. It would be rude not to."

I ignore her bullshit comment. "I'll tell you who does that, a girl. An immature girl who's been hurt by someone and takes it out on unknowing men. The real kicker is who you ended up being, and leaving without even telling me your real name? That was cool? Cut the shit, Everly."

"First, that's a horrible expression," she says, and I scowl at her even more than I was. God, this woman is infuriating. "Second, love 'em and leave 'em, isn't that your motto?"

"No."

"Oh, so all the women that line up on a regular basis to inspect your 'fire hose' is just an exaggeration?"

"It didn't use to be, but it is now. Has been for a while, but you refuse to see me."

"How is now different?"

"You," I admit. It's now or never. I've been giving her some space, waiting for her to see that I'm into her for more than just a quick and dirty fuck here and there. I don't want to hide this shit anymore. I've wanted her right from the start. I just didn't want to admit it because of the fucked-up way we started, and because of Cameron. Now that there is a kid involved, though, I'm not waiting for her to figure out what I already know.

She rolls her eyes, arms tightly locked in front of her. "Oh, please. You aren't going to charm me like all the others."

"Charm you? I'm fucking serious, Everly."

"Not going to happen," she says with a shake of her head.

God, this fucking stubborn woman. "Why not?"

"Because I know this will never work, and it's better to be rid of you in my life."

A growl rips from me, and I charge forward. Her eyes widen, and I stop inches from her. I press my hand against her abdomen, and she lets out a gasp. "I'm part of you now. There's no getting rid of me. Ever!"

Our eyes lock, and I drop my forehead to hers.

"Why would you want to stick around?" she asks, and I hear the defeat crawling in.

"Because I want this. I want you, us, Ev. I want it all with you."

"Because I'm pregnant."

"No! Because I like you, Everly. Shit, that's such a dumb word. I more than like you, but I don't know a fucking word to describe it right now. Even with all your bullshit, with all the shit you've got going on in that crazy head of yours, I want you. I want you to be mine. You and me, exclusive. I think I knew, even after that first night with you, that you were different. I couldn't stop thinking about you. I would have asked you to stay the next morning if you hadn't disappeared on me. You being pregnant now with my kid, well, that's just a bonus. But this thing between us was there before the baby, and I have the text messages to prove it."

"Then why come to me now saying all this?"

"You fucking lied to me, remember? You played me and left me, which created a whole other situation thanks to your Dear

John. And I've tried. Don't you dare try to say I haven't. I also tried to give you some space with you turning me down left and right. Next time I won't because obviously you can't get out of that head of yours."

"Do you have any idea what it's like to be the one that always does all the right things? Always the one with the good grades, who's praised daily by parents and a brother who think you can do no wrong? The baby of the family?" she says with anger, but there is also a tremor filling her words. "I'm twenty-five years old, Niko, and I'm still being treated like that little girl my family always had up on a pedestal."

"You want me to call you Princess now?"

Her eyes narrow on me, and she ignores my comment. "I had no life experience when I met Tate, and I fell. Then I fell flat on my face. Of course, that was two years after I walked around thinking that I had the best boyfriend in the world, only to find out he's been screwing every chick within a four-mile radius."

I look away but quickly flip my gaze back to her. I can feel my nostrils flaring, but I say nothing. I know I've been with a lot of women, but I never lied to one of them about what was happening between us. Never made a promise to commit to more than I knew I was ready for. She's placing blame on me that doesn't qualify in my case.

"That's right. You know exactly what I'm talking about because you're just the same as he is, aren't you, Nikolas?"

"I'm nothing like him!" I growl at her, and for a minute I take a step back. When I realize what I've done, I square my shoulders and look her directly in her eyes. I don't want to scare her, but she needs to know. She needs to understand that I'm not him, but she's determined to vilify me because of this guy.

This isn't going anywhere. I'm so pissed right now, and I know there is no way to get through her thick skull right now.

"Even if you're not the same, Niko, I'm not sure I can trust that."

"Trust me, you mean." I make it a statement, not a question because that's the root of the problem here. She doesn't trust me even though I've never done anything to cause her not to. "That's the root of the issue between us. I don't think it's fair, Everly, that you place the blame of another man's sins on my shoulders. I've never once lied to a woman I've been with, and I haven't lied to you."

She doesn't say anything and just shrugs like she did that first night that I found out who she was after she lied to me.

"Maybe you should think about who the liar is in this situation and evaluate your issues instead of putting them on me. Unlike you, I started off with nothing but the truth. So far it's looking like Tate's bad habits have rubbed off on you, and now you're saying I'm the one you don't think you can trust? I don't fucking think so, Ev. It's me that shouldn't trust you, but I've laid out my feelings as bluntly as any man can, and you still keep pulling the same bullshit card! You want to place blame on someone? I suggest you start by looking in the goddamn mirror!" I yell at her, my temper rising to the point that I'm ready to punch the wall.

She stares for a moment, stunned by my statement. Good. Maybe she should fucking marinate on that for a while, but not with me standing here.

"I need to get out of here before we both say something we can't take back later." I grab my bike helmet that I'd placed on her entryway table when I walked in and stop at the door. Without turning to look at her again, I take a deep breath before speaking. "Don't do anything without letting me know, Everly. I should have a say in this. I have a right to know. Stop being selfish, and think about the fact that this is more than about you and your past. It's more than me. There is a baby now. Our baby, and I'm not fucking going anywhere as long as you're carrying my kid. So grow up, little girl. Things are about to change regardless of whether you like it or not."

I don't wait. I don't look at her. I close the door and walk to my bike, start her up, and get the hell away from Everly fucking Hayes. For now.

Chapter Twenty-Two

Everly

I WAIT A MINUTE or two knowing Niko is home after seeing his bike parked out back. I knock again, louder this time. I know it's stupid, but after our talk the other day, I keep having these thoughts of Niko with other women, and as much as I try not to, I get upset. I heard what he said. I believe that he believed what he said, but I just can't get past my issues. It's too hard, especially after everything with Tate.

He said I was selfish. Maybe I am, but only about certain things. The thought of Niko being with someone else causes actual pain in my chest. I keep ignoring it. Pushing him away only to pull him back when it gets to be too much alone. As much as I'd like to believe what he said, I'm just not ready. I'm still trying to come to terms with the fact that I'm going to have a baby. He just needs to let me deal with one thing at a time.

I need him to know that I'm not saying no, but maybe, and only maybe after I've adjusted to what will be my new life as a mother. He should understand that. I mean, he should be freaked out too and trying to adjust to the fact that he's going to be a father. I think about that for a moment, and the last time we saw one another at my place. He was mad, sure, but he didn't seem that freaked over my being pregnant. Unless . . .

Maybe he decided after all that my issues aren't worth the aggravation. Perhaps my days of silence has him thinking that he made a mistake by telling me he wanted more. Maybe he changed his mind, and he's already moved on to someone else?

Oh, God! What if he's in there now, sharing that body of his with some other woman? Shit, I shouldn't be here. I shouldn't have come without calling, but there is no way in hell I'm leaving now. God, I can't take these hormones! I feel like I'm three different people sometimes. These pregnancy mood swings I keep having are ruling everything in my life right now, and I hate it. If I'm not throwing up, then the people around me, specifically Alyson, are asking me if I need a priest to perform an exorcism.

Screw it. He's just going to have to prove me right.

I raise my hand and bang again. Harder this time, determination now strengthening my pounding, but as I let my fist fly again toward his door, Niko opens it. And oh God, I'm struck stupid by his near nakedness.

"Oh, God. Holy Christmas. Fucking hell just froze over and took me." I think I just said that out loud because Niko is giving me a look that says he thinks I'm out of my mind, but holy shit!

Niko is standing in front of me, soap in his hair, towel barely wrapped around his slim waist, showing off that gorgeous, lickable V he has below the towel and the happy trail that my mouth just literally salivated to, remembering all the memories of its taste.

I watch and follow with my eyes as beads of water slowly roll down his rock-hard-abs, and I'm pretty sure I just licked my lips with a smacking sound that could be heard out on the street.

Niko clears his throat, drawing my eyes back up to his face and that cocksure smirk he always wears. God, he's beautiful. I'm speechless . . . I. Am. So. Screwed!

"Everly," Niko says, but it's the stern, business-like way that he says it that gets my back up. Like he's my boss and I'm late for the first day on the job. Whatever. He's the one opening the door with no clothes on.

"Jesus Christ, Niko! Go put some clothes on for crying out loud!" I'm a flustered mess, caught between wanting to sink to my

COCK sure

knees in front of him or slam my lips against his. The temptation needs to go.

"You're kidding, right?"

"Well, no! You're freaking naked! Do you usually answer your door soaking wet and naked? What if some of your bits and pieces were hanging out? Jesus."

I try to pull myself together, but Niko without clothes is a sin. Niko without clothes and wet . . . I swallow hard and look away.

One side of his lips draw up into a smirk. He's having way too much fun at my expense.

"Some of my bits and pieces? Did you just call my cock and balls *bits and pieces*, Everly?"

"No!"

"Could have sworn I just heard you say just that."

"Well, you heard wrong." I stare him in his eyes because there is no other safe place for me to look right now that doesn't involve looking at his naked, wet skin.

"For your information, I only answered my door, naked, but with all of my bits and pieces covered, because some nut job was pounding on my door, and I thought someone was dying."

"Did you just call me a nut job?"

"Yup. I sure did, but you don't seem to be bleeding or anything, so I'm going to ask you—are you dying, Ev?" His voice is calm and even, a hint of amusement in his tone.

My eyes dart around, trying to look anywhere but at him. "No, I'm not dying! Don't be ridiculous. And I'm not a nut job! I'm not the one streaking my poor unsuspecting neighbors at my front door, Niko."

"You just stomped on my front door like a swat team about to bust it down looking for drugs or some most-wanted convict, Ev."

"I did no such thing! I knocked." He quirks one of his brows up at me, and holy hell is he sexy.

"You knocked, huh?"

"Yes. I knocked. Loudly." He smirks at me and then pulls the door all the way open, waiting.

"Well, then, are you going to stand there all day, or do you want me to traumatize my neighbors with my bits and pieces, formerly known as the beast?"

I snort at the mention of the beast. Not too long ago we were having fun flirting back and forth via text messages and phone sex. Look what that did. That fucking monster knocked me up, and I'm mad at it, so for now, it's bits and pieces to me.

"Make yourself comfortable. I need to rinse the soap out of my hair."

"You're not going to put some clothes on first?"

"Ummm, not before I rinse the soap out of my hair, Ev. I usually do that before I get out of the shower, but well . . . You know why I had to cut my shower short, now, don't you. What's wrong with you? It's not like you haven't seen everything before. Or, you know, worshipped it."

I swallow hard, trying to ignore his comment, and walk in when Niko moves to the side, opening his door wider to let me in. I hear the door close, and then Niko walks past me toward the bathroom where I can hear the shower still running. It's then I get to finally see the tattoo that moves across the back of his shoulders. A large, flying black bird, maybe a crow, is drawn onto his skin, but I can't make it out in the quick glance.

"Well, obviously I've seen all . . ." I wave my hand up and down his body without going near him. ". . . that, but that doesn't mean that I want to talk to you and view all of your anatomical refinements."

"Anatomical refinements?"

"Yes! Anatomical refinements! I came here to talk, Niko. To you, not Mr. Happy there."

"Mr. Happy?"

"Yes! What the hell are you now, a parrot? Jesus! Just finish your shower please, and then put some clothes on. I'll just wait here."

"Ah, yeah, okay then." He eyes me strangely, but then it appears he's holding back a smile. Whatever. I'm here to talk about my future. Our future, and I can't do that with skin showing.

"As I said, make yourself comfortable. I'll be out in a sec." He pulls the towel from his waist as he gets to the door; his cock is half-mast and jumps, causing me to gasp. Just as he turns to close the half-opened door, he winks at me and instead pushes it all the way open so that I can see him through the transparent shower curtain.

"Holy Christ!"

I'm in hormonal overload; my eyes are stuck on the blurred profile of the beast that pumped a baby in me. I swear that it's getting bigger and that the room has turned into an oven.

My tongue swipes across my lips, gaze locked on him. I haven't even sat down, still standing in the same spot, trapped.

I thought I'd known lust in my life, but the feelings I remember are a smoldering ember compared to the inferno created by Niko. He hasn't even touched me, and I'm burning.

And he wants me.

And I want him.

I don't even notice I've stripped out of my T-shirt until I'm unbuttoning my shorts, letting them slide to the ground, flip-flops off with each step toward the man I so desperately need right now. My bra and panties are the final casualties to this lust that's driving my actions.

My brain has stopped and lets my body take over, seeking the only one that can fill every part of my mind, body, and soul.

I pull the curtain to the side, making Niko snap his head toward me. His eyes darken as they trail down my naked body.

"I'm sorry," I say as I step into the shower with him. The water is hot against my skin, and I arch toward him.

"Is this your way of apology?" he asks, his eyes wandering down and back up.

"This is me admitting how much I want you."

He steps forward, hands on my hips as he draws me in, his cock hard and trapped between us. "About fucking time."

His fingers tangle in my hair, fisting it to pull me closer as he presses his lips to mine. There's no asking for permission, his tongue slipping into my mouth. Just his kiss, his tongue against mine, makes me wet.

One of his hands slides between us, then trails down until he's slipping between my legs, his fingers running across my clit. I draw in a sharp breath, my eyes wide as I arch into him.

"I want to take you into the bedroom, throw you on the bed, and hate fuck the shit out of this pussy." His voice is all gravel and sex, his touch possessive and hard.

I blink at him, confused and aroused by what he just said. He moves his hand down further and finds my slick slit. A sharp breath leaves me as he pushes two fingers into me, eyes locked on mine. I wrap my arms around his neck, holding on. He knows what he's doing, where to touch, how to have me struggle for breath in seconds.

"Is this what you want, Everly? Do you want me to make you come? Is that all I'm fucking good for?"

"N-no," I whimper.

"Then what are you apologizing for."

"For being a bitch. For being scared. For thinking you wouldn't want this baby." Tears fill my eyes and his movements slow, his eyes softening.

The hand in my hair lets go and moves across to my face, his thumb wiping away the fallen tears. I'm crying, something I blame on the hormones, and he still has me on the verge of coming.

"Shh, baby. Don't cry. Why would you think that?"

"Because you're not a one-woman kind of man."

He pulls his fingers from me, making me shudder as they graze my clit.

"Even if we aren't together, I would always want to be with my child. And even if I didn't want to be with you, which I do, why would that make you think I wouldn't want to be a father?"

I can't stop the tears, the hiccupping sobs as I hide my eyes behind my hands. This crying can go away. I hate it, and it's all I seem to be doing lately. That and vomiting, which can also stop.

"Because why would you want to deal with me for the rest of their life?"

It's not until this moment that I realize the insecurity that I've been harboring. Inside, I'm still very much the nerdy girl geeking out over her brother's hot best friend.

He doesn't say anything, just stares. It's unnerving, and I'm about to jump out of the shower and get the fuck out of here and away from this situation I've put myself in when he presses his lips to mine and pushes me up against the shower wall.

I cry out from the cold of the tile hitting my warm skin, but he doesn't give me time to adjust as his hands grab onto me and pick me up. My legs wrap around his hips, and I can feel his hard cock between us, its length sliding against my slit.

"You like to pick me up," I say against his mouth.

A chuckle leaves him. "Because you're almost a foot shorter than me. I need those lips closer."

"I think you just like throwing me around."

"Mmm, pocket-sized for my pleasure."

"I'm not that short."

"You are to me."

He continues to slide against me but doesn't enter. "Niko, please . . ."

"What?" He's grinning at me, knowing full well what I want.

"Fill me. Please."

A growl rumbles in his chest. "First, you need to do something for me."

"What?"

"You need to get all negative thoughts out of that head of yours. Or do I need to fuck them out for you to listen to what I've been saying for months."

I stare at him, frozen in excitement, in knowing I want him to make good on his threat.

"Fuck them out it is."

With one thrust, he's inside me, and my head is back against the wall, mouth open.

Fuck.

I can't breathe. Only feel. His thick cock giving me the delicious stretch, filling me completely.

How did I ever think I could turn this down?

"Fuck, baby, I never knew it could feel this good," he says, his teeth scraping along the column of my neck.

"What?"

"Being bare, fucking without a condom," he says the words between thrusts, but I can't help the way they make me squeeze around him, causing an "Oh, fuck" to leave him. They weren't meant to be sexy, but somehow, they were.

"I'm sure you've done it before." With all the women he's fucked, I can't be the only one.

He shakes his head. "No, this is my first time."

"Second," I remind him.

He lets out a groan and smashes his lips against mine.

"This is how we should have made a baby," he says, his hips drilling his cock into me harder.

"Against a shower wall?"

"Sober."

And I understand. This feeling, this all-consuming desire that is all for him, is so powerful. The raw connection of baser instincts.

"I'll make sure you fucking remember how it feels from now on."

He pulls me closer, his head buried in my neck as he presses me harder into the wall. Each thrust seems to go deeper, hit harder. My eyes lose focus as I let go and just feel.

That's all he will let me do. His hands dig into my ass cheeks, his thumbs around my hips as he moves me up and down his shaft in time with his thrust. Pounding, relentless. Over and over until my breath begins to stutter, eyes rolling back as everything tightens, then abruptly snaps.

The screams leaving me are echoing around the small bathroom. As I come down, aftershocks rock me, and guttural moans fill my ears.

I feel each twitch of his cock deep inside me. It's different than before, unrestrained. His chest heaves with each harsh breath that blows across my skin. The air makes the droplets that have cooled move around my skin, causing goose bumps to pop up.

Niko blindly reaches to the side to turn the water off, sliding me across cool patches of tile and making me hiss. The water isn't matched in temperature to the tile, but it's getting there, the heat waning.

Once the water is off, Niko locks eyes with me. He hasn't pulled out.

"That's how I'm going to remember it."

I blink up at him. I'm still coming down, my brain scrambling to catch up. "Remember what?"

He cups my cheek, his thumb running across my lower lip. "How we made our baby."

Once again, the red glare of Niko's bedside clock is the first thing I see when I open my eyes. Shit. It's almost ten thirty at night. I've been with Niko for hours and completely lost track of time. The need to flee kicks in and I turn to look at Niko, who's sleeping soundly next to me.

We never did get to talk.

His hair is all over the place, and I have to hold myself back from caressing his face as he sleeps. I don't want to leave, but I don't know if I should stay either. Slowly, I try to make my way out of bed in search of my clothes in the living room.

Where the hell is my bra?

"Where the fuck do you think you're going?" Niko growls into my ear, making me freeze. His fingers wrap around my waist, pulling me back against his warm chest. "You thinking of running out on me again, Ev? Leaving another fucking Post-it note?"

Was he ever going to let that go? Then again, he didn't really know how dependent I was on the yellow sticky notepads.

"Running? No, not running. It's called leaving. Going home. You know, your usual?"

A growl rumbles through him. I've done it again, thrown his past in his face. It will be a hard habit to break. Why do I keep doing that?

"Nothing has been usual since I met you."

My heart thumps in my chest. Nothing? That makes me happier than it should. I step away and he lets me go, so I lean over to pick up my panties.

"Three months."

"Three months, what?" I ask, securing one flip-flop.

"You're the only woman I've been with in three months, Ev. You're the only one I can get it up for. The only woman I want to get it up for. The only one I even think about."

I stop my search and turn to look at him; his expression is solid. He couldn't be serious, could he? Only me in three months? I know his track record.

"I don't bring women back to my place," he continues, stepping to stand in front of me.

I shake my head. "You brought me home with you."

He pulls me to him, his lips running up the column of my neck, sending tingles across my skin.

"I don't sleep with chicks I fuck."

"You fell asleep with me."

His breath is hot, and his fingers slip around my torso and between my legs.

"I don't stay for breakfast."

I draw in a breath, my back arching as the few articles of clothing I collected fall back to the ground. His fingers dip inside me, rubbing against my clit with each slow, agonizing stroke.

"I don't call, and I don't text women."

"You called and sent me—" He doesn't let me finish, placing his finger to my lips.

"But for you," he says as he pulls me flush to him and grinds his cock against me. "I've broken every one of my rules. You know why?"

My hips move in time with him, a blaze heating me from my core.

"Got an answer for me, Everly?"

"N-no."

"Because you're not just some chick."

"I'm pregnant with your baby."

The thick ridge of his cock rocks against me as his hand grabs my ass, pulling me ever closer.

"Fuck, it's so hot when you say it in that fuck-hot sexy voice."

A whimper claws its way up my throat, escaping in a stuttered, high-pitched, body-shaking consumption. He's assaulting me on multiple fronts, chipping away at the emotional walls I've built to protect myself.

A few more hard strokes of his fingers, then they're gone. He trails his hand up to rest on my abdomen, gaze locked on the spot.

"It's more than my baby growing inside you. Although, I have to tell you, Ev, that makes me feel good as fuck." His eyes find mine. "Like I've marked you, and now you're all mine, but aside from that . . . It's you that's special. From the moment I first saw you, it was just you."

"Just me?" I ask softly and in disbelief.

"Stay. Don't leave. I want you to stay the night with me. Next to me. All night. I want to know you'll be here when I wake up in the morning, Ev. Don't run," he says and then stares at me. Waiting. The uncertain look on his face does me in, and it's then that I decide to let him in.

"Okay," I say as I take his hand, and we walk back into the bedroom.

We climb back into bed, and I lay my head onto his chest. Whatever thoughts I had of leaving and going home are now gone, a feeling of contentment overcoming me.

"I'll stay," I whisper to him.

His arm comes around me, and he squeezes me. My mind keeps repeating everything he just said, and all I can think about is just me and the fact that I'm going to have breakfast with Niko tomorrow.

"I like my bacon crispy."

"Your what?" he asks.

I look up at him. "Breakfast, tomorrow. I want crispy bacon."

He lets out a low chuckle, and I can't help it—I smile too. I'm having breakfast with my cocksure "baby daddy." The boy I crushed on since I was a kid is now very much a man, and I'm sleeping in his bed telling him how I like my bacon. Who would have thought?

"Okay."

Chapter Twenty-Three

Niko

SHE SNUGGLES INTO MY side, her head on my chest, and takes a deep breath before her whole body relaxes.

"I like this Everly. She's honest with what she wants, with how she feels," I say, a content hum vibrating in my chest.

Everly's fingers move across my skin in lazy circles, and I'm almost drunk on how good it feels. "I don't know how to stop," she says.

"Stop what?" For a second I think she's talking about her touch.

She tilts her head back, eyes catching mine. "Being a bitch to you. Not trusting you."

"I guess the question is why? What about me brings that out?" I ask as I run my hand up and down her back.

"You were my childhood crush, and my heart is a broken, untrusting mess right now. I'm scared you just want me for sex, like all the women you've been with, and the first instant I let you in, you'll devastate what's left of me."

Fuck. She's hurt and lashing out, and I end up being the target because there's something between us that I know is more than sex.

"You're not a mess, Ev."

"Yes, I am," she argues. "I'm a broken mess. And it's even worse now."

"You may be broken, baby, but you're not shattered. There is a big difference."

"Maybe, but it's so much more, Niko."

"Because of the baby?" I ask. We never did get to discuss whatever it was she came to talk about.

She nods and gives a little sniffle. "I'm scared."

"There's nothing to be scared of. I'm here with you, and we'll do it together."

I can feel the wetness of a tear slide down my chest, and I take hold of her hand, pulling it up to my lips. A soft kiss while I pull her closer. She's shaking, crying. Vulnerable in front of me for the first time.

"I don't know about babies or what to do. I never babysat. I don't know the first thing about being a mother or about how to let you in."

"I don't have any answers there. The only thing we can do is be there for each other, help each other, and in that, maybe you'll see there's more to me than you think."

"Like what?" she asks. I know she doesn't mean it to hurt, but it still stings how little she seems to know me.

"Like a man who is loyal. Who values family, friendship, and love."

"Friendship . . ." she trails off. "And there is the number three thing that is making me a disaster."

"Cam."

She nods. "I started this by lying to you on a night you were helping out a friend. You were there, waiting for me, doing everything Cam asked of you and I deceived you, but in the end, that won't matter to him. He's going to hate you, and it'll be my fault."

My lips form a thin line. She's a little too honest. I almost wish she would lie to me about Cam's reaction, but I know it's the truth. No matter who started it, the bottom line is I had sex with his sister. Even worse, I got her pregnant after I found out who she was.

I went after her because I wanted her. So much so that I forgot about my promise to my best friend. All I wanted was more time with her.

"It's going to suck when he finds out, I'm not gonna lie. I'm going to get the shit beat out of me."

Everly gasps, her brow furrowed as she looks up at me. "I never meant to hurt either of you. I never wanted that."

I shrug. "I never meant to knock you up. Shit happens."

"That's it? Shit happens?"

"Trust me; I'm not looking forward to a fight with Cam. He's an attack dog when it comes to you, and I am definitely not safe."

"Then let's wait on telling him," she says.

I scrunch my brow as I look down at her. "And keep up the lie that it's your shithead ex's kid?"

She nods. "I don't think I can deal with it right now."

"No, Everly. It's gonna have to be dealt with."

"I know, but give it a few weeks . . . or months."

I heave a sigh and shake my head. "If we wait too long, it's only going to be worse. It's better just to rip this Band-Aid off as soon as possible."

"Please? I promise that we will tell him, just not now. We can tell him together."

"I don't think that's a good idea, but I'll wait a little longer, Ev," I concede.

"Thank—"

"But not much longer," I say, cutting her off. "He needs to know, and it's best if he hears it directly from me."

"I don't know about that, but thank you." She leans over and places a kiss on my chin.

"Everything is going to work itself out, Ev," I say as I pull her tighter just to feel her as close to me as possible. "Try not to stress, and take care of you and our baby. Let me worry about your brother. Okay?"

"Yeah, okay."

"You're what?" I ask into the phone. Everly called at one of the worst fucking times with Cam only a few feet away.

"I'm going to tell my parents this weekend. Cam's going with me," she repeats.

"That's great—I can't wait to hear all about it," I say, sounding a little too cheerful.

There's a whispered, "Fuck," then a loud sigh. "Is he close?"

I step out the back door where a couple of guys are sitting at the picnic table and keep walking until I'm hopefully out of earshot.

"We have the same shift tonight."

"I'm sorry, I should have sent a text first."

"No, it's fine, really," I assure her. The last thing I need is to give her any type of barrier. "I want you to call. Just know if he's nearby, I'll speak in some code until I can get away."

"Are we spies now?" she whispers into the phone. "If so, can I be some sexy, confident femme fatale?"

"Trust me, baby, you're already that."

There's a moment of silence, and I pull my phone back to make sure we're connected. I begin to wonder if I pissed her off somehow when she comes back. "Hold on," she says, her voice a bit strangled.

Total silence takes over, but it shows we're still connected, so I wait. It takes a few minutes, but then she's back.

"Sorry, I didn't want you to listen to that." Her voice is rough.

"Are you okay?"

"Nothing but my regularly scheduled vomit session."

Ah. "Gross."

"And *that* is why I didn't want you to listen."

"Are you able to keep anything down?" I ask. If she's not getting any nutrients, that can't be good for her or the baby.

"A little, but not much."

"That's not good. You should talk to the doctor to see if there's something to help. There has to be." I don't know much about pregnancy, but I know about humans, and we need food to survive.

"I have my first appointment on Tuesday, which is another reason I'm calling."

"I'll be there," I say, not even letting her ask me.

"I haven't even told you what time."

"Doesn't matter. Besides, I have the night shift on Tuesday. And anyway, if I were scheduled, I'd switch with one of the guys."

"Niko . . ."

"Stop, Ev. I *will* be at every single appointment, no matter what."

"Even the checkups?"

"Yes, this is important to me, too. I don't care what I have to do to make sure I'm there, but I will. I told you we'd do this together, and I meant it. All of it."

"You know, you're making it hard not to like you."

A chuckle leaves me. "Good. It's about time you noticed what everyone else knows is fact."

"And what's that?"

The guys at the picnic table are all looking at me, Jenkins is making kissy faces in my direction. I flip them the finger and smirk.

"That Niko Callahan is a god," I say loud enough for the assholes to hear.

There's laughter, and I can hear a banging. "A god?"

"Baby, don't even try to bring me down. You can't. You've prayed for me, and I'll make you pray again and again. You'll worship me on your knees."

"Cocky fuck."

"Sure am."

She lets out the cutest giggle. "I'll text you the information for the appointment."

"Thanks."

"Oh, and Niko?" she says just as I'm about to hang up.

"Yeah?"

"Stay safe, okay? I need you." The way her voice wavers is like a knife in my chest. Reminders of the dangers of my job suddenly mean more, make me want to be more cautious and less gung-ho because now I have someone who needs me. I have two who need me.

"Always. Good luck tomorrow."

"Gym tomorrow?" I ask Cam, knowing full well he has plans. Fuck, I hate this lying shit, but Ev needs some time, so I'll give it to her, but not too much.

He shakes his head. "Sorry, man, got a family thing. Lunch with a side of revelation."

I scrunch my brow. "Revelation?"

"Everly's telling Mom and Dad."

I clap my hand down on his shoulder. "Better you than me." And that's the truth. Then again, I can see his parents handling the news a lot better than Cam will.

"Why the fuck couldn't you have a little sister so you could understand my pain?" he grumbles.

"I've got sixteen cousins, nine of them boys that ask the same thing."

"Ah, the Callahan clan."

I punch his shoulder. "Dipshit, we're Irish, not Scottish."

"No, *they* are Irish. You're only half." I shake my head at him because he's an idiot. "So how do family reunions and holidays go? Do you bring baklava to serve with the boiled corn beef and cabbage?"

"Asshole. You know, you've been ragging on me a lot lately. Are you not getting attention down south? Ya boys lonely?"

"Oh, I'm getting lots of action, unlike your celibate ass."

"Yeah, okay. If you say so, Cam."

"Which reminds me, can Niko come out and play tomorrow night? I need to let off some steam."

I shake my head. "Such a jackass, and no, I can't."

Cam blows out a breath. "You were so much cooler when you were single. Come on, we've got the alarm inspection to do."

I get up and follow behind him. This is how our relationship has always been, and I want to keep it that way. But he needs to know about Everly and me. The sooner, the better.

Chapter Twenty-Four

Everly

TELLING MY MOM AND Dad that I am pregnant is awful. I feel like a teenager. Just getting the words past my lips is the most strenuous thing I've ever done. Sitting across the table from them, watching their faces go blank in shock.

"I don't understand," Mom says, blinking at me. Apparently, she doesn't like the idea of being a grandmother yet. I thought, "I'm pregnant," was pretty clear.

"What is there not to understand, Linda? Our daughter is pregnant."

She shakes her head. "I spent years drilling into your head safe sex."

"Mom, it happened, and I'm not a teenager. I'm twenty-five, have a successful career, and own my own home. You and Dad were younger than I am now when you had Cameron. I was on birth control but didn't use a condom. It's rare, but it happens." Not lies. I was on birth control, and that was my fault. The condoms, however, were an oops that shouldn't have happened.

"Watch it, Everly. We were also married when we had your brother. You've just told us that our only daughter, our very single daughter, is pregnant with her first child after abruptly moving across the country with no warning, selling her home there and buying a new one here, and taking a new job. Excuse your mother for being a little shell-shocked as this is a lot to take in. We expected Cameron to come home one day and tell us he got some poor young lady pregnant, but never did we expect this news from you." I knew my dad would feel this way, so I'm not saying anything because he is right.

"Is it Tate's?" Mom asks, her brow scrunched.

I steal a glance at Cam who quirks a brow at me. He doesn't believe me, and with good reason. The problem is, I can't tell anyone who the father is right now.

"I'm not with the father, but that doesn't matter. I'm perfectly capable of taking care of a child on my own. I just wanted you to know."

"Of course it matters! Everly, he has a right to know that he has a child coming. Is that why you came home?" my mother asks, but my father just stares over my shoulder looking out of the window behind me.

I shake my head. "No. I left because Tate was a lying, cheating piece of pond scum, and I had to get away."

"He's harassing her." That has my father's attention. He turns and looks at me and then my brother.

"Cam!" I hiss, glaring at my brother. His intentions are good but unnecessary. Tate is harmless, just annoying.

"Do we need to get the lawyer on the phone? File a restraining order? He has a legal right, but he has legal obligations as well. We can get our attorney on this right away. He won't have a chance in hell if he's harassing you while you're pregnant."

I roll my eyes. "A restraining order? Dad, he's over three thousand miles away. He's just a pest. It will die down."

"Ev, it's been over three months. How often is he contacting you?" Cam asks, and I want to kick him.

My phone chooses that second to go off, and I let out a groan and look up at the ceiling.

Thanks, Tate, you fucking asshole.

Cam picks up my phone and turns the screen toward my parents. "Speak of the asshole," he says and presses the green button on my phone, accepting the call. "Hello, Tate."

"Cameron!" I whisper-yell, trying to grab my phone from his hands. I can hear the tone of Tate's voice, but I can't hear what he's saying.

"No, asshole. This is her brother, not that it would be any of your damn business who the fuck answers her phone. You lost that right when you fucked around on my sister," he says, and again, I can hear Tate saying something, but I can't hear what his reply is.

I'm sure it's bullshit, but I still want to hear.

"Never mind all that shit. Save that BS for someone who doesn't know shit when they hear it. Listen up, Tate, and listen good, because I'm only going to warn you once. Stay the fuck away from my sister. Don't call, don't text, don't fucking email. She's done with you. I know she's told you because I've seen the text messages she sent you saying just that." Cam's eyes find mine, and he stares straight at me. "She doesn't need the stress on top of being pregnant, so do us all a favor and cut the shit. When she decides to talk to you, she'll contact you. Until then, fuck off, asshole!"

He is still staring straight at me as he pulls the phone away and hits end call, holding the phone out to me. I can feel the blood drain from my face in horror before it floods back in from anger.

"Cameron! What did you just do?" Oh my God. He just told Tate that I'm pregnant. He's going to think this baby is his! "I can't believe you just did that." I drop my head into my hands. Jesus . . . He just opened a whole new can of worms now.

Worst of all, Cameron is daring me to call him a liar, and I don't flinch. Not that I have any reason to. He told Tate that I'm pregnant, nothing about Tate being the father.

"This is ridiculous. We're going to change your number. Right now," Dad says.

I shake my head. "Dad, I did that a few weeks after I moved here, remember? It didn't do any good. Within a week he got ahold of the new number. Probably from one of my friends who believed his bullshit and felt sorry for him."

"Then we'll get you a number under our plan."

"Richard, we can't do that. He's the father of our grandchild." Mom turns to me. "You are going to give him a chance to fix things, right?"

I shake my head almost vehemently. "No."

"The financial damage alone, Mom," Cam says. "He knows how much money she has, and I would not put it past him to extort money."

As much as I hate to admit it, Cam's right. It would get ugly, and he would use the child as a pawn.

What am I saying? I'm beginning to believe what they believe, that Tate is the father. What the hell did I just get myself into? This isn't good. This is getting worse by the second.

"He knows how much money you have? What does that mean?" Dad asks, his eyes wide.

I hold my hands up. "He knows I have a trust fund, but not the amount. But, Dad, I make six figures, which is about twice what he makes."

"She can leave the father part of the birth certificate blank; they're not married. She has no obligation to list him," Cam suggests.

Dad's eyes go wide, and he looks to Mom. Doing that spells scandal. People would find out, would talk.

My head is killing me, and the stress of the situation is taking its toll. I'm almost to the point of screaming out, "Niko is the father, all right? Nikolas Callahan fucked me one night after a few too many drinks." However, that wouldn't do any good right now. It would only make this conversation worse.

"When is the baby due?" Mom asks after a minute of silence.

"Um, March first."

Mom blinks and looks at me. Stares at me more like it, her fingers ticking on the table. She's counting, and I realize the problem with my lie.

The numbers don't match.

I lock eyes with her, pleading not to ask, not to question.

She purses her lips and gives a little nod. "Well, that leaves us plenty of time to figure out how to handle the situation."

Dad slams his hands on the table before pushing his chair back. "Cameron, let's go make a drink."

Cam and I exchange looks before he pulls back and follows Dad to the parlor where his cognac supply is.

Oh, boy.

We watch them head down the hall before Mom gets up and sits in the chair next to me. "Everly, who is the father?" Mom asks in a whisper, making sure Dad and Cam are out of earshot.

I shake my head. "I can't tell you. Not yet."

"Everly."

"Please," I stress. "I'll tell you, I just can't right now."

She nods and wraps her arms around me. "I love you, sweetheart."

"Love you too, Mom."

She pulls back, a forced smile below her worry-filled eyes. "Well, what's done is done, so now we need to get ready for the coming bundle of joy." A sharp "Oh!" combined with her eyes going wide and her mouth popping open means only one thing, and probably a lot of money. "We can get Clara Langley, you remember her, right? She designed your cousin Kiki's wedding. Anyway, she's a party planner, and I just love how she handled the wedding. After that, Sarah McMillan hired her for their annual season-opening party down the cape, and it was to die for."

"Mom, seriously? I haven't lived here in almost eight years."

She blinks at me. "That doesn't mean we don't have family or friends we want to invite."

"Your socialite is screaming."

"Oh, hush," she says with a roll of her eyes. "Just answer me this . . . is there going to be an issue with the father?"

I shake my head. "No. He surprised me. He was angry when I told him he didn't need to be involved."

"Really? Do you love this man?"

I roll my eyes. "Mom."

"I'm just asking."

"It's complicated right now, and maybe in a few months it won't be so complicated."

That seems to appease her, and for the first time since I told her our family is expanding, a genuine smile lights up her face. "All right, well . . . Where are you going to put the baby's room?"

"It's a good thing I bought a three bedroom."

It's been a stressful, annoying, lie-filled day, and I'm exhausted. This feeling of ick and disgust is why I hate lying. The only reason I'm doing it is for Niko's sake. Not entirely accurate, but mostly. He's the one who will be damaged the most when it comes out.

"Oh, hi, Everly," Grant says as he exits the door not ten feet from my own.

"Hey, how's it going?"

He nods, and I can hear Jojo whining on the other side of the door. It's been a few years since I shared a wall with someone. "Good. You?"

"Not bad. About to rescue your dog and take her upstairs for a snuggle."

He laughs, a sound that warms me. It's smooth, natural. The fact that he's handsome and sexy only adds to his appeal, but it doesn't escape my mind that he doesn't hold a candle, in my mind or body, to Niko.

"Without me?" he asks, a shy smile on his lips that makes me miss the cocky one I dream of.

"Girls' sleepover. No boys allowed," I say. It's the gentlest way I can turn him down. My life is way too complicated right now to even entertain the idea of being with Grant. He's the safe one, but I don't want safe. I want cocky.

Grey eyes, muscular arms, tattoos, and lips that make me weak.

He nods. "Well, I better get going. Have to pick up Ella. Good seeing you."

"You too."

He jogs down the steps, then turns back. "Oh, I almost forgot, I'm having a party next weekend. Would love for you to come."

I give him a polite smile and nod. "Sounds great. Text me the details."

The second I'm through the door, I blow out a breath, lock the door again, and trudge my tired ass upstairs. The exhaustion sweeping me has been intense lately, coming in waves. More than once this week I found my head against my desk mid-afternoon and have been scared out of my mind when my phone rang, or someone knocked on my door, startling me awake.

Then there's the vomiting. I'm so tired of having my head stuck in the toilet or sink or trash can. I've lost five pounds in the last two weeks because I can't keep any food down. Dry heaves are the worst. I thought it was called morning sickness, not all the damn time of the day sickness.

It sucks. I just want to curl into a ball, pull the blankets over my head, and sleep until it goes away. I do just that when I hear my doorbell ring. I let out a groan and ignore it. No way am I getting up. I finally feel like I can fall asleep without puking myself awake.

The bell rings again, followed by knocking. I take a deep breath in and pull myself up into a sitting position, waiting for the dizziness to pass. It doesn't seem like whoever is at my door is going away. I toss my legs to the side of the bed and pull myself up.

I don't feel so bad right now, and so I make my way slowly downstairs to the door. I see his silhouette and know right away who it is. Even though I know it's him, I'm still never prepared to see him, and as usual, my heart races along with those butterflies I get in my stomach that has nothing to do with morning sickness.

"Niko? What are you doing here?" I ask.

He pulls his arms up with a multitude of bags hanging from his hands. "Dinner."

I open the door and let him by. Was this planned and I forgot? Did he message me? I'm tired and confused and, after the day I've had, not sure if I'm happy or annoyed that he showed up possibly unannounced.

"Seriously? What is all this?"

"Well, I didn't know what you'd be craving, so I kind of just bought a little of everything."

I can't help the way my lips draw up. It's sweet. It really is. Niko is trying; he's just a little too early in the process for crazy food cravings.

"Thank you."

He beams at me. "You're welcome."

"I'm not sure I can eat right now, but you can eat."

"Why?" He tilts his head to the side, inspecting me. A look of concern crossing his handsome face. "Now that you mention it, you look pale, Ev. You okay?'

"I think so. They say it will pass hopefully once I'm out of my first trimester."

"What will? Looking like you're dying? Whatever is going on, it can't be good for you or the baby. You look really pale."

"Gee, thanks!"

"I don't mean it like that, babe, but you look like you feel terrible. If you're not going to go in, at least eat something light?"

"Yeah, maybe," I concede before leaning over to look into the bags. "What did you bring?"

He smiles and starts pulling containers from the bags he set down.

"I've got a little of everything. Wasn't sure what you'd be craving, so I even brought pickles and ice cream. Neapolitan, so you can pick a flavor." He lets out a laugh.

"Pickles? That doesn't sound good with ice cream, Niko."

"What? I thought all pregnant women liked pickles?"

"I don't know about all women, but that doesn't sound appealing at all. It sounds pretty gross." I hold my hand over my mouth. "Yeah, no to the pickles and ice cream."

"Okay. It's gone," he says, throwing the pickles back in the bag and slipping the ice cream into the freezer. "Noted. Just don't puke because I'll likely throw up with you."

That makes me giggle. I start to walk to the kitchen, but my bell rings again. Who could that be? Then it hits me.

Oh shit! "What if it's Cam? Go hide!"

"Everly . . ."

"Please?" I plead. He blows out a puff of air before conceding.

"I'll go this time, but Everly, he needs to be told. This is my kid too. Things are different now, and I don't want him to find out from anyone else. It's only going to make things worse."

"I know. We'll tell him. Just not yet, okay?" He doesn't say anything, just walks from the room. I turn and go to my front doorway, but when I get there, I see that it's not Cam, it's Grant. I open the door to Grant and find his daughter, Ella, standing beside him, a wry smile on her dad's face as he rubs the back of his neck.

"Ah hey, Everly. Did I catch you at a bad time?"

"Hi! Can you have dinner with us? We're making burgers on the grill, and Daddy burns them."

I laugh at the little girl's straightforwardness. "Hi Ella, right?"

"Yes, and you're Everly. Daddy said we could ask you to come over for our cookout. Can you come over? I just got a new Pinkie Pie. You can play with it if you want to."

"Pinkie Pie?"

"It's a toy horse. My Little Pony. She's addicted to the show, and the dolls." He rubs the top of Ella's head, and I have to admit, the two of them are cute. It's evident to me that little Miss Ella has her dad wrapped around her finger.

"Ahh, I see. Well, I'm delighted that you would trust me with your pinkie pie, Ella, but I'm afraid I'm not feeling very well today, so I've been resting this afternoon. I only just got up a few minutes ago actually."

Her little face falls, but then she looks up at her dad before speaking again. "That's okay. I can bring my Pinkie Pie over for you. She always makes me feel better when I have a belly ache. Daddy says she's got magic."

"Oh, no, sweetie. I wouldn't take your new toy, but thank you for offering. I feel special that you would let me borrow your favorite new toy."

"Not that one. My first Pinkie Pie. The one that my mommy gave me. Daddy says that because she gave it to me, that she gave it her magic before she died, and now Pinkie Pie watches over me so that when I'm not feeling good, I'm not alone."

COCK sure

Oh my God, her mom died? How awful. She's so young. I look up to Grant who looks away, but it's brief. He changes the subject quickly, and I know that he's not willing to say anything. Well, that explains where her mother is. I crouch down in front of her so that I'm eye level with the little girl who sounds much older than her six years of age, and I try not to fall over.

"I bet your mommy would be very proud of the fact that you were extra kind to me knowing I didn't feel well, but I think I'll be okay. So you just hold onto that treasure your mom left for you, and maybe, when I'm feeling a little better, we can have another cookout. How does that sound?"

Ella's face lights up, and her colossal smile takes up almost her entire bottom half of her face. She's beautiful. Grant is going to have his hands full with her once the boys start knocking.

"That sounds good. Yay, Daddy! She's going to eat over at our house when she feels better. That's okay, right, Daddy?"

"Sure, sweet pea. Why don't we let Everly get some rest, though, and we can start the grill. Then you and I can take Jojo for her walk after dinner. Sound good?"

"You're gonna have to give Jojo something else, Daddy. She didn't like your burgers last time either."

"Your burgers sound rough, neighbor." I laugh, then look back at Ella who's holding her dad's hand now. "I'll see what I can do when we have our cookout. I might even have some treats for Jojo when I come by."

"I'm going to tell her! She knows what treats are. She shakes her tail." Ella wiggles her butt to emulate Jojo. "Daddy says that means she's happy to see us or she's just excited for food. Do you have a dog too?"

"Ella . . ."

"It's fine. No, sweetie. No dogs yet. My parents have dogs, though. I love them, but my mom won't let me keep them, so I just visit."

"Oh." She looks as if she's contemplating her next question, but Grant picks her up.

"Well, I'm sorry you aren't feeling well. Let me know if you need anything. I'm just next door. I'm going to take her home and feed her before she talks your ear off."

I laugh again and stand up now that Ella is almost eye to eye with me while she's in her dad's arms.

"Let us know what day next week you are available. I'll buy the meat if you promise to cook it. Ella's not lying about my cooking skills. I'm terrible, but I'm getting better."

"Hey. At least you try. My brother couldn't even boil water when he moved out of my parents' house. Pretty sure he's still the take-out king. You at least get an A for effort. I'm sure it's not that bad." He scrunches his nose up, and it's cute. I immediately wonder how Niko will be once our child is here. Oh crap! Niko!

"Well, thank you for inviting me. See you later, Ella."

"Mmmm hmmm, Daddy, can we go walk Jojo now?" He shakes his head at her and then smiles at me as he heads for the stairs.

"Hope you feel better, Everly. Talk to you soon?"

"Oh yeah. I'll remind myself to look at my schedule. Thank you!" I yell and close the door.

I pad down the hall and find Niko leaning against the kitchen island. His arms are crossed in front of him, and there is a scowl plastered on his face. Ignoring him, I pull out a pad of Post-its and write a note, sticking it to the fridge. Out of the corner of my eye, I see Niko shake his head.

"Happy to see I'm not the only one who gets the star treatment."

I quirk my brow at him. "Never going to let that go, are you?"

He shakes his head, then gestures toward the front door. "Who was that guy you were talking to?"

I scrunch my brow. Guy? "You mean Grant?" I roll my eyes as I glance over to Niko and his steely gaze. "He's my neighbor. You know, the owner of the other half of this building."

"He seems friendly."

I cock my hip to the side and lean against the counter. "Really?"

"What?"

"Niko, we're not in a relationship," I remind him. "You're not allowed to be jealous."

COCK sure

"You're carrying my kid," he says as if that's enough.

"And he has a kid that was at the door with him."

"What's your point? He was totally using the kid to make his move on you. Does he know that you are carrying my kid?"

I match his stance, arms laced in front of me, and I let out a huff. "It may be your kid, but I'm not yours. You just charge over here without calling, expecting me to be free. What if I had a guy over? What if I had Grant over?"

His eyes narrow and rounds the corner, towering over me in a flash, his hand slipping between my thighs, making me gasp.

"Oh, Ev, you know it's only me who makes you feel this way. My cock makes you come so good. And weren't you going to stop acting like an ice queen, and stop pushing me away?"

My whole body slouches. "I'm sorry. Sometimes I feel like I'm two people lately, maybe three."

His hand moves around my hip, and he pulls me closer. "You know how you can make it up to me?"

"On my knees?"

His tongue swipes across his lips. "Oh, baby, that's one way and so fucking tempting right now." He groans, his eyes heavy as he reaches to adjust his cock. "You distracted me, and as much as I'd love to fuck your mouth, I want you to see that there is more to this than just sex. What you can do to make it up to me is agree to go out to dinner with me on Tuesday."

"I suppose I could do that, but what if I start feeling bad?"

He steps even closer, his hand slipping around my waist, his body pressing against mine. I reach out and rest my hand against his chest, feeling the hard, taut muscle beneath his shirt.

"We can play it by ear. I'll be here, no matter what. You'll agree to let me help and take care of you if that happens, and then you'll agree to be mine and stop this shit about other guys as an attempt to push me away."

Heat spreads through my body, and I can't help running my hands over his chest, around his shoulders and up around his neck. Everything about him is hypnotic.

"Okay."

"Okay, what?"

"Okay, I'll be yours."

He leans down, his lips ghosting mine. "About fucking time." He growls before devouring my mouth, and I forget everything else but Niko.

Chapter Twenty-Five

Niko

EVERLY: TOO BAD YOU can't be here for dinner. That's the message attached to a photo of a large pot of chicken and dumplings Everly is making.

For the first time in a long time, I wish I had weekends off. Not that I work every weekend, but when my girl says she's making chicken and dumplings and is sexy as fuck, it's hard to be away from her. She said she was feeling better today, but it seems to come in waves. At least she's been able to eat a little more lately now that she's in the second trimester.

It's only been a month, but she's officially mine. The dinner date didn't happen, thanks to our baby, so we did Netflix while resisting the chill part. In the end, the chill part went down. I can only resist her sexy body against mine for so long. There are still things we need to work out and things her non-trusting ass needs to work on, but at least she's finally let me in.

Since then, we've kept it pretty low key, just getting to know one another better.

Niko: Tease. Save me some. I'll be over as soon as I can. Don't eat it all! I type back.

Everly: Hey! I'm eating for two. We'll try and save you some, but I make no promises, Daddy. ;)

Niko: You calling me daddy does shit to me. Don't do that while I'm at work and I can't do anything about it. :/

Fuck! I'm not kidding. I like the sound of that. Not only from her, but I'm finally settling into the fact that I'm going to be a father. I want to be around her more not less, but with her working, my crazy schedule, and the fact that Cam doesn't know about us yet makes seeing her even harder.

This downtime is killing me. While no fires or accidents are good, there's only so much work we can do around the firehouse before it's all done. Which is why I'm sitting in this recliner, watching a Patriots preseason game for a few minutes. It's also an excuse to get out of the kitchen while Ferrell cooks his shit. We need to buy the guy some cooking lessons. He burns everything.

My phone buzzes with another notification, and it takes a moment for the pic to come through. The second it does, I let out a groan, my head falling back against the chair as my dick wakes up. It's another picture of the chicken and dumplings, and it's not in the pot. She has her shirt off, her bra lifting her tits up just right, and there's a trail of creamy sauce and dumplings pooling and sliding around her cleavage. This woman is going to be the death of me.

Everly: Oops.

Oops?

Niko: You're a cruel woman. I type back.

Fucking dumpling tease. I'll show her. Granted, my shift isn't over for seven more hours.

Everly: I showed you mine, you show me yours.

I look down at the text. She couldn't be fucking serious, could she? Then again, it wouldn't be the first dick pic I've sent her.

My dick is more than excited to participate. I look up and glance around. The room is empty, so I grab onto the waistband of my pants, letting my cock free. It's an adjustment to get in the right position, and I snap a pic.

"Dude, are you taking a dick pic?" Cam asks from the door.

I jump, the waistband snapping against my shaft right as my thumb presses the send button. "Motherfucker," I hiss and cup my poor cock. "Asshole."

Cam's head is back as he lets out a loud laugh. "Shit, that was priceless." I narrow my eyes at him and flip him my middle finger. "Still your mystery chick? It's been months, man. Am I ever going to meet her?"

I nod, knowing I need to tell him the truth. It's bad enough I'm lying to my best friend, that I did something I swore to him I wouldn't do, but we've stretched it out even further than I'd like. Lying isn't my thing.

"Not yet. I'm still getting used to this one-woman thing."

Cam nods and pats my shoulder. "I get you. How's it going?"

Another lie or omission is coming as I scramble for a response. On one hand, it's going great, but Cam wasn't kidding about the fucking mountain to climb to gain her trust. Then add in the baby growing inside her that I can't even tell him about because then I know he'll put two and two together.

"Our schedules make it hard to go out much, so it's more indoor time."

"Sleepovers," he says with a wink. "I'm just glad you found her."

Found her. Fucked her. Got your baby sister pregnant.

Fuck my life.

Usually it wouldn't be an issue, but when Cam finds out he met her twenty-five years ago, there's going to be a fight. As much as I want to tell him, I can't. I promised Everly. Plus, we agreed to be together when we tell him.

Fuck, I can't even tell my best friend I'm going to be a father. How excited and scared I am. How I'm falling in love with the mother of my child. Isn't that what best friends are for?

I need to talk to Everly. We have to figure out how to tell him, and soon.

"Me too. She's got some issues, but I want her and want to help her get over them."

"That's awesome, man. Really. I'm happy for you. Am I ever going to get this chick's name?"

I stare at my phone and the new message from Everly, but the name at the top doesn't match. My phone still shows the name Alyson.

Everly: Now who's the tease?

"Alyson," I say and turn the phone toward him. He shudders and then screws his face in disgust.

"Dude, I did not need to see your dick pic."

I turn it back around and roll my eyes. "That wasn't what I was doing."

"Maybe not, but it's there, on the screen, staring at me."

I roll my eyes at him. "Whatever."

"So, Alyson? Ugh, that name reminds me of the royal Payne. I mean, Everly's best friend. Jesus, I hope it's not her, just saying. Though she is kind of your type."

"What's she look like?"

"Curly brown hair, chipmunk cheeks, olive green eyes, and big red lips. She's got a big rack and, this is hard for me to say, banging legs. Her last name is Payne, and it fits her because she is a pain in the ass."

I laugh. "Nope, not her."

"For the best. That chick is going to drive some unlucky bastard to drink." He shudders as if the thought alone scares him.

"Don't most women?" I shake my head and smile.

Cam chuckles. "Touché, my friend!" He stands and holds a clipboard up to his chest. "Put your dick away and come on. We've got to do a vehicle inspection and then some prep work for the BC inspection next week when we're done."

"We're doing that with Tomlinson from Ladder Two, right?"

Cam nods.

"All right, give me a sec, and I'll be down."

"Hurry up, Romeo." he says as he leaves the room. I sit for a minute thinking about how things are probably going to change between Cam and me. God, this is fucked.

Picking my phone back up, I shoot a text off to Ev.

Niko: *Terrific! Your brother just walked in on me sending you a dick pic.*
Everly: *OH MY GOD!*
Niko: *Yeah . . .*
Everly: *What did you tell him?*
Niko: *What do you think I told him?*
Everly: *I don't know. That you are doing phone sex as a side job? It's not like I know what the normal protocol is when your friends walk in on each other sending dirty text messages. LOL*
Niko: *There isn't one, and it's not funny. We need to tell Cam. He's asking me questions about you, and I hate not telling him the truth.*

She isn't taking this situation as seriously as I am. She's scared, and I get that, but I don't want Cam to hate me even more than he already will by drawing this out.

My phone rings. I answer it, seeing that it's her. "I can't talk. I've got something I need to do here at work." There's more aggravation in my tone than I intend, but I don't like this situation we've created.

"Oh, then why are you answering if you are heading out on a run—isn't that against the rules?"

"It's not a run. It's something we have to do here. Not emergency related, or I wouldn't have taken the call." I can hear the edge still in my voice. Usually I'm happy to have her call, but my mood soured, and I'm apparently taking it out on her.

"Oh, okay," she says, and I can hear the uncertainty and hurt. Fuck. "So, can you talk for a second?"

"Yeah, but that's all I have is a second."

"What was Cam asking you about me?"

"He didn't know it was you that we were talking about, but he knows that I'm involved with someone, and he wants to meet her."

"Oh, thank God!" She lets out a relieved sigh. "I thought he suspected something and was being an ass to you."

"No, but I don't like this. I want to tell him, and I want to tell him as soon as possible, Ev. I'm not a liar, and he's my best friend. I can't even share that I'm about to become a father."

"I know. I know, and we will. I just wanted to adjust to us being an us first before we bring my brother into the mix, you know?"

I blow out a breath and rub my face. "Yeah, I get that. I understand and want that too, but at the same time, I don't want to lose my best friend. Cam is more than that. He's like my brother. Blood or not, losing him as a friend is going to kill me."

"You're not going to lose Cam," she says with certainty. "He's going to be mad, I'm sure, but he'll get over it."

"Do you know your brother at all, Ev? He hates liars just as much as I do. He would probably get over this, but he won't trust me anymore because we are lying to him about us. I know you want to wait, but it can't. Find the time for us to sit down with him or I'm going to do it alone, but he needs to know."

"Okay. Soon, but just give me a little more time."

"Everly, it's been over a month."

"I promise. Soon."

There's silence between us. "I have to go."

"Call me later?"

"Yeah. I'll try. If not, then I'll text you. He's on tonight."

"Okay. Stay safe, Niko." It's there again, stronger this time, the hurt and uncertainty.

"Ev, I'm not mad," I tell her, unable to stand that fucking tone in her voice. "I'm just frustrated. Okay?"

"Okay," she says, but I can still hear it.

"Get some rest, and I'll call you when I get off."

A final goodbye, and I end the call. I close my eyes and blow out a breath. When I open them, I see Bishop standing in the doorway, looking at me.

"I'm working on it, okay?"

His eyes lock on mine, then he nods before turning back into the other room.

If there was any doubt in his mind that there might not be anything between Everly and me, I just gave him every confirmation he needed.

Chapter Twenty-Six

Everly

"EVERLY?"

The sound of my name makes me blink, but I can't pull my head up from my desk.

"Everly, are you okay?"

"That's a two-sided answer. No, I'm not okay, but yes, I'm fine."

"What does that mean?"

I slowly sit up and look up at my assistant. "Lance, if you just started a new position, how long would you wait to tell them . . . God, I'm going to throw up again."

"Do you need another trash can?"

I swallow it back.

"Everly, are you sure you're okay? I know I've only worked for you for a few months, but I think we've gotten to know each other in that time. I'd like to think we've grown to a level of friendship."

I blow out a breath and nod. "I'm pregnant."

He blinks at me. "Well, it's not mine."

A chuckle springs from me and the first smile all day. "Thanks, I needed that."

"Being pregnant does explain some things. Do you want to talk about it?" he asks.

"I suppose it's going to be noticeable soon."

"Well, you've lost weight, so you have some time before it becomes too noticeable, right?"

Lance must be more observant than he lets on to notice I've lost weight. "I'm not sure it works that way. Besides, I've started to gain the weight back, and it's all in my stomach. Right now is the first time all week that I've had an issue."

"How . . ." He scrunches his brow. "How pregnant are you?"

Another chuckle crawls out. Such a man question. "One hundred percent pregnant. Forty-five percent uploaded."

His lips pull up into a smile. "Numbers I can understand."

"I'm due March first."

He nods. "That is a predicament, especially with the fiscal year end being April first. However . . . Can I be honest with you?"

"I would prefer it."

"They wanted you pretty badly at this location. They waited a year and would have waited longer. While they may not like you taking time off less than a year after your transfer, I can't see it being an issue. Truthfully, if it were, you could sue the shit out of them. One thing I know for sure is they don't discriminate. That is in your favor. I say just be honest and tell them soon. Give them plenty of time to find someone to cover you while you're out on maternity leave."

"Yes. I think you're right. I'm going to tell them. Sooner rather than later. Thanks, Lance."

"You're very welcome." He looks over at me, and I see sympathy. "Do you need anything else while I'm still here?"

"No. I'm not going to be here much longer anyway. You can head out now if you're done for the day."

"You sure?"

"Positive. See you in the morning." I wave him off.

"Okay. Don't stay too long. You look tired."

"Not you, too," I say with a laugh.

He puts his hands up and backs out of my office door. "Good night, Everly."

I need to pack it up. He's probably right about how I look. I feel tired. I just want to go home and put my feet up and relax.

Screw it. I'm going home now to do just that. I wonder what Niko is doing? Maybe I can get him to bring me something yummy. Hopefully him. I haven't seen him in days, and I miss him. As much as I've tried to fight it, to fight falling completely head over heels for him, I don't want to anymore. At least not tonight.

As the weeks pass I continue to stay in my Niko bubble, refusing to accept what I know needs to be done. I've kept Niko from telling Cam for two months now, and I hate myself for it. I'm being selfish and I know it, but I just can't stand the thought of Cam hating Niko. It kills me to think Niko could lose his best friend because of me. Which is an emotion I can't handle right now on top of everything else.

It's also because I'm still hesitant, still afraid that Niko doesn't really want me. We've been so happy, but when that strain on his friendship comes, where will that leave us? Will he blame me and leave?

The scenarios pop up unbidden and send me into a panic. I don't want to lose either of them. I want to hold onto this for as long as I can.

Before I could even text Niko, he messaged me to say he was heading over at seven. Five minutes till, I pull my door open and the sight that greets me leaves me feeling all kinds of want. God, I'm in trouble, but I don't care.

"Hi," I say. I can't help the smile the covers my face when I see him at my door, the way my heart speeds up when he gives me that cocky smirk.

"Baby, you look good enough to eat."

I roll my eyes as I step aside to let him in. "When are you going to let the dessert thing go?"

"You will always be my favorite dessert."

I shake my head. "Corny."

He slips his hands around my waist. "Corny? What do you have that tops that?"

"I missed you."

His smile falters, then his eyes soften. "You win."

"I really did miss you," I say.

"I know."

I purse my lips and slap my hands against his pecs. "Don't Han Solo me."

He leans down and presses his forehead to mine. "I really missed you, too." He blows out a breath. "In fact, I propose no more three-day droughts."

I link my fingers with his and pull him, walking backward toward the kitchen. "Sadly, it's the reality of your work schedule, but I have a solution."

"Oh yeah? Will I like this solution of yours?" His eyes widen. "Does it include you on all fours?"

A giggle escapes me. The man always has sex on his mind.

"Not exactly, but I guess it could lead to that, and other things like early morning or very late night wake-up calls." I hold out my hand to Niko who is now looking at my hand with his head tilted to the side.

"What is this?"

I can feel the heat flood my face. "Um, the key to my front door."

"Why?"

I look up at him, my heart slamming in my chest. Did I make a mistake? Shit. Did I read into us wrong somewhere? I thought I was what he wanted. "Because you're my boyfriend and I think you should have one."

He stares at me, and I'm completely confused on what he's thinking.

"You are so fucking adorable when you're acting shy."

I let out a relieved breath that I didn't realize I was holding. Looking down to the floor, I hook my fingers into his waistband and pull him closer. "Shut up."

He slips his finger under my chin and tilts it up, his bright grey eyes boring into me. "Thank you. I've never . . . this really means a lot, Everly."

I'm dumbstruck as I stare into his eyes. Why do I always doubt him? Why do I still think the worst? Is it because I doubt his sincerity due to his past relationship record or because I have doubts that he genuinely wants me?

"What time am I picking you up tomorrow?" he asks.

"Picking me up?" I ask, confused. "Why would you be picking me up?"

"You have your ultrasound tomorrow, right? I didn't screw up the date, did I? I could have sworn it was tomorrow afternoon."

I blink at him. "No. It's tomorrow, but I just figured you'd meet me there."

"Everly, we're going to see our kid tomorrow. I don't know about you, but I'm nervous as fuck. I figured we could grab lunch first and then head over to your appointment."

"I didn't take the whole day off from work. I still have a meeting that I need to go to first thing in the morning and then a conference call right before I can leave. I figured half the day was better than nothing, so I'm going to leave from work."

"That works too. I can check out my baby mama's fancy office," he says.

I roll my eyes. "I hate that saying."

He ignores me and continues. "Maybe if you're good, I'll come christen your desk. We can play dirty boss and sexy secretary. I'll take your calls while you blow me under your desk."

"Wow! Sounds tempting, but I don't want to traumatize my real assistant so early. I think he might stop bringing me lunch when I forget to go out and get a sandwich." Though I do really like the idea, I'm not going to let him know.

"Not a very manly job, but I guess it wouldn't matter to a *male* secretary."

"Be nice, Niko. Lance is very sweet, and he's the best assistant I've ever had. I lucked out in that department. All this time I've been doing everything on my own. He makes things so much easier, and I'd like to keep him, thank you very much."

Niko rolls his eyes but then smiles his Cheshire Cat smile. "Fine, I'll behave. What time should I pick you up?"

I eye him warily. Yeah. I don't trust that smile. "Around noon? I should be done around a quarter of. That will give me time to finish up and then we can head to that little Chinese place on Mass Avenue before my appointment."

"Noon works for me. I've got the whole day free. I'll probably get a run in first unless Cam wants to hit the gym early. Either way, I should be there early. Parking isn't the greatest near your office."

"Well, you don't have to come to my office. I told you we could—"

"Nope." He cuts me off. "I'll be there. It will give me a chance to come up with some role-playing ideas while I wait." I quirk my brow at him, and he stares back. "I was serious about the dirty boss shit. Now that I have that vision in my head, there is only one way to get it out," he says, and there is a fire in his eyes that always burns when he mentions anything to do with us and sex.

Speaking of sex.

"You know, I was reading in my pregnancy book that a woman's sex drive can increase during pregnancy."

His lips twitch up, and he pulls me closer. "You don't say."

"Yup." I nod. "Says so in the book."

"Where is this book? I think I should read it too. You know, so I know what to expect."

"I don't think so."

"Why not?" he asks, both eyebrows raising in surprise.

"Because it's called *What to Expect When You're Expecting*. Last time I checked I was the one that was growing an alien inside her. Us women need to keep some things a secret and decide when we choose to tell you other things, like the fact that some women get horny when they are pregnant." I smile at his facial expressions as I explain my reasons.

"I don't think that it's a book meant for just the mothers, Ev. That seems a little ridiculous. I could go out and buy my own, and they would sell it to me because they can. Good try, though. Now go get the book, baby."

"Nope. You can buy your own," I say as sassy as I can without laughing. "But, I may have picked up a book for you."

"How to bang your hot, pregnant woman? Because I don't need a book for that. I just need you to put your beautiful mouth to other tasks."

"*Other* tasks?"

He leans down and kisses my neck while he guides my hand down until I can feel how hard he is against my palm.

"Your mouth stretched around my dick." His hips flex, pushing him further into my hand.

"Then what?"

"Then you suck on it like a lollipop until I can't take it anymore and spread your pussy open to fuck you like I haven't seen you in months."

I gasp in mock incredulity. "Such crudeness, sir. I am a lady in a delicate condition."

"You think you're funny, don't you?"

I bite on my lower lip, failing to fight a smile as I look up at him as shy and as innocent as I can manage.

A groan rumbles through him and he pushes down on my shoulder. "Oh, sweetheart, are we roleplaying now? Giving me that fucking innocent act?"

Playing along, I give no resistance and drop down to my knees. He sheds his shirt before his fingers deftly work his belt open, then his jeans. I can't look away as I watch him twitch before he lowers his pants and underwear just enough for his cock to pop out. His fingers wrap around the base and he tilts it toward me. I lean forward, mouth open, ready to wrap my lips around him when he pulls it away. I glance up at him in confusion, and his eyes are heavy and dark, his smirk full of mischief.

Firm warmth smacks against my lips and my attention returns to the item of my every sexual desire. Barely a swipe of my tongue before he moves it again, causing me to quirk a brow at him. He taps my lips again and again; I try and touch it, and it's gone. One more tap to my lips, but this time I don't let him play his game. Rising up slightly, I grab onto his hand holding his shaft with one hand and his jeans with the other, tugging as I lean forward, taking him in my mouth.

"Fuck," he hisses, moving both hands to my head, fisting my hair.

He's so lost, so thrown off balance, that he flexes his hips while holding my head, fucking my mouth. After a minute he slows, his fingers unknotting from my hair. There's pure fire in his eyes, mouth slack as he looks down at me.

"Baby, that . . . shit . . ." he trails off, his head falling back as I bob up and down at a slow, teasing pace.

He groans with each swipe of my tongue and the sounds send a zing of heat straight between my legs. After a minute, his hand moves to cup my cheek, slowly pushing me off.

"You are too fucking good at that, but it's been a long, exhausting day, and if I come in that beautiful mouth, I don't know if I'll be able to make it to a round two."

He leans over, his hands slide under my arms, and he picks me up effortlessly. Like always, he uses his strength to draw me to him. Our lips meet at the same time as our stomachs, my legs wrapping around him.

"Then where do you want to come?" I ask, loving the way his eyes seem to darken even more as he lets out a groan.

He turns around and steps forward, setting me down on the counter. His hands fist into the waistband of my yoga pants before he pulls, yanking them over my ass before stepping back to get them down my legs.

I gasp when his hands rest on my inner thigh and he gives a sharp push. There is fire rushing through my veins, my breath sharp, loving the energy rolling off him. It's hot, chaotic, and darkly alluring.

This is one of those moments, the ones that tell me how much he needs me, quelling the ever-nagging thoughts that I'm not enough for him. Because in this moment I know just by the way he's looking at me that I am *everything*.

"I'm going to come in my favorite place," he says, exciting me further.

Slowly, his hands create a path that stokes the fire inside me with each inch. Moments like this I feel like I'll go mad, desperate for him to stop teasing me and just take me. His thumb flicks across my clit and I cry out, my legs tightening around him, pulling him closer. The length of his shaft slides against my clit, a sensation that causes a shudder to consume me.

"And where is that?" I ask, noticing how breathy my voice has become.

His forehead rests on mine, his hips rocking against me. "Fuck, baby, you're torturing me."

"I'm torturing you? How?"

"Because I'm exhausted." He pulls his hips back and nudges the head of his cock into my opening before sliding forward. My eyes lose focus as my nails dig into his arm.

"So good," I manage to say.

"I'm exhausted, but all my dick wants to do is try and put another baby in you." He pulls almost all the way out before slamming back in.

"Fuck!" I cry out. "I . . . t-that's not possible."

He begins a scorching rhythm that propels me faster and faster to a blinding explosion.

"Oh, I know," he says through clenched teeth. "But my dick still wants to try."

He slams into me harder, faster until I can't think. Until I can barely breathe. Once again consumed by Niko.

"Fuck, yes!" I lock down, my nails digging into his back, the tightening in my abdomen feeling seconds from snapping.

His hands move down to my hips, pinning me in place. I can't move, can't think, can only take the intensity that he gives. I freeze, drawing in a stuttering breath, then snap. A scream leaves me as I clench down on him, and mind-whitening pleasure moves through me.

"Fuck, fuck, fuck!" he roars, slamming hard into me, pushing as far as he can get.

I barely comprehend that he's coming, my mind still blissfully clouded. His head falls to my shoulder before his arms give out and he leans over, sending my back down to the counter. His abs press against my stomach and I know that soon this position will be impossible for a little while.

"So what book did you get me?" he asks, his breath hot against my shoulder.

"*Be Prepared; A Practical Handbook for New Dads*. It's got all the goriness and truth."

"Did you read it?"

"The first few pages. It scared me and I had to close it."

"Too much truth?"

I nod. "Horror movie level truths for after, but with a fun spin."

"So a *Cabin in the Woods* type feel?" he asks. I nod again. "Okay, we can handle it. I mean, people do this all the time."

"You sound like you're trying to convince yourself more than me."

"I know it's going to be hard, and the fantasy of us with our baby is not reality, but I know we'll be okay."

"How do you know?" I ask.

He smiles at me, the one that makes my heart skip, and he cups my face. "Because I have you."

Chapter Twenty-Seven

Niko

THERE'S A REASON I don't venture into downtown Boston; the traffic is brutal, even midday. I padded an extra hour on my drive time and ate half of it by the time I parked in the garage of Everly's building.

Walking in, I pass by her car and remind myself to talk to her about car shopping. With the weather turning colder, she needs to get something that can get through our sometimes brutal Boston winters. She's been putting it off, not wanting to get rid of her BMW. I told her to just park it at her parents' house for now because she needs a car with a backseat.

And all-wheel drive or four-wheel drive.

I'm tempted to give her my Tahoe so that I know she and the baby are safe.

As I wait for the elevator, I pull out my phone to double check her floor. When the doors open, I step on and hit the button for the fourteenth floor. It's a steady ride up with no stops.

When I get off, there is nobody at the receptionist desk, so I continue with Everly's directions to go left. I pass by offices and cubicles, earning more than one questioning or lust-filled glance.

Just as I get to her office, I slow, catching the eyes of an uptight-looking suit that's manning the desk outside her office.

"Can I help you?" he asks.

"I'm here to see Everly Hayes. She's expecting me," I say.

"She doesn't have any more appointments for today. What did you say your name was, again?"

"I didn't. Who are you?"

He stares at me and shakes his head. "That isn't usually how this works, guy, but I'll humor you. I'm Lance, and now you are?"

"Lance? As in Lancelot?" I ask him. What kind of name is Lance? Already I don't like this guy. He rolls his eyes at my question, and I want to just tell him to get out of my way so I can get my girl, but I'm at her job. I don't want to make shit uncomfortable for her.

"No, as in just Lance. Now, are you going to tell me your name so that I can see if Ms. Hayes is interested in seeing you, or are you going to stand here all afternoon trying to measure my dick?"

Is this guy fucking kidding me? "Measure your dick?"

He blows out a breath and rolls his eyes as he picks up the phone. "Everly, there's a man here to see you, but he won't give me his name. Were you expecting someone, or should I send him on his way?" He ignores me and holds the phone to his ear.

"Everly?" This prick obviously knows Ev on some personal level if he calls her by her first name. What the fuck? "What do you mean some guy, and I'd like to see you try to send me on my way, buddy." This moron needs someone to put him in his place. Send me on my way? Un-fucking-likely. "Of course she's going to see me, asshole. I'm her baby daddy."

"Niko!" I hear her shout from the receiver the dumbass has pulled away from his ear. More than likely did that on purpose, too. "I'll be out in a second, Lance. Have Niko wait for me, please."

"If you say so, Everly."

Of course she says so. What the fuck is up with this guy? He hangs up the phone and points me in the direction of the chairs in a waiting area. I start to walk away, but the fucker rubs me the wrong fucking way, and I can't stop myself.

"For the record, pretty GQ boy, nine and a half inches, that's what I'm working with. That's what she likes, and I know for a fact that she's not complaining seeing as she is currently baking my kid in her oven. Just wanted to make you aware of that, you know, in case you get any ideas that include whatever you're packing under that tight-ass suit you got on there, Mr. Not-Fucking-Gay secretary."

His mouth screws up, and I can see the way his jaw ticks. "I'm an executive assistant. And assistant does not mean gay, asshole. Why don't you go sit down before I get fired for punching my boss's baby daddy with the nine-and-a-half-inch dick," the smug son of a bitch says.

I snort and stand in place.

I'm not letting this asshole get the best of me. Screw that, and screw him. Fucking secretary.

He's lucky we're at Everly's job because if we were outside or somewhere else, I'd knock his stuck-up ass the hell out, wrecking his pretty-boy face. That alone would go a long way in making me feel better about the fact that Ev's fucking assistant is a straight guy and probably close to my age. He reminds me of Bishop with his stupid shoes, gelled up hair, and the stupid face that the chicks flock to.

And. He. Works. With. Ev. This is bullshit. He's got to go. I'm just going to have to let her know that I am not okay with this guy working as her assistant.

I'm not fucking moving. I look him up and down before I stand my ground and let him know what's up.

"I'm not sitting anywhere. I'm going to wait right here . . ." I point to the spot in front of me ". . . until my woman is ready to go."

His lips twitch, but he's smart enough not to laugh. If he knows what's good for him, he'll just pay attention and keep his eyes to himself.

"We have a doctor's appointment today. Gonna find out if my kid is a boy or a girl. That's what couples do. Ones that are about to have a kid together." That sounded stupid even to me, but I don't give a shit right now. If pretty-boy Lance here had any ideas about hitting on my girl, even if she is pregnant, he can get that shit right out of his stupid gel-haired covered head. Not happening.

He shakes his head and continues to pack up his desk. I guess he's about to leave for lunch. Good. I hope his GQ-looking face chokes on an ice cube or something. Anything that would take his ass away from this office and Everly.

Fuck. Now I wish I'd met her at the doctor's office like she said instead of coming here to her job. The situation has thrown me, and I'm acting and talking like some stupid gym rat that doesn't have two brain cells. Douchebag probably thinks my dick is all I have going for me, and the only reason Ev is with me when it's not, but this fucking weird feeling is making me dumb.

Cam said she had a gay secretary. He either lied or thought the same thing I did. Male secretary equals gay. Same thing we thought about the guy that cut his hair too, but we were both wrong about Omar. It turns out he was married with eight kids and cut hair on the side to make extra cash.

Fucking Cam.

I look over at pretty-boy Lance and give him a once over while he's not paying attention to me. There doesn't seem to be anything flamboyant about this fucker. That's for sure. He also just came right out and said he wasn't gay, so why am I still looking for signs that he's lying?

I wait a few minutes until finally Everly's office door opens and my beautiful girl appears. And she's not looking too happy.

"Hey, baby," I say.

No hello. No nice to see you. No thanks for picking me up, Niko. Nope. I get the ice queen.

Fuck.

This afternoon should be terrific.

"I'm heading out. I've left a few files for the Anderson account that Jim was looking for today. If you could just send a courier over to his office, I'd appreciate it, Lance."

"Of course, Everly. I'll take care of it first thing after lunch," he says to her, and she smiles.

I get the fucking ice queen bullshit, but she gives that fucking clown her teeth.

"Let's go, Niko," she snaps at me, and I'm left watching her twitch her little ass as she walks away from me and toward the elevators. I turn and see Lance is looking at her ass same as me, and I lose it.

"Keep your fucking eyes off her ass," I growl at him, causing Everly to stop and walk back to where Lance and I still stand.

"Niko!" she hisses at me.

She doesn't yell. Nope. She fucking hisses at me like some wildcat. Fine with me. Personally, I like it when her claws come out.

"Everly . . ." She looks at me, fire burning in her hazel eyes, and all I can think about is later tonight. It's going to be all about the hate fuck. My cock stiffens at the thought, and I want to pull her ass into her office so I can fuck her on her desk, making her scream my name and let Lance here know who owns that pussy. She looks over at Lance and her expression changes from pissed off to embarrassed.

"I'm so sorry, Lance. He's not normally like this. Next time I'll make sure I bring the muzzle. Trust me, though, his bark is way bigger than his bite. See you in the morning," she says and grabs my hand, dragging me along behind her.

The elevator opens just as we reach it and luckily it's empty. Maybe it would have helped me had it been occupied because as soon as the doors close, she unleashes her full ice-queen persona.

"What the fuck is wrong with you?"

"What's wrong with me? You're kidding right now, right?"

"No, Niko, I'm not kidding. That's my assistant! What if that had been my boss?"

"Yeah, your assistant, not your secretary, he doesn't like that. Why's your secretary a guy?" I ask.

"Why not?" she responds, then smacks me on the pec. "Since when did you turn all green-eyed monster on me?"

"Since your assistant is a fucking dude!" Fuck. She's my girl, and I don't want some other guy that close to her.

"I'm not arguing about this," she says, turning forward again. "He works for the company and me. He's great at his job, and I am not fighting about this."

"I don't like him."

She turns back to me, glaring. "You don't have to like him. I do!" she hisses.

"Are we going to go find out what we're having, or are we going to stand here all day talking about your asshole secretary?"

"You're un-fucking-believable right now." She shakes her head at me and rather than tell me off any longer, she stomps away toward the car.

"Oh yeah, angry make-up sex later. I'm all for it," I say out loud, but she keeps going. "Very very angry, hate, make-up sex. Even better, babe." She pulls the door open, gets into my Tahoe, and slams the door. I smile and walk to the driver's side. Once inside I start it up and turn my satellite radio on to lighten the mood. "Animals" by Maroon 5 comes on, and I see Ev's lips twitch from the corner of my eye.

Yup! Make-up sex indeed.

Chapter Twenty-Eight

Niko

TWENTY MINUTES LATER, AND we are finally checking in at her OB GYN's office. There are about eight pregnant women in all different stages of their pregnancies also waiting, and one woman with a newborn in one of those car seats with the handle. We take a seat next to the woman, and I see Everly looking down to the floor where the infant is sleeping with a pink blanket covering her. I hear another woman ask if it's a girl or a boy, and I want to roll my eyes. Unless she's blind, how the hell would you not know it's a girl with the bright pink blanket on her?

"She's very beautiful," Everly says to the new mother. "How old is she?"

"She's eight days old." She smiles back at Ev who is staring at the baby in complete fascination.

"Oh wow! You look fantastic for having just had a baby eight days ago!" The woman smiles at Everly and then looks down at her growing belly.

"Your first?" she asks. Everly places her hands on her belly and smiles back, her lousy mood from earlier gone.

"Yes. We're due in March." I grab her hand, and she looks over at me with something in her eyes I've never seen before. The woman's name is called, and she stands to collect her things and her new baby.

"Good luck!" she says to us and heads toward the nurse waiting for her.

"Hey," I say to her. "You all right?"

"What if we fuck this up?" she asks as she stares down at her lap.

"Fuck what up?"

"Being parents." She looks back up at me, her brow knitted. "I know there is a human being growing inside of me right now. I feel the baby, but seeing that little girl just now. That eight-day-old little person is sleeping helplessly in her little car seat . . ." She doesn't finish right away, but I see her lip tremble, and I have no idea what just made her start doubting herself.

"Baby, look at me." She looks over to me, and I know what it was now in her eyes before. Fear.

"This is such a fucked-up world. What if something happens? What if the baby gets sick? What if I don't know how to take care of it when it gets sick?"

"Everly, stop."

"We don't know, Niko. I know I sound crazy, but seeing that baby just made this feel more . . ."

"Real?" I ask.

"Yeah. I guess. I don't know. I'm sure it's just my hormones again, but I've been going full speed ahead with the house and the new job, my parents, Cam, and then you that I haven't let everything that's coming in the future sink in, you know?"

I nod my head yes because I do know.

"We're going to be okay, babe. We can only try our best as our parents did, and if we fuck up, well we just do. Live and learn, and that's what we teach this baby that's coming. Women have been doing this forever, and I'm positive that you're not the first mother-to-be to have the same doubts and fears. It's normal."

"Aren't you scared?"

I laugh at her question. "Fucking petrified, but I have something that grounds me when those fears kick in."

"What's that?"

"You."

"Everly Hayes?" a woman calls from the entryway to the back rooms. I stand up and grab Ev's hand to help her up from her seat. We walk over to where the woman is waiting, and she smiles at us both before telling us to follow her to the ultrasound room.

This is it. The day we find out if we are having a girl or a boy, and I'm nervous. We just want the baby to be healthy, but I won't lie and say that I'm even more terrified of finding out we have a girl on the way.

I don't think I could handle a little girl. I wouldn't know what to do with a girl. A boy, yes, but little girls aren't my specialties. Not only that, but I know how guys are. Guys like I was as a teen and then as a man up until I met Everly. I'd go to jail over some pimple-faced little fucker trying to date my daughter.

No, God wouldn't do that to me. I told Ev it didn't matter, but it does. I need a boy.

"If you could just unbutton your pants and place this on the lower half of your belly, the technician will be in shortly. There is a chair for you over there, Dad, so you can watch the monitor while we do the ultrasound," the woman says and then closes the door behind her.

I walk over and drag the chair over to sit next to Ev who's now lying back with her belly exposed.

"I'm nervous," I say to her.

"Me too, but I'm also excited, if that makes sense?"

"Yeah," I say quietly to her, squeezing her hand. If this is how we feel during just an ultrasound, I can't imagine what will happen when she's ready to give birth.

"Niko?"

"Hmm?"

"I'm glad that I have you, too."

We sit and wait for a few minutes before the ultrasound technician makes her way into the room we are in. "Good afternoon. Everly Hayes?"

"Yup! That's me," Ev says, not sounding like herself.

"My name is Lisa, and I'm going to do your ultrasound. I understand that you would like to know the sex of the baby as well today?" she asks, looking at the both of us.

"Yes. We both want to know," Ev says and smiles.

I nod, and the woman starts to type a few things on the machine's keyboard.

"Well then, let's hope this little peanut feels like cooperating with us today, and I will see what we can do to help you guys pick out the right colors for your baby."

"You can't always find out the sex of the baby by ultrasound?" I ask, confused. I thought this was an absolute when the doctor told us she was scheduling her ultrasound.

"Well, not always. You're right at twenty-one weeks, and it's easier to get a good picture a little later in the pregnancy."

"But you'll still be able to see? How accurate will it be?"

"Sometimes the baby will turn away or cross its legs in a way that makes it difficult to see, but I'm pretty good usually, so let's see what I can do for you two. Any allergies to latex?" she asks Ev, and I'm half tempted to answer for her knowing from experience, but I don't want Ev mad at me during this.

"No," Ev replies.

"Okay, good. Let's get started, then. I'm just going to put some of the gel on your tummy. It might be a little cold. Sorry about that," she says to Ev, but she's not really talking to anyone. Sounds more like words she says one hundred times a day, which I'm sure, being an ultrasound tech, she does. She moves some kind of device onto the jelly shit she just squirted on Ev's belly.

"Do you mind if I ask questions?" I ask her, because I want to know what she's doing exactly and what it is that I'm looking at. I'm clueless. I see nothing but black and white shit on the screen.

"Not at all. Most of my first-time parents do."

"What am I looking at exactly, and how does this allow us to see the baby?" I ask, noticing the way Ev's head bobs. It seems she wants to know as well.

"Well, this thing right here is called a transducer." She motions down to her hand. "It uses inaudible sound waves to produce a two-dimensional image of the baby while inside the mother's uterus. The sound waves bounce off solid structures in the body and are transformed into an image onto the screen here," she says, pointing to the images. "Solid parts, such as bones and muscles, reflect sound waves and appear as light gray or white like here." Again, she points at the screen. Now that she is explaining it, I can see exactly what I'm looking at. I think. "Soft or hollow areas, like the chambers of the heart, don't reflect sound waves and appear dark or black. You see that there?" she says, pointing to the black spot that appears to be blinking rapidly. "That's the baby's heart. Looks good." She smiles at Ev and me before looking back to the screen and typing on the keyboard in front of her.

I stare at the screen in awe of what Ev and I have created. The other part of me is now even more afraid of the type of father I'll be to this baby. Ev isn't the only one doubting themselves, but I didn't want her to freak out even more. If anyone will be excellent at parenting, it's her. I look down at Ev and squeeze her hand. She doesn't look at me, though. She's enraptured, her eyes unblinking at the image of our baby on the screen. I notice a few tears roll from her eyes, and she swipes quickly at them.

"Hey," I say, and she finally turns to look at me. "You okay?"

"Yeah."

"Then why are you crying, babe?"

She shakes her head at me, swiping again at her face as the tears roll freely now down her face. "These are happy tears, you goof. I just can't believe we made a little human."

I lean down and place a kiss on her forehead. I can't help but share her happiness because I was just thinking the same thing.

"We did. Now the question is—are we having a little boy or a little girl Callahan?" I look toward the screen and the tech, who is still taking measurements of everything she sees.

"Well, the baby isn't in the best position, but I think I got a look a few seconds ago. Let's see if we can get a better look," she says as Ev and I wait.

Geeze, this is nerve wracking. I watch along with her, and I swear I see something between the baby's legs that looks male.

God, please let it be a boy. I mean, healthy is good, but I don't think I can handle girls.

Holy shit! What if it is two?

I clear my throat, and Ev and the tech look over. "Umm, this thing can tell that there is more than one baby in there too, right?"

Ev's face turns a few shades of white, and I'm glad it's not just me that would probably fall to the floor if we got that news. The tech laughs and turns back to what she was doing.

"It does, and I think I only see one baby in there." I let out the breath I was holding and hear Everly do the same.

"Think?"

"Well, it's not guaranteed, but I'm pretty sure I see only one baby. It has happened before where one was hiding out of sight, but that's pretty rare. Same goes for finding out the sex. As I told you, we can be wrong, but I'm usually pretty good. Like now. See that?" she asks and points to what I thought I saw earlier. "I'm trying to get the baby to move a little more, but I'm almost positive that is a penis."

"Sure looks like it to me," I say with my chest puffed out. "I mean, I don't know how many you see a day, but it looks pretty big for a baby not even born yet. Definitely hereditary. Ow!" I say when Ev hits me very close to my cock. "You want to watch where you hit, babe, or this might be the last baby we have with my good co . . . What the hell, Everly," I say when she slugs me again.

"Niko. Pretty sure that you don't need to let the poor woman here know that the baby has a matching penis to his dad's. Shut up!" I rub the spot where she hit me and back up a little out of her reach. The technician laughs but ignores us for the most part. "Besides, she said maybe. She didn't say it was a penis for sure."

"I don't know, babe. I see something there."

Ev huffs at me in agitation. Guess that conversation we had where she said she didn't care what we had was BS. Apparently, she wants a little girl.

"Of course you see something there. Girl parts are something too." She rolls her eyes and then turns her head back toward the screen. "Is everything else good with the baby?" Ev asks, and I feel like a jackass for not asking the same question.

"Everything looks good so far. Just waiting for this little peanut to move one more time. There! There you go, love bug," she says and clicks some buttons again on the keyboard, only this time a few pictures start printing. She rips them off and hands them to Ev, and I move closer to see. She typed the words "Hi Mommy and Daddy. See you soon! Love Baby Boy Callahan."

Holy fuck!

"We're having a son?" I look, and now it's me that feels like crying. I don't, of course, because that would make me a mangina, but I want to. "I mean, we're having a boy, Ev." She smiles down at the pictures the woman handed her, and maybe I was wrong about her wanting a girl. I'm just happy to see her smile at the news.

"We're having a son," she whispers. I kiss her head again and then look at the pictures.

"Thank you, Everly." She looks up then. "Thank you for this. We're going to do our best. I know this already because you're his mother. So, thank you for our son."

"Okay, I'm all done here. Everything looks good. You can use the paper towels there to clean up and meet me outside. Your OB will let you know when your next ultrasound will be, but usually not until closer to delivery unless there is a need before. Congrats!" she says and heads for the door.

"Thank you," both Ev and I say as she leaves. Ev gets up and pulls her pants back up after wiping off the slimy shit she had on her belly. I offer to help, but she waves me off, so I give her space to do her thing. The entire time I can't stop the Kool-Aid grin from sweeping my face. I'm sure I'll be wearing it for the rest of the day. Hell, maybe the rest of my life.

Holy shit! I'm going to have a boy.

"Why is there never any damn parking?" I ask, circling the block for the third time. We just had a celebratory dinner, and I'm ready to do some other celebratory things in the comfort of home.

Everly shrugs beside me. "I don't have a problem."

"You have a reserved spot," I point out.

"There!" Her arm stretches out, pointing to a spot fifty feet ahead. There's an SUV just down the way that must have pulled out.

I swoop in, determined not to lose the spot even if it is a few blocks away. When we get out, the cold air hits me. The weather can't seem to make up its mind.

"It was seventy yesterday," Everly says as she folds her arms around herself.

I step up next to her and sling my arm over her shoulder, pulling her close. "Gotta love the fall."

"It's making me miss California."

"Well, I wouldn't be there."

"Yup, not missing it now," she says, looking up at me with that beautiful smile of hers. I can't help but lean down to press my lips to hers.

I love walking with her, going out with her to dinner or the movies. Strange to admit, but I think she is what my life was missing. I don't miss the single life. At all. Because I have her, I'm happy.

"I'm full, but I also want dessert," she says, rubbing her stomach.

"Oh, baby, I can help you in that department."

She shakes her head and giggles. "Not the kind of dessert I was talking about. Your little boy is hungry."

Little boy. A boy. I still can't believe it.

Today was the day. I don't care either way, but when the technician said the baby is a boy, I was happy.

"But, I am definitely down for some dessert after, well . . . dessert," she says with a wink.

Shaking my head, we head into the house and close and lock the door behind us.

"Ugh, I *have* to get out of these clothes."

I follow her up the stairs. Any chance to watch her ass sway, I take. You can't even tell she's five months pregnant from this angle. Not from the front or back, only the side.

I watch from the doorway as she throws her clothes off, stripping naked, giving me a good look at her sexy body that is somehow even sexier with her stomach sticking out. She tosses clothes around the closet in a huff.

"Nothing fits," she growls, finally deciding on some sleep pants and a T-shirt I left here.

I lick my lips because, damn, she looks good in my shirt. A little collarbone is showing, the shirt dwarfing her, showing off our size difference.

"Just tell your mom you need clothes. You'll have five boxes on your doorstep in days."

She turns to me, eyes wide. "Don't joke about that." Her tone is so serious I can't help but laugh. "I'm serious, Niko. I told her in passing I needed a dress for a holiday dinner and a few days later there was a stack of boxes from Nordstrom on my porch."

After getting a couple of glasses of water and a plastic cup Everly has filled with Frosted Flakes for her dessert, we settle onto the couch. The first trimester was so rough on Everly that she's just gained back the weight she lost. There may be a few extra pounds, but they are all in the bump her stomach has gained. It's a gentle slope, but laying back on the couch in my oversized-for-her shirt, it does, in fact, bump out.

"I can't wait to tell my mom," I say as I reach to run my hand down her side and across her stomach.

"You haven't told her yet, have you?" Everly asks.

I shake my head and sigh. "Sometimes it's hard to get ahold of her, and the times we've connected haven't been at ideal times."

"Cam was around," she says, and I nod. "You should call her now."

I purse my lips. "Seven-hour time difference. I'll give her a call in the morning."

"That has to be tough. Why did she go back?"

"After Dad died, she went through an awful depression."

Everly laces her fingers with mine. "It was sudden if I remember correctly."

I nod. "A heart attack, which was not expected. He was in good health; there were no warning signs."

"I can't even imagine."

"She couldn't even get out of bed the weeks following. My aunt was here, her sister, who suggested she go back to Greece. It was hard for me. It felt like I was losing both my parents in a small span, but I knew it was what was best for her. Her sisters and family are all still in Greece. I was an adult, albeit in college."

"Was it what was best?" she asks.

"For her? Yes. She lived in Boston, but Greece is her home. I Skype'd with her back in those days. A few weeks and, while she still missed Dad, she came back to herself."

"That had to be hard on you," Everly says. Her brow is furrowed as she brushes her fingers through my hair.

"When are you going to tell your parents we're having a boy?" I ask, changing the subject. It's a hard topic for me to talk about because I do have issues with my mom leaving me. I love her, but it messed me up.

"Probably this weekend."

"Family lunch?"

She nods. "Mom's excited. I have a feeling there will be much shopping going on this weekend. She'll want to decorate and get clothes and . . ." she lets out a sigh. "I love my mom, but she sometimes goes overboard."

"First grandchild syndrome."

"Yeah. Without a doubt. I have a feeling she's going to spoil this baby rotten, so be prepared."

I laugh at her statement, but I'm good with that. "Spoiled isn't a bad thing as long as he knows that he will still have to earn things that he wants and doesn't expect. I have faith in your parents. After all, you and Cameron aren't rotten."

"No. We both learned early on that we wanted to make our own way. It's why we both barely touch the money Mom and Dad set aside for us when we turned of age. It's there if we need it, but we don't depend on it. I usually pretend that it's not there."

"That's what I'm talking about. Your parents made sure you two were grounded. I don't doubt that they won't be the same with our son." She nods her head yes as she piles more cereal into her mouth, and I laugh. "How is it that you even manage to make eating Frosted Flakes look sexy as fuck?"

"You're crazy," she replies after she swallows what's in her mouth.

"I think so, too. Crazy as fuck for you."

She bites her lip and reaches for the remote, turning on the TV and bringing up the guide.

This is what I love. Being with my family.

Finally home.

Chapter Twenty-Nine

Everly

"YOU ARE SO BEAUTIFUL," Niko says as his hand slips under the hem of my shirt.

"You're distracting me," I say as I scroll through the TV menu looking for something to watch. I'm about to throw on Netflix if I don't find something soon. Then again, I love Niko's hands on me and I've learned that the longer I ignore him, the more persistent he gets. The more persistent he gets, the better it is. I just have to hold out, which is a very difficult task.

He hums against my neck, his breath warm, lips ghosting across my skin.

"That's your fault for being so enticing."

"I wasn't so enticing ten years ago," I remind him. "What if I looked like I did then? You wouldn't have looked twice at me."

He pulls back. "Are you calling me shallow and saying I only like you because you're beautiful?" I nod. "Not possible."

"Why is that?"

"Because right now you have no makeup on, you're in an oversized T-shirt and baggy pants, your hair in a messy ponytail, and you are so cute I can't keep my hands off you."

I stare at him, watching him, waiting for something like "Just kidding," but it doesn't come. His eyes are soft and he's looking at me like I'm the only woman in the world. I jump at the feel of his hand cupping my face.

"I was a stupid kid."

I reach over and pick up my glasses that I use when working on the computer and slip them on. "How about now?"

His eyes widen. "Jesus . . . do you have a pencil skirt because you are the naughtiest naughty librarian I've ever seen."

I shake my head and roll my eyes, partially to cover how much I want to kiss him and am holding back. "I still don't think you would have noticed me."

"You're wrong, Ev. My dad told me that one day I'd meet a woman who would knock me on my ass, and he was right. It's more than your looks that blew me away, it was all of you."

I stare at him, processing what he just said, unable to comprehend it. *Me?*

His hand slips under the waistband of my panties, his fingers sliding against my clit, making me jump and suck in a sharp breath.

"I never knew a pregnant woman could turn me on so much, but fuck, baby, watching your stomach grow, knowing I did that. That's *my* baby growing in *your* body," he growls, pushing his fingers in deeper as he pulls me closer. "*Our* baby boy."

I can't help but reach up and grab onto his shirt, my forehead in the crook of his neck. "Niko," I whimper against his skin before a moan slips out.

This is what I was waiting for. The way he touches me is somehow more intense, his desperation spreading like wildfire across my skin. This isn't about just his wants, his needs. It's about intimacy and a relationship and two people trying to make it through the roller coaster of life together.

It's so much more than "just fucking" and I can feel that with every swipe of his tongue, every touch, and every kiss he gives me.

My hips rock into his hand without thought. Sheer drive for pleasure moves me. Desire takes over, spiraling me down.

"Niko . . . Niko," I whisper against his skin over and over. His hand speeds up, driving his fingers faster and faster until I've got his shirt clenched in my hands and my muscles tighten, pulling him closer.

"Come on, baby." He runs his lips along my shoulder before I feel his teeth sink in at the base of my neck.

My eyes pop open, a silent scream as I come undone in his arms. His fingers slow before retreating, leaving me a boneless mess. I'm still coming down when he yanks my pants down my legs and spreads them apart.

He wastes no time settling between my thighs. I draw in a sharp breath as he pushes inside me before a low moan spills out. Nothing ever will feel as good as Niko. Reaching up, I cup his face in my hands and pull his lips down to mine as he sinks all the way in.

His hips retreat, but as his arms wrap around me, pulling me closer, he slams back in.

"My belly is starting to get in the way," I say before losing all thought as he continues. His hips rock in a slow, sensual motion.

"Guess we're going to have to get creative," he says.

I love it when he's like this. While sex is always fantastic with Niko, when he's slower, tender, I feel a connection with him on more than just a physical level, which is already extremely strong.

His eyes are locked with mine, and each thrust makes words I'm not sure I'm ready to say to him sit at the edge of my mouth.

I love you.

I love you. I love you. I love you.

A mantra just for me, for now.

It's not just the moment, it's the truth. I can feel it in my heart and in every fiber of my being. I fell well and truly in love with Nikolas Callahan. No longer an unfulfilled teenage crush.

His breath mingles with mine, his eyes dark as his brow furrows. A groan leaves him and he presses his lips to mine while his movements speed up.

I grab onto him, pulling him closer, holding him to me as he slams into me one last time. Erotic groans fill my ears, and I can feel each twitch of him inside me.

"That was just for now," he says after a minute.

"For now?"

"Oh yeah, I still owe you a hate fuck for earlier."

My eyes widen as I stare at him, a smirk on his lips. Soft and sweet or hard and dirty—it doesn't matter. I am his forever.

"Let me see, let me see," my mom squeals as soon as I walk in the door.

"Hi, Mom. Good to see you, too."

Dad laughs from behind her. "She's been so excited. I think she just can't wait to figure out what she's shopping for."

"Oh, hush, Richard. This is our grandbaby."

I pull out the sonogram pic from my purse and hand it over to my mother's greedy hands.

"Oh, my goodness! Look at . . ." She reads the print on the picture. "Baby boy."

"All I see is a blob," Dad says as he steps back to grab his coffee cup.

Mom rolls her eyes, which suddenly go wide as she stares down at the picture.

"Let's just go frame this," Mom says, suddenly dragging me and the sonogram away from my dad.

I glance at Mom, then back at Dad who just shrugs at me. We move through the house about as far away from him as can be before slipping through the door leading to the basement. She makes sure to close the door behind us, and once we're down, she pulls me further from the stairwell.

"Are you okay?" I ask her, completely confused by her behavior.

She turns on me, her eyes wide. "Baby Boy Callahan?" she asks, her voice on the edge of shrill as she points to the typing on the sonogram.

My mouth goes slack. Shit. How did I not remember that? When Niko called him baby boy Callahan, the technician must have written that when I wasn't paying attention.

"Is that why you wouldn't tell me who the father is? Because it's Niko's?"

I can feel the tears well in my eyes. My mind is entirely blank. I hate these hormones. Unconsciously I start to rub my stomach. I don't know if it's because it feels like the baby is doing somersaults or to soothe me.

"Everly Cassandra Hayes, answer me."

I nod. "Niko is the father of my baby," I say. It's almost freeing as much as it is frightening telling my mom.

"Cameron doesn't know, does he?"

I shake my head. "I don't want them to fight."

"Sweetheart, he's going to find out."

"I know, and we're going to tell him," I tell her. We will, we just haven't yet, and I know it's my fault. I'm the one dragging it out.

"How long has Niko known?"

"Since right after I found out."

"Everly . . . it's been months."

"I know. Cam told him I was pregnant, and he figured it out pretty fast. I didn't even get the chance to tell him."

"Cameron still thinks it's Tate's. He and your father . . ." She trails off.

"What? What are they doing?"

"I don't know, but I do know they are keeping an eye on him. You need to tell both your brother and your father. Now."

I shake my head. "Niko has to be here."

"Sweetheart, you've weaved yourself a web of lies that need to be cut down."

"I know, and we're going to tell him, but together."

"Everly." She's getting that stern tone to her voice. The one that used to snap Cam and me back into behaving.

"We are, Mom, but he wants to be the one, so he has to be there too."

"Okay, but this isn't my secret to tell, and I won't lie to your brother. Tell him, and tell him soon. It's not fair to put others in the middle of this."

"I know, Mom. We are going to tell him."

She nods her head at me and then smiles. "A little boy! How wonderful!"

"It is. For a while there it didn't seem real. Then I heard the heartbeat. That was something, but seeing your baby, even if just on that ultrasound screen, it's just amazing." I sniffle, trying to hold back more tears.

It seems all I do these days is cry. Happy, sad, neutral, hungry? The answer is to cry.

"Oh, sweetheart, you are going to be a great mother to this little boy."

"What if I screw up? What if I break it or something?"

She laughs and hugs me. "Don't be silly. You won't break him. You'll see. Once he's born, your instincts will kick in. You'll know what to do, and what you don't know, I'll help you with. You're not alone. I have to tell you, though, I feel so much better now that I know that Niko is the father," she says, and I lift my head from her shoulder, wiping away my tears.

"You are?"

"Of course I am. I mean, this is my grandchild so I will love him no matter what. I already do, and he's not even here yet, but when you first told your father and I that you were pregnant, well . . ."

"I know. You were disappointed in me."

"Not disappointed, Everly. Worried."

"Worried? You didn't think I could do this on my own? I mean, I know you expected more from me, but I've been doing things on my own for a long time, Mom. I haven't even touched my trust fund. Well, I did to put the down payment on my house, but I paid that back when my house in California sold. I work my butt off every day, and I can take care of myself and this baby if I need to. On my own."

"We know that. That wasn't why we worried."

"Well, then why?"

"Because you shouldn't have to do something like this on your own. This should be the happiest thing to ever happen to you in your life, and you should be sharing these moments with someone who cares and loves you. Someone who will love you both. Having your brother and then you after is something your father and I will always treasure. Even the hard times. I don't know what I would have done without your father by my side the whole way. I was a mess the entire time I was pregnant with Cam."

"You were? You always seemed so natural at raising us. Why were you a mess?"

"There is no parenting manual. There is nothing that tells you that you are right or wrong when it comes to raising your children. Once you start a family, you just have to wing it. Follow your gut and your heart. Your dad was the one that was cool as a cucumber. I think I hyperventilated the entire first and second trimester of my pregnancy with Cameron."

I can't help but laugh at her. "Well, in all fairness. You were carrying a little devil. Maybe that was your body's way of telling you that you should be scared."

"Everly Hayes, that is not nice," she says sternly, but her lips twitch. "Not nice, but not untrue. Your brother was a little terror as a toddler. Even worse as a teenager." She shudders, and I can't help but laugh. "If your father were not around to help me keep your brother on track, I don't know where Cameron would be right now. That, and his friendship with Nikolas. Once those two became friends, Cameron changed, and for the better. Some of his friends before Nikolas used to make your father and I cringe. He just hung around with everyone no matter where they were from or what they did. Scared the shit out of us both."

"Mom!"

"What? It's not like you've never heard me cuss. Besides, I've heard you and Alyson say much worse, so hush."

I hold my hand up, pretending to lock my mouth with a key and throw it behind my back. She's right. I'm afraid to ask what she's heard Aly and I talk about over the years while I was still at home. Alyson was a wild child and pretty much talked me into everything we did. I was always the big chicken, afraid to get caught.

"Anyway, knowing that it's Niko that is the father makes me breathe a lot easier. I know your father will feel the same way."

"What if it were Tate's?"

"I didn't know Tate very well. What I do know about him now, I don't like. We have known Nikolas for a long time. He had a tough time after his father passed away. His mother moving back to Greece was also hard on him, but he stayed here. Stayed in college, finished and followed your brother when he became a fireman. That wasn't what your father and I wanted for Cameron, but we raised you both to follow your own path and respected his decision. Nikolas did too, and apparently felt the same way Cameron did. My point is, he was always a good boy, and he's an even better man. Give him a chance to let you see that, and you'll know what I mean about not doing this alone."

"Niko has been great. I was prepared to do this alone, but he's been there beside me since day one."

That seems to surprise her, which confuses me after all the hype she was throwing his way.

"That shouldn't surprise me, but at the same time, I know what he and your brother have been up to. So, I have to ask again, now that I know who it is, do you love this man?"

I blink at her. Do I? It's a simple question, but an answer I only seem to know when he's inside me. I've kept from thinking about because I'm still afraid I'm not enough for him. That little, geeky Everly Hayes will never be enough for him. No matter how much I've changed, deep down I'm still the same.

"Yes," I say in a strangled whisper, a tear slipping down my cheek.

Chapter Thirty

Everly

THE SMELL OF WHATEVER Niko is cooking has me on cloud nine. The baby and my stomach are practically jumping, and I have no clue what it is, only that it smells good.

"Please tell me you don't plan on doing one of those really awkward pregnancy photo shoots or want to do one of those stupid gender reveals," Niko asks from his spot in front of the stove.

If I didn't feel the same way about both of those things, I might be offended. It's the new, trendy thing to do, but not for me. "Last time I checked, my name was Everly Hayes, not Beyoncé."

I look at him and attempt to emulate one of Niko's famous smirks that he's always throwing my way, but I'm sure I look ridiculous. He laughs when I do it and then shakes his head at me. I ignore him and laugh with him as I step up beside him, looking at the meal he's preparing for his baby and me.

"Besides, the only person I want to see me naked and pregnant is you. And we'll tell who we want to know, not the whole damn world."

He smiles and wraps his arms around me, a humming sound vibrating in his chest. "I really do like to see you naked."

The feel of his lips against my skin is something I don't think I'll ever get used to. Warm and electric, I crave it every moment of the day. My once crush is my now boyfriend and creator of my growing baby bump.

"How did your mom take it? You never did tell me." With his mom half a world away, I'd forgotten that we needed to tell her. Then again, I haven't told my father or brother who the real father is yet because we are still trying to figure out how to tell Cameron. Mom won't keep it a secret from them for much longer.

He draws in a sharp breath. "Yeah, that. I got chastised big-time in no less than four languages." He runs his hands soothingly over my stomach, making me notice I've tensed up. "I was told to make sure I treat you right and take care of you and all the things I'd already planned on doing."

"All the things you'd already planned on doing?"

He sways with me in his arms, a low chuckle against my ear. "Oh, I have many things planned, but I don't know if you're ready for them."

I swat at his arm. "Tease."

"Says the biggest one of them all." He softly kisses down my neck. "She also said she'd come and help when the time gets closer."

"How did she react when you told her who I was?" I ask.

"She was a bit shocked and worried. Time is moving fast on us, and we really need to tell Cam."

I nod in agreement. "I know. My mom knows now, so that's one less person."

He looks down at me. "How did that happen?"

"The sonogram. I somehow didn't notice the whole Callahan part."

His mouth pops open, then snaps shut as he nods. "Oh, yeah. Plus, all the paperwork has my last name."

"Well, you are responsible for all this," I say, pointing down to the weird distended curve my stomach has become.

"Damn straight." He smiles down at me.

"Maybe that's how we should tell Cam."

The smile leaves him, and he turns back to the pot, his arm still around me. "If we're flippant about it, he'll be more pissed off."

"True."

"Baby Callahan," he says as he runs his hands around my stomach.

Niko drops down to his knees and pushes the hem of my shirt up. There isn't a defined bump, more like my entire abdomen is sloped, and it's definitely noticeable. I haven't "popped" yet, but it's been weeks since any of my clothes fit. That has resulted in many shopping trips with Mom, who has already spent way too much. She is even setting up one of the extra bedrooms as a nursery for when the baby comes to visit.

I smile as he nuzzles the bump and presses his lips to my skin. "How is Daddy's baby today?"

Does he understand how much that melts me? How sexy that is?

Our bubble of happiness is interrupted by my phone going off. I glance over at it a few feet across the counter and turn back to Niko. The light atmosphere that surrounded him is gone, and his eyes are slits as he stands.

"Is that him again?" he asks, glaring down at the phone.

I nod.

"Jesus, Ev. There is something wrong with him."

I let out a sigh, tired of this fight with not just Niko, but everyone. "I really thought he would have stopped months ago." True, the calls and texts have slowed down, but I still receive one form of communication nearly every other day, a vast improvement from the half-dozen daily attempts the first month I was here.

"Obviously you are as addictive as I've been saying since that first night."

"Says the man I haven't stopped thinking about since I was eleven."

He lets out a chuckle, but it quickly morphs. "Seriously, he worries me."

"Think he's going to take me away from you?" I ask, wrapping my arms around him, trying to get back to the lighter vibes.

"Yes." Niko's tone isn't playful. He's dead serious and the air changes as my smile fades. "I worry about your safety. We know he's here. In Boston."

I narrow my gaze on him. "How do you know that?"

His jaw clenches, and he looks away.

"Nikolas, you tell me."

He grinds his teeth, making the muscle in his jaw jump. "Your dad hired someone to let him know if Tate's name came up on any flights."

"What? Why would he do that?" Mom hinted at something like this, but wouldn't or couldn't tell me.

"Because you're putting blinders on when it comes to him. Cam listened to all the voicemails, read all the text messages. The guy is not stable."

I shake my head, unable to believe it. "He's an annoying gnat, nothing more." They don't know him as I do.

Niko stares at me, his jaw continuing its tick, and his brow furrows and un-furrows like he's warring with himself on telling me something.

"He landed in Boston three days ago."

All the light leaves me while a chill moves up my spine. "W-what?"

"It's a round-trip ticket."

"It could be for work," I argue as I try and wrap around my head that maybe Cam was right. Why does he always have to be right?

"Maybe, but I'm pretty sure whatever brought him here, you are the real reason he came."

"It's all just so overwhelming," I say, stunned. This is not where I thought my year would take me. I'm happier than I ever was with Tate while simultaneously scared out of my mind about having a baby.

"What is?"

"This situation I've gotten myself into."

He blows out a breath. "You've been putting your head in the sand too long on some things, refusing to deal with them."

Maybe he's right. I've put Tate out of my mind just as I have talking to Cam. Very ostrich-like—if I don't acknowledge them, they don't exist. "I've got a lot on my plate."

"I understand, baby, but there are two big things you need to deal with."

"I know. I'm going to tell him. Both of them. Soon."

The doorbell goes off, then again and again.

"Shit! Cam's here."

Niko's eyes pop open. "What? How can you tell?"

"That's his ring, his sign."

Niko shakes his head. "You two . . ."

"Go upstairs."

He looks at me and nods before slipping down the hall and up the stairs. Panic fills me with each step toward the front door.

I blow out a steadying breath, then throw the door open. "What are you doing here?" I ask, quirking my brow at him.

"What, a brother can't come visit his sister?" he asks in mock offense.

"Unannounced? Were you raised in a barn?"

"I was raised in the same giant house you were, kid,"

I roll my eyes. "It's called a phone."

Cam goes silent, his hand up to his ear with his head cocked. When I try to speak, he throws his hand over my mouth.

"Nothing. Nobody is here," he says a minute later as he lets my mouth go. "So, you're alone. Am I cramping your alone time?"

"That's not it. It's just what if I was unavailable."

"Unavailable? Doing what, screwing your baby daddy?"

"Ugh, I hate that term."

"You're not screaming out in denial."

I freeze. Shit. He was testing me. "I was so put off by your baby daddy terminology to process the rest of the gibberish coming from that mouth of yours."

"Whatever. Besides, I think I should be offended you didn't call to tell me."

Shit, he's right. I've been avoiding him some and should have contacted him.

"I'm sorry, Cam."

"Uh-huh, feeling unloved right now." He walks into the kitchen and over to the pan on the stove. "Sis, are you cooking?"

"Yeah . . ." I trail off, hoping he doesn't ask what because I wasn't paying attention to what Niko is making.

"Ooh, you making moussaka?"

What did he say?

"Um, yeah. You know it?"

He nods. "Crappy name, but Niko has a great recipe for that. Shit's good."

I step up to the stove and look in as I turn the burner off, not wanting to burn whatever is cooking. I'm not even sure what Cam said, but I play along with it. "Does he? I'll have to hit him up to compare. What brings you by, brother dear? Not that I'm not happy to see your ugly mug."

He purses his lips, his eyes narrowed. "Oh, you are lucky you are pregnant right now. Those are fightin' words."

"Seriously? You're going to listen to what comes out of your sister's mouth versus all the chicks swarming you?"

"You wound my pride," he says.

I narrow my gaze on him. "Seriously, what's up?"

"Well, a little birdie told me that you have something to tell me."

My eyes go wide. "They did? And who is this little birdie?"

"Mom."

My heart stops beating for a second, then kicks into high gear to catch up. He's in way too good of a mood for her to have mentioned anything about Niko and me.

"What did she say?"

"Ev, seriously? What happened this week? A certain doctor's appointment?"

"Oh! The ultrasound."

"Seems there's a pic of my niece or nephew. Mom wouldn't tell me which."

"No? Why not?"

He shrugs. "Not sure. She was a little weird."

"Well, sad to say, I left the picture at work," I lie. "But I am pleased to announce that you have a nephew on the way."

He breaks out one of those megawatt smiles that gets all the women going. "Yeah? A boy?"

I nod. "Yeah, and I'm going to need your help."

There's no flicker in his smile, still beaming as he wraps his arms around me. "Always here for you, Ev."

"Thanks, Cameron."

He straightens and glances down at his watch. "Well, I was just swinging by on my way to the station."

"You're working tonight?" I ask as I wonder what all the crap was about when he first got here.

"Yup."

"Niko, too?" I ask as I walk him to the door.

"We don't have every shift together. Jesus, Ev."

"It wouldn't surprise me if you did, the way you two are joined at the hip."

"Brat." He turns the doorknob, then looks back at me. "Oh, almost forgot, are you free next weekend? I've got Saturday off and wanted to see if I could take my little sister out to lunch."

My mouth pops open. "Holy shit, are you asking me on a sibling date?"

He shakes his head and sighs. "Weirdo. And yes."

"Love to." I blow him a kiss.

He winks at me. "Text you later, kid."

"Stop calling me that!" I yell after him. I can hear his laughter from the other side of the door, slowly drifting away. Peeking out the window, I wait until he's in his truck before turning and running upstairs.

"That was the perfect opportunity," Niko says as soon as I enter the bedroom. He's sitting on the edge of the bed, leaning over with his forearms resting on his thighs. It's then I see how draining on him the situation has become. "I'm tired of this." I can only nod, but I'm still not ready. I may never be. "I know you're scared."

"I'm n . . ." I trail off and look to the window. "I've had so many changes this year, and the thought of one of my biggest supporters not talking to me . . . I don't know if I can take it. I don't want Cam mad."

"Baby, he's going to be mad, we know this. He'll be way madder at me then he will you, though. But we have to make it right with him. That's what's important."

"You're right."

"I'm tired of the lies."

I nod and try and stop the shaking of my hands. "Me too."

"They don't do anyone any good."

"He's off next Saturday," I say as I lock eyes with him.

"So am I."

I swallow hard. "We'll tell him then. On Saturday."

He nods and pulls me into his arms. "It'll be okay. Cam loves you."

"He loves you, too. I don't want that to stop."

"Don't worry about me."

"How am I supposed to do that?" I tilt my head up and cup his face in my hands. "When you're all I think about."

He presses his lips against mine. "Good, because you are all I think about, all I breathe. Everything about me is all for you."

I stare up at him, transfixed. All for me?

Chapter Thirty-One

Niko

I STARE DOWN AT my watch, counting how much time I have to get Everly home and then to work. Another appointment. They seem to be happening more and more as Everly's pregnancy progresses. I'm happy with each visit when they tell us everything looks good, but do they have to happen so often? Today was thankfully close, happening at the hospital she'll deliver at.

"Niko?" I hear my name called and turn to see who it is.

"Siobhan?" I say as one of my favorite cousins approaches me. I haven't seen her in a while, and she's a welcome sight after so long.

"Oh my God!" She steps forward and wraps her arms around me. "How have you been? I haven't talked to you in so long."

"Christmas two years ago? You should have called."

"Pot calling kettle." She's not wrong, but my life has been crazy busy, and that was before Everly and the baby.

"Hey, I'm not the one who changed their number."

She rolls her eyes. "Could've gotten it from Charlie," she says, a slight Irish accent coming through on her brother's name, a habit picked up from growing up in an Irish household.

"Ditto. What are you doing here?"

"Ah, it's my day off, but a friend of mine delivered her baby after my shift, so I'm visiting." Her brow furrows as she looks me over. "What brings you here? Everything okay?"

I nod. "Things are great."

"Yeah? Well, look at that smile you're sporting. What're you up to?"

"A baby boy Callahan."

Her eyes widen. "Oh, God, that is great. Seriously wonderful. How far? How come no one told me?"

"She's twenty-five weeks, and we haven't told anyone just yet. It wasn't exactly planned."

She laughs at me. "Most of them aren't. I work as a labor and delivery nurse, remember? I hear some crazy stories. We had a woman in a few weeks ago that had no clue she was pregnant. She went to the ER with back pain and thought she had a herniated disc in her back. It turns out she was thirty-nine weeks pregnant and had back labor. Boyfriend came home on leave from the military and apparently left something behind."

"Oh wow! How do you not know you're pregnant? I mean, I'm not a woman, but Ev is already all belly. Did she not notice she had one?"

"It happens. Some women don't get their periods. Some still have bleeding when they're pregnant. It can be light or a little heavier. That's not always a sure way of knowing, but she honestly didn't look pregnant due to her build. Good thing she wasn't a smoker or drinker. The baby was born strong and healthy. Once the shock wore off, the mother was actually thrilled once she held the little girl," she says, and I just can't imagine not knowing you had a child coming into the world.

"That's a crazy story," I say because it is.

"I know, right?" She smiles at me, and I'm glad I ran into her. I've missed her. She was always more of a sister when we were younger than just a cousin. Or at least I wanted her to be. Out of all my cousins, she was the one I hung out with during anything family related besides Charlie. She didn't judge and was a genuinely good person.

"So when do I get to meet her? What's her name?"

"Everly. Everly Hayes."

She tilts her head to the side, and I see the moment the name clicks with her. "As in Cameron Hayes? Your best friend, Cameron?"

I laugh and nod my head to confirm. "That would be the one. It's his younger sister."

"Well, I have missed out on a lot, haven't I, cousin?"

"Maybe a little bit, but it's all good. We can get lunch, and I can catch you up. I want to know what's going on with you, too."

"Not much, but yes! We should all do lunch together. Bring Everly. I'd love to throw you guys a baby shower," she says as she rifles through her purse.

"Yeah, you'll have to talk to Ev about that. I don't usually do that stuff."

"Well, cuz, you'd better get used to it because it's your baby too. It will be Jack and Jill."

"Jack and Jill? What the fuck is that?" I say entirely perplexed with her train of thought. She just laughs me off, grabbing a pen and a piece of paper from her bag.

"Don't you worry about it, silly man. Everly will know what it means. All you need to do is show up. Here's my number. Call me next week, and we can compare work schedules so we can make a date." She hands me her number and then hugs me again. I squeeze her back, and even though I have no idea what Jack and Jill is, I can't wait for her to meet Everly.

"It was so good to see you, Siobhan," I say and step back

"It was good to see you too, Nikolas. I better run. Don't forget to call me!" she says as she makes a quick retreat.

I turn back and Everly is standing in front of me, her expression a mix of anger and sadness.

"Everly?"

"Why?"

I scrunch my brow. "Why what?"

"You made me believe you, Niko. You made me think I was the only one, but the truth is you're still looking for your next lay."

"What the hell are you talking about, Everly?" I can feel the tension rising. Feel her walls returning brick by brick as she prepares to shut me out.

"You took that girl's number; did you give her yours too?"

My eyes widen when I finally understand. Shit. "You have the—"

"The wrong idea? Yeah, you're right about that. It's funny. I'm pretty sure I've heard that same line before. It's exactly what my ex said to me when I walked in on him fucking another woman. Do you guys go to some training and all of you learn the same shit to say when you get caught?" She shakes her head, and I see tears pooling in her eyes.

"Ev, baby, you *do* have the wrong idea."

"I had the wrong idea in thinking *this* was going to work, that I could trust you and that maybe, one day, we would be a family. How fucking stupid. After everything, how could I be so stupid? Goodbye, Niko." She turns and storms off.

I stand there, watching in stunned shock, trying to figure out how my life went from pretty perfect to shit in two point five seconds. There's no way I'm letting her walk away, and it only takes a few strides to catch up with her.

I reach out and grab onto her arm, stopping her. "Everly, wait. You don't understand."

"Let go of me!" There are tears running down her cheeks, and she's pulling to get away, her entire body bowed away from me.

"Everly!"

"No! Just leave me the fuck alone!" she screams, and I let her go. People are looking at the scene, and even though I want to go after her, I'm still in shock at how everything just went down.

After two days of no contact with Everly, I understand entirely how Tate feels. She won't pick up my calls and doesn't return them either. Text messages go unanswered.

A few months ago she was a mess, and now I'm the one that's a mess.

"Dude, you need to eat," Cam says as he tosses a plate down in front of me.

I shake my head. Hunger left me when Everly did. What's worse is that she isn't staying at her house, and I have no idea where she is. I want to ask Cam about her, but I know what can of worms that will open.

"What happened?"

I shake my head. "She saw me talking to a woman, exchanging numbers, and she flipped."

"And you don't see the problem here?" Cam asks, clearly taking me for an idiot. "What the fuck were you doing talking to another chick?"

I stare at him. "Siobhan Callahan."

His eyes go wide and his mouth opens, still waiting on the food inches from it. "Your hot-as-fuck cousin, Siobhan?"

"Yeah, I knew you had the hots for her."

"Who doesn't?"

"Me. I only have the hots for my girl and now I can't get her to talk to me."

"Dude, I would hope you didn't have the hots for your cousin. That's fucking gross," he says in disgust. "Didn't you explain?"

I throw my hand up in the air. "She wouldn't let me! She caused a scene and yelled at me to leave her the fuck alone."

Cam doesn't say anything to that, just looks down at his plate for a second. That's just great. He's been busting my balls about her since we started, and now a look of pity crosses his face. If he only knew that "she" in this scenario was his sister. I might have been able to ask for his help on this, but I'm fucking stuck trying to figure out how to get her to talk to me on my own.

What's worse is the plan was to tell Cam this weekend, but if she refuses to let me explain, to talk to me, that conversation is out the window for now.

"Just eat. If we get a call, I don't want to have to carry your ass out of a burning building because of you fainting," he finally says. You know you're good and truly screwed when Cameron Hayes is being the concerned and rational one.

Fuck my life.

Chapter Thirty-Two

Everly

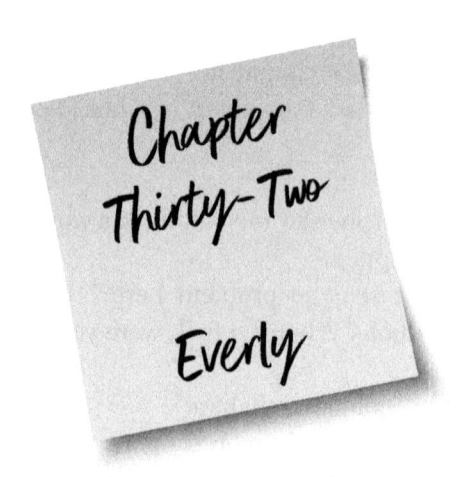

THE WHITE GLARE OF the screen begins to strain my eyes, but it's not until my phone vibrates next to my desk that I'm able to tear myself away. Niko's name flashes across the screen, but that's not the strange part. What is off is which phone it's showing on. Niko has always contacted me on my work line, but now it flashes on my personal phone.

I'm about to turn all my phones off so I'll stop seeing his name, but if they both go just to voicemail, I'm afraid he will show up at my office.

My life is utterly fucked. How did I get into such a twisted mess? I'm a few short months from having a baby, and I refuse to talk to the father.

He was talking to another woman, which doesn't really bother me, but it's the fact that she gave him her number and he took it after he told me again and again that I was what he wanted. He convinced me to trust him, to care for him, to open up to him, and then turned on all that at the first pretty girl in his path.

Then again, that might not have been the first. He could have been with other women this whole time.

"Just stop, Everly," I say to myself with a sigh. I know Niko isn't a cheater, but I just can't help the out-of-control scenarios my overactive imagination comes up with.

I know I'm in a fucked-up emotional state and probably overreacted, but I'm also stubborn as hell and right now unwilling to admit that the entire situation could be a fuck-up on my end.

My poor assistant, Lance, has been keeping his distance from me for the last few days. I'm sure he's afraid I'll start crying again, and he won't know how to deal with me. He's been so great with dealing with my crazy mood swings that I gave him today off. I figured that the more I do to bury myself in work, then the less time I'll have to think about Niko. Unfortunately for me, I'm hungry, and that means I need to get my own lunch or see who will deliver.

Screw it. I need some air anyway. I grab my bag and coat and head out to grab my lunch. At least food always makes me feel better.

It's past lunchtime, but I don't seem to care. I ended up grabbing a sandwich and then on the way back to my office, I stopped in this little children's boutique. I thought it was a great idea until I picked up a few things and started to text a picture of something I thought was adorable to Niko. Of course, I'd caught myself before sending it, but that just put me in a worse mood than before.

The elevator dings, letting me know that my floor has arrived and as I step off, I blink and am met with large, piercing grey eyes. Niko.

"What are you doing here?" I ask him. The receptionist isn't at her desk, and I don't know if that's a good thing right now or a bad thing. I'm not ready to have this conversation with him, and I just want him to go.

"Well, I fucking wonder." He steps closer, seething. "When do you plan on answering my calls, seeing as how you've been avoiding me?"

"I thought my lack of response would have been sufficient."

"It's not that fucking easy when you're carrying my kid."

"Shh," I hiss as I look around. "Keep your voice down."

His brow scrunches, and he glances around. "I hate to tell you, the baby bump between your hips is a bit of a giveaway that you're knocked up, or are you telling people that you swallowed a watermelon?"

"Of course not. Don't be an ass, Niko," I say and walk into my office. Niko follows behind me and closes the door. "Obviously people know, but that's not what I'm talking about."

"Then what are you talking about?"

I throw my hands in the air. "You! Coming here, to my place of employment and yelling our business to anyone within a hundred-foot radius."

"Maybe if you hadn't avoided my calls and texts all week, I wouldn't have had to come here to find you."

"You know where I live—that would have been more convenient," I say, knowing I was at my parents' house, glued to my phone as I talked to Aly.

He takes a step closer. "If you'd been home, that might have worked. Even if you were home the four times I went over, would you have let me in?"

I stare at him for a second before moving my gaze down to my coat that no longer zips around my midsection. "I don't know."

"And there's the problem. After all these months you're still running, and I want to fucking know why."

"Does it matter?" I ask.

"Hell, yes, it does. You didn't even let me explain. You just shut me out just like you did that asshole. One small problem is that we're connected for life. I'm not leaving, not running. I'm here, waiting for you, and you keep running. I'm telling you right now, Everly. You running isn't going to stop me from chasing you. I'm not fucking going anywhere, so get used to it."

A flutter moves through my chest as words my teenage self dreamed of fall from his lips. He's waiting for me, not me chasing him.

"You wouldn't be saying that if I wasn't pregnant. I'd be just another girl you fucked."

"That's not true, and you have never been just another girl that I've fucked."

Okay, if he's not going to leave, then I'm done here for the day. I push past him, opening my office door, moving toward the exit. "Whatever," I say. "You can stay and talk to yourself, but I'm done here."

There's a loud sigh behind me before the squeak of sneakers on the granite floor. Niko reaches me right as I step out into the elevator and ask the woman to press the lobby button for me. She smiles and does it, oblivious to the tension that is between the man that just followed me in here and me.

"I don't want to continue this conversation," I say as Niko steps up beside me.

"I don't give a shit. It's a conversation we need to have because your crazy hormone-driven ass isn't fucking thinking."

The woman next to us turns and looks over at Niko and then me. I smile before speaking.

"Sorry," I whisper like Niko isn't standing right next to me. "He has Tourette's syndrome. Completely harmless. Just cover your ears and ignore his mouth. I do it all the time." She turns away from me. I don't know who she is, and I don't care at this point. I just want away from him.

"Everly . . ." he growls.

"Take your meds, buddy. They really do help," I say and ignore him.

The elevator dings again and finally we are in the garage of my building. I walk out, the lights on my car blink as I deftly click the unlock button to make sure I can get in to get away as soon as I reach it. He's still on me, beside me, angry and seething, and I really just want to kiss him.

Fucking hormones.

"I have a doctor's appointment next Wednesday at eleven," I say as I pull open the door and sit down. Niko's hand shoots out as I try and close the door.

"We're not done, Everly."

"See you Wednesday."

He lets out a sigh, and I close the door, allowing me to back out and away from him. He doesn't bother trying to chase me further, and I'm grateful. I can't do this today.

I blow out an unsteady breath, a tear slipping down my cheek as I make my way out onto the roadway. What the hell is wrong with me? Niko hasn't missed a doctor's appointment and has been a doting boyfriend, and at the first possible sign, I look for a reason to push him away.

Why am I doing this to both of us?

The traffic takes me nearly an hour to get home, and I can't wait to get out of these clothes and relax. I finally popped a few weeks back, and each week since, my stomach gets bigger and bigger. I just want to relax, and I am missing the ability to have a nice glass of wine to unwind. That part of being pregnant sucks. Maybe I'll take a nice, hot bath with the lights dimmed and some lavender candles.

I drop my keys in the dish, my purse on the table, and hang my coat on the hall tree before I head up the stairs toward my bedroom. Maybe Chinese would make the perfect dinner, or perhaps Italian, or even some Mexican. God, a good burger sounds divine right about now with a side of onion rings.

I wonder if I can get each restaurant to deliver without them all arriving at the same time. I'd much rather they didn't judge me for wanting food from more than one place, in one night. That's all I need. The Mexican food delivery driver is showing up while I'm piling moo shu pork into my mouth from the Chinese driver that just left.

After changing into some lounge pants and a T-shirt, I continue debating my dinner options on my way to the kitchen. I turn the corner and stop, my eyes wide as I stare at a figure sitting on one of my island bar stools.

My blood runs cold as I stare into the green eyes that once melted me but now, seeing them so suddenly, frightens me.

"Hey, darling," he says with a smile so broad that shows all his teeth.

"Tate, what are you doing here?" I ask as the hair on the back of my neck rises. I'm trying not to freak out, but he's in my house, sitting in my kitchen as if we have done this a million times and like he has a right to be here. Is he serious?

My gaze flits around, trying to find out how he got in when I see the busted-out pane of glass on my backdoor. Which means he somehow climbed the six-foot privacy fence to break in unnoticed.

"You broke into my house?"

He holds out a bouquet of flowers. "Well, I wanted to surprise you, and I didn't see another way to do that, so yeah. I'll replace your window, darling."

"Tate, why did you break into my house?"

"Come on. Don't be like that. How else was I going to surprise you and give you these?" he says and pulls a bouquet of long-stemmed red roses from the table. "Happy birthday, Evie."

Birthday? Oh, crap. In all that's going on with Niko, I've forgotten my own birthday.

"You weren't answering your phone, so I had to find a way for you to talk to me."

I don't like the look in his eyes. There's something off. Maybe Niko and Cam were right.

We were practically living together in California. I didn't think he was the kind of man that would lie and cheat on me, but now that I know that he's not the man I thought he was, I can no longer stand to be in the room with him, never mind hear him call me Evie. No. He lost that right the first time he stuck his dick into another woman that wasn't me.

"Now we can celebrate together."

"Tate, I don't know what is going on, but we're not together. I'm pregnant, if you couldn't tell."

His gaze shifts down. "What your brother said was true?" He stares down for a moment, then locks eyes with me. "We're going to have a baby? I'm going to be a dad?"

"No, *we* are not having a baby. *I'm* having a baby. You are not involved in any part of this."

"What does that mean?" His expression drops and he looks around, jaw locked. "Are you cheating on me?"

"To be cheating on you, we'd have to be together. And not that it matters, but *you* were the one cheating on *me*!"

"Evie, listen. I've been trying to get you to talk to me for months. To explain. Things were so stressful at work, and I swear it will never happen again."

"I don't care. And stop calling me that. I didn't listen to what you had to say, Tate, because I didn't—and don't—care. Screwing around, lying to me, you don't get another chance. It's over. It's been over. The minute you chose to fuck another woman, it was over. The moment you chose to stick your dick in another woman was what sealed our fate as a couple."

"Everly . . . it's not that simple. We're connected now. I won't let you go. Our child deserves to have both of its parents, and I won't live away from the two of you any longer. I've already started the process of transferring here. It's probably going to take a few months, but that's okay. I can fly back and forth for a while, but I will not walk away from our child, and I'm not walking away from you."

"Tate . . ."

"No, Everly. No more. I know you were upset, but I told you, I made a mistake. I'm human. I won't do it again. Enough of this ignoring me. It's time for you to grow up and start thinking about more than yourself. There is another person involved now."

"Are you fucking kidding me?" I yell at him, snapping because I've heard enough. "You manipulating son of a bitch!"

"Everly, watch it," he growls out at me.

"No, Tate. You watch it! I'm not yours to push around. This isn't your baby. Thank fucking God for that one!"

"I don't believe you."

"I don't really care what you believe. The baby I'm carrying doesn't share a goddamn thing with you, and I'd appreciate it if you'd leave."

"Everly . . ."

"Now!"

He slams his hand down on the counter, making me jump. My mouth pops open as I watch his face redden, the skin contorting into a mask of pure anger.

"That should be my child!" he says, grabbing my arm.

"Calm down."

It's like a flip is switched, the anger suddenly gone, replaced by a sad smile. "It's okay. I'll raise it like it's my own, but the next one will be mine. I can't help it if someone took advantage of you."

"Took advantage?" What is he talking about?

"I know that I hurt you, darling, but I swear to God that is all behind us now. You were hurt, and you wanted to hurt me back. Done. We're even now. I'm not mad. I understand why you did it, but it's over. I wasn't ready, but I'm ready now, Everly."

I hate it when Cam is right.

The baby spins inside me as I begin to shake. I don't know what happened to the Tate I spent two years with, but the man in front of me, this manipulating sociopath, was never even a glimpse of his personality.

"You can come back if you want. I know how much you love Cali. I can stop the transfer."

"No, I can't. I don't even want to go back."

"Okay, then I'll let the transfer happen, I'll move here. We'll be a family."

"We will be nothing, Tate. Nothing. We are over, and there is no getting back together. What part of that don't you understand?" I say and start to move toward the door. His hand snaps up and grabs hold of my forearm, pulling it up as he yanks me closer. I arch away, cringing from the sting in my arm.

"Don't say that! Don't you fucking say that! You're mine. Ever since that day we met at the museum."

Museum? "That's when I thought you were someone different than you are now! Or someone I guess you've always been, but you hid it well the entire time we were together. Tell me, Tate, how many other women were there?" I ask, trying to sound strong, but my voice wavers.

I don't want him to think I still care, but what he did still hurts no matter the fact that I've moved on. He broke something that I don't think I'll ever get back.

I'm sure he can feel me shaking. "Tate, you're hurting me. Let go."

"I would never hurt you. I didn't mean to hurt you before. I just need you to hear me out, darling. Just . . . let's sit down and talk. We can fix th—" He doesn't finish what he's saying and I look up, hoping he'll just go.

Tate's face contorts, and he lets out a groan, his grip loosening. In my periphery, I can see the hand wrapped around his arm, squeezing. The energy radiating from behind me can only be one person because it's nothing but a crackling heat. Nothing but the overwhelming presence of Niko.

The fear falls from me, relief rushing in.

"Take your fucking hand off *my* girl," he says as he steps out from behind me. Tate's fingers let me go, and Niko crosses his other arm in front of me, sweeping me behind him. "And get the fuck away from *my* son."

The hairs on the back of my neck stand up, a shiver zipping down my back. Niko all primal and protective and projecting so much strength is a heady combination. I've never seen him this way. His jaw is locked, lip curled up into a snarl as he sends a death glare to Tate.

"What the fuck are you talking about? Who the hell are you?" Tate asks as he rips his hand away.

"No, you don't fucking get to ask any questions. You need to be answering some, like how the hell you got in here."

"How did you?" Tate counters.

"With my fucking key. Now answer the question before I lose all patience and beat the breath from your body."

Just as I start to move away from Niko and toward my phone, Tate tries to grab my hand. "Evie, don't do this. He's not me. You will never be happy with anyone but—" He doesn't finish his words, and suddenly I'm pulled back behind Niko again.

There is a crunch as Niko's fist meets Tate's face. "I told you to take your fucking hands off my girl."

There is a multitude of emotions from excitement, fear, and swooning that are running through my already messed-up emotional system.

Tate is bent over, his hands covering his face. "What the fuck! You broke my fucking nose!"

"You're fucking lucky I didn't bring my fire ax with me, asshole! I've got plenty of friends who would help me hide chopped-up parts of your body."

Tate's eyes widen. "This is who you are involved with? He's a lunatic!"

Niko steps in front of me again, blocking me from Tate's view. "Leave. Now. Before I call the cops."

"You don't know me!"

"I know enough. She told you to leave her alone. That means you don't call. You don't text, and you don't fucking come to her house. You show up here again, and I'll do more than just break your fucking nose. Now leave!" Niko yells, causing me to jump. I've never seen him this angry before.

Tate stands up. Blood is pouring from his nose, but he's stopped holding it. Instead, he brushes his pants off as if the floor soiling his suit pants is worse than the blood that has now stained his white shirt.

"I'll be in touch, Everly. I'm going to demand a paternity test. I have rights."

Niko starts laughing, and for a minute I forget that Niko just punched my cheating ex in the face. He's smiling as if Tate just told him the earth was flat and not round.

"That's fucking funny?" Tate says, causing Niko to stop laughing.

"It is," Niko says as he stalks toward Tate, who finally decides to show some fear at the fact that Niko is in his face and that he's a threat. "It's funny because if you think for one fucking second that the baby she's carrying is yours, you're even more out of your fucking mind than I thought."

"I'm not out of my mind. You're delusional if you think that I'm just going to walk away without knowing for sure that the baby she's carrying isn't mine."

"You are if you believe that I'm going to let you stress out the mother of my child. Now get out before I break more than your face and then call the cops."

Tate doesn't say anything right away. He just looks at Niko and then over to me before he turns and walks to my front door. "I'll be in touch, Everly. You can count on it," he says before closing the door.

Niko stands there for a minute, and I see that even though his back is to me, he's flexing his hands almost like he's fighting the urge to go after Tate or to calm himself down after the confrontation they just had.

"Are you all right?" I ask, and he turns to look at me. The anger on his face is quickly switching to one of concern and anxiety. He stalks toward me, pulling me into his warm body, and I can't help it, I bury my face into his chest, and a sob escapes me; the fear finally allowed an outlet.

"Shhh, he's gone, baby. I'm not going to let anything happen to you," he says in a soothing tone. "Either of you. You hear me, Ev? He will never put his fucking hands on you again. I'll kill him before I let him touch you." He pulls back, searching me from the head down. "Did he hurt you? All I saw was his hands grabbing you and you telling him to let go, and I almost lost it." I can't help it and laugh. "What's so funny?" I'm sure he thinks I've lost my mind after what just happened.

"You did lose it, Niko. Pretty sure he's going to try and press charges. You probably broke his nose."

"He broke into your fucking house, Everly. I don't give a fuck what he does, but I doubt he'd go to the police after the breaking and entering he just did. He deserves more than a damn broken nose."

I nod my head because I forgot about that. The adrenaline that I felt run through my body now has me crashing. I begin to shake uncontrollably, and I feel ridiculous that I can't stop myself.

"Hey, why don't you sit for a few minutes, okay? Maybe we should go to the hospital and get you checked out? None of this is good for you and the baby." He walks me over to the sofa and we sit, Niko's arms around me, and I tremble in his arms.

"No. I'm okay. I just need to sit for a few minutes. I didn't realize how scared and angry I was until you got here and told him to let me go. I honestly didn't expect to see him again."

"We knew, Ev. I don't know why you didn't see it, but your brother and me and your father all knew he wasn't going to walk away. Not after hearing about all the text messages and phone calls he was making to you."

I don't say anything to that because he's right. I don't know why I buried my head in the sand when it came to my breakup with Tate, but I just didn't want to think about him anymore. It's the main reason I left California, my job, and my house and moved back here.

"I'm just glad that I showed up when he was here. I don't want to think about what that asshole would have done had I not been here to throw his ass out."

"He thinks the baby is his," I say as I rub my hand on my belly and think back on everything Tate just said to Niko and me before he left. "He's going to come back. Probably try and force me into a paternity test."

"Like hell he is. If he wants proof, we can get something from your doctor stating how far along you are. He knows the baby isn't his. He's just looking for an excuse to stay in contact with you. The timing is way off unless there is something else I don't know?" He looks down at me, and I shake my head no, eyes wide.

"Of course not!" I say. "I wouldn't lie to you about that. I know I fucked up in the beginning, but Niko, I would never lie about being with Tate and you, and I would never lie about who fathered a baby. He's yours. I've only been with you since coming back home, and before that, it had been a good month since I was last with Tate and that was when I lived in California. Tonight is the first time I've seen him since I left there and moved home."

He pulls me back in and holds me tight. "I believe you, baby. I just wanted to make sure."

"I'm sorry," I say.

"For what?"

"For making it so that you have to question my trust when I'm the one who keeps questioning yours. I'm going to make it up to you. I promise that I won't lie to you again."

"I already trust you, Ev. It's not that. I just needed to ask," he says, but he asked, so I know there is still that small doubt. I meant what I said. I'm going to earn his trust. Our child deserves two parents that respect and trust each other. But first, we need to figure out how to make Tate leave me alone. My head's a mess. Finally, my shaking subsides. I just want to lay down and sleep until tomorrow. I'm emotionally drained to the point that I just want my bed and Niko's arms around me. I wonder if Niko would stay with me tonight. At least until I fall asleep.

Chapter Thirty-Three

Niko

I WANTED TO KILL that fucker! I still want to break him. I would have done more than punching him in his face had Ev not been there. I felt myself lose it when I saw his hands on her, and I snapped. I don't remember ever feeling that kind of rage go through me.

I hold Everly closer to me and make the decision I know needs to be made. Cameron has to know that this bastard is here in town. I won't leave her now, and if that means Cam finds out, then so be it. I can't worry about that shit right now. Everly and the baby are what is essential. My friendship with Cam will have to wait until I know she and the baby are safe from that fucker

"Ev, I need to call Cam."

"What, why?"

"Because, baby. You can't stay here."

"But this is where I live. It's my home. I'm not letting Tate force me from my home again."

"Everly, you cannot stay here alone. I have to work, and so does your brother. Tate doesn't know where Cam or I live. Worst case scenario, you can go to your parents' house, but I'm sure they'd be easier to find than Cam's." I look down into her red, tear-filled eyes, and my chest aches. "It's not forever, Ev. Just long enough for us to fix your window and get some kind of reliable security system installed here. Then you can come back."

"Okay, but what are you going to tell Cam?"

"The truth, Ev. We tell him the truth." She nods, and I'm relieved as hell she's agreeing. I can't do this shit anymore. All the hiding and lies are fucking killing me.

"Can we wait and do it tomorrow?"

"Babe..."

"I promise, tomorrow we will both sit him down and explain everything to him. I'm just tired, and I don't think I can handle more tonight. I just want to get some things and get out of here so that I can relax and get some sleep. It's been a crazy night already."

Shit. She's right. I don't want to add to the stress of what happened tonight by telling Cam. There is no way that come-to-Jesus moment is going to be a quiet and relaxed conversation between Ev, me, and my son's uncle. One more day isn't going to hurt.

"Okay, Ev. We'll wait till tomorrow. Grab your things, and I'll call Cam to let him know what went down tonight and that you're leaving. I'll be out here waiting for you."

"Okay. It shouldn't take me long. I can always come back and get more later."

"Not alone," I growl at her. "You don't come back here until we get the window fixed and the security system set up."

I don't mean to come across as angry, but this dude just will not take fucking no for an answer. I know he knows the baby isn't his, but he's using it as an excuse to try and stay in contact with her. Trying to manipulate her.

Over my dead body. When Cam hears that Tate showed up at Everly's house and what he said to his sister, there is no doubt in my mind that he's going to blow his lid.

"I won't come back alone," she says and pushes up on her toes to kiss my cheek. "I'll be back in a few minutes."

"Good!" I say and slap her ass as she walks away. "I like you much better when you're sensible." She snorts as she heads toward the stairs. From behind you still can't even tell that she's pregnant. She's nothing but the baby belly, and it's sexy as hell.

I pull my thoughts away from my girl and dial Cameron's cell. Tomorrow can't come soon enough, but for now, he just needs to know that we have an issue.

The phone rings three times before he answers.

"Cam, I'm taking Everly to your place. You off tomorrow? We have a problem, and she can't stay alone." I listen as Cam's concerned questions come over the line, and note his tone of confusion. "Yeah. Tate broke into her place. I told her to pack a bag, and I'd take her out of here until we can get her window fixed and maybe have that guy Louis knows that works for that alarm company install one here for her before she comes back." As I listen to Cam and answer whatever questions he has, Everly walks back into the room holding two small bags. I take them from her and wait while she grabs her jacket and puts her shoes on.

"Yeah, we'll leave now. I'll take her to your place and stay with her." She looks up at my comment, and I shake my head, letting her know it's all good. I'm sure she figured we'd go to my place, but I knew that once Cam found out that he would want her at his.

"Of course I will. She's fine, man. Just a little shaken up and stressed out. She said she wants to rest. I'll grab her something on the way to your place, and we'll see you in the morning. Yeah, okay. Later, man." I click end and Everly just stares. "You okay?"

"Yeah. I just thought we were going to your place. I'm sorry if Tate showing up here made you re-think your wanting to chase me, but I had no—"

"You think that I would let that fuck scare me away from you? Are you serious, Everly?"

"I don't know." Her bottom lip trembles. "I'm sorry, Niko. I'm just tired and emotional, and I don't know what I'm saying. Let's just go. Forget I said anything." She starts to lift her bag that I left by my feet, but I stop her by grabbing her hand.

"Ev, look at me." She does, and I want to swallow her whole. She's so vulnerable right now and reminds me so much of the younger version of the Ev I knew as a kid. "I'm not going anywhere.

I'll be here for as long as you want me and even when you don't want me anymore, I'll spend all my time and energy making sure that you do again, eventually." I smile down at her and she laughs, tears filling her eyes. God, I hate seeing her cry. It fucking shreds me. "I'm not going to make it easy for anyone to push me away from you. If I wouldn't let you do it, what makes you think I'm going to let that asshole, Tate, get rid of me? It will never happen. You and baby Callahan here," I say, placing my hands on her belly. "You're both my family now. I don't walk away from my family. Ever."

She nods and wipes a stray tear away. I can't help but note the way she has her hand fisted in my shirt. Like that little bit of touch is enough to comfort her. If it is, I'm okay with her never stopping touching me.

"Let's go get you settled at Cam's and then get you something to eat. You can get a good night's sleep; then tomorrow after Cam gets home from the station, we can tell him that he's going to be an uncle."

"He already knows he's going to be an uncle," she says, rolling her eyes.

"Yeah, but he has no clue that he's my kid's uncle."

Chapter Thirty-Four

Everly

SLEEP EVADED ME MOST of the night after the incident with Tate. We made it to Cam's house in less than fifteen minutes, and all I wanted to do was sleep. At least that's what my body wanted. My brain, on the other hand, had other ideas. I've tossed and turned for over an hour now and wish now more than ever that I could actually drink alcohol. I wouldn't be so miserable if I were curled up with Niko, but staying in Cam's unfamiliar home, in his spare bedroom, isn't conducive to Niko in bed with me. Especially since we have no real idea of when Cam will be home. My guess is first chance he gets, he'll be here.

A few hours after we got to Cam's, Niko got a call that Tate was on a plane back to California, which made me breathe a little bit easier. However, it did not send Niko home. Cam didn't feel I was safe yet and asked Niko to stay. Unbeknownst to my brother, it was no hardship on Niko.

It did make it harder on me because Niko was a few feet away and all I wanted was his arms around me. He didn't feel comfortable sleeping with me in Cam's home until Cameron knew about us. I need Niko more than I care to admit.

Luckily, or unluckily, depending on how our conversation goes this morning, we plan to sit down and tell my brother everything today once he gets home from work. I guess we won't have to hide anymore. I'd be lying if I said I wasn't worried about Cam's reaction to the news. More so of his response toward Niko.

I never wanted to come between the two of them or their close friendship, but somehow I've managed to do just that. I'm praying that Cam will be okay, but the part of me that knows my brother realizes that won't be the case. I just hope that he can get over it and not push either one of us away.

When the sun lightens the sky, I head out to the kitchen. Niko is asleep on the couch, and I stop in front of him. He is breathtaking even asleep. I take a quick listen for Cam before leaning over and brushing a few strands of hair from his forehead, placing a kiss. I'm not sure what time he was getting off, but better safe than sorry.

I make every attempt to be quiet in the kitchen, but Cam's granite counters make every dish I set down clank and echo.

There's a sharp intake of breath before Niko stirs. His hair is sticking up in all directions, and his eyes immediately find me. After a stretch, he pads over to me.

"Cam home yet?" he asks.

I shrug my shoulders, and he looks over at the clock on the stove. A smile forms on his lips as he steps up behind me, his arms slipping around my waist. I guess it's safe to say that means Cam isn't home yet.

"How are you doing?" He presses his lips against my neck, and I relax back into him.

It's not enough, but it helps to quell the buzzing in my veins.

"Couldn't sleep."

He rubs his hands over my bump and sighs. "Baby, that's not good."

"I need you." My voice is more of a whine than I intend.

He turns me around and rests his forehead on mine. "I know. Me too." His thumb brushes away a tear that slides down my cheek. "Why don't you go sit down? I'll make breakfast."

With a nod, I reluctantly leave the comfort of his arms. Niko takes over, breaking the eggs as I turn to sit at the table so I can watch him work.

"What does Momma and baby Callahan want?"

My stomach growls, our baby flipping, ready for food as well.

"Scrambled eggs and bacon on cinnamon raisin bread with a slice of cheddar."

Niko shakes his head and smiles. "A little weird, but not too off the charts."

"I didn't want pickles today."

He quirked his brow in question. "I thought you weren't down with the pickles."

I shrug. "The cravings kicked in last week, and they are getting weirder and weirder. When is your shift today?"

"I have today off. That's why us talking to Cam today works out. Well, for the most part. I go in tonight."

His schedule is all over the place, and I begin to wonder what he's going to do when the baby arrives. We haven't talked about it yet, and I don't know if he gets paternity time.

The bacon pops in the pan while I watch Niko move around the kitchen. He knows what he's doing, evident in the many delicious meals he's made over the past months. Unlike Cam, who can't even boil water without burning a pan, Niko's mother taught him to cook.

"Are you okay?"

I didn't realize I'd spaced out, Niko's words shaking me, and I nod. "Just thinking."

"About?"

I turn, looking away from him, and swallow hard. "He scared me, and I'm afraid he's not going to stop."

The sound of the frying pan clanking onto a different burner rings around the room before Niko's footsteps echo. He cups my face, turning me to look at him. Grey eyes that hold a fire stare back at me.

"I'm glad that you are finally taking this guy seriously, Ev, but I won't let him anywhere near you, do you hear me? That fucker will never lay a hand on you."

He presses his lips to mine before dropping down to his knees in front of me. The feel of his hands on my stomach makes the baby spin, but I don't think Niko can feel him. I reach out and brush his hair back; his black hair is silky between my fingers. This is the connection I so desperately need right now.

"I honestly never thought he would act like that. I realized when he cheated on me that I didn't know him, but yesterday made me see that I never really knew him at all."

"People hide in sheep's clothing. It happens, and you learn from it, Ev, but baby, I won't let anyone hurt you. I'll protect you both for the rest of my life." He leans forward and kisses my belly. "You're my family, my life."

"What the fuck is going on here?"

My gaze snaps toward the voice, eyes widening as my mouth pops open.

Shit! Cam.

His jaw is locked, eyes blazing as he stares at Niko's hand which is still on my belly.

Niko slowly stands, his touch leaving me as he faces his best friend. He steps toward Cam, his hand out. "Listen—"

Cam cuts him off, rushing forward, grabbing Niko's shirt and pushing him backward until his back slams against the wall.

"I told you to stay the fuck away from her!" Cam growls, baring his teeth.

"Cam, stop!"

I'm powerless to stop anything, stuck as an observer. We knew Cam wouldn't take us well, but I'm not prepared for this violent of a reaction from my brother.

"This is your only fucking chance to come clean. Have you fucked my sister?"

Niko throws up no resistance, his eyes locked on Cam. "Yes."

A snarl rips from Cam as his arm swings back and collides like a freight train into Niko's jaw.

"Stop!" I cry out, tears falling as I watch the one thing I didn't want to happen play out before me.

"You son of a bitch! I thought you were the one person I could trust. How could you?" he asks but doesn't wait for an answer before his fist connects again with Niko's face. I hear bones crack, but I can't tell whose bones it is.

"Cam, please, stop," I beg. My plea goes unheard or ignored, punches flying. Either way, this has to stop or they are going to kill each other. I grab the plate that Niko had out for our breakfast, and I throw it against the wall. It lets out a loud crack as it shatters and falls to the ground. Both men stop and look at where the plate now lays in pieces on the floor, then their eyes turn to me. Breathless, bloodied, and nostrils flaring from their brawl, Cam pushes away from Niko who then walks toward me.

"What are you doing, Ev? You could have fucking hurt yourself or the baby." He takes my hands in his and looks me over.

"Tell me you're not the father," my brother growls at Niko, who looks at me, knowing this is it. It's now or never. Can't get any worse than this, can it?

Niko turns to Cam as he wipes his mouth with the back of his hand, a thin line of red left behind. "I could never do that. He's my son."

"You son of a bitch. I warned you not to fuck with my sister. Now you fucking knocked her up, and you've got another chick—"

"Stop!" I yell at him. "Just listen, Cameron!"

"And you! You have no idea that he . . ." Cam trails off, his eyes wide. I know then the pieces are snapping into place. All the little lies and omissions from both of us over the past seven months I'm pretty sure are running through his mind, adding up. "She's your Post-it note girl. Everly is the one who ran out on you."

"He didn't know who I was, not that it matters," I say.

Cam turns toward me, his lip curled up into a snarl. "He didn't know who you were? Are you fucking kidding me, Everly?"

"It's the truth!"

"How fucking long?" he asks, and I'm confused. He knows how far along I am. "How fucking long have you been fucking my sister behind my back, Niko?" he yells at me, but the question is for Niko.

"Since the night she got back into Boston," Niko says and stares my brother in the eyes.

"He's not telling you everything, Cameron. Just listen and stop screaming at everyone."

"I'm having a case of what-the-fuckitis right now, so excuse me if I'm not treating this whole clusterfuck with kid gloves. Pun intended, yeah?"

"Cameron . . ." Niko says, and my brother turns toward his front door, opening it.

"Get the fuck out of my house," Cam says, pointing to the outside of his door.

Niko nods, moving to the couch to grab his bag and keys. I follow behind him, pulling his hand back so he won't go. Niko turns and stares at me, a look of sorrow on his face, and it crushes me to see it there. He knew this would happen. Knew that Cam wouldn't forgive him, but he has to. If he would just tell him everything, then maybe Cameron would turn some of his anger toward me and not just blame Niko.

"No, wait! Cam, just listen. I know you're angry, but this isn't all on Niko. Actually, it's—"

"Everly," Niko says and shakes his head no while squeezing my hand. I don't understand. Why won't he tell him that it was me that started this?

I can't ask him here, but if he's leaving, so am I.

I walk past Cam and into my room for the same. My heart hammers in my chest as I throw my clothes and toiletries into my overnight bag.

"I'm not done with you, Everly," Cam grits out when I emerge from the bedroom.

Niko takes my bag from me and slings it over his arm before holding his hand out to me, waiting for the other bag.

"I'm not a kid you can ground. I'm a fucking adult, Cameron, and I don't have to do what you tell me to. I'm with Niko. I'm pregnant with his baby, your nephew, and I'm going to stay with him. This wasn't how we wanted to tell you, and that's on me. Unfortunately, this is how you found out." I lace my fingers with Niko's. "I'll talk to you once you've calmed down some, but I've had enough going on in the past twenty-four hours that I just can't deal with you too. If you are kicking Niko out, then I'm going with him."

"Everly . . ."

"No, Cameron. You're angry. I get that. I understand that. I'm sorry that you found out like this and that we didn't tell you sooner. That's my fault, but I'm not sorry that I'm with Niko. Call me when you calm down, and then we can talk about this."

Niko grabs my second bag and then my hand, and we walk out of my brother's home. I'm praying that we aren't walking out of his life too. I've never seen my brother so angry before, and that doesn't sit well right now.

Chapter Thirty-Five

Niko

"WHAT NOW?" EVERLY ASKS, drawing my attention after I merge in with traffic.

What does she mean? "Now you stay with me, obviously."

"Will that work with your dating schedule?"

I let out a groan, finally understanding. She's still off her rocker about Siobhan.

"Everly . . . I just threw my relationship with my best friend out the window for you. For fuck's sake, you just called me your boyfriend in front of your brother. You've been affectionate . . . I thought we were past that shit."

"I'm sorry," she says, but she doesn't sound convincing.

"You're it. My girlfriend, the chick who has my balls and my motherfucking heart."

She blinks at me. "Your heart?"

"Why do I have to be the vulnerable fucking one in this situation when *you're* the one with the hang-ups?" I ask her. Because that's how it always is.

"Well then, just tell me who that woman was. Is her number stored in your phone?"

"Yes."

Everly gasps, and I let out another groan. This isn't getting us anywhere.

"Just . . . take me to a hotel."

"Not happening. You're not leaving my sight."

"Why not?"

"Because I fucking love you and I'm not letting that motherfucker get near you two. And I'm going to let your suspicious ass stew a little more since you were an ice bitch to me for a week, not letting me tell you about my cousin, Siobhan Callahan."

In my periphery, I can see the fight drain from her, the blood leave her face. She slouches into the seat. "Your cousin?"

"Yes. I told her about the baby and she wants to throw a Callahan family baby shower for us." Somehow, she either didn't hear me blurt out that I was in love with her, or she's chosen to ignore it.

"How many cousins do you have? I don't even know much about your extended family."

I glance at her, trying to figure out what she's thinking. "Well, you know my dad was a first- generation Irish American, and my mom is from Greece. There are a few Greek cousins that I've only met a few times, but I have sixteen Callahan first cousins."

"Sixteen?"

I nod. "Irish Catholic. Dad was one of six. Siobhan is one of five from Dad's Irish twin brother, Sedan."

"He had a twin?" she asks.

I shake my head. "Irish twin."

"Well, yeah, he's Irish."

A chuckle erupts as I realize the issue. "Irish twins are siblings born within twelve months of each other."

"Oh."

"Dad's the only one who had one kid, and everyone blamed my mom for that, but the truth was she miscarried and never carried to term after me."

"Why would they blame her for that?"

"Some of the family didn't like that he married a Greek girl and not a 'good' Irish girl. They kind of ostracized him, and I became the black sheep of the family."

"Why?"

"Because I'm the son of the Greek woman who stole away their poor Lonan. Not everyone feels that way, but there are some who don't approve of my existence. My mother's family wasn't crazy about my mom not marrying a Greek either, but they didn't push her away like my dad's side of the family did."

"That's crazy!" Everly cries out. "Not that there's anything wrong with your parents, but you were innocent."

Suddenly, Everly starts sobbing, tears raining down her face. It's so sudden, so strange, I pull off the road and throw the car in park.

"Baby?" I ask as I undo my seatbelt, then lean over to cup her face.

"I'm s-sorry," she manages to say between hiccupping sobs. "I'm sorry I was such a bitch. I'm sorry for not trusting you. I got scared."

"Why were you scared?"

"Because I'm in love with you, too." I smile at the words I've been waiting to hear from her lips, ignoring the pain in my own.

"Your lip," she says, reaching out to ghost her fingers over the large split I can feel in the swelling of my lip.

"I'm lucky he didn't knock any teeth out."

"I've never seen my brother like that before. He was so angry."

"I knew he would be."

"Why didn't you tell him everything?" she asks. "Why didn't you want me to tell him that it was me that lied to you, that this was my fault?"

I let out a breath and try to explain to her the best that I can. This isn't going to just blow over. "Because regardless of how it started, Ev, I knew after, and I still didn't tell him. I didn't know who you were when I took you back to my place that first night, but Cam knows that I knew at some point, and I still didn't tell him. I lied. That's not something he's likely to get over tomorrow. I broke a trust that we've always had between us. One that I'm not sure I can ever earn back."

"He was trying to tell me that you had other women, wasn't he?"

"Probably, but he also knows that I've been talking about just one woman for a while now. No matter what he was going to say to you, he knows that I haven't been fucking around. He's been bitching at me for a while now to snap out of what he called a funk, but it wasn't what he thought."

"It wasn't?'

"No. Not at all." I lean forward and rest my forehead on hers. "When are you going to understand that all I see, all I've been able to see since you steamrolled into my life again, is you."

"But, you've never been committed to one woman before. You said that yourself. What if you get tired of me?" Her breath speeds up. "What if I get so big carrying this baby that you don't want me like that, and you want to go back to fucking other women?"

I groan at her words. God, this fucking dickhead did the worst possible thing a person could do to anyone by cheating and lying to her.

"Ev, I'm a very sexual man. I'm not going to try and bullshit you here. I like sex. I've had lots of sex. I've been with a lot of different women over the years, but I've never lied to them, and I've never led them to believe I would give them more than a sexual relationship. I've never wanted more than that. I have never wanted to commit to anyone before you. I've never been ready so when I say I like sex and I mean . . . I like lots of it."

"Oh my God. Enough Niko, I get it, you like fucking sex. I don't want to listen to this anymore. I'm hungry. My feet hurt and I'm hormonal. That's never a good combo so shut up, because I swear to God, Nikolas Callahan, if you start listing off the bimbos you've slept with next and rate them, I'm going to rip off your beans and frank and grab the ketchup!"

My eyes widen, and I sit back on my side of the car. "Well that was a fucking visual I don't want. I don't think I'll ever get that out of my head, but baby, you didn't let me finish." Before she can start again, I place my hand over her mouth, shushing her, then smile as she glares daggers at me.

She reaches up and pushes my hand away. "What? I didn't say that I'd skin your one-eyed snake."

I shake my head but can't help the shudder that runs through me at the thought she just planted in my head. This woman could be vicious if I'm not careful. I won't ever forget that fact. Last thing I want to see is her Bobbit impersonation.

"What I was going to say was . . . I only want to have lots of sex with you. No matter how big you think you are, I will always see you as my beautiful woman. I only see myself having tons of sex with *you*. And if you're too tired or feel unsexy, for whatever crazy reason you have conjured up in your head, I'll just have to prove to you that you are who I want. Whenever. However. Forever."

She sucks in a breath when I say the last word, but I'm not done.

"I want to have more babies with you, Everly, and if that's not what you want right away, well, then we can just have fun practicing for the future. Don't push me away. Have faith in me. For once, have faith in *us*. Don't punish me for my past and for Christ's sake, baby, don't punish me because of yours. I'm *not* him. I'll *never* be him. I watched how my father looked at my mother my whole life, and he worshipped the ground she walked on until the day he died. I want that. I want you."

Everything is silent as she stares at me, processing all that I've just said.

"Where did you come from, Nikolas Callahan?" she asks, making me smile. Not the response I was looking for, but shit . . . I'll take anything but her doubt when it comes to us.

"Well, you see, that's not something that I like to think about. We obviously both know where babies come from, babe, but that is not something I like to remember."

"Niko, your parents obviously had sex."

I roll my eyes at her and then cover her mouth with mine. Lifting away from her, I look into those beautiful hazel eyes of hers, and it's then that I see it.

"You're my home, Everly Hayes. I'm pretty sure I loved you that first night we were together. Hell, if I'm honest with myself, probably even when you were a kid."

"Ummm that's kind of weird, but I'll take it. I do think you're just saying that, though, because I was just a kid and you were a teen."

"I was, but you are misunderstanding me. It wasn't the type of love that I have now for you, beautiful girl. I was always jealous of Cam."

"Jealous, why?" She looks perplexed.

"Maybe jealous is the wrong word. It wasn't a bad feeling. Envious is a better word. He had you. I was an only child, and you worshiped the ground he walked on. He protected you at every turn. I wanted that. It's why I didn't want you to take the blame in all this. I don't want things to change for you and him. He's your brother. Your family. He'll get over being upset with you and all will be right again."

"What about you?"

"You let me worry about me. Just don't stress yourself out worrying about your brother and me. I'll deal with Cameron when it's time. What happens after that is for me to worry about, okay?" She eyes me warily, but then her eyes soften as she looks me in my eyes.

"You've got it wrong, though, Niko. I worshiped the ground both of you walked on. It wasn't just Cam."

I smile at that. "I wouldn't mind you worshiping the ground we're on now if you know what I mean?" I wag my eyebrows at her, causing her to laugh. "I love you, Everly Hayes. We're taking this journey together, and I hope that we'll take many more in the future. With or without your brother's blessing. I'm not going anywhere."

"I love you, too." She leans up to kiss me, and for now, my problems with Cameron are on hold. For now.

Chapter Thirty-Six

Everly

"OKAY, SWEETHEART, THEY'VE GOT the security system all set up," Dad says as he ends the call with the dispatcher from the security company. No one has let me back into my house until the proper precautions are up, so I'm happy that the security system is finally in place. It's been very disjointed the past week and a half without my stuff. More importantly—without my body pillow.

"Thanks, Dad," I say, looking at my father. I know that he's worried about us and taking care of the installation of this new security system on my house has at least put him a little more at ease.

"I want you and my grandson to be safe," he says as he draws me in for a hug and runs his hands up and down my arms. "I have to tell you how relieved I am that Tate isn't my grandson's father."

"Mom said you would feel that way. I'm sorry, Daddy. I didn't want to lie, but I was worried about how Cam would react."

He nods. "Niko is a good man. I know he'll do everything he can for you two. Cameron is angry and hurt right now. Give him some time. The two of you is a bit of a shock, but in a way, I'm not surprised."

Niko and I got here a little while ago. He had to work later and didn't want me to be alone when he wasn't home, so we came here. My mom grabbed Niko as soon as we walked in the door claiming she had some things for him to help her with, but I knew she wanted to give my dad and me a few minutes to talk alone. Now that we're alone and he mentioned Niko, I'm curious to hear what he has to say.

"Why do you say that?"

"You don't remember our talk? The one where you were adamant you were going to marry Niko."

I shake my head and roll my eyes. "Dad, I was twelve."

"You were *very* adamant."

"Well, I can assure you that was not my intent when I moved back."

He laughs. "Maybe not, but as I said, I'm not surprised. You followed your brother and Niko around anywhere they would let you. If your head wasn't buried in one of your books, you were hightailing it after those two boys."

I laugh at the memories. I was pretty bad.

"That was puppy love, Daddy. I had no idea what real love was. I was just a baby."

He looks over at me, searching. "And what is it now, Ev? What kind of love do you have for Niko now?"

I think about his question for a moment, but not because I'm unsure. I want my dad to know that this is real. After Tate and getting involved with Niko so soon after. Plus, the fact that it started out on a lie.

"I love him. Not because he's the father of my baby. He's everything I wanted, and I didn't even know I was looking for. I was really hard on him in the beginning, but he stuck it out with me. He's put up with my mood swings and all of my insecurities, and he's still here. He even put the baby and me before his relationship with Cam, and I know that it's killing him."

My father nods his head in understanding. "Niko and Cameron have been friends a long time, sweetheart."

"I know, Dad."

"Best friends."

"I know that too. Why are you telling me something that you know I already know?"

"Because, Everly. He can be your best friend, too. That doesn't have to change what Cam and Niko have."

"That's why it's killing me to see him so hurt over the fact that he feels as if that door is closed now. That Cam will never forgive him, and they'll never get back their friendship."

"Talk to Cameron."

"I tried, but he was so mad he wouldn't listen. He lost it and punched Niko without even giving us a chance to to tell him anything."

"I heard, but Everly, if you explain things to your brother, make him see that this thing with Niko isn't going to go away. That you love him. I'm hoping that Niko returns those feelings, am I right?"

"He does. He's not only told me, Daddy, but he's shown me how much I mean to him. This thing with Cam is one of them."

"Then show him. Let him see that this is it for the two of you. It's not his worst fear. Your brother has always scared away the boys when it came to you. When he left for college, you'd have thought he was your father and not me. He grilled me on who you were to stay away from and the places you and Alyson liked to go and forbid me to allow you to go to these places."

I bust out laughing because I know that his demands on my parents had more to do with Aly than they did with boys back then. Pretty sure that hasn't changed, but I won't let that distract me from the current situation I have with Cam.

"I can imagine that list."

He smiles and shakes his head. "I wasn't that dad, but I did keep an eye on you. I knew I could trust you to do right by your decisions in life, and I also knew that you had your own mistakes to make and to learn from. Cam needs to know that this is your life. It always has been, Everly. You've marched to your own drum for a very long time. Even when you were a child following after two boys that weren't your age. If someone told you no, you did it anyway, just to prove to everyone that you could. I'm proud of you and everything you've achieved already. I know that you're going to be the best mother, and Niko will be a great father. Your brother will see that too."

He hugs me, and I don't say anything else, just place my head on his shoulder and sit with my dad for a few more minutes. We both hear the front door open, and then my brother's voice calls out to my mom who's hopefully still outside in the garage with Niko. Guess there is no better time than the present.

"Talk to him, Ev," Dad says.

I take a deep breath and make my way out of the room in search of Cam. I just hope I can fix this between Cam and Niko because I really want them both in my life without the tension, and I know Niko wants his brother back.

I walk toward the kitchen where I find Cameron drinking a glass of water, his back toward me.

"Hey," I say, and Cam stiffens, but doesn't stop drinking and says nothing in return. Guess he's still mad, but he didn't tell me to go to hell yet, so I guess that's a good sign. "We planned on telling you."

"When? After the baby got here?" Cam growls. "Was I just going to see him in the delivery room and have it click then just what the fuck has been going on?"

No, he's not calmed down.

"Cam."

"No, Everly. It's not like this is a few weeks after finding out, this is months. You're six months pregnant. Merry fucking Christmas and a Happy New Year to me."

"It wasn't like that, Cam. Niko wanted to tell you in the beginning, but we were just figuring things out. We never meant it to go on for so long. For what it's worth, he never meant to go against his word."

"But he did. He promised me! For crying out loud, Ev. I asked him to keep an eye out for you because fucking Jake was sniffing around you, and I didn't want you to get hurt. You deserve better."

"Cameron, I'm telling you that it wasn't like that at all," I say.

"But it wasn't Jake I needed to worry about, was it?" he says, talking over me. "No . . . Niko had already made his play for you and lied to my fucking face every time I asked him about this woman he was seeing."

Niko steps out from the doorway. "It's was my fault, Cameron. Don't yell at her like that."

Cam glares at him and shakes his head. "No, don't even try—"

"I told him my name was Alyson," I say, cutting him off. "He didn't recognize me, and I lied to him. He's wrong. It wasn't his fault, Cam. Be mad at me because I'm the one that started this."

"Oh, I'm plenty mad at you, little sis, but even if you were the one that first night, I know damn well it wasn't the only time." He turns to Niko. "So, when was it? When did you sleep with her, knowing full well who the fuck she was?"

"That night at The Sinclair," Niko says without pause. "You know how I'd been, unable to think of anyone other than her. Well, to you, she was my Post-it note girl. That night we had too much to drink, and I couldn't fight against it any longer. I didn't want to. I put my loyalty to you and our friendship on the line."

"For pussy."

I cringe at Cam's words.

"Watch your mouth, Cameron. She's still your sister. I'm not going to stand here and let you disrespect her in front of me."

"I wasn't talking about my sister. At least I didn't know that I was. That the woman you were losing your goddamn mind over was Everly, but you let me go on and on about this woman. Never once calling me on my shit and telling me that the woman that I was bad mouthing, the woman that left a fucking Post-it note on your cock was Everly."

"Cameron!" I whisper-yell at my brother, looking toward the other rooms where my parents are probably listening. This isn't the place for this, but he's not going to stop when he's this angry.

"I know you, man," Cameron says to Niko. "You have never in your life committed to one woman. Not one, and there have been many," he says looking to Niko and then to me. I can't deny what he's saying because I know he's right. I've always known that Niko and my brother were the epitome of manwhores, but that doesn't mean people don't change.

"Why her?" he asks. "Why of all women did you have to go after Ev?"

Niko shakes his head. "It just happened, Cam. I didn't know who she was when I met her at the pub. I know that's not an excuse because eventually I did find out and I continued to see her. It wasn't something that I decided on a whim. You saw me, man. You saw how fucked up I was when she thought I was fucking around on her with my cousin Siobhan. You know that I haven't been with anyone else. Of all people, man, you know," Niko says to a stoic-faced Cameron.

"And how do you know she's not just a shiny toy for you?"

"This isn't something that's just going to pass, Cam. You're not wrong about my past. I've never wanted anyone, until her. It's something I can feel in my bones. It wasn't done to anger or hurt you, it was done to appease every fiber of my being that screamed out for her," he says, and I'm no longer wondering what my brother is thinking because I'm too busy hanging onto every word that Niko says about his feelings for me.

"How do you know it's real or just because of a mistake?"

"Getting pregnant was an accident, but not a mistake," he says to Cam. "My son was never a mistake." Niko looks to me. "Baby or not, Ev, there is no way I would have been able to stay away from you," he says and then turns back to my brother. "I've never felt like this before. Never thought I'd want to, to be honest. I don't want to go back to the time before her because I know now what it's like to love someone."

I can feel the tears trailing from my eyes as he says things to me that up until recently, I thought would never be more than a childhood fantasy. Here he is, years later, admitting he loves me in front of my brother, and my heart is bursting.

Niko walks to me and pulls me close to him then turns back to Cam. "We're going to be family. It doesn't matter if you approve or not. We'd both rather that you did, and that you were a part of this. I'm asking you to please be part of it, Cam. You're my brother."

Cam shakes his head. "I wish that were true, Niko, but I really fucking can't stand you right now, and I need to leave before I make you a fucking bloody mess on the floor of my parents' house," he says before turning and walking away.

My eyes widen as I watch my brother's back disappear around the corner. A moment later the back door slams so hard the windows rattle. I look over at Niko, who's hanging his head. If that didn't reach my brother, I don't know what else will.

"I honestly thought we were getting to him," I say, saddened by his reaction.

"He's fighting it, and it's going to take a while to break through to him, if ever." He looks down at me sadness etched in his handsome features. Lifting a hand, he reaches up to trace my cheek with his fingers. "What?" he asks when I just stare at him.

"You really do love me," I say, but it's not a question. I know. What I said to my father was all true, but hearing it again just cements it for me.

He nods. "I do. So fucking much, baby."

"You have no idea how long I've waited for you."

"Since you were twelve," he says with a chuckle and that cocky-ass smile of his.

I smile at him and brush a strand of hair from his forehead. "Sounds about right."

Chapter Thirty-Seven

Niko

MY SHIFT STARTED TWO hours ago, and it's the first shift I've worked with Cam on at the same time since the shit that went down with Ev happened. He switched shifts with Bishop and Jenkins pretty much every shift for the past two weeks, even working on Thanksgiving Day to avoid me. Bishop told me that he and Jenkins decided to tell Cam no this week in hopes that we'd "work through our shit," as Jake put it.

Needless to say, it hasn't been going well. We are about to head out on a call, but as Cam and I both move to take our usual positions on the truck, Cam makes it clear that working shit out isn't going to happen anytime soon.

"Stay the fuck out of my way," Cam says as we climb onto the truck.

The siren blares, and we're off. It takes longer than it should to weave through the traffic, but the cause of the call is blatant when we round the last corner.

A three-decker apartment building with flames shooting out the second-floor window.

There are people in the yard wearing pajamas, staring up at the building. A couple of guys move to the hose, two for venting, while me, Cam, and Jenkins run into the building. We all head off and start the process of making our way slowly through the place, searching for residents while the others try to get control of the fire. The site is burning faster than we can look. What started in the basement apparently shot up the walls and is now burning from the top down. A few minutes later, I hear the chief call it over the radio.

"Hayes! Callahan! Jenkins! Get out now!" he calls over the scanner.

We immediately stop our search and turn back in the direction of the front door. My heart is hammering in my chest as I try to see through the smoke and get out before the roof collapses. I'm twenty feet from the door, about six behind Jenkins, when I hear a loud crack. The ground shakes, and there's a scream over the line as I turn to look at Cam, but he's not there. I stare into the haze trying to see anything, but all I see is smoke and debris, the heat from the fire making moving closer almost impossible.

"Cam!" I yell and head back to where he was.

A massive chunk of the floor above is missing, giving a view of the flames licking at the ceiling of the second floor. More debris falls as the structure fails, dropping down all around me, but I refuse to leave without Cam.

He was only about eight feet away, but the fallen section starts at six. It's at the point now where I can just see maybe two to three feet in front of me.

"Cam, can you hear me? Cameron!"

There's a low groan over the line, but I can barely hear it over the roaring of the flames and the harshness of my own breath. I start moving furniture and chunks of fallen joists until I reach the main slab that came down. I see yellow glints from the reflectors on Cam's gear. He's half under the section of floor, flames all around him.

"Fuck! Cameron, can you hear me?" I ask but get no response. He isn't moving, not trying to get out from under the weight.

Another section falls, and the chief is yelling in my ear. There's no time, so I grab onto Cam's arms and pull, praying that I'm not doing more damage, but I don't have a choice. There's no time. I grab him, but I only get a few inches before his gear gets caught in the debris.

There's a reason I work out, a reason I strengthen my muscles as much as I can; because of this job, and moments like this. With one hand, I grab onto his belt and the other I grab onto a joist. I don't even count to two before I pull in two different directions—up on the beam and out on Cam.

It does the trick, and I'm able to pull him out from under the weight of everything. There's still no response from him, and I can't even tell if he's breathing.

"If you survive this, you're not giving me any more crap about your sister," I say as I kneel down and grab one arm. I pull it across my shoulders while I dig one shoulder into his stomach, the other arm wrapping around his leg before I press through my legs to stand.

The fire is raging even more, bits of the building crashing down all around us. Each step is hard and heavy and as fast as I can move with his dead weight on me. The heat from the flames is fucking unbearable, and I want out of this gear, now! Finally, I see the door and the light just outside. We make it through the door, a loud crash behind me as the third floor gives way, billowing smoke out around us.

I make sure we're clear before letting the fatigue take me down to the ground. The guys are swarming around us, grabbing onto Cam and lifting him from my shoulders in time for the EMTs to grab him.

I pull my mask off, drawing in a full breath that only makes me cough. All of my muscles are wiped, and I fall the rest of the way to the ground.

"He's breathing," Bishop says, leaning over me. He's got an oxygen mask in his hand that he places over my nose and mouth. "Good job."

"Every . . ." deep breath ". . . body . . ." another breath ". . . out?" I ask as I draw in the clean, highly oxygenated air.

Jake nods in confirmation. "Everybody is out."

I'm happy everybody is out, but just because Cam is breathing doesn't mean he's okay. Glancing over, I watch as they load him into the bus and slam the doors. I need to go with him. I need to get to the hospital and make sure he's going to be okay. If something happens to him, all that I can think about is that the last conversation I had with him was with him angry as hell at me for being with his sister behind his back. I don't want that to be what I remember if he doesn't make it for some reason.

"Callahan, there's another bus coming, and I want you on it," the chief says.

I shake my head. "I'm fine, chief. I'm going to go, but just to find out about Hayes. I just need a minute."

"You're going to the hospital so you can get checked out. Don't give me any shit, Callahan."

I give him a nod, knowing it's useless to argue with him. Also, I'll be close to Cam and can keep up to date on how he's doing. "Hayes is in good hands, Niko. He'll pull through this. No way is that jackass is going to check out on us so soon. Not when his main purpose in life is to be a pain in my ass," Chief says.

I want to laugh and tell him he's right, but he wasn't conscious. Until I see him awake and yelling at me again, I'm not going to be able to think straight. "I need to let his family know," I say to him.

"Don't worry about that. Just get yourself checked out, Callahan. I'll see you at the hospital."

Shit, my phone is at the station, and I don't know Everly's number. Maybe it's better I don't call her yet anyway. She'll probably freak out, and I don't want her upset right now until we know what exactly is going on with Cam. I'll figure out how to get word to her after we know more.

"Callahan! Your ride's here," Bishop yells. Good. Let's get this shit over with so I can find Cam.

An hour later and I'm at the hospital. They're about to give me my walking papers, setting me free to go find out more about

Cam. Last I heard he was still unconscious, and they were running some tests. The door flies open, and Everly runs in. There are tears streaking her skin, and a sob wracks her when she sees me and wraps her arms around me, burying her face in my neck, and holding onto me like she's not sure I'm really here. She finally pulls her face from me, and her red, puffy eyes meet mine. I wipe a few of the tears that keep rolling down her face.

"Hey, baby," I say, a small smile on my face. I didn't want this. I knew she'd freak out.

"How is he?" she asks.

"How did you know?"

"Your chief called my parents."

Of course he did. I should have known.

"How is he?" she asks again. Panic is coming off her in waves.

"Shh, baby, I'm not sure yet, but you need to calm down. I don't want you going into early labor."

"I'm fine, Niko, but when I heard that Cam and you . . ." she trails off after the words come from her pretty little mouth in a rush.

I lock my fingers with hers and draw her over to the chair. "I know he's stable, but they're still looking him over. We haven't heard anything else from the doctors since he was brought in."

"Are you okay?" she finally manages to ask, her eyes darting around my face while she inspects me with probing fingers.

I nod. "Just tired. It's been a long night."

"Thank you for saving him," she says, and I realize that tonight could have gone so wrong.

We could have lost Cameron. Hell, I might not have gotten out with him, and I wouldn't have gotten to see Everly again. I wouldn't have been here for the birth of our son.

I can't help but pull her closer, her head moving to rest in the crook of my neck while I let my head fall against her shoulder. Her baby bump sticks out so much more now, almost creating a physical wedge between us. I rest my hand on her stomach, my fingers making circles when I feel a bump against my palm.

I stop, then resume, figuring it was probably a muscle twitch.

I feel it again, but this time I know it's not my imagination.

"What is that?" I ask, moving my hand around her swollen belly.

"Hmm?" Everly looks to where my hand is. "Did you feel him?"

I turn to look at her. "That was him?"

She smiles and nods. "He's doing all sorts of moving around right now."

"That has got to feel . . . weird," I say in awe. I place my hand back down, hoping to feel it again.

She gives a little laugh. "It takes some getting used to. After the initial weirdness of having something move inside me, I get excited knowing that's our baby. Wait till you see the outline of his foot on my stomach. I saw that today and freaked out." I laugh at her face, but I'm sad that I missed it.

Another thump, this one longer and drawn out against my palm. I stare down at my hand in complete fascination but am pulled out by a sharp hiss from Everly.

"What?"

She presses against her side. "He's just using my liver as a punching bag."

"That doesn't sound right, babe. I don't know how you women do this shit." I shudder.

"I'm just happy it's not my bladder he's punching right now. I feel like the elderly folks that lose control over their bladder and pee themselves. At this rate, I cough or sneeze, and I'm afraid I'm going to pee. I need to go buy some adult diapers to make sure I don't embarrass myself in public." She screws up her face, and I can't help screwing with her.

"Hmm."

"Hmm what? I just told you that I'm not looking forward to peeing on myself when your son starts using my bladder for a pillow, and all you say is hmm?"

"I was just thinking, I've never been into any of that shit, but for you, I'd consider making an exception."

"Exception for what?"

"Golden showers." Her eyes grow wide as saucers, and I hold back my laugh, keeping my face completely serious. She looks like a fish out of the water right now. Her mouth opens and then closes with words she can't seem to find. Finally, I can't take it, and I let out the biggest roaring laugh.

God, I needed her tonight. The fire. Thoughts of what could have happened tonight when Cam and I went into that three-decker. Cam getting hurt. Just everything, and all I could think about was her.

"What the hell, Niko?"

"I was kidding, babe. It was a joke. I'm not into that shit at all, and as much as I love you, I draw the line on letting you piss on me."

"Jesus Christ, Niko. Don't say shit like that to me. You had my hopes up for a minute there. I was going to ask you how you felt about scatophilia, but now that I know you're joking, I feel weird. Thanks."

"What the fuck is that?"

"It's the paraphilia involving sexual arousal and pleasure from feces."

I stop laughing at her, and now I'm the fish out of the water.

"Got ya!" she laughs.

My expression drops. "Now that shit was not funny. I thought you were serious."

"So did I." She smiles but then looks toward the door when the nurse comes in.

"He's awake if you want to go see him," the woman that came out earlier says to us. "His nurse is just taking his vitals, but you can go in."

"Thanks," I say and look at Ev. "I know you want to see him, but can I have a minute alone with him first?" I ask, and her face softens. "I won't take long, and then you can come in and fuss over him." I smile a little, and she nods.

"Of course. I'll go call and let my parents know that he's awake. They were an hour away when they got the call and are heading here from Rhode Island."

COCK sure

"All right. I'll see you in a few minutes then," I say and kiss her head before she walks away to call her parents.

I make my way toward the room the woman told me Cam was in. The door is open and the curtain is closed, blocking my view of whoever is behind it. "Hello?" I say softly. "I'm looking for Cameron Hayes's room."

A nurse pops her head out from behind the curtain and smiles at me. "He's here. I'm almost done if you want to pull that chair over and have a seat. I'll be out of your way in a sec."

"You don't need to run off already, do you?" I hear a raspy voice say.

When I look inside, it's then that I realize that the voice was coming from my best friend. Relief floods me when I see his baby blue eyes open, a small smirk appearing on his face.

"I just woke up, after all. I'm pretty sure I could use a sponge bath. Isn't that what you nurses do for your patients?" he says to the poor girl who's redder than a tomato right now.

"I don't think you're ready for that just yet, Mr. Hayes, but I promise that as soon as the doctor okays you for a shower, I'll send in Hester. Hester is the best aide on our floor."

"I seriously doubt that," he rasps out. "Her name is Hester. What kind of name is that? Doesn't even sound sexy or feminine." He screws his face up, and I almost want to laugh.

"That's because Hester is a male aide. Not at all feminine. I'll be back to check on you in a little while. Don't try and get up, Mr. Hayes. Doctor's orders," she says before walking away.

I can't help it. I laugh as Cam's face goes from disgust at the mention of Hester to absolute disgust at the thought of Hester being a male who's going to help him shower later.

"Shut up, Callahan. Why are you in here, anyway? Shouldn't you be getting checked out yourself, asshole?"

"Already did. I'm good. You're the one that went all lights out on me, man. Scared the fucking shit out of me," I say, and I mean it.

I didn't say anything to anyone, but the thought of Cam not making it really fucked with me. I don't know what I would have done had something happened to him, and on top of that, he wasn't speaking to me.

"I'm glad you're okay, then," he says and looks away. "I'd hate to have been the one to have to teach your kid how to play ball. I suck at sports."

Hope blooms in my chest. He's throwing out an olive branch, and I'd be a dumb son of a bitch not to take it right now.

"I hate that we're not speaking," I tell him, staring him straight in the eyes. "Your sister and I are having a baby, and I want my best friend there. I love her, man. I know you don't think I'm good enough for her, but I'd like to prove you wrong."

Cam looks away and then back. "What the fuck do you mean? I'm speaking to you now, dumbass."

"You know what I'm saying, Cameron. Tonight was crazy. It's part of the job. I know that, but for the first time I had someone that would have been hurt and lost had I not come home." My brow furrows as my jaw clenches at even the thought of the agony it would cause her. "On top of that, she would have been devastated if she lost her brother while he was still angry with her. Fuck, man, I would have been, too."

He doesn't say anything for a long moment.

"Thank you," he says.

I nod my head at him. "You don't need to thank me. You would have done the same for me if the situation were reversed. I know that."

"Yeah, I would have. I would have had your back just like you've always had mine." I start to open my mouth to agree, but he's not done. "That's why finding out about you and Ev the way that I did ... Well, it was fucked up, Niko. I heard what you said. That day at my parent's house. I believed you. I just wasn't ready to deal with the fact that you didn't think our friendship was important enough to tell me to my face that you were fucking my sister."

"Cam, it's not like that. I'm not just—" He waves me off.

"I know it's not like that now, but that's what I thought at the time. She's my kid sister, man, and you've been more of a brother to me than anyone else has in our crew. I've known you since we were kids. I just didn't expect you to not come to me with something as important as my sister."

I don't say anything because he's right. I owed it to him to go to him as his friend. No, as a man, and let him know how I felt about Ev, but I didn't. I let the situation get to a point that our friendship was damaged, and for that, I honestly feel like shit.

"It's going to take me a little time, but I'll work it out on my own. I just need some time to adjust. That all right with you, man?" he asks, and my head comes up at his words.

"Of course. I understand," I say and walk toward his hospital room door. "I'll go let Ev know she can come in now. She was calling your parents to let them know you were awake." I walk to the door and turn my head back to him. "I'm glad you're okay, Cam."

"Me too, brother. Me too."

Chapter Thirty-Eight

Everly

"I DON'T KNOW WHAT we're going to do with all this stuff," I say as I look around at box upon box filled with baby stuff. Two giant baby showers, and a Christmas where my mom went overboard, and we're fully baby equipped.

"I thought the one your mom threw was huge," Niko says, and I laugh. His cousin Siobhan wasn't kidding when she said she wanted to throw us a huge shower for the baby. Nearly every cousin or their wife turned up, plus his aunts and a few uncles who were dragged to the event.

"Turns out your Irish side was just as big and generous." There are going to be a lot of Thank you cards to write, and my hand is cramping at just the thought.

"As I said, some are trying to make up for their parents' prejudice."

"This might be my favorite gift," I say as I pet the quilt that rests on the back of the rocking chair.

Niko nods.

It was a gift from Cameron. A specially made and designed quilt with a firefighting teddy bear on it. I love that not only did he come up with the idea for such a sweet gift on his own, foregoing pulling from our baby registry, but a gift that he commissioned after his and Niko's fallout.

"He's excited to be an uncle," he says, happy that my brother has finally accepted that Niko and I are together and that we are going to be a family. It took a few weeks, but Cam has slowly warmed back up to Niko. Which is evident in the quilted design. He even had Callahan scripted on it.

In the past few months, Niko has pretty much moved into my place. He spends all his time here. Though I think this week I'll buy a king-sized mattress and headboard. My queen is a little cramped with all the pillows *and* Niko. I look around at all of the gifts we got, and I'm amazed at just how much you need to care for a baby.

"I didn't realize just how much of this stuff you actually have to put together," I say as I look at the boxes containing the crib, changing table, and stroller.

"I want to grab a quick shower before I head to work, but I promise that I'll start putting the crib together when I get back."

"And after you sleep."

He nods. "We can just do a few things as we go, but the crib should be first," he says and kisses my forehead before walking over to his duffle bag packed with his clean clothes.

He starts pulling out a few things, looking for one of the shirts he wears to work when I reply, "Yeah. Although, I'm not sure when we'll put him in it. I kind of want his bassinet in the room with us for a while when he first comes home."

I look at Niko to see if he's okay with that. I know he works crazy hours and sometimes double shifts. When he gets home, he sometimes just crashes first before anything else. Having a newborn baby in the room with us at first probably won't appeal to him, but I want him with us for the first few weeks, maybe even the first few months.

He walks toward me, placing a kiss on my lips this time and smiles.

"I like the idea of him being close to us. I wouldn't want it any other way. Besides, with you breastfeeding, it would probably be a lot more convenient if he was right next to you in his bassinet."

"How do you know that it will be more convenient? Have you breastfed a baby before, Nikolas?" I ask and am met with his beautiful grey eyes and that one, cocky, yet sexy-ass raised eyebrow.

"Babe . . ." he says, and then nothing else. I cross my arms when he just stares at me, waiting for him to answer my question, but he doesn't. He merely shrugs at me before going back to rummaging through his bag.

"You know I hate when you do that, right?"

"When I do what?" he asks.

"When you blow me off with a shrug rather than answer a question. That thing you do." I pout.

Niko shakes his head and chuckles a little. "Oh, that I do know. You did it to me more than a few times, and I wanted to grab you and put you over my knee. It pissed me off every time you did it. Guess your bad habits rubbed off on me."

My mouth pops open. "I have never done that to you. You are such a liar!"

"Don't go there, baby. You will lose," he says with a smirk before changing the subject. "You going to be okay without me for the night?"

I roll my eyes. "It's not like you haven't gone to work and left me alone before. Of course, I'll be okay."

"I know that, but it's been a long day. You look dead on your feet and to be honest. I was worried earlier."

"Braxton hicks," I assure him. "Perfectly normal at this time. You heard the doctor say that I could expect them."

"I did, but . . ."

"You also heard him say that it was perfectly normal. If I get them again, I'll watch the clock and time them." I run my hand across my very round stomach. "It's not time for him to come out yet, Niko. As much as I'd love for him to vacate my big fat vessel, he's still baking."

"Hey, there is nothing wrong with how you look, Everly. You are the sexiest pregnant woman I've ever seen."

I roll my eyes at him again. "Yeah, well, when it's time to give this little guy an eviction notice, you better believe I'm going to be the happiest woman ever. As for you, you're just saying that because you like screwing me doggie style, seeing as how I've gotten so big and that is the most comfortable position for me when we have sex."

"While I won't lie and say that I don't love seeing you on all fours, baby, the truth is I'd fuck you upside down while standing on my head and you'd still be the sexiest woman I've ever seen."

I crack up at the visual he just planted in my head. "I can't see how that would even work, but okay."

"Ev, you need to get that shit out of your pretty little head," he says and walks over to where I'm now sitting on the bed. "I love you." He kisses my right cheek. "Every." Then he kisses my left cheek. "Single." He kisses my nose. "Part." And then he leans down and kisses my belly. "It wouldn't matter if you weighed one thousand pounds. You're not going to get rid of me. Accept it, Ev. You're stuck with me for the rest of your life." My heart is fluttering a mile a minute at his words. "Now behave so I can get ready for work. I'm jumping in the shower."

We haven't had a conversation about what's going to happen after the baby gets here. I mean, we're together. He hasn't officially moved in, but he's here every night that he's not working. I get up and walk over to my dresser and open two drawers. With a handful of clothes, I begin emptying them, making space for his clothes. I don't want to seem pushy, but he's been living out of that damn green duffle bag for a couple of weeks now. He takes his dirty clothes home and comes back with clean ones once he's done with his shift at the firehouse.

Maybe it's time I let him know that I'm done pushing him away. I want him to stay.

I finish emptying a few more items from the drawers for him and decide that the closet is another place in my house that he can have. Not all of it, of course, but at least a part of it. When I'm done, I hear the water shut off in the bathroom and I wait.

As usual, when he's naked I lose all rational thought. Niko naked and wet, though? I have no words. I just stare, and I'm pretty sure I drool.

"Stop looking at me like that when I can't do anything about it," he says and drops his dirty clothes in his bag.

"You know it would be easier if you just threw your dirty clothes in the laundry basket over there," I say, pointing to the corner of the room.

"Yeah, but then I'd have to get them later, and they need to get washed," he says, completely missing what I'm trying to say. Maybe I'm too subtle. "Besides, I need to grab new clothes when I go home, so I'm not always being ogled by you while I'm naked."

"Yeah, right. You like being naked just as much as I like seeing you naked, so stop telling me things that aren't true."

Niko waggles his eyebrows up and down. I laugh at him and shake my head while watching him pull on his boxer briefs.

"I was thinking . . ."

Niko's head snaps toward me, and he blows out a breath. "Oh shit. That's never a good way to start a sentence with you. Do I need to sit down?"

I scrunch my brow and scowl at him. "Stop it. I'm serious."

He holds his hands up. "Okay."

"I was thinking that instead of going back and forth so much, and since you're here most of the time, you might as well bring more clothes here," I say, and Niko stops dressing to look at me, giving me his full attention. "It's not a big deal or anything."

I look toward the empty drawers I cleared out and left open for him. He follows my gaze and walks over to the dresser.

"You are giving me my own drawers, babe?" he asks. His voice is sounding a little huskier than it usually does.

I shrug when he looks back at me, my eyes darting to the ground. Why is it always so hard to accept that he wants to be in my life? That we're together? He loves me, I know that, but sometimes I still feel like I'm twelve years old, blushing every time he looks at me.

"I cleared some closet space too. You don't have to use it. I just thought I'd offer the space. It's a good place to hang your work clothes."

His eyes are smoldering when he looks back at me. "Fuck it." He storms over to me and leans down, smashing his lips to mine.

I let out a squeak, my eyes wide, while his hands slip into my waistband and pull my pants down. Without a word, he spins me around and pushes down on my back, leaning me over the edge of the bed.

"What?" Is all I manage to get out before I feel the thick head of his cock press into me, stretching me.

"You're gonna make me late," he says as he slams into me, sending a flash of sparks to radiate through me. Each time he bottoms out, that shock sends tingles shooting through my body. "Always have to go and make me hard before work, so this'll be a quickie."

"But I didn't do anything," I manage to get out between moans he forces from me.

His fingers dig into my hips. "You practically fucking asked me to move in with that shy, innocent look after staring at me like you wanted to swallow my cock whole and looking sexy as fuck with my kid inside your belly." He leans over, his breath hot against my ear. "If you haven't figured out that you just standing there turns me on, apparently I need to be fucking you more to remind you."

My fingers fist the comforter, unable to focus my eyes, just enjoying the pleasure.

"Fuck, yes," I cry.

His hips pick up, slamming into me faster and faster, making my eyes roll back.

"You better come quick, baby."

"Just a little more," I beg, focusing on nothing but him until my eyes roll back

"Fuck, fuck, fuuuck!" he yells, thrusting against me one last time, his cock jumping. His groans send me over the edge and pleasure snaps through me, my body spasms.

Strength leaves us both, and Niko falls down on the bed to the side, taking me with him.

"Ask me," he says between pants.

It takes me a minute to use my brain. "Do you want to move in with me?"

"Yes," he says with a kiss onto the top of my head.

I shudder as he pulls out and turn to look back at him.

"Well, I was clean."

A giggle slips from me. "Dirty boy."

His lips twitch up into a smirk. "For you? Always."

He heads back into the bathroom to clean up while I lay on my side. A smile plays on my lips as sleepiness starts to take me.

A swift kick to the ribs has that idea gone and me rolling onto my back and holding my side as I let out a hiss through clenched teeth.

I feel the bed dip beside me. "You okay?"

I give him a nod. "Just your son practicing his soccer skills. Help me up?"

After cleaning up, I put on some clothes, watching as Niko pulls his Newton Fire Department T-shirt over his head.

"Give me a call for anything," Niko says as he leans down and presses his lips to mine.

"Anything?"

A groan slips from him. "When I get back . . ." he trails off.

"When you get back, what?"

His lip pulls up into that smirk, and he winks at me. "See you in the morning, baby. Sleep tight."

"Goodnight."

"I'll set the alarm on my way out."

I nod, but then my head snaps toward him. "No, wait." He stops and looks back at me. "I'm going to go grab that bag of baby clothes from the trunk of the car first. I want to get them in the wash tonight, so I'll set the alarm when I come back in."

"Everly, I don't want you lifting shit when I'm not here. It can wait until tomorrow when I'm back. I want you to stay off your feet, baby. You've had a long day, and you should rest up. You already overdid it today."

"Niko, it's one bag that probably weighs less than five pounds, if that. I'm pregnant, not disabled," I say, and he eyes me skeptically. "I promise that I'm only grabbing the bag of clothes. The rest are in here already. The heavy boxes are all yours. Now get going before you are later than you already are for work."

He lets out a huff of air before walking back to me and crushing his lips to mine. Kisses like that from Niko always seem to cause my brain to misfire, and I'm breathless by the time he pulls away.

"Okay, but fucking hell, woman, you are stubborn. Thank fuck we're having a boy because I don't think I'd be able to handle two Everly's under one roof." I laugh at him as he walks away, shaking his head. "I'll lock the door for now. Get some rest, baby," he calls over his shoulder.

"Will do, Daddy!" I say, and I hear his faint groan before the front door closes and he's gone.

Minutes after he leaves, I turn on the TV and crawl under the covers. It doesn't take long before the day takes its toll and my eyes get heavy. Baby clothes are forgotten, I fall asleep and dream of my life going forward with Niko and the baby we have coming.

There's a dip in the bed that stirs me, then the sound of the TV rushes in only to be silenced. I hadn't realized I'd fallen asleep.

"Niko?" I ask, my eyes opening only to cringe against the light emanating from my bedside table.

My stomach drops as I look at my bed, at the man sitting on the end. It's not the black-haired, grey-eyed man of my dreams. Instead, it's the brown-haired, green-eyed demon of my nightmares.

As I stare at him, I wonder if I am in a walking nightmare. If in seconds I'll wake up, startled, but safe with Niko beside me.

"Why are you here?" I ask.

"You are mine, Everly," he says as if that is explanation enough.

My muscles are tense as I stare at him, trying to muster as much strength as I can. "Tate, you need to leave."

"Then you went and whored yourself out," he says, ignoring me. "Letting some inferior punk come in you and knock you up. That should be my child you're carrying."

A chill moves through me as I pull away from him and into more of a sitting position. "Niko is going to be back any minute. Please, just go before things get ugly," I say, hoping that he'll leave rather than risk another confrontation with Niko.

"Since when did you turn into such a fucking liar, Everly?" he spits at me. "I know he's not coming back. I watched him leave, and from the looks of the clothes he was wearing, I'd say he's not going to be returning anytime soon."

His hand starts to pull the sheet that is covering me. I grab it to stop him, but he pulls it harder, exposing my legs.

"What are you going to do, Tate, force me to be with you?"

He scoffs at my question. "Of course not. I've never had to force any woman to be with me."

"Then what are you doing?" I ask.

"Looking. There is nothing wrong with looking. Pregnancy suits you, baby. You have that glow people always say women get when they are carrying a child."

I don't know what to do right now. He's gone from one person to another in a matter of seconds, making me even more uneasy than I was when I awoke to him sitting on my bed. I glance over and eye my work cell phone that I plugged in before I went to bed.

It's then that I remember my personal cell is still under my pillow. I placed it there in case Niko called me from work in the middle of the night. Tate sees me looking at the one plugged in, and it's then that he gets up and grabs my phone. He unplugs it, turning the power off and placing it in his pocket away from my reach.

"Wouldn't want you calling anyone before I've had a chance to talk to you, Everly," he says, his tone sending a shiver down my spine. "I mean, I came all this way just for you. The least you can do is hear what I have to say before you go calling your mental boyfriend."

"Niko is mental? You've broken into my house, again, and you're calling him mental?"

"Get dressed, baby," Tate says. "Let's go for a ride. There's something I want to show you." He walks to the door and opens it. "I'll give you some space, but I'm waiting right here."

"I'm not going anywhere with you, Tate," I say, surprised that my voice doesn't waver because everything inside me is. "It's midnight, for crying out loud. If you want to talk, then come back tomorrow at a normal hour, and I'll talk to you." I pull the pillow in front of me, feigning modesty, bringing the other cell phone with it.

After figuring out by touch which is the bottom, I hit the home button and wake it up. The phone icon is in the bottom left corner if I remember correctly, and I pray that I hit the right app. In my periphery, I spot the color green and move my thumb to the center. Niko was the last person I spoke to so he should be the person that my phone redials when I hit the call button.

"You can either get up and get some clothes on, or you can come with me dressed as you are," he says with a snarl before changing it to a smile. "Your choice, darling."

"Close the door then, so that I can get dressed."

"Why? It's not like I haven't seen it all before. Stop stalling and move that sweet little ass."

"Tate, please. Please, just go," I say once more, hoping that he'll do it, even though the truth is I know he's not leaving.

He wants me to go with him, but I know that no matter what, I need to do everything in my power to stay here in my house until someone shows up. He looks disheveled. His hair is sticking out from his hands continually running through it. During the time we were together, Tate only did that when he was nervous about something. I don't know what he has planned, but I'm not going with him. I want him to leave, but knowing that isn't going to happen without my going with him, I figure the next best thing would be to try and get him to talk to me here until Niko or someone can get here.

"No, Everly. I've been trying to talk to you for months. To explain everything, but you ignored me. You just cut me out of your life like I was never even there. You packed your things and just left without a word. I begged for you to listen, said the words please and sorry until it didn't make sense, but you wouldn't listen!" he yells as he slams his hand against the door frame making me jump. "You wouldn't talk to me, but you're going to listen now."

"I'll talk to you now, Tate," I say, trying to calm the shaking, hoping that Niko answered the phone. "Let me get dressed, and we can go downstairs and talk. I'll make you some coffee or whatever and we can talk."

Tate's head tilts to the side. "Now you want to listen?"

"Yes." I nod. "You're right. I didn't give you an opportunity to explain. I was hurt, and I didn't want to hear what you had to say. I owe it to you to at least hear you out. To explain," I say and hope to hell I sound genuine because I sure as hell can't stop my hands from shaking. They give me away, show him that I'm scared out of my mind, but I'm willing to say anything to get him to back off. He stares at me for a minute, saying nothing, and I have no idea what the hell is going through his mind.

"Tate?" He turns his back to me but doesn't move.

"Get dressed, Everly. I'll give you some privacy, but I'm not going to lose the one shot I have to make you see that we're good for each other. You don't throw away something like we have due to a misunderstanding," he says, and I want to yell and rage at him about his choice of words, but I don't.

I have to think about the baby I'm carrying and the fact that if I fight him right now, I could hurt my son. My yoga pants are still on the floor from where I took them off earlier, and I throw them on as fast as possible with my belly being in the way. I fell asleep in nothing but my panties and one of Niko's tees, so that will have to do for right now. I don't want Tate to change his mind about talking downstairs, so I slip my house slippers on and walk to the door, tucking the cell phone into the waist of my pants so that he doesn't see.

I walk past Tate and pray that he's calm enough now to be reasonable. "Come on, I'll make you something to eat too if you'd like. I could use a late night snack myself," I say to him, but I don't look back to see if he's coming. It's not until I get to the top of the stairs that I feel his hand pull me to a stop. I turn and look at him, and I see a hint of sadness in his eyes that wasn't there before.

"It should have been me."

"What are you talking about?" I ask, genuinely puzzled at his rapid change of thoughts. He reaches out with his other hand and places it on my belly. I freeze not knowing what he's going to do, and the fear for my child is something I've never in my life felt before.

"This baby should have been mine and yours, Everly. That doesn't matter to me, though. I'll take care of it as if it were my own, and we can have another after. You'll see. Everything is going to work out. We have a long drive, darling, so let's go grab you a jacket, okay?" he says, and I know that sticking around here isn't going to happen.

"Tate, I'm not going with you. I want to talk to you, but here."

He shakes his head and tightens his grip. "I can't show you what I want to show you here. Let's just get a coat for you and some shoes and then we can go—"

"No!" I yell and pull at my arm, ready to run away, needing to get away, but at the twist, I feel my heel slip off the edge of the top step. The momentum throws my weight toward the stairs, my center of mass shifted due to the baby, and I reach out to grab onto something as I feel myself start to fall.

"Everly!" Tate's hands and body come forward and try to grab my arm again, but it's too late.

A scream leaves me as I wrap an arm around my stomach to protect the baby and tumble down the stairs. I finally come to a stop, and the last person I think of before everything goes black is Niko.

Chapter Thirty-Nine

Niko

"HEY, BABY," I SAY into the phone, but there's no response. "Baby? Everly?"

"Get dressed, darling. Let's go for a ride. There's something I want to show you," a male voice says, and the blood in my veins freezes. It's from far away, not directly into the phone.

What the fuck? I pull the phone back to double check that it was Everly that just called me and sure enough, it's her number, but that's not her, so what the hell is going on?

"I'm not going anywhere with you, Tate. It's midnight for crying out loud. If you want to talk, then come back tomorrow at a normal hour, and I'll talk to you."

Tate. The blood freezes in my veins, and for a moment, I stop breathing.

I immediately hit the recording app and put the phone back up to my ear.

"You can either get up and get some clothes on, or you can come with me dressed as you are. Your choice, darling," he says, sounding muffled, and my fucking blood boils.

"Close the door, then, so I can get dressed," I hear her say more clearly.

"Why? It's not like I haven't seen it all before. Stop stalling and move that sweet little ass."

Fuck. Fuck. Fuck. That motherfucker!

I run through the station without a word, almost taking Jake out as I get to the door.

"Whoa! Everything—"

"Call Cam. Get cops to Everly's. Now!"

That's all I can get out as I run to my truck. It's fucking cold out, and I don't have a coat on, but I don't care.

"I'm coming, baby." As soon as I get to my truck, I've got the key in the ignition, gear in drive, and foot on the gas before my door is even closed.

"Tate, please." I can hear the fear in her voice, and it rips at me. "Please, just go."

I wanted to believe we'd solved the Tate problem, but somewhere deep down I was afraid he would come back. The evidence was there that he wasn't right.

"No, Everly. I've been trying to talk to you for months. To explain everything, but you ignored me. You just cut me out of your life like I was never even . . ." his voice fades in and out, making it hard to make out what he's saying. ". . . just left without a word. I begged for you to listen, said the words please and sorry until it didn't make sense, but you wouldn't listen!" his voice booms out. "You wouldn't talk to me," Tate says to her, and the distance that he has between him and her cell doesn't stop me from hearing the desperation in his voice.

"Keep him talking, baby," I say, not knowing if she can hear me or not, but I feel like I need to say something until I can get to her.

"I'll talk to you now, Tate. Let me get dressed, and we can go downstairs and talk. I'll make you some coffee or whatever and we can talk."

"Now you want to listen?" I hear him reply.

"Yes. You're right. I didn't give you an opportunity to explain. I was hurt, and I didn't want to hear what you had to say. I owe it to you to at least hear you out. To explain."

"Tate?" I hear her say, and it's killing me not knowing what the fuck is going on.

My heart hammers against my chest, fear and anger boiling inside me. I'm going to kill him. I'm going to motherfucking kill the bastard when I get there.

"Get dressed, Everly. I'll give you so. . ." the connection of the phone being able to pick up his voice drops out again. ". . . make you see that we are good for each other. You don't throw away something like we have due to a misunderstanding," he says to her, and it's all I can do not to break my fucking teeth from grinding them so hard.

This guy is fucking dead if he touches her! The phone sounds worse, and I can hardly make out what he's saying now. Fuck!

I'm stuck, the traffic not moving, completely immobilized which can only be due to an accident at this time of night, unable to do anything but listen to the woman I love play nice with this fucking nutcase. I can hear her tone, I understand the tremor there, and it's killing me right now.

"It should have been me," I hear Tate say, just barely audible at this point. I have no idea where she has her phone, but it keeps making noise, and those sound drown out their words.

"What are you talking about?" I finally hear her say.

"Baby, keep calm. I'm coming. Son of a bitch, get the fuck out of my way!" I yell at the cars in front of me, laying my hand on the horn of my truck. There is more muffled talking and what sounds like movement, but I have no idea. I have the phone on speaker now so I can get through this shit. The phone is quiet, and I look at it to make sure I didn't lose her. That's when I hear it.

"No!" Everly's screams pierce through.

"Run, Everly. Get out of there," I yell, but the problem is, I have no idea where in the house they are.

I can hear the sounds of something, and my blood runs cold at what I overhear next. Tate, not Everly, and he's coming through loud and clear, leading me to believe he's close to her. It's what he says that has me pushing my foot down on the gas and fuck whoever gets in my way.

"Fuck! Everly? Everly, can you hear me, sweetheart? I'm going to get help, okay? You're going to be okay. Wake up, Evie. You have to open your eyes, darling. I bought us a house. That's what I wanted to show you, but you're so stubborn! Oh, Jesus. You're bleeding. Fuck! Everly, wake up. Please, Everly. Fuck! What do I do? I don't know what to do!"

I lose it and start screaming into the phone. I don't care. "You're fucking dead! You hear me, motherfucker! Dead!"

My leg bounces, and I spot a side street I can turn on to get away from the traffic. It might get me there faster even with all the twists and turns. A little off-roading, and I press down on the gas. I just need to know that she's okay. I hit 911 on my cell and give them her address. I feel better knowing that Bishop called it in already, and I end the call.

Fuck. Finally. I see her house up ahead, and I don't slow down. The light from her entryway is coming through the open door. I can't see anyone as I pull up, barely putting my truck in park, jumping out and running for her front steps.

I see someone appear at her front door, and I'm ready to bury this fucker right now, but as I get closer, he turns around, talking into a phone. Not Tate, her neighbor with the little girl, Grant or some shit.

"Where is she?" I yell, and he points to the door.

"They said not to move her, man. They're on their way. Two minutes ETA," he says, and I ignore him. All that matters right now is me getting to Ev.

I run past him, and that's when I see her. My blood runs cold. She's not moving. Her arm is bent at a weird angle, and there is blood on her face, from what, I have no clue. I fall to the ground beside her.

"Everly, baby, can you hear me? Come on, baby, open your eyes." Nothing. I move my hands gently over her and then place two fingers between the bone and the tendon over her radial artery to check for a pulse. I let out a breath once I find it. I want to grab her, but I know not to move her. The sound of sirens close by is the best sound I've ever heard.

"Ambulance is here. Is there someone I can call for her?" her neighbor asks, and it's then that I remember Tate.

"Where is Tate?"

"Who?" His brow is scrunched in confusion, and he shakes his head. "There was no one here when I found her. I was in the kitchen when I heard something banging on the stairs, but it wasn't my stairs. When I didn't see your truck outside, I got nervous, and that's when I came out. The door was open, and she was on the ground at the bottom of the stairs."

"Did she say anything to you?" I ask him, and his head shakes back and forth.

"No, man, she was unconscious when I got here which was only two minutes tops before you pulled up."

I nod my head and move to the side as the EMTs come through the doorway. I know one of them, and he knows Cam as well.

"How long has she been down?" he asks, and I just want him to get her to the hospital.

"Maybe ten minutes or so. She's thirty-five weeks pregnant," I say, and he starts checking her vitals while his partner brings in a stretcher and neck support.

"We're going to take her to Newton Wellesley. You following behind?"

I shake my head. "I'm not leaving her. They're mine."

He nods. "You can ride in the bus with her then. What's her name? Age? Anything else I should know?"

"Everly Hayes, twenty-six. Nothing that I'm aware of. She just had her appointment a few days ago, and I don't remember hearing anything that you would need to know. I'll call Cameron. He's her brother, so he'll know if I miss anything."

He looks over at the mention of Cam but doesn't say anything. He and his partner both count it off and then move Ev so she's on her side when they place her gently back so that she is flat on the backboard and ready to move to the stretcher. They lift her up and place her down, immediately strapping her in. I move out of the way until they start running her to the ambulance, following quickly behind.

"I'll close up her house, Niko. I'm praying for her and the baby. If you need anything, just ask!" Grant yells, and I wave him off.

I know he means well, but I don't care about her house. I don't care about shit right now except Everly and my son.

Chapter Forty

Niko

"**HANG IN THERE, BABY. You're doing great.**"

I've said the same thing about one hundred times already, and each time I say it, Everly lays there, eyes closed, unresponsive.

They told me to keep talking to her, but I don't know what else to say. I'm scared. So scared for her. Seeing her still form laying at the bottom of those stairs . . . I shudder thinking about it, and I want to go to the police station and kill that motherfucker right now.

Apparently, Tate came back to the house after they took Everly away in the ambulance. He told the cops he left because he wanted to find help, but the fucker could have done that by calling 911 from her house while she laid at the bottom of the fucking stairs bleeding.

Cam thinks he freaked out after Ev fell down the stairs and ran like the fucking coward that he is, but then came back for his cell phone that he'd apparently dropped along with hers at some point while they were at the top of the stairs. He more than likely realized it was still at Everly's house and if she died, he didn't want the police to know he was ever there.

Thank God her neighbor Grant pointed him out to the cops who took him in for questioning and then arrested him. Grant said he recognized him from the last time Tate stopped by her house uninvited and seen him leaving, holding his hand over his bloody nose. Fuck, how I wish now that I had beat him to death back then. Not sure what charges they are going to throw at him, but if I have anything to say about it, his ass is going to fucking jail for a long time.

They wanted me to come to the police station and give them my statement, and I told them no. They can come here if they want it, but I won't leave Everly. They went to work right away and checked everything out when she first got here. She has a concussion, broken arm, and a lot of bruising. Other than that, we won't know anything more for a little while longer. For now, it's a waiting game.

They have her hooked up to all these machines. Some are for her, and a few are for the baby.

His little heart is beating like a war drum through the monitor to my right, and I feel comforted by it. I know it means my son is a fighter. Just like his mom. I just keep waiting for her to wake up. I know she's going to wake up. We need her. I need her.

There's a knock on the door behind me, and I turn around, hoping it's good news, but the disappointment must show on my face when I see it's just Everly's best friend, Alyson, the girl she pretended to be when I first found out that she was Everly Hayes. God, that seems like so long ago. We've come so far since then.

"Anything?" Alyson asks, and I know she's just as worried as I am right now.

I shake my head no and turn back to hold Ev's hand, my other hand resting on top of our son where he's been for the past eight months, protected in his mother's womb. I haven't felt him move at all since they brought Everly in, but I hear his heart. I just keep touching her stomach in hopes that he'll move. I just need him to give me a sign and for his mother to wake up.

"They're going to be fine. You know that, right, Niko?"

"Yeah," I say and pray that it's true. "They both have to be. I don't honestly know what I'd do if I lost one of them, or fuck . . . if I lost them both."

"You can't think like that. Ev's a fighter, and this baby, your son, he's a fighter too. Never forget that. They'll pull through this, and you two will be right back to driving each other crazy, and then the baby will be here driving you crazy together."

I smile at Aly. Or what I hope is a smile. I know she means well, but until I see Ev's beautiful hazel eyes open, I'm not going to relax.

"Hey," Cameron says as he enters the room, slowly closing the door as if he doesn't want to disturb anyone. "Anything?"

I shake my head, but keep my voice to myself. I'm tired of talking. I only want to speak to Everly.

"My parents are both here. They want to come in and see her, but the nurse said only two at a time. I thought maybe you'd like to go home, shower and change—"

"I'm not going anywhere. I'm sorry, Cam. I know you are just trying to help, and they want to come in, but I'm not leaving." I try to finish, but Alyson interrupts my protest before I can say anymore.

"You don't have to leave, Niko. Cam and I will leave, and we'll have Ev's parents come in one at a time. I'm sure they'll understand. Right, Cameron?"

Cam looks over at her, and for a second and I can't tell if he looks shocked that she's speaking to him or that she is speaking to him as if they're friends. These two can never be in the same room with the other, so if it doesn't last long, I'm ready to throw them both out the minute they start with their usual shit.

"Yeah, umm, right," Cam says to her just as calmly as she spoke to him. It serves to remind me that this situation is seriously fucked up because everyone is completely out of their element right now. "I'm sure they'll understand. I'll talk to my parents. We'll let them decide who comes in first. You sit tight, Niko." Cam's hand rests on my shoulder. "She's going to pull through this, man. They both are. They're Hayes, after all. We've always been fighters. There is no way Everly will let anything happen to her or my nephew."

I know she wouldn't let anything happen, but this is out of her control. It's out of everyone's control.

"Positive thoughts, man. You have to have them. They need you to stay positive." I nod again, because what else can I say? "I'll let my parents know. We'll be back in a few. Call me if anything changes, yeah? We won't be far."

"We?" Alyson says.

"Yeah, we can let them visit, and you and I can go grab some clothes for Niko. It will be quicker if you sit in the car, give me more time to run in and out without trying to find parking."

I look over toward Alyson who looks as if she's just swallowed a lemon. Apparently, the thought of being alone and in such proximity to Cam doesn't appeal to her, but when she notices me looking at her, she schools her face, and it's like watching one of those face transformations they do on those makeup infomercials they show late night on television. If I wasn't so nerved up right now, I might have laughed at them both.

"That okay with you, Aly?" Cam asks, and I know it's for my benefit right now. Cam is never this calm around Aly.

"Yeah, whatever I can do to help my friend. If helping you helps Niko stay by her side, then I'll go. Just don't piss me off, Hayes, and make me regret it later," she says and starts to walk out of the room, Cam following behind her with a smile on his face.

An alarm starts blaring, making us all jump. Both Cam and Aly stop their exit and turn to see what is causing the noise. It's the monitor that is hooked up to Ev's stomach. The one monitoring our son.

A few seconds is all it takes for a swarm of nurses and doctors to storm in. Their words are gibberish, but some I know and the floor falls out from beneath me when I hear them barking out orders.

The baby is in distress.

Another alarm goes off, and my entire body begins to shake—it's one of Everly's monitors.

"What's going on?" I ask but get no response. They're all running around.

Cameron steps up to me and grabs my arm.

"We have to go."

I yank my arm from his grip. "What the fuck are you talking about? I'm not leaving them."

My mind is racing, not computing that they're taking her away.

"Sir, we need you to wait outside, please," one of the nurses says to me, and I shake my head no.

"Niko, let them do what they need to do, man. You don't want to be in their way. Come on." I hear Cam, but I'm not leaving until I know what's happening.

I start to ask another nurse what's going on when I overhear the doctor yell out to let the OR know they are coming as they turn Everly onto her side. What the fuck? I don't get the chance to hear more as they start pulling her machines down and making them portable and start to move her entire bed out of the room.

"Wait! No! What are you doing?"

"Mr. Callahan," one of the nurses says as she steps up. I don't know which one because my eyes are locked on Everly's disappearing form. "They're taking her into surgery. They need to get the baby out now."

I shake my head, disbelieving what she's saying. "It's too early. She's only thirty-five weeks."

"It's necessary. The baby is in distress, or we wouldn't do this right now."

"I'm going with her!" I yell at her, but she's giving me a look that shows me nothing but sympathy.

"I'm sorry, Mr. Callahan, but I need to go see what is going on. Someone will be out as soon as we know more or once they are both stable. I promise you they are in good hands," she says and walks swiftly through the doors I'm not allowed through.

A tear opens in my chest. The sentence is crushing because I don't think I can handle losing either of them.

Cam's shaking next to me as he runs his fingers through his hair. I walk over to a chair and sit with my head in my hands, not knowing what else to do at this moment, feeling the most helpless I have ever felt in my entire life.

As I sit there with my eyes on the floor, my mind racing through nothing but Ev and me over the past eight months, I feel an arm going around my back, and I look up.

"She's loved you since she was just a little girl, Niko. I think her dad and I knew she'd never grow out of it, too," Ev's mom, Linda, says as she squeezes me a little. "When I saw that ultrasound picture with your last name on it." She smiles at me. "I wasn't surprised. I think that if she'd never gone to California and stayed away so long, you two would have found each other sooner."

I think about that and remember back to that night at the pub when we first saw each other after so long. I knew she was different for me than other women I had been attracted to, I just didn't realize it at the time. Or maybe I did, and I just didn't want to sound like such a pussy by admitting it to anyone, never mind myself.

"She's always been stubborn, my Everly. You tell her she couldn't do something, and she'd do everything to prove you wrong. I think meeting Alyson helped her come out of her shell in many ways, much to Cameron's chagrin of course." She lets out a small laugh as I shake my head.

I look over to my best friend Cam who is leaning against the wall watching the doors where they took his sister through, but I know he's listening.

"My point is, if Ev can help it, she won't let anything happen to that baby and she'll fight because even as scared as she's been, Everly wants to be a mother to that little boy more than anything," Everly's mom says and I know she's right, but the part that keeps playing in my head is her saying "if she can help it."

That's what scares me the most. None of us have any say over what happens right now, so we are all just forced to sit and wait.

I don't know how much more I can take at this point. This wasn't how this was supposed to happen. I was supposed to be in there with her. Right by her side while our son made his way into this world.

Instead, I'm forced to wait a hundred feet from them while they cut her open and pull him out. What if something goes wrong? What if I lose them?

My chest is so tight I can barely breathe. I can't sit still. I need to move. I need to be there with her. With our child. I need to be holding her hand. I need to be doing something other than wearing a fucking hole in the carpet of the waiting room.

A door opens, and I hear a familiar voice call my name. "Niko?"

I rush forward and wrap my arms around my favorite cousin. "Siobhan."

"I saw Cameron downstairs. How is she?"

I shake my head. "I don't know. They took her almost an hour ago, and nobody has come out."

She nods and holds her hand out. "Stay here. I'll see what I can find out."

It's then I notice she's in her scrubs, her hair pulled back in a ponytail. I watch the door as she walks out, hoping someone walks in.

"Who is that?" Richard asks. I can tell from his tone that he's already thinking the worst. I turn, but before I can respond, Linda swats him on the arm.

"That's his cousin, Siobhan. The one that threw the baby shower last weekend. She's a nurse in the maternity ward here."

Richard's mouth pops open, and he seems contrite. He's been like a father to me for a long time and tried to fill the role after my dad died, but he knows my history. I don't take offense to where his mind went.

"Forgive me, Niko," he says. "I didn't mean it to come out like that."

I shake my head. "Nothing to forgive. I get it, we didn't tell anyone for a long time, and it takes some getting used to."

"It's not that. One day, you two will have a daughter, and then you will understand. It's instinctual to protect your little girl, even when it isn't needed."

When Siobhan returns, there's no rush in her steps. Her face is ashen, and she won't look at me.

I shake my head. "No. Please, no." My whole body vibrates and the strength leaves my legs, sending me down to my knees.

Siobhan drops down in front of me. "The baby is out and okay."

"Everly?"

Her brow scrunches. "She's hemorrhaging."

There's a strangled gasp from Linda followed by a sob.

"The fall caused damage they couldn't see. They're doing everything they can to stop the bleeding."

The door opens, and I look to find Cameron and Alyson step in. One look at me, and they rush forward.

"What's going on?" they ask in unison.

"Everly is bleeding out," I manage to choke out.

"Oh my God!" Alyson cries and covers her mouth with her hands.

"The baby?" Cam asks, and I feel like an asshole for not asking about my son, but she said he was out and okay.

I want to see him.

I need to see him.

"Where is he? Can I see him?" I ask Siobhan, whose face lights up with something I can't place. I just want to see my son until I know Everly is going to be okay, and she looks like she's on drugs.

"Well, you see there is something else, but before I tell you this, I want you to know that it's not a bad thing. I mean, you still have time to return everything you got from the showers. I can do it for you so you won't have to worry about a thing."

"What the hell are you talking about, just say it!" She's scaring the fuck out of me right now, and my nerves are already shot to hell.

"Sorry. Well . . . you have a daughter."

I stare at her, trying to understand her words. "What?"

"You and Everly have a girl, not a boy," she says, smiling like the cat that ate the canary.

What in the fuck did she just say?

"She had a girl?" I hear Alyson say from somewhere to my left, Ev's mother mimicking her question.

For a moment, the fear I had for Everly is put in the back of my brain as I try to comprehend what my cousin just said, and I think I might throw up. I sit back down in the chair I was in earlier, shocked, saying nothing when Cameron comes and stands in front of me. I look up at him, and he's wearing a face I'm sure looks similar to my own, but less severe, but at least he's able to speak.

"Looks like we'll need to invest in firearms courses and get those shotguns ready. Not letting these little fuckers near my niece until she's fifty years old," he says, as severe as I've ever seen him.

I want to agree, but I'm still replaying Siobhan's words in my head on a loop.

"You have a daughter. You and Everly have a girl, not a boy." I look around the room at everyone standing around with apprehensive smiles on their faces. They're all looking at me, waiting.

"What the fuck am I going to do with a girl?" I say, earning a few chuckles.

Everyone except Cam, who sits next to me, placing one hand on my shoulder. A sign of his understanding because his next words echo my current thoughts.

"What indeed, bro. What the fuck indeed," Cam repeats and for once, I know he's on the same page that I am. Neither one of us knows what the fuck to do with a baby. Throw in a baby girl, and we are fucked.

Chapter Forty-One

Everly

MY EYELIDS ARE HEAVY, weighted down, and it's a struggle to open them. There's something wrong, or at least something not right.

It's not just my eyes; every part of me is a struggle to move.

Heavy.

Tired.

Pain.

I manage to groan, which makes the sound of footsteps to echo in my ears.

"Everly?" Niko's voice calls to me, but I can only groan.

"Baby, can you hear me?"

"N . . ." I swallow hard, my throat dry. I manage to work my eyes open enough to see him. "Niko?"

His head dips, his forehead pressing against mine as he expels a hard breath. The angle is odd and only adds to my confusion.

"Sss goin' on?" I say, and even I can hear that my words are slurred.

"You fell down the stairs."

My eyes widen, and I take a long blink. "Baby?"

"The placenta detached. They had to get her out."

I stare at him, my brow slowly furrowing. "H-her?"

His lips pull up, and he swipes the hair back from my face. "Seems there was an oops."

"Oops?" I'm so confused. He's just not making any sense.

"Siobhan said that it happens from time to time, though usually the other way around. Sometimes what they think is a penis, ends up being the umbilical cord blocking the vagina. Her words, not mine," he says, and I can tell by his tone and the look on his face that he's still yet to come to terms with the mix-up.

"How long?" I ask, not even sure what I'm referring to, but with every moment my head clears more and more.

"You've been out for three days." He tangles his fingers in my hair. "You scared me, baby."

All I can do is stare at him. If it were the other way around, I know I'd have been scared shitless myself, so I understand. It's the same way I felt when Cam got hurt, and I didn't know if he was okay and wasn't sure if Niko had also been injured when they were on the job.

Something I know I have to deal with as we go in the future. His career will always scare me.

"We don't have any girl's names," I say, changing the subject. My brain feels slow, still working through what is going on.

"I've got a list going."

"You do?"

He takes my hand in his and kisses my palm. "It got bad, Everly. You've had two blood transfusions. For a few hours, all I had was her, so I focused on her and tried not to freak out about the possibility of losing you."

"How is she?" I ask, suddenly acutely aware that my body is empty.

"Tiny, but perfect," he says with a smile. "Very tiny."

"Very tiny?"

"Four pounds, eleven ounces. She's strong. They kept her in the NICU for a few days just to make sure. Her bilirubin levels were high, so they kept her under a light to help bring it down. Jaundice," he says, and I feel completely lost at the information he's throwing at me. Not understanding any of it, but in awe that he does.

"It's going to be fine, baby. All is good. From what I was told, it's not at all uncommon. Trust me, she's perfect. Your mom is in with her now. They have to give her formula for now."

"I want to breastfeed," I say as my hand moves to my now empty stomach. I'd gotten used to the baby inside me, and suddenly, he . . . she's gone. In what was a literal blink of the eye for me, but days for Niko.

"I know, and you'll be able to, but not until the meds and shit are out of your system. She's doing fine on the formula, but they said you could pump to keep the milk supply coming, then when you're ready, you can try," he says, and all I want to do is cry.

I've missed the first few days of my daughter's life. I have no idea what she looks like, who she looks like. Tate stole that from me. How I could ever have been with that man for two years and not have seen that he was a wolf in sheep's clothing makes me feel horrible about myself.

"Hey," Niko says and turns my head toward his concerned face. "It's going to be okay, Ev. It's over. He's not going to bother you again. You, me, and our daughter will be fine. We have many firsts to celebrate in our future."

"I know, but this is all my fault. If I had listened to you, Cam, and my dad about Tate, maybe it wouldn't have gotten to this point. Maybe we could have stopped him before it got to him in the house like a deranged stalker. Maybe—"

"No, Everly. This is not your fault. It's his. He is the one that wouldn't take no for an answer. How were you supposed to know that he would go to the lengths he did? There's something not right upstairs, baby, and there is no way that you could have known he would do what he did. None of us did. Trust me, though, we all know now, and it's being taken care of," he says, his tone turning angry.

"I don't understand."

Niko slides his hand down my arm and picks my hand up, kissing the back of it. That's when I notice my other arm is heavy and glance down to find my arm is in a cast.

"Tate broke in again. You called me." His brow scrunches. "He was talking about taking you somewhere. At the time, I had no idea what was going on, but he claims that he bought a house for you, him, and the baby to live in. Told the police that he was there to surprise you, but that when you were walking down the stairs, you slipped and fell." Niko blows out a breath through clenched teeth. "I know he's full of shit about how it happened; he wasn't giving you a choice but to go with him. I heard you tell him to leave, Ev. I heard everything. Scared the shit out of me. I tried to get to you, but . . ."

The memories circle in my mind, and I know I'm not going to forget this for a very long time. "I forgot to turn the alarm on. I-I fell asleep, and I didn't set the alarm. When I woke up, he was sitting on the end of the bed and I just, I tried to get away," I say, trying to think of everything that happened. "He . . . he grabbed me." I can see it, like watching a movie. "I managed to wrench my arm from his grip, but we were at the top of the stairs."

Niko swallows. "I'll never forget seeing you at the bottom of those stairs. I thought you were both gone."

"Where is Tate now?"

"The police took him. He left you there but apparently came back to your house right after the ambulance brought you here. For now, he's locked up. They're trying to throw everything they can at him. Breaking and entering is one and because you were home at the time he'll get more time. That is just one of the charges, though. They plan to charge him with attempted kidnapping since he tried to force you against your will to leave your home. They'll need a statement from you, but not today."

"I don't have to see him, do I?"

He shakes his head. "Probably not until the trial. I honestly don't see them letting him go with all that they have on him right now, and from what your brother told me, they have been working with the DA to see what else they can stick him with. He'll likely go away for a while, so don't think about him right now, baby. The detective on this case took my statement the morning after you were brought in. That, along with the recording on my phone, and

I'm sure he's done. He can lie all he wants, but I heard him, have proof, and now that you're awake, you can tell them your side, but not until you've rested more. He's not going anywhere."

All I can do is nod. I know he didn't push me. I fell. That was an accident, but he scared me. He wasn't giving me a choice but to go with him even though I asked him to leave, so I have no sympathy for him right now. He broke in again. I'll tell the police the truth, but I agree that he needs to answer for what he did. I wouldn't have fallen had he not broken in.

For now, I just want to see my daughter and spend my time thinking about our future. Mine, Niko's, and the baby girl we didn't know was coming.

"What are we going to do with all the boy stuff?" I ask.

A soft chuckle comes from Niko. "Oh, my sweet woman. Have a little faith in me," he says and chuckles. "Well, okay. I'm lying. It has nothing to do with me. It's all your mom and my cousin. Your mom already has her social circle on it, with Siobhan helping. Don't think we need to worry about that, but I know one thing they can't do for us."

"What's that?"

"Name our daughter." He smiles. I think for a minute about what he just said, and it hits me.

"I think I have one."

"You do?"

"Yes. I know we were thinking of Nikolas for a boy. I'd like to keep that still."

"Umm, Ev. As much as I'd love to name our child after me, I don't think Nikolas is gender neutral," he says, and I laugh.

"Not Nikolas. Nicole."

He thinks for a minute before replying. "You want to name our daughter Nicole?"

"Not exactly. I was thinking about something you just said a minute ago, and that made me think of the perfect name for her." His puzzled look is almost too funny, but I decide not to drag this out before he calls the nurse to medicate me due to my not making sense to him.

"Faith."

"Faith?"

"Yes. Faith Nicole Callahan. I want to name our daughter Faith because that is precisely what we have in each other. What we need to always have in each other and our family. Mine, yours, and our own. Nicole is after you. Or at least it's as close to your name as I can come up with. What do you think?"

"I think it's beautiful, just like her. Just like her mother. I love it, and I love you, baby." He leans down and kisses my lips. If it were any other time, I'd be on cloud nine after a kiss from Niko, but right now all I can think about is meeting our daughter.

"Can I see her?"

"Of course. Let me go find out how to make that happen. I'll be back in a few minutes." He kisses my head this time and then takes off out of my hospital room.

"Faith Nicole Callahan. I can't wait to meet you, baby girl," I say out loud.

She may not have entered the world as we planned or be the boy we thought we were having, but I love her just the same, and I'm not going to feel complete until I have her in my arms. Her and her daddy.

Epilogue

Niko

DUE TO EVERLY'S HEALTH, she stayed in the hospital for over two weeks until she regained her strength and the doctors were convinced she was past the point of infection. Our daughter stayed as well, and I spent every day with them.

Linda made sure the house was ready for us since we were a little ahead of the time frame and therefore behind on the nursery. Per usual Linda style, she went a little overboard in the decorations, but neither of us minded.

"She's beautiful, Ev. Thank God she looks more like you than this ugly SOB," Cam says, and I smack him in the back of his head. I'd like to do more, but he's holding my daughter in his arms. I hate to say it, but I'm jealous of my best friend right now, because I want to hold my little girl and never let her go.

She's perfect in every way. Perfect from the wispy brown hairs on her head to her tiny feet. She's still small, but she gets bigger every day, just like my love for her.

"Okay, time's up, Uncle Cam. She wants her daddy."

"No, she doesn't. She's sound asleep, you dick!"

"Watch your language around my daughter, asshole. I don't want her first words to be penis."

Cam holds the baby tighter to his chest, preventing me from taking her from his arms without waking her, and I want to punch him.

"You do realize that you just scolded me for saying dick and not penis after you called me an asshole, right?"

"That's because you are an asshole who needs to watch his mouth around my kid. Now give her to me."

"You two are seriously twisted. Give her to me, Cam. I need to wake her anyway to feed her."

"Of course! Can't have *my* niece being hungry. After all, Uncle Cam is going to make sure she has lots of fun and is spoiled fucking rotten!"

Carefully, Cameron places Faith into Everly's good arm. She still has the cast on, but is managing better than I thought when it comes to holding the baby.

Fuck, I almost can't stand how much I love seeing Everly with our daughter.

"Cameron!" I growl at my best friend, and he shrugs his shoulders.

"Deal with it, penis. She's going to love me more," he says. I shake my head and decide internally if I want to kick or punch him in his nuts when the doorbell rings. "Saved by the bell. I'll get that. I don't want to see my sister's boob when she pulls it out to feed my princess."

"Seriously?" I say to his retreating form.

Whatever. God, he's an asshole sometimes. I take a seat next to Everly on the bed as she nurses our child and the most calming feeling of fullness hits me.

I'm happy.

I love Everly Hayes, and I'm so in love with our daughter that I don't know what to do with myself.

"I want more of these," I say as I caress the top of Faith's head.

"More of what?" Everly says, looking down at our daughter while she helps her to latch onto the other breast to feed. It's only been a few days since she's been able to breastfeed her, the drugs finally out of her system, but it seems to be going well.

"More little Everlys."

Her head comes up, eyes looking into mine. "I think we should probably hold off on more babies for a while. I mean, we just had this one; let's get used to being parents of one before we start adding little Nikos to the mix, okay?"

"Little Nikos?" I ask with a smile. She doesn't say no to more, and that makes me happy for right now.

"Of course little Nikos. I thought we were having a boy the whole time I was pregnant with this little angel. I'd mentally prepared myself for a boy. Hell . . . I might have even seen my therapist more than once with panic attacks over the fact that there was going to be a walking, talking smaller version of Niko Callahan with your DNA and some of Cameron's, seeing as he is my brother. I love our baby girl to death and wouldn't trade her for the world, but now that I've adjusted to the thought of a little Niko, I'd love a son."

"With me? You want more babies with me?"

She rolls her eyes. "What kind of question is that, Nikolas Callahan? Of course with you! God, Cam is right, you are a penis."

I can't help it. I start laughing, and it does nothing to wipe the scowl off Ev's face. In fact, it makes me laugh harder.

"What is wrong with you? You sound like a hyena. Be quiet. Faith is falling asleep!" she hisses at me, and I stop laughing, wiping the tears from under my eyes. I stop and watch her pull Faith up and onto her shoulder, lightly rubbing her back. I stare at them both in awe.

I can't imagine my life without them. What I'd be doing right now had Everly not moved home and back into my life when she did. I don't want to live another day without her and Faith by my side.

"Marry me," I say, and I mean it. I feel it with every fiber of my being.

"W-what?" Everly stammers out, an insecure expression on her face.

"I said, marry me, Everly Hayes. You are my reason for everything. Until the day you walked through that door at the pub, my life was shit. I just didn't know it. I was living, but my life was meaningless until you. You and Faith are my life. I don't want to miss a day in hers. I want to be there every step of the way. From her first tooth, first word, first steps. Hell . . . I want to be there when she goes on her first date when she's thirty-five. I want to buy a shotgun in preparation for the first unworthy asshole that tries to break my baby girl's heart, and I want to practice shooting his dick off for doing it. Marry me, Everly Cassandra Hayes. Be my wife. Have more little Everlys with me. Be my family forever."

She blinks at me, and when she speaks her voice is soft. "You know you can still be there for her, by her side for everything you just said without us getting married. I'd never stop that, Niko. Never."

"I know you wouldn't. That's not what I want, though, Ev. I want you. I want you and her. I love you. I want our family to be a real family. I want the big house, and the minivan and—"

"I am not driving a minivan! I'm also not getting rid of my BMW." I stare at her for a few seconds. Waiting. Hoping that I'm not wrong about this. "I just don't want you to feel obligated because of Faith. I'd understand."

"Everly!" I growl at her. Gently, she manages to put Faith down into her bassinet and turns to me.

"I just want you to be sure that we're what you want for the long haul. I just—"

I cut her off and slide my hand into her hair as I pull her mouth toward mine. The kiss is urgent, intense, and full of everything I feel for her. I want her to feel what she means to me, and right now, this is as far as I can go considering she just had our baby and is still on the mend.

"I'm so sure about this that it's all I've been able to think about. I've wanted to marry you for a long time now, but I knew you wouldn't believe my reasons for asking you, so I waited. I thought I lost you when I found you, unconscious on the bottom of those stairs. I thought I lost both of you and it knocked me off my straight line. Everly, you're in my bloodstream, baby. Don't make me bleed out. Say yes. Say yes, and make me the happiest man alive, because any man on this earth that doesn't have their own Everly Hayes by their side, well, I don't want to think about that man because he's a dead man without you. Make me the lucky one. Say. Yes."

"Okay," she whispers and wipes tears from her eyes.

"Okay? What's that? It's yes or no, baby. Not 'okay.' Christ, you're a handful!" I smile and look down at her beautiful, tear-streaked face.

"Okay, yes. I'll marry you," she says a little louder this time. "But only if you repeat it."

"Say what again?"

"Say that your life was meaningless without me and that the baby and I are your life."

"You are my life, baby. You and Faith are everything and more. I'm not letting you go."

I don't get to say any more to her as the loud shouting from downstairs interrupts the rest of what I wanted to say. Instead, both Ev and I turn at the sound of loud voices in the hallway, and as much as I don't want to spoil our moment, it's already ruined when the tone of my best friend's voice has me getting up and making my way to the front of the house.

"Stay with the baby. I'll see what that's all about," I say without giving Everly time to respond. I make my way toward the two heated sounding voices, but I stop and listen where I am rather than making my way to the end of the hallway.

Huh . . . oh, this should be interesting. I have no idea what is going on between the two of them, but I now have an idea. I can't wait to throw this in his face.

"Turnabout is fair play, brother," I say to myself and listen for another minute, deciding that they can handle this without an audience.

Turning on my heels, I make my way back to my soon-to-be-wife and daughter. The thought alone has me grinning like a lunatic even when I hear the front door slam shut.

When I get back up to the bedroom, Everly's snuggling a pillow, her eyes shut as the lack of sleep takes over. I climb up on the bed and pull the pillow form her arms, earning a furrowed brow and some groans before I pull her to me and have her snuggle into my side.

This is how we were always meant to be.

Cameron

"Are you coming in or not? I don't have time to stand here all day, sweetheart," I say, knowing it will piss my sister's best friend off.

I've known Alyson since she was a teen. Alyson and Everly went to high school together, and we have never gotten along. We had a very small window of civility a few years back after her brother died. I thought things between us would change, but I was wrong. My tolerance level for Aly is usually zero on a scale of one to ten, and that's being nice. I don't know why the fuck she always pisses me off, but I'm usually delighted to know that those feelings are mutual. I fish, and she gives it right back. Although, something has changed between us, and as much as I want to regret it, I can't, but that doesn't mean I have to be nice to her or even like her.

"Fuck it! Stand out there all day if you want. I'm going back upstairs."

"What's your problem?" she asks.

"My problem? I don't have a problem, sweetheart. You have a problem?"

"Whatever, Cameron. Excuse me. I'd like to see my friend and her daughter if you don't mind," she says with the haughtiest attitude I've ever seen on a woman.

Well, fuck her. "Whatever. We both know running away is what you're good at. So run along, little girl."

She stops dead in her tracks and whips around toward me, fire in her eyes. If I didn't know better, I'd say she had smoke coming out of her nose. Huh . . . interesting.

"What the fuck is that supposed to mean?"

"Just what I said. You're used to running away when you don't like something, so go ahead and fly away, little bird."

"I'm not running. You're crazy."

"If you say so. It looks like you're running to me. Why is that, Alyson?"

"I don't run!" she screeches.

"Obviously you're running from something, with all the nameless fucking you've been doing."

"Really? And what are you running from, Cameron Hayes? Because from what I've seen, you do plenty of your own nameless fucking!" she says, seething.

Oh good. She's mad now. When isn't Alyson Payne angry?

"First off, babe, I'm not running from shit, and I always get their names. Sometimes I even get breakfast in bed. Eggs and bacon or Mickey Mouse shaped fucking pancakes with strawberries and whipped cream."

"Oh, I'm sure you do, asshole."

I ignore her comment and keep going. This fucking woman infuriates me to no end. "You know why I always get their names, have breakfast, and sometimes even dinner? Because I'm not a bad guy. I might see them again or I might not, but I don't run. I walk, and I always make sure that when I leave satisfied, she's satisfied, and if she's not, well, I rectify that shit real fast, so we are both happy. So, no, baby, I don't run. You, however, run through men like water."

"So now you're saying I'm a whore?"

"No. You just said that. I said you are running from something. What is it, Aly?"

"No. What you just said was that you could fuck whoever you want, get their names, have them make you Mickey fucking Mouse pancakes, which by the way is fucking ridiculous all by itself, and you're somehow *not* a whore? What are you, ten?"

I start to answer her smart remark, but she keeps going and doesn't breathe between words.

"You need your man card pulled, buddy. Maybe someday you'll get it back when you don't eat fucking Disney shaped pancakes, but that's beside the point. You're saying it's okay for you, but if I do it as a woman, I'm running from something or a whore. That's just some bullshit, Cameron. It's a bullshit double standard."

"You're putting words in my mouth."

"Really? Then what are you running from, Cam? You've no wife. No girlfriend. Just fuck buddies. Why is that, huh?"

"I keep telling you, and it's not because I'm running. I just haven't found the right one that I felt was worth settling down with."

"Well . . . don't fucking look at me!"

"Oh, trust me, sweetheart, I'd never make that fucking mistake again. I'm looking so far away from you it's not even funny." She glares at me before pushing past me and taking the stairs two at a time. I shut the door and follow behind her, but keep far back enough that she can't kick me down the stairs. I don't trust her evil ass for even a minute and would put nothing past her. I reach Ev's door as the she-devil my sister calls a best friend knocks lightly on, and I stand to the side.

"I don't hear anything," I say. "Maybe they fell asleep, and you should just come back later, preferably when I'm long gone." She turns, and if looks could kill, I'm confident I'd have died twenty times already.

"Well, gee, dumbass. Maybe you should go and come back later when I'm gone. You'd do us all a favor if you weren't here polluting the air with all the bullshit that comes out of your mouth. That and noise pollution."

A throat clears from behind both Aly and me, and I turn to see Niko standing there with the door to Ev's room open.

"Oh, hey, Aly. You here to see Ev and the baby?" Niko asks her with a bit of an uncomfortable look on his face. I'm sure he's heard enough.

Aly snorts out a sound that sounds like a cross between a pig and a wounded dog, and I just stare at her and try and look disgusted. "Well, I'm certainly not here to see this asshole. Are they awake; can I go in?"

"Sure. Ev just fed Faith, but she's always hungry, so I'm sure she'll be awake soon. Go ahead in and tell Ev I'll be back in a sec." Niko gives her a half smile, but I know this look. I'm not in the mood to explain this to him right now, but fuck if he's going to leave it alone. He grabs my arm, dragging me down the hall before he stops and crosses his arms over his chest.

"What the fuck was that, Cam?" Niko asks.

"What was what?"

"Don't play dumb with me, brother. You know damn well what I'm talking about, but just so we can cut past all the bullshit I know you're about to spit at me, be blunt. Are you fucking Alyson? Your sister's best friend?"

I narrow my eyes at him. "You do realize you fucked my sister, right, and that you were my best friend when it happened?"

"Was?" he asks, his eyebrow raises as he looks at me.

"Still are, but that doesn't mean I have to explain to you who I am or who I'm not fucking, so cut the shit, Niko."

"Fucking hell! You are!"

"No, I'm not!"

"Dude, I've known you since we were kids." Niko quirks his brow. "I know when you lie, and fucker, you are lying right now."

"I'm not lying because I'm not sleeping with Alyson."

"Not now, but you have. I just heard the two of you, and the sexual tension between you two would cut concrete in half right now, so spill it."

"Fine. We fucked around, but it was a long time ago. End of story."

"I knew it! How did I miss this? I've known you for years and didn't put two and two together until today. That explains the hostility the two of you have. Explains a lot! Why not just sit and talk to her?" Niko says with that dumb as fuck smile of his.

"What the fuck, Niko, are you my friend or fucking Dr. Phil? Just drop it. I'm going to see my niece. Stay out here and hold the door for thing two in there as I'm sure she'll be leaving as soon as I enter the room."

"Who's thing one?" Niko says, and I ignore his question. Now that he knows, I'm positive he's going to bust my balls whenever he sees Alyson and me in the same room. Asshole.

I turn and haul down the short hallway to see my sister and niece before Niko has a chance to dig any further. It's none of his damn business anyway. I may not be sleeping with her right now, but that doesn't mean the thought of that attitudinous mouth of hers wrapped around my cock in the near future isn't on my to-do list. Now I just have to get her on the same fucking page, which is easier said than done. Alyson Payne gives new meaning to the phrase, "Game on," but I've never backed down from anything in my life, and I'm not about to let a girl with the big mouth and attitude take me down to her five-foot-four-inch level.

"Game on, sweetheart. Shit's about to get real fucking interesting."

Also Coming 2018 from K.I. Lynn and Olivia Kelley

Cam and Aly sitting in a tree, K.I.S.S.I.N.G?

Find out in Cocktailing, the next book in the Cocksure world!

K.I. Lynn is the *USA Today* Bestselling Author from *The Bend Anthology* and the Amazon Bestselling Series, *Breach*. She spent her life in the arts, everything from music to painting and ceramics, then to writing. Characters have always run around in her head, acting out their stories, but it wasn't until later in life she would put them to pen. It would turn out to be the one thing she was really passionate about.

Since she began posting stories online, she's garnered acclaim for her diverse stories and hard hitting writing style. Two stories and characters are never the same, her brain moving through different ideas faster than she can write them down as it also plots its quest for world domination . . . or cheese. Whichever is easier to obtain . . . Usually it's cheese.

Olivia Kelley grew up in Boston the oldest of six children. After her first son was born prematurely at only twenty-four weeks, she became an active advocate for parents of disabled children, sharing her own experiences with others. Sadly, he passed away in 2005 at the age of only fourteen. She has a firm belief that you live your life as a lesson. Learn from it and let it mold you into the best person that you can be.

While caring for her son, she turned to reading to escape the reality and stresses of her everyday life. Up until recently, she spent years working corporate America and the Marketing and Public Relations for many different authors in the romance community.

Her first book, *Cocksure,* is co-written with her friend, *USA Today* Bestselling Author K.I. Lynn, and due to release January 2018.

She currently resides in Boston, Massachusetts, with her four children and one very naughty cat. She's social media-addicted as well as a reading addict and loves to meet new people. Look for her on Facebook under Olivia Kelley!

CPSIA information can be obtained
at www.ICGtesting.com
Printed in the USA
BVOW08s0635280118
506478BV00001B/55/P

9 781948 284011